T0375255

Books by Susana Aikin

WE SHALL SEE THE SKY SPARKLING

THE WEIGHT OF THE HEART

Published by Kensington Publishing Corporation

THE WEIGHT OF THE HEART

SUSANA AIKIN

KENSINGTON BOOKS
www.kensingtonbooks.com

KENSINGTON BOOKS are published by
Kensington Publishing Corp.
119 West 40th Street
New York, NY 10018

All Kensington titles, imprints, and distributed lines are available at special quantity discounts for bulk purchases for sales promotion, premiums, fund-raising, educational, or institutional use.

Special book excerpts or customized printings can also be created to fit specific needs. For details, write or phone the office of the Kensington Sales Manager: Kensington Publishing Corp., 119 West 40th Street, New York, NY 10018. Attn. Sales Department. Phone: 1-800-221-2647.

Kensington and the K logo Reg. U.S. Pat. & TM Off.

ISBN-13: 978-1-4967-2516-5 (ebook)
ISBN-10: 1-4967-2516-6 (ebook)

ISBN-13: 978-1-4967-2515-8
ISBN-10: 1-4967-2515-8
First Kensington Trade Paperback Printing: June 2020

10 9 8 7 6 5 4 3 2 1

Printed in the United States of America

To N.J.A.

I open for thee thy mouth.
I open for thee thy two eyes.
I have opened for thee thy mouth with
the instrument of Anubis, with the iron tool
with which the mouths of the gods were opened.
—*Egyptian Book of the Dead: Papyrus of Ani*

CHAPTER I

It's only nine in the morning, but the sun is already sizzling over the skin of the city. Its blinding rays reflect off every angle and shoot into my eyes, making me squint. In the absence of sunglasses, which I've forgotten at home, my head is beginning to throb with heliophobia.

I'm about to turn the key in the old metal gate lock when my cell phone rings and Julia's voice breaks through. "We're almost there. Can you check that everything we need is in the kitchen? Also, please come up to the gate when I honk. We'll need help getting out of the car."

"Sure," I say, and she hangs up.

I push the rusty metal frame open as the thought hits me that I've no distinct memory of the last time I stepped through this door. Could it be more than six months, one year even? I peer at the row of dry lilac bushes that border the path leading up to the old house, and remember how we decided to not fix the failed automatic watering system and let the garden go. It now feels like genocide. But I've been living in a fog for the last two years, just trudging along from one day to the other. It's also true of my sisters, Marion and Julia. The three of us are still struggling to adjust our lives in the aftermath of Father's death. As if we'd been stunned. I close the gate behind me and make for the shaded porch. The heat is mounting by the minute.

August in Madrid can be an experience close to that of a North African desert. Dry, burning winds teeming with fine dust sweep through the empty streets and avenues during the long hours of insufferable, blistering sun. Only the night brings relief. Meanwhile, the masses have fled to beaches and mountain villages, and those left behind take refuge inside air-conditioned buildings or in the older-style shaded apartments during the hours of sunlight, like desert critters hide under rocks and sand away from the blazing sun. Those are the hours when only mad dogs and Englishmen roam the streets, as Father used to say.

For the last weeks I've been entrenched in my apartment, secluded away from the swelter. Agreeing to take my vacation in September has landed me with unending reams of correspondence, while Marcus, my indulged business associate, travels along the Baltic coast of Western Pomerania with his family. What on earth would drag me out of the comfort of my air-conditioned sanctuary to come spend a hot day inside an old, abandoned house?

Remorse shoots through me as I catch sight of the beautiful, faded façade at the end of the path. Its granite walls hang with ivy and honeysuckle, like a forgotten oasis of green creepers ensconced away from the surrounding yellowed garden that has been guzzled by drought. The proud, nail-studded door under dark wooden rafters stares out to me from the deep porch, while adjacent tall windows steal shy, opaque glances through wrought-iron grilles. I step onto the salmon-tiled portico and walk around the patio chairs where we used to lounge at night by garden lanterns. Their once red-and-gold striped cushions are now bleached by the sun and covered in grime.

A rush of trepidation takes over as I consider what I will encounter when I step inside the house. I think of the closed, dark, dusty rooms, of the silent corners full of books, pieces of furniture and multifarious exotic objects that lay quietly waiting for something to happen, for someone to save them from the mass grave of an abandoned house. Julia has a point about the place having become a bit uncanny. The last thing I remember was it being full of strange noises, creepy with mysterious footstep sounds and disquieting creaking, particularly after dark. It could be that there's plenty of wood in floors, beams, and bookcases, which might be contracting and expanding with temperature changes. There was also a moment when the wanderings of country rats under the rafters could have explained the noises; only that the din remained after a team of exterminators accomplished a mass execution. It was then that Julia started to joke about it being haunted; and her jokes turned to eerie suspicions of unresolved issues that are still affecting our lives. Are we then associating commonplace phenomena of closed-down houses with our memory of the heartache and rage that has swept through this one particular abode?

I follow the path up the stone steps that lead to the veranda. Around me the garden is a sorry mass of dry grass, ropey weeds, and thorny thistles over a bed of cracked earth. It used to be a classical British garden, an extension of perfect lawn surrounded by shapely rose bushes tended around the clock by a gardener under Father's strict supervision. But we have let go of everything, my sisters and I, buried our heads in the sand hoping that our grief for the past, for our loss, for the house itself, will dwindle away with sustained neglect. Our carelessness is also reflected in the swimming pool, once a sparkling blue basin of water, and now just a dirty pond of dark green scum bubbling with mosquito larvae and other aqueous vermin. The statue of the flute-playing faun boy standing to its side is also weather-beaten and pockmarked, with eye sockets covered in patches of yellowed lichen.

How strange that once much-beloved objects, structures, or places can end up in states of such forsaken wastefulness. Luckily some things are impervious to the slack of human beings, like the chain of mountains I'm now gazing at from the veranda. Their longevity is so much more enduring than ours. I'm only thirty-three years old, but for them it's been around two hundred and fifty million years since they first erupted from the belly of the earth.

I lean on the iron rail and gaze at the smooth line of blue peaks wrapped in wreaths of clouds. Why is it that from this point I can turn around and look safely at our family house? When we were girls, we used to talk about its magnificent French windows as being the eyes of the house, and the paneled door, the mouth, always gaping toward the mountain range on the horizon, and drooling at the sight of our beautiful garden. That patch of lush green surrounded by restless trees peering inside windowpanes into long rooms with terracotta floors and whitewashed fireplaces.

My phone vibrates in my pocket, startling me. It's Julia. "Anna?" Damn, I've forgotten about her request. She says, "Listen, I've had to stop at the shop to buy more flowers for the ceremony, so it will be ten more minutes before I get there. Did you check the stuff in the kitchen? If something's missing I need to know now."

"Got it," I say, hanging up and rushing inside the house. The large butcher block sitting in the middle of the old kitchen is clumped up with all sorts of plastic bags and boxes containing the various articles Julia brought in yesterday and that I'm supposed to check on now. I spot a torn piece of graph paper with a list scribbled in wavering, ornate handwriting. This is not Julia's, so whose is it? It resembles something like the calligraphy of a child from a past century. I go down the list and check that all items listed are somewhere on the table. *Twenty candles, at least eight of them white; three bottles of wine, can be the cheapest; two bottles of rum, preferably Cuban; any other two old bottles of liquor you might have around the house; a box of cigars, preferably Havana; lots of freshly cut rosemary; one or two whole coconuts—this is very important. One large bag of salt—coarse sea salt. White flowers, at least five dozen. A white tablecloth, well ironed. Sage, as much as you can get. And finally, we will need a new mop and bucket. And a broom, an old-fashioned straw broom. Footnote: Best not worry about the broom and coconut, we will provide it. And lots of love as always, signed D.* Who on earth is D?

I'm checking and rechecking that everything is on the table, when my eye catches the second footnote. *PS. Oh, and two kilos of lamb chops.* And this is where I stop. What kind of madness am I getting into?

It happens frequently that I give in to my older sisters' wishes just to avoid their tantrums. Julia, in particular, can be very difficult when antagonized. She's unable to rein in her explosive anger when things don't go her way, and can become a human steam engine in seconds. So, unless I'm totally determined to put my foot down over a life-and-death issue, I just humor her as if I were the older sister and she a distraught little girl whose needs better be satisfied in order to keep peace in the house. And when it comes to Marion, she's become such a volatile personality that navigating her moods is equivalent to walking on a field packed with landmines.

This time, though, Julia has gone over the top. She's been hammering me about bringing in this woman to cleanse our *haunted* house. And insisting that this person whom she calls a *santera*, an energy healer of sorts, and whom, mark you, she is picking up from a nursing home this morning, has supernatural powers capable of overcoming today's conked-out real estate market and propitiating a sale. What word did she use? A *limpieza*?

Sometimes I wonder at Julia. She's always been a mercurial personality, swinging from dreamy states of mind to episodes of fuming rage, from sullen moods to mischievous tomfoolery. And in addition to her bristling diatribes having become more frequent of late, there is also that other trait that seems to develop further as time goes on, that other interesting but also dangerous side of her: her uncanny fascination with the superstitious, with the outlandish, with the *dark and strangely beautiful*, as she would put it. Although I can't say it's a unique trait of Julia's, since it's widespread in the family. Father was obsessed with Egypt and dark art at the end of his life; Marion's passion for bullfighting and matadors is intense enough to be considered an exotic superstition, and Julia's love for anything and all Cuban is a near religion. Sometimes I think I'm the only one in our lineage who's been saved from losing her marbles.

I reconsider my decision to go along with this absurd scheme. A *cleansing* of the house? A magical ceremony to expedite its sale? Do I even want to sell the house at a time when the market is collapsed, when we would have to give it away for peanuts?

A honk shakes me out of my absorption.

They're here.

I walk up to the gate through the garage. Julia's car is parked outside on the street. She winds down the window. "Everything okay? Please help her out, while I gather the rest of the stuff."

I walk around and open the car door. Two immensely swollen feet clad in oversize sandals drag themselves out onto the pavement followed by a pair of elephantine legs under a long white linen dress. A small hand reaches out and grips mine with unexpected strength. With a few firm, gentle tugs, I help her get on her feet. She's not as heavy as could have been anticipated by her volume. As I stand beside her, I get a scent of her flesh, a heavy odor like treacle, sweet and intoxicating. I'm taken aback for a moment. It reminds me of *membrillo*, or quince jelly, that dark, sugary, solid marmalade that Nanny used to serve with soft cheese for dessert on Sundays. Something in me relaxes.

Julia hands me a walking cane from the back of the car, and the old woman threads her arm through mine and holds on tight, hugging me closely in her grip, as we walk slowly through the gate, down the garden path and into the house.

"Aren't you going to say hello?" The suave Cuban accent whispering at my side rings a distant bell in my head. I turn and look at her for the first time and instantly recognize the dark slit eyes with their hypnotic stare, the thin smiling lips, the oval head framed by waves of obsidian hair falling down to the shoulders. The memory of that one afternoon some fourteen years back shoots through my mind, razor sharp. Nothing seems to have changed in her face; only the body has muted, being now hugely bloated in the abdomen and extremities. But the head hasn't changed a bit. And then, those eyes! A strange feeling wells up, an unease, as I reflect that no time has seemed to elapse since we last saw each other, as if there was no gap between past memory and present encounter.

She smiles, watching me closely with penetrating eyes. "It's been a while, hasn't it? But I've had you in mind—as I always do with those I feel drawn to."

Yes, I too remember her very well.

"Hello, Delia," I say.

CHAPTER 2

It had been hot, torrid, as that infamous summer of 1995 crawled toward its end, and I found myself at the house in yet another blistering August afternoon that can only be imagined in remote deserts, the air so stifling there was nothing to do but collapse into a slumber in some shaded corner of the house. The legendary siesta of the Mediterranean provinces; inevitable, when even lingering about the house is unbearable, never mind the streets. Father was abroad, probably sweating profusely under a different sun that would return him home red as a lobster and full of outlandish objects to add to his exotic collections. Marion was in London, and Julia lost somewhere in the vicinity with Alina, her lover. I was alone in the house. Exhausted, I crept onto my bed and stretched out, belly down, over the mattress. My eyes lingered on the stripes of light blazing through the drawn venetian blinds dancing with particles of dust; only the buzzing sound of a trapped housefly disturbed the hefty silence as I descended into unconsciousness.

All of a sudden I was jerked out of my slumber by a flutter of voices followed by a loud shriek and a huge splash. The pool! Someone falling in the water! I scrambled to my feet, limbs drunk with sleep and mind edging on panic, and dragged myself toward the window. As I pulled up the blinds, the image of a woman fully clad in white, floating belly up in the pool, made me gasp. The body was still, with the afternoon breeze steering the white drapes of the long dress around her shape and spreading out the strands of her long black hair away from her head like a black star. Her eyes appeared tightly shut, resisting the bright sparks of light glitzing over the water.

I ran downstairs. Julia and Alina stood in the patio beside an ancient-looking woman. The three of them looked toward the pool in silence. I relaxed.

Julia turned around. "Didn't know you were here. You look like you just woke up from a hundred-year nap. This is Señora Virginia," she said introducing the old woman, and then motioning her head toward the water, added, "and her daughter Delia."

"I saw her from the window; it gave me a fright," I said.

Señora Virginia sighed. Myriad wrinkles surrounded her mouth and eyes, but a sharp gaze shone above the dark-skinned cheekbones. She seemed out of a photographic history book on rural life in the nineteenth century, something about her weather-beaten appearance, her old-fashioned dress, the way her long gray hair was tied up at the back of her head.

"No need to be so paranoid. People jump in the pool all the time," Julia said with a smirk.

"People jump in the pool in bathing suits," I said.

"And sometimes without . . ." Alina said, looking at Julia with mischief. She was dressed in a short saffron tunic over her round thighs. Her short pixy hair glistened with pomade, and her eyes were accented with thick eyeliner. In contrast, Julia wore denim shorts with an old T-shirt and shaggy Converse shoes. Both looked out toward the pool, while Alina stood closely behind Julia, combing her hair with her fingers. I disliked Alina; she engulfed my sister to the point of estranging her from everyone else. Particularly from me. Julia had been my closest sister, my best friend, all my life. It was always Julia and me. Marion was my heroine growing up, but Julia, my accomplice, my partner in crime. But when Julia met Alina three months back at the Escuela de Bellas Artes, the Madrid art school, where they both studied painting, something instantly switched. Julia became nothing short of intoxicated with her newly found friend, and wasted no time plunging into a steamy affair. From that point on the two became inseparable—they even seemed to walk around as if they were conjoined Siamese twins. Every effort on my part to befriend Alina, and retain access to my sister, failed. Everyone, and everything, had become excluded from their private bubble of paradise.

I clicked my tongue and walked toward the pool. When my shadow darkened the edge of the water, Delia opened her eyes and squinted at me, shaping her thin lips into a crooked smile. "I was too hot—I didn't make it to the changing room." She closed her eyes again and moved her arms to paddle around the water.

Julia and Alina settled Señora Virginia in a chair in the shade and motioned me toward the kitchen. Once there, Julia opened the liquor cabinet.

"Anna, would you hide all these under the kitchen sink while we get Virginia some water? She's asked us not to give Delia any alcohol. The woman has a problem. So no matter what she says or does . . ." Before I could open my mouth to protest about this bizarre request, Julia and Alina dashed out carrying a tray with cups of water. But in those days I'd still do anything Julia asked, so needy I felt for her approval, particularly now that Alina had come between us.

I started moving the bottles under the sink, when I felt a shadow fill the door space behind me. Turning around I saw Delia standing at the threshold, water dripping all over into widening pools at her feet, and wondered how she'd gotten out of the pool, bypassed Julia and Alina, and made it so quickly to the kitchen. Her white dress clung to her flesh, revealing her curves, her underwear, and her dark nipples. Her hair fell in waves over her shoulders, drip-dripping, like thin, dark, twisted hoses. She stared at me hypnotically, onyx pupils shimmering inside long slit lids.

"All you girls are so beautiful, each one attractive in a different way," she drawled in a suave Cuban accent. "But you, you're special."

I couldn't take my eyes off her. She reminded me of a black Madonna statue or a kachina doll, with an ageless sort of beauty. She could have been thirty-five or sixty.

"Do you need to change into some dry clothes?" I asked.

"First I need something to drink. I am very thirsty."

"Can I get you coffee? Water with ice?"

"Actually, I have low blood pressure and need something with lots of sugar right now." She pointed to the bottle in my hand. It was an old, half full bottle of anisette that had been in the cabinet for as long as I remembered. Most of its contents were crystallized around the neck.

"This is due for the garbage," I said, feeling tension mounting in my arms and shoulders.

"Not really." She stepped into the kitchen. I watched her small feet bringing in a trail of water. "I just need a shot to balance out."

In one unexpected, graceful leap she was by my side. She put her hand on my arm. "Your skin is so smooth, almost like silk," she said. "And that blue dress really enhances your figure."

She was very close, and the proximity of her beauty increased my strange sense of intoxication. She had an oval face with high cheeks and a delicate nose. Her lips were crimson-red and very thin, like the curved blade of a small scimitar. I looked into her eyes, but they were hard and shiny, like a dark mirror, impenetrable to the gaze. With one swift movement she grabbed the bottle's neck. But I didn't let go of the body. For a moment we got into a tug of war.

"Be kind, and let me have a sip," Delia pleaded.

"I can't," I said, securing my grip further.

Delia licked her lips. "I'll tell you your fortune if you do." Small beads of sweat formed along her hairline. "I don't need to look at your hands to know that you will have lots of money. Lots! And I see a lover, a beautiful man. How passionately you will love him. But, oh no, there's conflict!" She pierced my eyes with her pitch-black stare and I began to feel dizzy.

"I don't believe in that nonsense," I said.

"You don't believe in your destiny? You're a strange girl!"

That instant Julia and Alina burst into the kitchen, and Delia pulled the bottle out of my hands. She stepped back, and put it to her lips.

"Delia, you promised!" Julia said, while Alina gave me dirty looks.

"I'll just take a very small shot," Delia said. Julia and Alina lunged toward her, but Delia was already drinking. She closed her eyes as the thick transparent liquid slid into her mouth. When she reopened them, the dark mirror of her pupils had been replaced by a mischievous glint. Julia sighed, and yanked the bottle away from her. Alina clicked her tongue.

I stepped outside into the patio. A few feet ahead, the velvety surface of the pool rocked softly, dappled with the shade of bushes and trees, and the sky was turning pink behind the blue line of distant mountains. Virginia sat at the table cooling herself with a small lacquered fan. Her face was drawn, forlorn, with a sort of crippling fatigue, as if she had lived far too long on this earth.

"For God's sake, isn't this woman a consummate drunk?" I say when I get back to Julia, who's still getting things out of the car.

Julia ignores me. She gathers a stack of old newspapers and loads them onto my unwarned arms. "We'll need these for wrapping."

"Julia! I just asked an elemental question."

She sighs. "Yes, she did have an alcohol problem, but she pulled herself together in the end. And she got handed down the gift after her mother's death. Now she's a powerful healer, even more so because she's had to overcome an addiction."

I'm aghast. "Great. We just bought a gazillion bottles of liquor, and this woman is going to drink them all and bless the house."

Julia eyes me with fury. "What's the matter? Can't people have a past? I told you she's clean now. It is some kind of poetic irony that someone who's been immersed in shit would come to cleanse our house, don't you think? After all, it takes knowing one's demons to be able to lug someone else's out. Specially when it comes to big, fat, hairy, and thoroughly revolting specimens like our own."

Julia has her moments with words, when she rises above her grouchy persona and puts together metaphors that can be sharp and amusing. But today she's just full of crap.

"Look," I say, exercising my utmost patience. "Let's rethink this for a moment. We can still call it off. We'll pay her, of course; make her some coffee and take her back home. In exchange, I promise to devote all my energy in the coming months to moving this sale along. I'll look for another agency, advertise it independently on the

Internet, hire someone to give an overall coat of paint and fix a few things here and there. And of course, do a thorough clean-out of the property."

Julia eyes me with disdain. "What, you think that with all your brilliant business skills you're going to solve the problem?"

"I'm sure that if I put my mind to it, and if we adjust the price, we'll sell. Yes."

"You don't get it, do you?" Julia scans my face with narrow eyes. "Don't you realize this whole thing is beyond us? Have we even sorted out the damned place in these two years? I'm not even sure we've emptied the refrigerator all this time. Don't you see? We can't deal with it, we're petrified."

She pauses for a beat and looks away.

"He's still here, you know."

"C'mon Julia, isn't that going a bit too far?"

"Don't pretend you don't know what I'm talking about."

We lock eyes. I feel the skin on my arms contracting into goose bumps. I say, "Sure he's here. So is Mother. And anyone else who's ever lived in the house is also imprinted somewhere in its memory."

"Don't compare. Mother is here as an angel. Possibly the only angel the house has known. But he's quite a different matter." Julia lowers her voice. "Listen. I had to come last week to let the electric company in and I could hardly walk through the rooms. I just wanted to scream. Even the electricians made a comment on the weirdness of the place. I didn't even dare open the door to Father's study."

I take a deep breath. I'm too overwhelmed to say anything. It's been a long time since the thought of the study crept into my mind and overshadowed my mood. But I totally see how Julia couldn't open it up. That room was the last bastion of Father's desperation, the last refuge of his self-hounded mind. It *is* the darkest room in the house.

"Anna, can't you stop questioning everything to the last detail? Why does your opinion always sound so weighty, so practical, so know-it-all? Just suspend judgment and trust me for once, will you? Just this once."

I stare at Julia and realize I'm beginning to feel exhausted with all this arguing. I wonder if it's worth keeping up my resistance. The reality is that all three of us have been unable to approach the house. We still haven't managed to remove the smallest piece of furniture, not even one book, a trivial ceramic vase, or a washcloth. The closets in Father's room are intact, his old electric shaver sits in the bathroom; his coat still hangs on the peg behind the door. The house is exactly as it was the day he was taken to hospital, a preserved mausoleum. This might actually be an opportunity for the three of us to regroup and start sorting things out in good old practical fashion.

"All right, let's just go through with it then," I say.

Back in the kitchen, Delia is sitting at the table in a large chair. At her side stands a short man dressed in white. Julia and I deposit all the bags on the table, and the small suitcase at her feet.

"This is Constantine," Julia says, casually. "He's going to be helping Delia today."

Constantine looks at me, and nods. He is a youngish fellow, with a small chubby body, scanty light brown hair, and a peculiar face that sort of ends up in a pout. The skin over his cheeks is marked with acne scars, and he has a squint on his right eye that makes it stare off toward the wall; a sort of strabismic eye, with an independent life of its own. It adds to his disquieting appearance. Where has Constantine come from? Was he in the back of the car minutes ago? How come I hadn't even seen him when I was helping Delia out?

"Constantine," I echo.

"Yes, that's me," he says, perking up. "I'm sort of the sorcerer's apprentice." His strange face breaks into a shy, candid smile.

Delia snorts with laughter. "Sorcerer's apprentice! That's a good one! Come on, Constant, get to work, there's a lot to be done. We have to hurry if we want to finish by today. I can already feel this is going to be a big job." She seems to be totally at home, sitting here in our kitchen as if she owns the place. She turns to me. "One thing I'm going to need, dear, is a large pot of real strong coffee, with this heat and all. In Cuba we never used to start anything without first drinking coffee. The sacred brown liquid that sanctifies all action under the scorching sun."

As I set about making coffee, I sense a strange, deep unease. Something in me is conscious of an inevitable drift already pulling us all onto the tracks of an unknown adventure ahead. A thought pricks my mind. This is my last chance to turn around, pick up my bag, and walk out of the house.

But I don't.

Instead, I pour the coffee into the filter basket and snap down the lid.

CHAPTER 3

Julia sits at the table across from Delia. "Can you give us a rundown on the day's plan?"

Delia's eyes gleam with restrained laughter. "Oh, Julia, my dear, beautiful, ravishing Julia, how impatient you are, how much in a hurry to sell your house. How can I give you the day's plan when we are working with Los Santos, the Saints, and El Espíritu Santo, the Holy Spirit? You can't tell them when to do things, they decide the time and the place, when to start and when to finish. So, NO!" Delia bangs her fist on the table, making us both jump. "From now on there is no schedule and you'll just need to wait until THEY decide it's over. All right?"

I place a cup of coffee and a sugar pot on the table in front of her, and she stirs three spoonfuls of white granules into her cup.

She savors her first sip. "That having been cleared up, I shall give you a rundown on the rules of the day. Number one, from now on, nobody touches anything related to *el trabajo*—the job—unless I request it. Number two, nobody drinks alcohol or smokes inside the property until we are done. And most importantly, number three, nobody—NOBODY, you hear? Nobody follows us into the rooms where Constant and I are working—under no circumstance. And nobody goes into any of the rooms that have already been cleaned. All right? So now, clear off somewhere else, because Constant and

I are going to build the altar right here in the kitchen. I'll call you down when it's ready." Delia stands up from her chair and grabbing her cane, pokes Julia playfully to prompt her to get up and leave. "Oh, and one more thing—bring me another bunch of flowers from the garden."

Julia gasps. "More flowers?"

"You've been cheap with the flowers," Delia says. "We need more. Don't you know they will represent Los Muertos, the spirits of the dead that inhabit and bless the house? Do you want them to feel short-changed? Off you go!"

"But, Delia, the garden is barren; it hasn't been watered for a couple of years. There's no flowers left," Julia says in a whiny voice.

"Bring anything green then, tree branches, something."

"The only flowers left are oleanders," I say. "They survive drought."

Delia stares at me for a moment, pensive. We all wait on her, full of suspense.

"But, Delia, aren't oleanders . . ." Constantine starts to say with a small voice.

Delia lifts a hand to indicate he should hold his thought. Then she says, "Oleanders will be fine, given the circumstances. Please bring in a decent bunch of them."

Julia and I fumble around the kitchen drawers for a set of clippers, but only find a set of large shears, and we make for the garden. Constantine closes the kitchen door behind us.

We walk along the veranda toward the giant willow tree where a bunch of old wicker furniture basks in the shade under its long, sweeping branches. At the far end, tall boxwood hedges border the rows of oleander bushes sprinkled with bright flowers that shimmer in the sun. I trail behind Julia and observe her long body, her slim, tanned legs, her sandaled feet brushing over the parched lawn. Her strawberry-blond hair blazes against the sunlight, refracting golden rays that spill over her orange shirt and white capri pants. There is something especially radiant about Julia today, an unusual sheen that speaks of change, of some new opportunity ahead. But at the same time she looks wrapped up in herself, forlorn. I want to ask her many questions, I know she's going through something, I know she's thinking about Alina. But it's not easy to get Julia talking; she tends to be a miser with personal information these days. I just follow behind, shears heavy in my hand.

When we get to the oleander bushes, we stand for a moment, unsure of how to approach felling the thick stems with their clusters of fuchsia-colored flowers. If Spain had to have a national flower, at least the south of the Peninsula, and more recently in the central plain, it would be oleanders. Their beauty combined with their hardiness have made them popular in landscaping, not just in private gardens, but also along hundreds of miles of highways and roads. They sway in the wind along roadsides and freeways as one whizzes past in cars, their flowers gleaming under the sun, their stalks rooted deep in arid, rainless soil. But viewed from close by, there's a hostility about them. Their dark green leaves grow in clusters and are narrow and leathery; their stems are covered with an oily, sticky substance that gives out a rancid stench, contradicting the sweet, intoxicating scent of the flowers.

I hand the shears over to Julia, but she doesn't take them.

"Remember Nanny didn't let us play around these bushes when we were little?" she says.

"She didn't?"

"She said they were very poisonous, that they gave seizures to dogs and horses who nibbled on them."

"I think that might have been one of her old wives' tales," I say.

"I don't believe so, Nanny knew a lot about plants and herbal medicine."

"She also used to tell Father not to plant hydrangeas in the garden, 'cause they prevented the girls of the house from marrying." I laugh.

"I don't see why you laugh, that's exactly what has happened in this house." Julia's face is somber. "I don't like these flowers at all. I don't even feel like cutting them."

"I don't mind," I say. "It'll be good for the bushes, they haven't been trimmed in ages."

"Oh no, but you can't." Julia takes the shears from my hand. "Only I can cut them."

"Why?"

"Because, this is part of the *limpieza*, and I'm the one who's been initiated to do it."

I'm incredulous. "Initiated?"

"Yes, Anna. Initiated. As in a ritual. This very morning." Her eyes are beginning to blaze. I want to laugh again, and ask *In the nursing home?* But I know we'll get into a squabble, so I hold back my mirth.

Julia cuts the flowers and passes them over to me. I know she's seething at my disbelief. She works quickly with a sort of fury, head bent down, hair falling on her cheeks. At times she struggles to cut some of the thicker stems with both of her hands on the scissors. Soon we have a bunch of twelve or more sticky branches speckled with pink flowers. We stand for a moment, rearranging them into a manageable bouquet. When I lower my gaze toward the bushes I see how brutally Julia has cut some of the stems. They stand in shock, hacked and oozing a thin whitish sap. Julia can display out-of-control behavior when she's irritable, and this has become part of our dynamic of late, since we've gotten into bickering about almost anything. I make a mental note not to sound skeptical again. After all, I've agreed to this ceremony, or whatever it is.

But now Julia seems to be musing about something else. "You know, she still has lovers," she says.

"Who? Delia?" I ask with bewilderment.

"She is seventy-five and still has lovers. Don't you think that's something?"

"Have you met any of them?"

"She's introduced two of them at the nursing home. You know, a couple of guys who are not that old yet, who are somehow functional."

"Lovers as in real lovers?"

"Yes. She's very explicit about it."

"Hell!"

"Impressive, isn't it?"

"She's connected to Alina, isn't she?" I ask, conscious of the dangerous terrain I'm getting into. "Have you heard from her recently?"

"She calls sometimes from Miami."

I search Julia's eyes. "You still love her, don't you? You want money to move to Miami, don't you? Is this what this urgent selling of the house is about?"

"I haven't been badgering you about Marcus, have I?" Julia snaps. "So don't question me, it's none of your business."

She's defiant, furious. For a moment, I'm taken aback. What has come between us in the last year? We used to be such close, inseparable friends. I can't remember one time when being in need I didn't have Julia's shoulder to lean on. I can't remember one weekend when I didn't seek her out to go hang around for whole afternoons or evenings at my apartment or hers.

"Please, let's not quarrel," I say. "Let's be cool today."

Julia inhales deeply as if to sober up. "All right." Then she adds, "Let's head back to the house. I still need to open doors and windows for the *limpieza*. You can come along if you like. But no questions." She takes the bunch of flowers from my hands and walks away.

"I'll catch up with you in a minute," I say.

I'm not ready to go inside. I lean over the veranda, and turn my gaze to the mountains. In a few hours the heat will rise further over the long plain that leads up to the sierra and make it swoon under a haze so thick, it will resemble a desert mirage. Then, far off on the horizon, the line of mountains will blur into images of recumbent sleeping giants, big clunky bodies cloaked in groves of trees and rocks sticking up against the sky, their folded arms and legs sprouted with bushes and flowers, their eyes shut under layers of dirt. How many times must we have stood here, Julia and I, making up stories about the sierra, wondering at its ever changing form like a kaleidoscope, where sun, fog, and snow paint different pictures every day, every hour, and trigger wild imaginings. And then, can I ever forget all those times I was ravished under the dreamy brow of these same mountain gods?

Do I really want to sell this house? Even putting it in the hands of real estate agents is something I've agreed to just to humor my sister Julia. I understand her circumstance, her needing money, wanting to move on. My situation is very different. I don't need money. I don't need to sell. I don't want to, either. I am content with my lot at the moment. My company is soaring, I get along reasonably well with my business partner, and I absolutely love my beautiful duplex apartment in the heart of the city. What can be missing?

Furthermore, this house is much more than a house to me,

it's closer to the idea of a nation. It's like a small country in itself planted on Spanish soil, a tiny dominion from which I've always drawn my identity. We didn't think of ourselves as living in Madrid. We lived in Cambrils number 4. Although of British descent because of Father and Spanish because of our mother, we didn't think of ourselves as either British or Spanish, but as citizens of our own unique, rich, diverse world. A miniature state with its own rules, its own mixture of cultures, its own aesthetics, its own chain of mountains. With even its own twist of the English language, a tongue stuffed with a zillion Spanish terms and literal translations of impossible words from a variety of other languages. To friends and acquaintances our house was always a wonder to visit, full of exotic art, exuberant collections of strange objects, and beautiful furniture brought from different places; cartloads of books on art, science, and literature. We always had visitors from faraway countries, whom Father entertained as business guests, and who kept us abreast of what really was going on in the world. It was like no other house I had ever known, or will probably ever know. And despite all that has come to pass between these walls, growing up in this amazing place was the best thing that ever happened to me. How can I let go of it now?

Back in the kitchen the altar seems to be well underway. On the table, which is now covered by an embroidered white starched cloth, bottles of wine and liquor have been arranged in a semicircle, inside of which the million candles, all lit up, sparkle around a strange collection of objects contained in coconut shells: colorful beads, necklaces, cowrie shells, cigars. Picture cards depicting saints in extravagant attire stand against bottles and candleholders. On opposite sides of this arrangement, multiple vases hold the white lilies and daisies Julia bought before, and the oleanders we just cut. At the feet of it all, three sticks of dark wood, the likes of which I've never seen before, pile upon each other, side by side with a kitchen grater and a handbell with beautiful, ornate carvings on its handle.

Delia turns to me. "I know you're the youngest, but you strike me as the most responsible person in this house. From now on, I'll communicate with you about anything I need."

I shrug my shoulders.

She eyes me for a moment. "You're not really into this, are you? You're just being bullied by your older sister."

Constantine laughs from the other end of the room. "That's what older siblings do. My brothers used to bully me all the time, they used to beat me, make me do all sorts of awful things—even after I was grown up. Until they met Delia, and then they never bothered me again."

"That's what happens when you're under the protection of a Cuban *guardiana*," Delia says. "There's no more nonsense then. Only hard work! So now, get going!"

I can't believe the level of this conversation, and I just stand eyeing Constantine warily as he bends over and picks up a bucket of water and a mop. Then I remember Julia telling me how part of the *trabajo* would consist of mopping the entire house with some sort of blessed water. And swishing around a whole coconut with a straw broom! Holy shit!

Delia nudges me. "Time to leave." She waves me out of the kitchen. "Constantine, I'm ready to start! We'll begin with the living room upstairs, but first let's get our blessings," are the last words I hear before I step out the door into the patio. I decide to hide around the corner, to look discreetly through the small window into the kitchen. I'm not normally curious about other people's affairs, but this whole scene is taking on such a bizarre air, all this weird collection of items on the table. And the lamb chops sitting in the fridge!

From my hiding place I watch Delia haul herself out of the chair, take her cane and edge around the table to face the altar. She makes the sign of the cross over her chest repeatedly while reciting an unintelligible prayer, then picks up the bead necklaces from the coconut bowls and extends them toward the altar, as if in offering. I see Delia's huge arms rise with the beads, the flesh falling underneath them in long flaps, her small delicate hands placing the necklaces ceremoniously one by one around her throat and inside her white dress between her breasts. She motions Constantine to come closer, to put beads around his neck too, and into his shirt; all the time reciting the monotonous prayer which I can't understand. They face each other, each with hands pressed at the chest, then embrace twice, once on the right side, once on the left, and gently punch each other with opposite elbows. They turn to face the altar again, while Constantine picks up one of the cigars and lights it up, sucking hard at the brown cylinder until it catches; and then hands it to Delia, who starts puffing out the smoke toward the objects on the table. With her other hand she takes a bottle and puts it to her lips, but instead of swallowing the alcohol, she sprays it forcefully out of her mouth onto the altar, and at each one of the objects there contained. The flames on candlewicks flicker but don't go out. Then, taking up her cane in one hand and the handbell in the other, Delia starts toward the stairs leading up to the second floor. I watch her feet dragging to the tinkling sounds of the bell she's shaking, followed by Constantine, who carries the bucket of water and the mop.

A clawlike hand at my shoulder shakes me out of my voyeuristic fascination. "I thought we had agreed we weren't going to interfere with her *trabajo*," Julia said.

"She only said follow her."

"Same thing. And anyway, first you think it's a whole load of crap, and then you can't resist having a good look. Are we relapsing again into our old double standard mode?" I laugh while Julia smirks. She seems relaxed, finally.

We move away from the window toward the patio and sit down at the table. We look at each other for a moment, then she lowers her eyes and stares down at her sandals.

"I just got a call from Marion. She's on her way," she says. "And she's *really* mad."

"Why is she mad? Didn't she also agree to this?"

"She never returned my calls, so I've just told her about it."

"No wonder she's mad then."

"Anna, you're going to have to deal with her."

"Are you kidding me?"

"Nope. I'm not."

For the last few years I have been the mediator and peacemaker between my sisters, who've been at insufferable odds. Although, to be accurate, they've been rivals ever since I remember, and have always used me as a sort of buffer. When they fight there's no getting in between them, only standing back and seeing them go at each other like vixens. They only want me there as a witness so that at the end they can say, *See what she did to me? See the things she said?* as each tries to draw me into her cause against the other. It's hard to believe that the same controversies over toys and clothes have been transposed to money, management of common affairs, and other more adult-sounding subjects, but the pattern of their rivalry hasn't shifted. And although I am closer to Julia in age and daily camaraderie, and I see the mean, crazy side of Marion, I can never totally be on Julia's side, because of the tender spot I have for my eldest sister. As a girl, nothing Marion could do diminished her charisma in my eyes. Later, as a grown woman, the dazzling heroine was replaced by the tragic character she is now, and that brought her still closer to my heart. Julia knows my bias; it has always been one of her festering wounds.

"All right. If, in exchange, you promise to join me in proactive enterprises toward a future sale, while Delia goes about her job," I say, changing the subject.

"Proactive enterprises? Not me. I brought some work to do. I'll just sit out here and work on my sketches." She furrows her brow while the lines of her thin face align themselves downward toward her pursed lips, a sign that she wants to be left alone.

"C'mon, Julia, we could start an inventory of furniture and art pieces. We need to start getting organized."

But Julia is not in the mood. "I'll be honest and tell you that, besides being here for the *limpieza*, the only other thing I'm striving for is making an inventory of my *own* art pieces in the house. Supposing there are any left around."

Great, I think. Let's just be in our every-artist-for-himself mode here. But I don't say anything. I just sit back in my chair considering that the sun is close to its zenith, and the heat is beginning to soar.

The sound of a car door slamming hard pulls me out of my musing. Quick, heavy footsteps walk on the pavement toward the house and the gate clashes loudly after a few seconds. All sounds seem to stop for a beat. Julia and I sit motionless in our seats, as if frozen.

Then we hear Marion's scream. "I won't have any killings in this house!"

CHAPTER 4

Marion stomps into the patio. She is wearing a plum-colored summer dress and very large dark sunglasses that cover most of her face. She rips them off and stares at Julia with fiery eyes. "Stop this immediately, or I'll call the police!"

Julia jumps up from her chair, her sketches and pencils scattering all around. "What's your problem? How dare you walk in screaming?" she yells.

"What is *your* problem? How dare *you* organize this behind my back?" Marion echoes.

"Behind your back! I left you a dozen messages. You haven't returned one single phone call for over a week!"

I stand back, gauging the best strategy to approach the situation. The heat is rising quickly. Marion's lips are quivering. I take a few steps toward her. "Marion, everything's all right," I say. "It's not what you think."

Without even a glance in my direction, she flings out her arm to bar me from advancing. "You know nothing about this. Stay out!" I stop in my tracks.

Marion stares fixedly at Julia. "Call this off!"

"No way!"

"In that case, I'm calling the cops right now!" Marion fumbles in her purse for her phone.

"And what are you going to say?" Julia says, pulling a stupid face to mimic Marion. "Officer, there's an old lady blessing my house?" Marion freezes for an instant. Both of them are panting.

"This is no blessing. I will not stand for killings." Marion's voice is now edging on a hiss.

"Why do you always have to take things to extremes? *I will not stand for killings*, she said," Julia echoes in parody, then clicks her tongue and starts gathering her sketches from the floor.

Marion takes out her phone with trembling hands and dials.

"Is this necessary?" I ask her, beginning to feel unnerved. But she pays no attention.

"Police? There has been a break-in at my house. Yes, illegal immigrants, very scary people—"

"Stupid bitch!" Julia leaps up from the floor and lunges toward her. Marion steps back, losing balance for a second. The cell phone drops from her hand and crashes on the floor. The battery clatters out as it hits the tiles. Marion gasps but doesn't move. Her reddened eyes radiate hatred.

Julia stands back, body tense with mingy victory. "Sorry, but you brought this onto yourself," she says.

Marion kicks off her shoes and dives to the floor. She grabs a bunch of Julia's etchings and tears them up.

"Are you crazy?" Julia wails, scrambling to retrieve her papers.

From this point on, the fight will get seriously mean.

"Stop! Both of you. Stop this minute!" commands a thundering voice. There's a moment of freeze frame. We all turn heads and see Delia coming down the steps that lead into the patio. She descends with difficulty, cane in one hand, mop in the other as if it were a tall staff. Constantine hovers around her nervously, mumbling, "Slow down, Delia, you might fall. Please be careful!"

But Delia is unstoppable. Her large, white-clad body drifts into the patio like a glacier tongue gliding into a valley. Julia and Marion stand and compose themselves.

"Ladies, ladies, what is the matter?" Delia asks. "Did I hear someone talking about killing animals? Do any of you have questions that should be directly addressed to me?" She looks at Marion. "You must be the eldest daughter of the house."

Marion scowls. "And who are you, and what are you doing in my house?"

Delia looks at Julia and me, her face amused and incredulous at the same time about the fact that our sister is not up to date with the *limpieza*. She turns to Marion. "My name is Delia Santos and I have been commissioned by your sisters to clear and bless your beautiful house."

"That's all very nice, but I don't approve of the barbaric methods of your tradition. I won't tolerate sacrifices or blood-spilling in my property."

"Dear young lady," Delia says, "while it is true that some Santería rituals are like that, it's not the way I work. I'm a *santera palera*, a *santera* from the house of Palo. My power is at the altar, at the sacred *nganga*." All of a sudden she sounds as if she were reciting a script or a solemn prayer for a large audience. "I am a daughter of Changó and the Holy Spirit, of Santa Barbara, god of fire and thunder. I do not take life. Changó is behind me, and Eleguá, god of forests and roads, is here today as the opener of paths."

Marion crosses her arms over her chest. "I'm not stupid, I've done my research and I know *santeros* sacrifice chickens in their rituals, and much worse. You're not going to fool me."

Julia is about to open her mouth when I squeeze her arm hard, and she only says, "Ouch," but gets the message.

Delia stares at Marion patiently. "You are misinformed, young lady. *Paleros* do not perform blood sacrifices. I'm only here to bless this house, with the help of the Holy Spirit. You have nothing to fear."

"Is that right?" Marion's voice spills with contempt. "I don't care who you are, what you do, or what you think you're doing here. I am an owner of this house and I would like you to stop everything and leave immediately," she says with forced calm.

Delia stares at her with an unwavering smile. "All right," she says after a moment, and then turns to a petrified Constantine. "Constant, before we leave, you're going to have to smuggle out those old hens again! Jeez, they never do make it to the sacrificial altar, do they?"

Constantine sniggers. None of us laugh. Marion stares ferociously at Delia.

"Before we begin packing, let me make sure I have this right." Delia walks toward the table, while Constantine scrambles to place a chair behind her. Delia gives Constantine the mop and sits down, without taking her eyes off Marion. "So," she says in a casual tone, "you do not stand for killings?"

Marion blinks. A moment goes by.

"Are you a vegetarian?" Delia asks.

"That's none of your business," Marion says.

"Are you?"

"Of course not!"

"Then you stand for killings. Meaning, every time you eat meat, you kill."

"That's different. It has nothing to do with this."

"Doesn't it? It's the taking of a life with forceful intention."

"Yeah, for the intention of survival!"

"So killing for survival is appropriate. What kind of survival? Only physical?"

Marion looks perplexed. "This is total bullshit. I'm not having this conversation. Please leave!" And she turns around, as if to leave herself.

"Where is your fear coming from?" Delia calls after her. "Has anyone been killed in this house before?"

Marion stops in her tracks. She turns around and stares at Delia, her eyes radiating shock and horror. "What did you say?"

"I said, has anybody been killed in this house?" Delia pronounces her words slowly.

I see Marion begin to shudder. I don't like the turn this conversation is taking. I walk toward her and put my hand on her arm, but Marion shrugs me off. "What have you told this woman?"

Before I can answer, Delia says, "No one has told me anything. I am asking you. Has anybody been killed in this house?"

Marion looks at her as if the orbs of her eyes were going to explode. She opens her lips to say something, but she seems too agitated to talk. She leans on the wall and starts convulsing with repressed sobs. I walk over to her once more, but she holds up one arm to indicate she doesn't want me near.

"Leave her," Delia says. "Let's go back into the house for a few minutes. Let's give her some space. And dear, please make another pot of coffee."

We all leave the patio for the kitchen, Julia in the rear, after gathering the rest of her papers from the floor.

In the kitchen, Delia sits in a chair by the altar, and Julia and Constantine sit at her sides. Nobody talks. I set about making more coffee, while I listen for Marion in the patio. After a few minutes, I hear her footsteps move quietly away. But I don't hear the gate or her car starting up, which means she's gone somewhere else in the house. When the coffee is ready, I pour it into cups and take it over to the table.

I drink mine standing at the sink. I'm upset with Julia and Delia. I'm conscious of how crazy and melodramatic Marion can be, but isn't her vulnerability evident? What looks like all fire and poison always ends up boiling down to a small, breakable creature. Doesn't Julia know this too well? Isn't it obvious to Delia too?

Delia sips her coffee in silence. Then she says, "How many people have died in this house?"

"Why? Two," Julia answers.

"Only two?" Delia asks.

"Yes. Mother, a very long time ago. And Marion's fiancé, also a while ago."

"Her fiancé?"

Julia casts down her eyes. "He drowned in the pool."

"I see." Delia is pensive while she slurps up the rest of her coffee. Constantine raises his eyebrows in a gesture of sympathetic grief.

"Well, all the more important that we do this *limpieza*," Delia says. "However, there's nothing doing without the consent of the eldest daughter of the house. Now that she's here, if Marion doesn't give permission, we can't proceed." Delia sets down her empty coffee cup, giving Julia and me a hard look. I imagine she's holding us responsible for Marion not having agreed to all of this beforehand.

Julia sighs. "I know she's very upset right now. She's still traumatized by that awful event. But she's the type who can also be capable of great clarity. I think if Anna talks to her . . ." Julia looks at me across the room with pleading eyes. She's saying, *I know you're not one hundred percent into this, but please stay with me right now, please, turn Marion around.* She doesn't need to pronounce a word, she's asked me to do this type of thing countless times.

"I'll talk to her," I say. "But if she refuses, we'll stop everything. Promise?"

Julia nods.

I walk out of the kitchen into the patio, and then around the house to the main entrance. It's noon and the sun is at its zenith. The raspy song of cicadas comes thick from all corners of the garden. The sun falls hard on the tiled patio and the old chairs. The porch is hot under the wooden rafters overcrowded with ivy. I peep through the large window that looks into the living room, where Delia and Constantine had been working before Marion arrived. The room is silent. Some of the white-cloth-covered furniture has been moved around. In the middle, leaning against the large sofa, is the mop, and the bucket of water at its feet. To the side stands the broom and, on the floor leaning against its straw brush, sits a round, hairy coconut. Jesus!

I move farther to the library, where I also spy through the glass door. Marion's broad, plum-colored shape lies doubled up on the long sofa facing the empty fireplace. Her long, dark curls speckled with gray streaks cover her face. I know Julia has been making sure that all doors in the house are open, but now, in view of this one's rusty and deformed metal hinges, I wonder how she's unbolted it. It screeches horribly as I push it open, its frame grating against the floor.

But Marion doesn't move.

I walk past the long shelves jammed with books, a disorderly mass in all sizes and colors, the bulk of Father's prized art-book collection. I sit in the old leather armchair opposite Marion. I know her temper tantrum is mostly over, and that she might listen to me. Marion is a short-distance runner.

"I'm sorry. I should have called you myself to make sure you were okay with all this," I say.

Marion clears the hair out of her face with one hand. "I know it's all Julia's doing. I'm sure you don't really want this yourself. It's just that you always go along with her." There's a reproachful tone in her voice. Her face is puffy and reddened, her eyes opaque, as if she had been shedding hot, difficult tears. She's lying on her side, with bare feet and knees pulled up to her big breasts, showing a long cleavage under the plum dress.

Marion used to be slender, with a long graceful body, flawless white skin, and a curling mane of dark brown hair that fell in long ringlets to her waist. Father used to say she was the Pre-Raphaelite beauty among us, the Dante Gabriel Rossetti, while Julia was the Modigliani and I, the Picasso. He used to sit in this very room and bring down art books from the library shelves, his impatient fingers flipping the pages of the oversized volumes, searching for pictures and portraits to authenticate his allegation. When he found the portraits that proved his point, he would say, this is what Marion looks like, and this is like you, and this, you, and we would stare in confusion at the images on the page. In retrospect, I suppose in my case he meant some portrait of Dora Maar, Picasso's muse and lover. But back then I felt annoyed and hurt with his Picasso comparison, because what I had seen of his paintings of women like Jacqueline Roque and the Demoiselles d'Avignon were figures with stupid looking eyes, double noses, and childish primary colors all over their faces. Julia also complained about the small, blind eyes of the Modigliani women and felt embarrassed by their nudity. But Marion just sat smiling, intoxicated with silent pride, because Dante Gabriel Rossetti's portrait of Proserpine was the most beautiful of all. Then, anyone would have thought that of the three, she was Father's favorite. But secretly, I always knew better, because Father admired Picasso over other painters, as the greatest artist of his century.

"What have you told this woman? Did you tell her about Fernando?" Marion asks.

"Not until a minute ago," I say.

"So how come she is picking up on it? How come she's talking about someone getting killed?"

"Marion . . ."

THE WEIGHT OF THE HEART   31

"Seriously, is she seeing something we don't know about? She's a fortune-teller, isn't she?"

"She is not a fortune-teller. She's a *santera*. A priestess from the Santería tradition," I say.

"And what is Santería?"

"I don't know much about it," I say. "Julia explained it's a Cuban religion, some sort of mixture between African Yoruba religion and Catholic. Apparently, slave populations mixed their gods with Catholic saints in order to hide them from our evil conquistadors and clergy. Their priests and priestesses, the *santeros*, work with energy and perform *limpiezas*, symbolic ceremonies to clear obstacles. That's supposedly what we're going for here."

Marion thinks for a moment. "She might be able to find out hidden information about his death."

"I don't think that will happen."

"Why not?"

"Because," I say, exasperated, and then add, despite myself, "C'mon, Marion, will you never let go? It's been so long."

"Easy for you to say, it didn't rip your life apart!"

I sigh and brace myself for what's coming. We've had this conversation so many times, I have so often struggled with answers to her questions, I no longer know what to say. It happens periodically that Marion brings it all up again. And I hate revisiting the memory of that night and the physical nausea that wells up in me when I look back on the twisted sequence of events. But Marion is still trapped in this bubble of time, and always manages to pull me back into it. I'll admit she's tried to move on with her life. She's committed to her work as an architect at the city's Department of Urban Planning, and has become devoted to her weekly yoga practice, without which she *couldn't bear to face life*, as she says. She's also been half-heartedly dating Brian, a banker guy working for the Madrid branch of Lloyds, for the last five years or so; but to be honest, only due to his unrelenting insistence. Marion still lives in the past.

I look at her straight and see once more that image of broken glass behind her dark irises, a cracked surface where the outer world is reflected in split, asymmetrical forms. This is why looking at Marion is painful. Her broken self is always reflected in her eyes. It's hard to remember her without shattered eyes, at the time when she was all gentle smiles, and her soft gaze felt as cozy as a winter night by the fireplace. Marion, with her long brown hair and pale skin, her small, delicate nose and full lips, used to be considered a prime example of what they call an English rose, and although her basic beauty has survived the ravages of time, her eyes have not. Their smooth hazel surface was probably changed in one single instant, when the image of Fernando floating belly down at the bottom of the pool splintered her soul. She stood there, a single scream ripping endlessly from her throat, while her body struggled to remain upright, as if a fierce wind were blasting her off the ground. It was I who jumped in the water and tried to drag his body to the surface and toward the rail grips on the shallower side, where we might have a chance of hauling him up. I pulled him by the white shirt he had worn open over his smooth, olive chest only hours before. The small crucifix with a gold chain floated around his neck, weightless, glittering in the water. I struggled to avert my eyes from the bloated, pasty face that bobbed along as I tugged at the body, and from the leather shoe that was still on one foot. Dawn had hardly broken, and I was cold under its pale light. I shivered in the water while I held the lifeless mass, and waited for Marion's unbearable shrieks to finally bring someone to my aid.

I make an effort to shake off these images from my mind. "Marion, I just need to know if you'll be okay with the work this woman is doing in the house today. We just want to clear the air so we can let go of the house."

"Do you really believe she can clear away all that has happened?"

For a moment, her question reverberates in my ears, and the idea of the house as a condensed version of all that has taken place inside its walls fills my mind. Are spaces capable of retaining the impact of events within their structures? Can laughter, tears, love, and hatred linger endlessly inside rooms? Like silent echoes on an infinite rebound? I suppress a shudder.

"I don't know. She might at least help us get some closure," I say.

"Do you think she'll find anything? Some new clue we never considered?"

I want to kneel down and put my arms around her, hold her

bosom's warmth against mine to stop it from dissipating, from hemorrhaging away, as it's been doing for over a decade. But the distance that has ensued between us lately would never allow for my embracing her now. We're still holding on to the tension that arose between the three of us after our father's death, when instead of feeling united by grief, we all chose to go separate ways, as if branching off individually would make it easier for us to overcome the past.

"Marion, let's just do this, it can't hurt. Meanwhile we can make plans to empty the house for the sale."

"Do you really want to sell?"

My chest tightens. I look away. No, I don't want to sell. I couldn't bear to have this place torn from my life right now; it would feel like being skinned. I've only agreed to talk about the possibility to please Julia, but a part of me wants to believe it will never happen. It's all we have left. Our parents might not be here any longer, but the house still is.

Marion waits on my words.

"In a way I think it would be the best for us all. It would help us move on." I echo Julia's words. Why am I always fearful of antagonizing my sisters? I've always been wary of any discord among us. Even more so after Father's passing. We'd had multiple discussions and fallings-out. The topic of the sale of the house had become the main bone of contention. While Marion was against it, Julia kept urging us to put it on the market. I had first sided with Marion because I didn't want to deal with anything that would bring back memories. I just wanted to live in the present. Immersed in my company and my ultra-workaholic schedule. But there had also been some bad blood between us, after an old will Father had drawn up over ten years ago popped up during probate as the only valid document around. A will in which he designated me as his main heiress, plus the official executor—a will he no doubt thought many times of changing, but never did. I had immediately redistributed equally among the three of us whatever remained of our father's diminished fortune, including this ruinous house. But my sisters had retained a certain resentment toward me. Another one of Father's sweet legacies. We'd talked about it openly a number of times, and whereas Julia seemed more disposed to let go of her bitterness, Marion had a harder time parting with her grudge. She was the eldest, and although she didn't act like it at all, she had felt disrespected after having been officially wiped out of her authority in the family, and in the inheritance process. That was why being addressed by Delia as the *eldest daughter of the house* grabbed her. It was the first time anyone returned her, even if just symbolically, to her real place in the family.

Marion sits up slowly, wipes off her tears with the tips of her fingers, adjusts her dress over her knees, and takes up one of the couch cushions, hugging it to her breasts.

She looks through the window for a moment. "I'll admit that something in me has been wanting to chase out the ghosts of this old house."

I stare at her, surprised.

She releases the pillow. "I'm sick of living in their shadows."

CHAPTER 5

Down in the kitchen, everyone sits in silence. The altar is still ablaze, and the room feels like an oven. I think about the oleanders that Julia has brought in and arranged in vases, together with cool daisies and lilies, around bottles and coconut shells, and how soon they will wilt under the heat. Delia fans herself slowly with a small black lacquered fan. Constantine and Julia's faces are beaded with sweat.

"Marion is okay with the cleaning," I say.

"Is she all right?" asks Julia.

"She'll be fine."

"Good!" Delia says, heaving herself out of the chair. "Let's get on with it then."

Everyone trickles out of the kitchen, but I linger around for a bit. I look down at my phone sticking out of my handbag on the counter, and see I have a missed call. Marcus! What would he want all the way from Germany on a Saturday like this? I push the phone deep into the bag. I cannot possibly deal with it now. I'm feeling annoyed and morose. I want to be alone. I hadn't factored in the amount of emotional upheaval that this seemingly harmless *limpieza* would bring about. Marion's has already been triggered, but what if Julia's goes into one of her *sensitive* states? It could be more than I can handle in one day.

Delia's handbell rings on the second floor, accompanied by singing. Where in the house can I retreat to, to be as far away as possible from all this? To one side of the kitchen, at the end of the corridor, is Nanny's old room. We still think of it as her room, even so many years after she's been out of the house.

The room is small, with whitewashed walls, and sparsely furnished. The bed, pushed against the wall underneath the window, consists of a smallish mattress and box spring with a metal headboard, the type found in the *pueblos*, the old villages in the countryside. It's now covered by a shabby flowery bedspread festooned at the edges with thick, yellowed wool fringes that fall to the floor. A narrow, hand-carved piece of stripped pinewood serves as a bedside table. On top of it stands an old brass lamp ending in a bare bulb, and inside its only drawer, a tattered picture card of the Our Lady of Covadonga taped with scotch tape to the bottom. This had always been Nanny's patron, the virgin who inspired Christian warriors to fight against the Moors in the Reconquista of the Spanish Peninsula from Islam.

At the foot of the bed stands her old Singer sewing machine on ornate iron legs and treadle. Opposite the bed is the little white wardrobe that had for so many years belonged to the room Julia and I shared. I stand for a moment facing its mirrored doors, its silver linings so deteriorated that they only reflect images as abstract collections of colors and shapes. I observe my head as a splash of pinkish flesh topped by a blob of short black hair, my lower body in thick brushstrokes of green fabric over muscular legs. Along the beveled rim on the upper-right corner, the darkened opaque surface is still dotted with small islands of silver lining that reflect jagged images. For an instant, I watch fragments of my face reflected on these patches. A pointed cheekbone, the dip in the middle of my upper lip, a pale blue eye with tiny wrinkles at the corner; its pupil, contracted into that wistful look I so dislike, now stares back at me, a little peeved. What do I expect to find in this room?

I grab hold of the handles and open the wardrobe doors. Inside, on top of a darkened shelf, sits a moldy stack of old linen, on top of which is Nanny's frayed apron, neatly folded. Unbelievable that such an old relic should have endured. I reach out to touch it. Its coarse cotton feels thin, eroded. I take it out and lift it to my face. It smells musty, like mildewed kitchen rags. I unfold it and stretch it out before me. One string is missing, the other threadbare and torn. A tune creeps into my mind, and with it, the words of a Spanish children's song,

> *When I stepped on board,*
> *the boatman said to me,*
> *pretty girls go for free.*
> *I am not pretty,*
> *nor do I want to be . . .*

followed by the sound of a skipping rope and small feet jumping on the patio floor. Marion and Julia singing, taking turns at skipping and swinging the rope with Nanny. And I, too young to skip, watching impatiently to the side, begging to be taught, and pulling Nanny's apron strings loose as the only way to get her attention and boycott the game. Well, surely not this very same apron, but I swear, an identical one. Nanny always wore the same clothes. Year after year she bought the exact same items for day-to-day wear. Only on Sundays she wore a different dress when going to mass, a dark, silky garment buttoned up to her neck with small pearly studs.

I return the apron to the wardrobe and sit across from the bed in the room's only chair, another sober piece of simple wood that has been here since my earliest memories. On the wall beside me hangs a black-and-white picture of the three of us sitting with Nanny in some meadow, having a picnic. How old she looked even then, when she must have been only around fifty, seeing how small we were in the picture. I couldn't have been more than five years old, Julia eight and Marion ten. Nanny's hair was already totally white and pulled back into a tight bun at the nape of her neck, her brown eyes horribly augmented behind thick glasses, and her large matronly figure covered by the white apron, with thick chunky black shoes at the end of heavy legs. I always remembered her like that, as if she hadn't changed one bit in all the eighteen years I lived with her.

We called her Nanny but she was everything: maid, cleaner, cook, nurse, mother. She had come with Mother from their native city of Vitoria in the Basque Country, north of Spain. She had worked as a maid at Mother's family house since she was a girl, seen Mother grow up from infancy, and then joined her in her newly married life in Madrid. After Mother passed away, she stayed to bring us up. I have more memories of Nanny than of Mother. I grew up mostly in the kitchen and in Nanny's bedroom, slept many a night in this bed, hugging her body of solid flesh that smelled of bread soaked in milk.

In this room I'd always sit in this same chair, watching her do chores while asking endless questions. I remember her in the evenings standing at the ironing board by a tall pile of clothes, listening to soap operas on the radio, tear-jerking stories with names like *Simply Mary* or *The Subway Ticket-Seller.* Always stories of high drama, with young, beautiful, and innocent working-class women ravaged by social injustice and demon lovers. These radio shows were sacred, not just in Nanny's room, but in the whole country. Six in the evening was the moment when households would become paralyzed, and all housewives, maids, and nannies resorted to sewing, darning, or ironing clothes in solemn silence, glued to a nearby radio.

Although I never saw Nanny shed a tear, these were her tenderest moments. Otherwise, she was not a demonstrative woman; in fact, rather stiff, and sometimes even standoffish. She was, by her own definition, "a girl from the north," a tough matron from the highlands, from a country entrenched in timeless matriarchal tradition that not even the Romans had managed to subdue with their war-savvy legions and overwhelming technology.

"For centuries," she used to say, "women would face troops and marauders, knife and pitchfork in hand, having first safely hidden away their daughters in large ceramic pots used to store oil or wine in cellars."

But Nanny's life had not developed, at first appearance, along the lines of heroic legend. She started as a servant at the age of twelve, she had a sweetheart for a few brief months before he was killed in the Civil War by some macabre "friendly fire," and thereafter continued to work as a maid all her life. She never had children, never owned anything, left very little behind. However, in the real story behind all that, Nanny was, while she lasted, the custodian of our house. She ran the whole operation; she brought us up following the very complicated requirements of our household. It was a mystery how she adapted to a mostly English-speaking family, a wonder how fiercely she endorsed our manifold education with foreign schools, music lessons, ballet, and whatnot. She was the bedrock on which we all rested. She was the land, the peasantry that pulls along like an ox, carrying the weight of a motley, erratic, supposedly sophisticated crowd on its back.

Father was, of course, some sort of British version of the reincarnation of all those troops and marauders that her ancestors had fought, knife and pitchfork in hand. He was the impossible daily challenge Nanny had to contend with. To begin with, Father was the pickiest eater I ever knew. It didn't matter how much Nanny strived to produce delicious food for our table, he always complained. Especially if she ventured into British recipes, such as roast beef, Yorkshire pudding, or shepherd's pie, there was always some blemish to be found. The objections that became legendary were mostly against the most rooted elements in Spanish cuisine: olive oil and garlic. To Father, the smell of garlic and the strong taste of olive oil were daily maddening encounters, unbearable components of indigestible third-world food unfitting for the more delicate, evolved British digestive tubes. He told all kinds of stories about English travelers getting the runs as soon as they hit the greasy medieval-style casseroles and extravagant rice dishes.

Mealtimes were the hardest moments. The three of us sat around the table frozen with trepidation: Marion to Father's left, I to his right, and Julia by my side. Nanny would come in with the food and go around the table serving us individually. She always started with Father, and then stood back behind him, waiting for approval. All our eyes would be on Father as he began the ceremony of tasting the food. If the verdict was positive, he made no comment whatsoever, and after a moment everyone sighed with relief and started to eat. However, if the verdict was negative, he immediately put the plate aside, indicating with a wave of his hand that it should be taken away and substituted with something else. If the second offering was neither to his taste, he joked about living in a house with an empty pantry in spite of working so hard to make a living. Then he usually went into one of his favorite diatribes against backward countries.

"Do you know that when I arrived in Spain in the late fifties, people were so poor that they walked around in *alpargatas?*" he would say, as if denouncing an inexcusable historical situation. *Alpargatas* were a sort of espadrilles or sandals made with thick grass classically worn by peasants and poor farmers years ago. But what did that have to do with anything?

"And do you know what was the first thing they did to the girls who came from villages to be servants in households? They'd scrub their nails and their fingers, thoroughly. Teach them to wash their hands. Please translate to Nanny, I'm sure she has her own story about it." The three of us would sit paralyzed with embarrassment and pain for Nanny.

It wasn't that Father couldn't speak Spanish, he could. Despite his most ludicrous accent and making the most awkward grammatical mistakes, he got by. But he liked to do this kind of thing when he wanted to make inconvenient statements. In those moments Nanny, conscious of some abstract humiliation directed at her, would retreat into the kitchen and we would continue to eat in silence.

"Of course, that's not to say that Nanny doesn't have a noble heart, even if she has no education," Father would add, in a weak effort to diffuse the foul atmosphere he'd created. "You can always tell a genuine soul from a person's eyes. You can be honorable, even if you come from a lower class. And Nanny is like that. Why do you think I kept her after your mother died?"

In reality, it had been the other way around. Nanny had decided to stay and support Father after our mother died. A few months after the passing, her widowed sister had called from Vitoria and asked her to move in with her and help her with her own bunch of small children. Nanny thought about it carefully, and in the end decided her commitment was with us.

"She has our other sisters," she explained. "You have no one."

We really had no one. Estranged from Mother's family and far away from our Manchester relatives, we had no close blood relations to nurture us in such terrible moments. Father was devastated. He lost weight, he was sick frequently; he eventually took refuge in his work, two or more packets of cigarettes a day, and tall glasses of whiskey on the rocks in the evenings. He became a consummate workaholic, would leave very early in the morning with his briefcase and a cigarette dangling from his lips, and return late at night, shriveled, ashen-faced, stinking of tobacco and stale office furnishings. Sometimes, if he wasn't totally exhausted, he would sit by our three little beds and tell us stories. He was a good storyteller. His best tale was called "Anna and Her Toys," and in it, when we went to sleep, my dolls and teddy bears would come to life and wake me up. Then, I would dress up like a boy and go to a different world, sometimes taking my sisters with me, where we underwent countless adventures in which I was the heroine disguised as a miniature Robin Hood. I remember being magnetized by the tale, while my sisters smoldered with envy and wondered why he always favored this story above others. I guessed he was most sad for me. I was only five years old.

Those had been hard years for everyone. I only remember them in permanent autumnal or wintery mode. Dark, gray skies, short days and cold nights in which I would always migrate to Nanny's room.

On weekends, Father would sit alone in the living room, surrounded by papers and letters from his office, and work his way through them hour after hour. Meanwhile, we would sit downstairs in the TV room watching American television series, or hang around in the kitchen with Nanny. At one point or another, Father would ask for tea and the four of us would begin the hopeless task of making a cup of tea that would meet with his approval.

Poor Nanny, measuring up to the alchemical grind of producing a perfect, not just British, but specifically Mancunian, cup of tea. Even Mother had never mastered the necessary proficiency in all the strict but apparently necessary steps. There was the boiling of the water, not in any pot, but only in the designated kettle. Then the exact measuring of the tea from the tin decorated with Chinese figures, followed by the careful pouring of the water into the teapot, first in the empty pot to heat it up well, and then once again over the small mound of tea leaves at the bottom of the teapot, not forgetting to let it steep for exactly five minutes. And finally, the most challenging part was not just pouring the tea and not forgetting that the milk and two spoons of sugar were first to be deposited in the cup, but the act of delivering the full teacup without spilling any of its contents onto the saucer.

At that point Nanny needed to mount the stairs to deliver the cup to Father. She would haul her heavy body up the steps, one hand grasping the banister and the other holding the jittering cup of tea. Many a time, she would return to the kitchen in silent dejection, the flooded tea saucer still in hand, after Father had refused to drink the wreckage.

"One suggestion, don't fill the cup to the brim, *comprende?*" his voice would trail down the stairs, followed by, "Girls, please get her to understand."

To Father, Nanny was the representative of the third-world country we were stuck in. Of course, there were others. The gardener, the deliveryman who showed up regularly at our doorstep, his company employees he contended with daily, and so on. But the most immediate one was Nanny, and therefore always symbolic of all the ills and tribulations that one had to put up with in this bloody country. Vignettes of my sister's faces, exhausted and patiently waiting for him to wind down from his tirades against Spain, are etched in my mind. His unwavering lingo of vituperation will forever play itself in the depths of my subconscious. Talk of the goddamn nincompoop nation, the insolence and the laziness, the amateurish arrogance, the inefficiency, the imprecision of language, the loser's-paradise attitude, and so on.

Maybe at the heart of his raging discontent was Mother's death at a young age. Maybe the way her family had opposed their marriage because he was Protestant, and not Catholic like them. Maybe it had to do with the fact that after she died, he hadn't mustered the strength to relocate back to England.

"Just that a woman, a young woman, could have died of pneumonia in the late twentieth century," he would sometimes say, "that tells you how backward, how undeveloped this country can be.

If we had been in England that would never have happened, she would still be with us." But he never related the whole backstory, how Mother had been sickly all her life, how cutting off with her family in order to marry him had filled her with devouring grief.

Nanny had stood up against Mother's brothers at the funeral and defended Father when they accused him of not taking good care of her. And then, once we all returned back home, she stood in her black garments behind his chair as he wept, and shyly placed one hand on his shoulder. But that had been a unique instance of physical tenderness between them.

They lived in opposite sides of the house, like opponent winds across the compass rose, flurry breezes avoiding each other at best, and blasting gales contending fiercely at worst. And although Nanny's wind regularly seemed to be the passive, defensive force, the floodgate that could unbind her cyclone was any attack perpetrated against her most significant concern: any one of us, the girls she had kept safely hidden away in large ceramic pots used to store oil or wine in cellars.

The day after we found Fernando floating lifeless in the pool, a host of policemen and detectives had swarmed around the house until nightfall. When the last group left late in the evening after interrogating us for the third time, Nanny took Marion upstairs and tucked her into her bed and then went to the kitchen to warm up some milk and take a Valium from the medicine cabinet. After Marion finally went to sleep, she came downstairs and stood in front of Father in the living room, while Julia and I sat in silence on the long sofa across from his armchair.

"Mister James," she said, "I know you did not push that boy into the pool, I will put my hand over the fire in any courtroom if I have to. But I also know how you destroyed him, how you broke him so he wouldn't marry your daughter. I will stay for as long as it takes to nurse Marion back to health, and then I will pack my things and leave. I cannot work in this house anymore."

The final battle of the winds was unleashed. A force like a typhoon erupted through Father, a blasting stream of chilling onslaught. Nanny withstood the squall, the spears from the bloodshot eyes, the throbbing impulses in the fisted hands. Then, at the first spaced silence, she turned away quietly and went downstairs to her room. Julia and I followed her, crying, and I stood in this room holding on to her heavy body and begging her not to go, to forget Father's words, those cold, furious words. with which he had thrown her out of the house. But Nanny had reached the end of her rope, her knives and pitchforks were blunted by years of defensive grind. Meanwhile, Julia sobbed, crouching on the floor over the old-fashioned suitcase that Nanny had already brought down from the top of the wardrobe and was meaning to fill with her belongings.

Constantine's pouty face emerges behind the threshold of the door, or maybe it has been there for a while, observing my absorption. "Ahem," he whispers, "sorry to bother you, but Delia is saying she needs five pounds of coarse sea salt. I'm imagining that you wouldn't keep those amounts in the house, so . . ."

"Five pounds! Jeez, it sounds like a lot," I say, making an effort to pull out of my reverie and contemplate the quandaries of this new request.

"Well, you know, in this business some things that are minimal in the day-to-day get magnified, and some others that are humongous can be reduced to practically nothing," he says with a shy, raspy laugh, as if embarrassed at having revealed a great truth in an awkward, untimely way.

A truth I wish he'd kept in his arsenal of secrets, since all I'm concerned about right now is how to pull out of the depths of my trance. I look up at Constantine, who still lingers at the door, ogling my outstretched legs. Annoyed, I draw my knees together, while he averts his eyes, bashfully.

"Let me see what I can do," I say, and stand up, aching at having to extricate myself from Nanny once more, and mad about having to buy no less than five kilos of salt, which I suspect will somehow end up being rubbed into my wounds.

CHAPTER 6

I squint at the bright sunlight as I step into the patio.

Julia is sitting at the far end, her feet up on a chair. I stand behind her and peep over her shoulder at the sketch she's working on. The image of two women sitting on the beach under a parasol, looking out onto the ocean, drafted in broad charcoal strokes.

Julia looks up. "I know what you're going to ask. But don't count me in. I've done more than my share. Your turn to drive around looking for impossible ingredients."

I don't have the energy to argue, so I take up my handbag and go in search of Marion.

The library is full of green bottle flies. I've left the door ajar by mistake and they've buzzed in from the garden in search of shaded solace. But Marion seems unaffected by their droning charges against the windowpanes. She is sitting on the sofa, leaning back, with arms folded behind her head, staring at the ceiling. Is she day-dreaming one of her tragic dreams?

"I need to buy salt for Delia. Can I use your car?"

Marion stares at me, startled. "Salt? Whatever for?"

"Don't know. They need all kinds of stuff for their work."

"I'll drive you. That way, we can buy something to eat." Marion is back to a mellow mood. It amazes me how quickly she can undulate between emotional states. But one thing's always sure to get her on the upswing: food. Even just the thought of it.

We get into her car, a burgundy Toyota Corolla she's had since her return from London, eight years ago. Marion buckles herself into the driver's seat, adjusts the rearview mirror, and applies lipstick on her pouted lips. "Where to go on a Saturday afternoon in the middle of August to buy salt, I wonder?"

"There's only one place open right now in this neighborhood. That expensive, deluxe deli over by the main road," I say.

We drive slowly through narrow, labyrinthine streets along tall stone fences, behind which large houses stand surrounded by gardens collapsed under the midday heat. Sections of the road's bumpy, pebbled surface are splattered with gluey globs of violet mulberries from the trees lining the sidewalks. They stick to the car tires, making them roll over with a crunchy sound. Their sickly smell wafts in through the car window, a sweetish odor of crushed, rotting fruit that makes me feel queasy. It brings back images of Julia and me standing on ladders against their tree trunks, harvesting leaves to feed the silkworms we kept in shoeboxes under our beds. At night we dreamed of the silk fabrics we'd have, once the fat, white butterflies emerged out of cocoons and fluttered away. Until the day we found out that silk can only be extracted from cocoons from which butterflies never emerge. So much for little girls' harvesting dreams. But those same mulberry trees have pervaded; tops reaching farther into the skies, robust branches lush with heart-shaped leaves, throwing long shadows over sidewalks. Their yield of clumped, purple berries has likewise increased, and at this time of summer, mounds of wasted fruit decomposing on the ground greatly encumber pedestrians and cars.

It's ironic to think that the first time I saw Fernando, he and Marion were kissing under one of these mulberry trees, like a foreshadowing of their ill-fated love. Silhouettes wrapped around each other in the amber streetlight, lips fused under a mass of entangled black hair. Sensing my presence, Fernando perked up, still holding Marion's body tight, as if to protect her from a threat. In a flash I saw his pale, handsome face, with moist black eyes under firmly traced brows, and hair combed back like a movie star from the thirties. He wasn't much taller than Marion, but his wiry body stood graceful on strong legs.

Marion broke into a smile. "Don't worry, it's only my little sister," and she introduced us. I got a whiff of musky cologne mingled with his manly tang as he pecked my face. I also saw his two large gold rings on the fingers that held Marion's hand. They matched the golden chain around his neck ending in a small crucifix hung between the clavicles under his open shirt.

"If I wasn't already crazy about you," he said, looking at Marion, in a suave, hissing Andalusian accent, "I would definitively look up your sister. What a beauty she is!" I stood tongue-tied. I'd never seen Marion kissing anyone. I'd never seen such a good-looking man before.

Marion disengaged her hand from his. "I have to go. It's late. Will you call me tomorrow?" And they kissed again, with hungry, tender lips, and when they pulled away their eyes seemed to ache, anticipating the long wait before their next meeting.

"Until tomorrow then," said Fernando, and walked slowly into the night street, turning his head twice before his smile dissolved in the dark.

"Please, don't tell anyone about Fernando," Marion said, putting her arm around me as we walked to the house.

"Sure. But, why?"

"I want to introduce him properly to Father and Nanny."

"When?"

"Soon."

"How did you meet him?"

"I met him in a flamenco bar. He's a *torero*, a bullfighter, you know?" she said proudly. As we waited to be buzzed in to the house, I watched her face unfurled into an ecstatic smile, and her throat tense, as if holding down shouts of joy.

A week later, Marion took me to the bullring of Las Ventas for the first time. We drove in the small Seat 600 Father had given her to drive to architecture school, which was also burgundy. Burgundy has for some reason always been Marion's color. I even remember her that day wearing a long burgundy skirt over cherry cowboy boots. I'd never been even close to the Las Ventas bullfighting ring, nor had ever seen a bullfight, save for a few stolen glances at television sets in bars where the *corridas* were being broadcast. We parked the car on a side street and Marion hurried me toward the plaza. I was amazed at the huge circular building, a coliseum of terracotta bricks, with tall square turrets, horseshoe arches, and ceramic incrustations all over its façade.

"You can look at all this later," Marion said, pulling me by the arm. "We're late. I hope we can still find Manuel." I didn't have time to ask who Manuel was, as we were immediately spotted by a short, wiry guy with long hair pulled back into a ponytail and dressed in shabby jeans and a black shirt, who motioned us nervously toward him.

"Quick," he said after kissing us both on the cheek. "He's about to enter the ring." He ushered us through the main door, after nodding knowingly to the man who took entry tickets, and whizzed us through passages and corridors until we stepped out into the arena.

It was sometime past six in the afternoon, but the sun was still strong. I shaded my eyes to take in the immensity of the arena, glaring from its sand-colored circumference. The ring stood surrounded by climbing rows of stands already full of people. We walked down the rows until we came to two seats very close to the ring, apparently reserved for us, which Manuel pointed out. He then waited for us to settle down before signaling he was leaving, and would see us later. I felt uneasy as we sat among the crowd that was already standing up and cheering. I felt tired and listless. Although our seats were in the shade, the stone was still hot from the daylong swelter.

"Here he comes!" Marion said, pulling me by the arm to make me stand up. Bullfighters, picadors on dressed horses, and men in red shirts and caps poured out of one of the gates and started parading around the ring saluting the public. All was happening to a trumpet sound while the crowd cheered wildly.

Marion looked around anxiously among the *toreros*. "There he is! Can you see him? In the pink suit!" I looked and vaguely recognized Fernando's dark head of curls. He was walking between one row of matadors, and another of picadors with lances, mounted on horses. His slim body was packed into an embroidered suit that glittered in the sun. A short, brocaded jacket with heavily padded shoulders, tight trousers extending from the waist down and over the knees, salmon-colored stockings, and black ballerina-like shoes. The other *toreros* and picadors were dressed similarly in different colors: red, cream, blue. Some wore black oblong hats, but not Fernando. He walked along bareheaded. The colorful parade paced around the ring three times, greeting the crowd and paying respect to the dignitaries sitting in the main box, and finally exited through the same door they had entered.

Seconds later, a hatch-like gate opened and a bull sprang into the arena. Its dark powerful body was driven by long pointed horns; a mass of smooth, black muscles glistening under the sun. The bull galloped furiously around the ring, hurtling himself at the *barrera*, or wooden wall enclosing the arena, and charging at the *burladeros*, the narrow entrances where bullfighters and other personnel entered the ring or escaped bulls if they must. A few bullfighters stepped out with red capes and made attempts at passes, but had to be aided by others in order to get away safely. The crowd oohed and aahed in waves, standing at times to get a better view of the bull chasing the bullfighters or stabbing its horns into the wooden wall of the *barrera*.

"That bull's a cunning bastard, he knows more than is desirable," said a bald, greasy man sitting next to Marion. "I wouldn't want to be the matador who faces him today."

Marion shuddered and looked at me, and I knew that matador was Fernando and that was his bull. When I returned my eyes to the ring I saw one of the horses with the heavy padded skirt walking slowly across the arena, mounted by a man with a lance, the picador, and slowly approaching the bull. I noticed the horse was blindfolded, and my stomach tightened.

I stood up. "I want to leave. Please, I can't bear to watch this." But Marion ignored me; she was glued to the scene. After I protested again, she took my hand and pushed me back into my seat, "Just stay with it for a while, it will be over soon."

I sat down, feeling nauseated with fear.

The bull was very still in the middle of the ring, observing the approaching party, getting ready to charge. Then, in the spur of a second it flung itself into the horse, ramming against its flank as the picador thrust the lance into his back. Blood began to trickle under the metal spear, while the bull continued to thrust and shove the horse toward the *barrera*. At one point it stepped back for a few seconds, just before hurtling itself once more with lowered head and horns, so that as he lunged he lifted up both horse and man in the air. I gasped and felt my heart thumping wildly in my chest. Horse and man were suspended in midair for what felt like whole minutes, while the man jabbed at the bull again and again. The crowd around us cried wildly. Bullfighters came out of the *burladero* with capes and ran to the bull, swirling their red cloths over his head and back, to take him away from the horse. Finally the bull pulled away and charged against the capes, and the horse fell on the ground, struggling in silent pain while a river of dark blood gushed from his belly. I buried my face in my hands and burst into sobs.

Marion squeezed my hand. "I'm sorry. It's all right, they'll take care of him, don't you worry."

But the horse was already dead, or at least it had stopped moving and lay listless, while men in red caps and shirts helped the picador out from under its body. Then, they quickly brought in a cart driven by two steers and dragged the horse's body away, before they smoothed out the sand on the ring. All this time, *banderilleros* jumped into the ring, placing small sorts of arrows into the bull's back, but all I could see through my watery eyes was a bunch of multicolored lumps moving against the yellow sand.

"Please let's go," I said to Marion.

"It's okay, dear," said the bald man next to Marion. "You'll soon get used to it, and then really begin to like it. Everyone's a bit shocked the first time." I looked at Marion and saw with disbelief the eagerness with which she sat on the edge of the seat, looking out into the ring. Her body was vibrant with excitement, breathless for dramatic action. I knew I wouldn't be able take her away until the bullfight was over.

Suddenly, the whole arena grew silent while the matador walked into the ring to face the bull for the real fight. It was Fernando's time. Marion took my hand and held it tight against the seat. Fernando strode with ease into the middle of the ring, with head high and body upright. He carried a large red cape in one hand and a sword in the other. He walked slowly, hiding the sword under the cape. The bull stood still, eyeing him closely with small eyes, and didn't move, even when Fernando stopped a few feet before him. They seemed to size each other up for a few minutes while the crowd froze into silence. Then Fernando took a step forward, making a short, throaty sound, "Heh!" and coaxed the bull toward the cape. But the bull waited. Fernando went in closer. "Heh!" It took a third time stepping in before the bull charged. The crowd shouted, *"Olé!"* and the battle began. The bull went for the cape, looking to dig his horns into the man, and the man twirled around him, hardly moving his feet, just twisting his waist and swirling the cloth around the bull, one time after another, creating a whorl-like dance between red and black. The crowd was beside itself. Every set of eyes now followed Fernando's cape amidst roaring waves of clamor. Even I forgot about my apprehension for an instant, and marveled at his art, while Marion soared beside me, exploding with pride. Now and then, Fernando would turn his back to the bull after a number of swirls, and walk away. The bull stood panting, seemingly perplexed, blood still dripping down his back. Then one time the bull charged at him from the back, but Fernando swung quickly and drove him into the cape. From that moment on they engaged in quick, breathless passes, while the bull came closer and closer to Fernando's body each time. The crowd wailed in frenzy.

"Someone should be taking that bull away from him now," the man next to Marion said. Marion grabbed my hand again, squeezing it until I was in pain. Everybody seemed to be in a trance. The tension between man and bull was hypnotic. Fernando's movements were becoming shorter and sharper. The bull wouldn't yield. I saw Fernando's small body brushing against the dark gloss of the bull's flanks. I saw how the bull's blood had been smeared on his pink suit. And then in one quick second the tables turned.

The bull swerved its horns abruptly and caught Fernando's side. He tossed him into the air, tumbling him to the ground. Three other bullfighters rushed from the *burladero* with their capes. The bull kept charging at Fernando's fallen body. Marion screamed. The crowd screamed. Even I screamed. Finally a group of five bullfighters took the bull off Fernando, and others rushed into the ring and carried him behind the *barrera*. The crowd became silent with dejection.

Marion stood up, trembling. "Where are they taking him?" she asked the bald man.

"Down to the sick bay," he replied.

"Quick, let's go," she said, grabbing me again by the hand, and when I searched her face questioningly, she hissed in agony, "Please!"

"I don't think they'll let you in there, miss," was the last I heard of the man's voice before we started out of our seats and raced up the rows toward the back of the arena, passing by groups of confused spectators and bullring workers, while Marion slithered between passages and corridors as if she knew the place by heart, with me trailing behind. Finally, one of the security guards pointed to the end of a dim hall and we arrived at the sick bay. A smell of sweat, blood, and antiseptics wafted out into the corridor.

At the infirmary door, a male nurse in white scrubs stood barring our entrance. "Sorry, no visitors at this time. He's in critical condition." Marion let out a shrill cry, while I looked past him into the scene ahead.

The infirmary was a stark room with whitewashed walls. In the middle stood a table on which Fernando was lying, a large bloody slash between the right-sided ribs, exposed over his torso. To the side, next to a metal cabinet and an instrument trolley, lay Fernando's blood-drenched brocaded jacket over a chair. A doctor in a white coat, with a long face and sparse mousy hair, was washing the wound with large pieces of cotton wool and gauze. Fernando's face was contorted in pain, his eyes closed. The gash was like an open mouth, dark crimson granulated lips frozen into a voiceless cry. Surrounding the table was his cousin Manuel and three other men, two young and another one older. The latter was called Federico, as I would later learn, and was Fernando's disagreeable, but efficient, business manager. His drooping green eyes stared out wearily under dark bushy brows; long sideburns extended along thick vertical folds of skin surrounding his contemptuous mouth. His large head was out of proportion to his thin, shortish body, which was clad in an Andalusian country-style suit and riding boots.

He stared sourly at Fernando's wound. "You are a fool to work the bull so closely, it's unnecessary. You're too *chulo*, cocky, you'll be out for the season, and we'll lose a bunch of money."

"I can't believe you accepted that bull, Federico," Manuel said, "That animal's extremely vicious. And way too heavy. I wonder how the next guy will deal with him."

The other two guys agreed with Manuel. One was tall and lanky, dressed in an oversized gray suit; the other, slim and wiry like Manuel, with rotten teeth that showed when he laughed.

"Fernando could have handled him perfectly, if he hadn't taken stupid risks. Who lets the bull give such close passes? You might as well have asked him to give you a shave!"

The other men chuckled, and the one with rotten teeth said, "At least you'll admit he has *cojones*, and that's why the public raves about him."

"When *cojones* get you killed, that's the end of your *cojones* and of my contract!" Federico replied.

"You're lucky it didn't puncture the lung. It came real close," the doctor said. "We'll have to take him to the hospital. I'll just give him temporary stitches. But I can't give an anesthetic. We'll have to do this cold turkey," he added.

"That's where the *cojones* come in handy too," said the man in the oversized suit.

When Marion heard the words *hospital* and *anesthetic*, she cried out again, and only then did Fernando open his eyes and look in our direction. Then he said in a dull, assertive voice, "Let her in."

"No women in the room," Federico cut in. "Manuel, see that they leave."

"I said, let her in!" Fernando repeated in a stronger voice and made an attempt to sit up, but blood started gushing from the wound and the doctor made him lie down again. "Easy now. It's all right if they come in," he said, nodding to the nurse. The male nurse stood to one side and we stepped in.

The moment Marion walked into the infirmary, a sort of freeze frame descended on the scene. The conversation between the men stopped. They watched as she swept through the space with her long burgundy skirt over cherry-red boots and waist-length curls trailing behind, exuding that tragic grace only on tap for beautiful heroines soon to be mortally wounded; that Pre-Raphaelite vulnerability Father had impressed on her by matching her with Proserpine and the Lady of Shallot.

Marion reached Fernando's side and took his hands, tears streaming down her face. Fernando smiled weakly. His face was waxy and clammy, his eyes liquid pools of ink.

"I wish I hadn't insisted you come to this *corrida*. I don't want you to see me like this," he said.

"My love, you must promise never to step into that ring again. I couldn't bear to lose you."

He sighed. "That's not going to happen. Who would I be in your eyes if I become a coward?" he said with tenderness. Marion lowered her face toward his and they kissed. There was a sense of embarrassment in the men around them.

"Let's just turn off the lights and leave," said Federico in a mixture of pleasantry and bitterness. "The moment goddamned women walk into the scene . . ."

"C'mon Federico, give him a break!" Manuel interrupted, and led him and the other men out of the room, leaving us with just the doctor and the male nurse.

"He had to fall in love at this crucial moment in his career," I heard Federico's voice trail down the corridor, "and to make things worse, with a *guiri*!" *Guiri* meant foreigner, unwanted tourist, or outsider, and I was annoyed to hear the word applied to Marion and me. Although, yes, we were extremely removed from this strange world of rough men, bulls, blood, leather, and dust. But *guiri* meant American, or at least Anglo-Saxon, inhabitants from a faraway culture that would never understand Spain or its traditions, who could interfere with the natural order of custom and belief. Part of Fernando's reputation, as a poor boy who had stormed the bullfighting world with irresistible talent and courage, was now tied to his torrid romance with a beautiful *guiri* girl.

But Fernando and Marion were not effaced by Federico's words or any public opinion. They existed in their own separate bubble, oblivious of the world. They continued to pour passionate glances into each other while the doctor finished with his stitching, and

Marion squeezed Fernando's hand and stroked his face every time he winced with pain.

When the doctor was finished, Marion turned to him in a huff. "Doctor, please give me a blanket, don't you see he's cold?"

"The ambulance will be here any minute," said the doctor, and gave her a white sheet to cover Fernando, who had closed his eyes again and was shivering.

I was standing by the door, leaning with my back against the wall, observing them in silence, when the male nurse came over and stood next to me. He looked to be in his early thirties, with olive skin and sharp, hawklike eyes from which nothing seemed to escape scrutiny.

"Your friend is head over heels about Fernando, isn't she?" he asked quietly.

"She's not my friend, she's my sister."

"She needs to watch out for herself if she doesn't want to become a widow."

"What?"

"I've seen many *toreros*. This one is branded." I wanted to sneer at him, but that minute a security guard rushed down the corridor announcing the arrival of the ambulance, and everyone scrambled into a flurry of activity to move Fernando onto the gurney that was soon wheeled in.

We ended up not going to the hospital; although the doctor had to promise Marion that he would personally accompany Fernando all the way and stay with him overnight, if needed. She could then visit him in the morning, when he would be recovering in a room of his own. We drove back home in silence. Marion entered the house ashen-faced and, claiming she had a headache, refused to have dinner, ran up the stairs to her room, and locked herself in. Later on, I put my ear to her door and heard her muffled sobbing, as if weeping with her face buried in her pillow.

Fernando recovered, returned to the bullring only a few weeks later, and fought dozens of bulls until the end of the season. But Marion didn't quite recover. She failed most of her semester exams, lost considerable weight, spent her days in a stupor, and only came to herself in the evenings when Fernando came to fetch her to go for a walk, or to one of the flamenco bars. Her room filled up with bullfighting lore. She wore a black, wide-brimmed Andalusian hat and bolero jackets to class, and listened to flamenco guitar all day long. Beside her bed was a giant bullfighting poster announcing a *corrida* to be fought by Fernando Rios, El Niño.

She was madly in love.

In the beginning, Father took it all lightly. He received Fernando in good humor and called him *hombre*, man, and even had a conversation or two about the art of bullfighting, of which he knew nothing. Fernando would laugh and explain things patiently, not realizing that most of the time he was being put on by Father. When things became more familiar between them, the jokes became heavier.

"*Hombre*, how are those big bulls doing? I heard they give them sleeping pills before they come into the ring so that they're easier to tackle. The days of real bullfighting are over, aren't they!"

Or he would say, "I've always been told that matadors are very brave, you know, to face the bull alone in the ring and all; but then there's others who think that to be that brave you need to be totally stupid. What do you think? Are you that brave?"

Fernando would break into his charming smile. "Mister James, I admit to not being the most intelligent of men. As for the ring, I'm as brave as the next man. Most of it is luck. You see, Jesus and the Virgin Mary protect me," he'd say, and taking the crucifix that hung on his chest, pressed it to his smiling lips. "How else can a poor boy get away from the land and make a future for himself? I'd rather die by the horn than of hunger."

Fernando's good looks and gentle manners were disarming. He was perfectly groomed without any affectation, his clothes were always spotless, starched and ironed. He never failed to arrive with a gift for Marion or the household. There was an innocence about him, a nobility; like he belonged to that breed of men who are almost customized for the weaving of legends. Clean-cut, noble-hearted, fearless in the face of destiny, unconditional heroes. He had grown up in Cordoba, a province of deep Andalusia, the son of a poor *bracero*, farm laborer. At the age of sixteen he'd jumped into the bullring as a *spontaneous*, as they were called, and managed to stave a vicious bull off a well-known matador who was being gored. For that reason he got nicknamed El Niño, the kid, and given a chance to work in the *quadrilla*, or the matador's bullfighting team. Soon he was the rave of the bullfighting world, young and dauntless, and taking chances in the ring reminiscent of the old bullfighting masters. A *natural* they wrote him up; and as graceful in the arena as a dancer on stage. He had contracts for two whole years when he met Marion, and although probably making very good money then, still lived in a modest *pensión*, or bed and breakfast, in the heart of the old Madrid, with his whole *quadrilla*, when they were not traveling to the provinces to fight bulls in other rings.

We were all so taken by him, so engrossed in his genuine, gentlemanly ways—even Nanny couldn't resist coming out to greet him every time he visited—that we thought Father would grow into him too. But Father kept scaling up his mortifying comments, until it became clear that he would never accept Fernando. And the closer the bond between Marion and Fernando tightened, the brighter they shone together as a magnificent couple, the more his belligerence grew.

On Marion's birthday, when the small crowd of friends who were attending her party, including Fernando and Manuel, were watching the replay of a bullfight in which Fernando had broken records of swirling the *capote*, or cape, closely at the bull, Father suddenly insisted on interrupting and playing a video cassette in a VCR he had just brought from London. The film was *Ferdinand the Bull*, an old Disney animation from 1938, about a bull who refuses to fight in the bullring because he is a pacifist and wants to go back to smelling flowers in the meadows.

"The funniest part is that the bull is named like you—isn't that hilarious?" he said, laughing uproariously, with tears in his eyes. "Poor bulls, the things they have to go through!" And he offered everyone a glass of sherry to celebrate "*Ferdinand's* accomplishments."

Marion was furious and got up from the sofa, saying, "Let's all go for a drink somewhere else. I know a great bar," and without a glance at Father, she walked out of the room. Everyone picked up and started leaving after her.

Fernando got up too and nodded politely at Father. "Mister James, thank you for your hospitality, I will bring Marion back before eleven, as usual," and followed Marion out. Father saw them to the door, taking with him the red shawl Marion had forgotten on the chair, which he held cape-like, making passes at an imaginary bull as he hummed a *pasodoble*, the classical bullfighting tune, and said "olé" now and then.

When they were all gone, he walked back into the living room, still chuckling.

"It's not funny," I said.

"It is and it isn't," he replied, sitting next to me on the sofa and taking up his glass of sherry. "It sure isn't for the bull."

It wasn't fun for Fernando, either. His habitual, charming smile was beginning to fade from his face when he visited the house, and we could all see how downcast he was becoming as he lost footing with his girlfriend's father. Marion, on the other hand, became cold and distant with Father as he pushed forward his campaign against her matador lover. He'd started a relentless drive to erode her confidence in the whole affair.

He would typically open up a conversation at lunchtime by saying, "Bullfighting is not a sport, like cricket, tennis, or rugby. It's never a fair game, because no matter how the bull performs, he's always put to death in the end. It is just a cruel, gory spectacle for the entertainment of primitive, bloodthirsty audiences." Marion, sitting next to me, would tense up and start pushing her food around the plate.

"Well, what about fox hunting?" Julia would say in retort. "That doesn't feel like a fair game either, all those people on horses with lots of dogs hounding one little fox."

"What would you know, Julia? No comparison whatsoever!" Father said, always dismissive of Julia's comments. "Hunting is a noble sport, and has put food on the table for humans since the beginning of time."

"Who eats foxes?" Julia would insist in a smaller voice, well aware of her power to irritate Father.

"What do you mean, who eats foxes? You mean what do foxes do? They attack chicken coops, and ravage fowl; they impoverish and endanger farmers! They need to be dealt with, don't you think? Bullfighting is different, it's entertainment, it doesn't serve any economic purpose. It's like the Roman circus, distracting the masses with bloody thrills, pulling their minds away from the real problems, from the state of the nation."

"I'm just sorry for the horses," I would add, carried away by Father's fervor, and then immediately realize I was betraying Marion. For the moment Father enlisted a partisan opinion, he'd charge for the kill.

"And those men who call themselves matadors, with the pink and gold frills, all bells and whistles, their little ballet shoes and the red cape—they're just butchers posing as clowns, they have no sensitivity whatsoever for the animal, for the pain, for the absurdity of it all . . ."

Finally Marion would burst into sobs, storm out of the room, and run upstairs to lock herself in her bedroom.

"Hey, Anna! Aren't you getting out of the car?"

Marion is already crossing the street.

It takes me a moment to realize we've arrived at Sanchez Romero, the fancy, ultra-expensive supermarket. I step out into the blinding sunlight. It burns the back of my head and neck like a rod of fire. Seconds later I walk into the shop, where the contrast with the glacial air-conditioner is so dramatic that a wave of brain freeze benumbs me. The place is empty. Some Bach concerto for flute and violin or another plays in the background. We walk around the neat aisles stacked with all sorts of chichi products wrapped in colorful designer containers.

"Would there even be something as simple as salt in this place?" I ask out loud, irritated at the outrageous prices. A young guy clad in the store's navy blue uniform, stocking a shelf close by, says, "We do, miss. Just follow me." I follow him to the fish boutique section, where he disappears behind a door and brings out our five bags of coarse salt.

"Enjoy your feast of salted sole," he says with a smirk, as he loads them into my cart.

"Feast of salted sole?"

"You know, the recipe. I thought this amount of salt was for . . ." He falters.

"Oh yes, yes," I say, walking away. Of course, he's thinking I'm about to wrap a whole school of sole into tight jackets of coarse salt and grill them for a party. For what other purpose would anyone be acquiring industrial quantities of salt in a dainty place like this? If he only knew what other creative purposes are reserved for the use of this particular load!

As I push the cart down the aisles, I catch a glimpse of Marion, who is studying a shelf packed with bottles of wine. For a moment I observe her figure from afar, her round curves, the way she bends over to squint at labels, coyly curling her hair behind her ear. There is a delicate quality to Marion, a tearful softness that can escalate to hysteria, it's true, but also an absence of hard feelings, of a callous heart.

An unbidden quote from a forgotten author enters my mind, *Those who won't shed the salt of grief through tears, will later have to squeeze drops of blood to release their pain.* This is one of the main differences between Marion and me. She knows how to cry, how to dissolve her grief through sobbing. As for me, it's been years since I shed a single tear. Surely, the salt of my grief is well petrified by now.

I walk up to Marion, who's holding a bottle of red wine. "Don't bother to get any of those. We can't drink any alcohol in the house until the *limpieza* is over. Delia's orders."

"I'll buy a couple anyway, and keep them in the car for later. I also got us three chicken sandwiches—."

"Marion, I can't believe you don't know we're both vegetarians!"

"Never mind, you can take out the chicken and eat the veggies. Don't roll your eyes. I paid a fortune and can't return them."

We pay for the salt and the wine and make our way back to the car. Once inside, I sit back and relax. Whatever is meant for today, will be. I close my eyes and imagine the car from the outside. A small burgundy Toyota whizzing down the streets, hazed out by the vapor swirling from the asphalt.

CHAPTER 7

The moment we get back to the house, we're engulfed by a thick smell wafting out of the kitchen, a pungent, acrid smell surrounded by a zesty cloud of garlic. Someone is cooking meat. Not just meat, but the infamous lamb, to be more precise. I'd forgotten about the chops in the refrigerator. Marion looks at me in amazement, as if demanding an explanation, but I shrug my shoulders. We cross the patio and enter the house.

Inside, the smell is even stronger and the smoke coming from the candles on the altar is nothing now, compared to the fog that pours out of the huge frying pan where Delia is sautéing the lamb chops with a pile of garlic and herbs. Constantine stands by her side, mesmerized.

"Don't just stand there! Get me some thyme and black pepper," Delia says, with a hint of irritation.

"Sorry, Delia, there's only a bit of oregano left in this jar. The cabinets are empty. No spices." Constantine hands her a big empty glass container with a few green wisps at the bottom.

"The recipe won't be the same, then. Pass the white wine." Constantine steps over to the altar, takes one of the bottles among the saints and coconut shells, and gives it to Delia. I seek to make eye contact with Marion to express my shock at this last action, but I find her totally engrossed in what's going on in the frying pan. Delia turns around to look at us. She's wearing a flowery apron over her white dress, something she must've brought along in her suitcase, because I don't recognize it as part of the household.

"Oh, here you are! Just in time." She smiles, wiping the sweat from her forehead with the back of her hand.

My eyes are beginning to water because of the smoke. "Do you need the salt?" I say, confused.

"No, not the salt. I would need decent spices for the chops, but no matter. I was saying you're just in time to eat." She turns to Constantine. "Bring over the large plate." Constantine carries an oblong platter to the stove, where Delia piles the lamb chops with a wooden spoon.

"Ready!" Constantine says with satisfaction, and he carries it all out into the patio.

Delia scoops up a bottle of wine—again from among the saints on the altar—and a loaf of white bread. "We're eating out in the patio, it's too hot in here." We step out after her. They've already set the table under the grapevine, with plates, silverware, and glasses for the wine. Constantine brings chairs.

"Where's Julia?" I ask.

Julia walks in from the pool. "Sorry, I couldn't stand the smell in the kitchen." She sits down and glares at Delia. "You know Anna and I don't eat meat, don't you?"

"That's a pity," Delia says. "The Orishas want everyone to participate in the banquet when they're performing a ceremony."

"The Orishas?" I snort, incredulous, thinking it's all a joke. Julia gives me a don't-you-dare kick under the table.

"Yes, the Orishas," Delia says, unfazed. "What, you thought that I was just cooking by the altar for convenience? Cooking and partaking of food is done for our saints, the Orishas. And Orishas like lamb chops." She makes the sign of the cross and closes her eyes in silent prayer for a moment, then breaks the loaf of bread and offers Constantine a piece. She pours wine into their glasses and they start to eat. Julia and I look on warily.

I've never liked lamb. For as long as I can remember, I've felt nauseated by its smell. Father used to like roast lamb with mint sauce served for Sunday lunch, and that became a recipe Nanny mastered to such an extent it even got her a compliment or two. But the most disgusting lamb dish I saw Father eat didn't happen in our dining room, but on the road, on a trip we took one summer to a beach town on the southern coast. We were driving through the arid, central plain of La Mancha, the very turf of Don Quixote's ramblings, a flat extension of yellowed sunburned fields, and stopped for lunch in a restaurant along the road. It was a medieval-style den, with dark brick walls hung with old ceramics, stuffed bulls' heads and strings of garlic. We sat around a table, my sisters and I squeamish at the greasy, rancid smells that wafted out of the kitchen. Then Father ordered one of their menu specials: baked sheep's head. Baked sheep's head! We all gagged, wondering at our father's sanity. Where had all his gastronomical scruples gone? After all the criticizing, all the deprecating tirades against Spanish food, he now decided to try a dish from the deep Castilian past? After a while, the waiter, an older, dried-up man with a green-hued face, emerged from the kitchen with the sheep's head on a platter, and set it on the table in front of Father. I covered my eyes with my hands and only allowed myself to peep out of the slits between my fingers. I could see the head still had the eyes on, though glazed over horribly after the baking. I thought I was going to throw up. Both Marion and Julia looked sickened too. But Father ignored our reactions, and just turned the platter around, looking at the head from all angles. Then he proceeded to pull it apart with his bare hands, chewing delicately on the scarce pieces of cooked tissue embedded along the sad skull, while my sisters and I exchanged revolted glances in silence.

I'm afraid I'll never be able to erase this scene from my brain as long as I live. Its memory regurgitates every time I smell cooked lamb. Maybe Julia's vegetarianism comes from the same traumatic source. However, it didn't affect Marion in the same way. I look at my older sister now as she watches Delia and Constantine like a hawk, her sandwich untouched on her plate.

"You sure you don't want any, Marion?" Delia says. "You said before you weren't a vegetarian."

"I'm not."

"So, here." Delia serves her a pile of chops and pours wine into her glass.

"I thought we weren't supposed to drink while the *limpieza* was going on," Marion says.

"I also thought you'd given up drink altogether," I add.

"Don't you worry about any of that now," Delia says, her black eyes lengthening into long slits. "All of this is done for the Orishas," she adds, and I see her thin crimson lips open into a smile that trembles with deep, suppressed laughter. But Marion doesn't appear to notice anything at all; she's fixed on the feast before her, delight all over her face.

None of this surprises me. Marion is one of those persons too involved with the serious stuff of life to give any thought to jokes or facetious behavior. She can be mellowed into situations because she never reads between the lines. She lacks the guile to think or act strategically. She tends to approach situations squarely. In that way she had been like Fernando. They dealt with life as the matador deals with the bull. Head-on.

When Marion realized that Father was intent on breaking up her relationship with Fernando, she made a clear-cut decision. She would marry him as soon as possible. So she brought him one day to the house and requested that Father see them privately in his studio.

When I opened the front door to let them in, I sensed an air of melancholy in Fernando. He had been gored again at the beginning of the season; the bull's horn had carved a nasty, deep wound into his thigh. He was back in the ring again, although he hadn't recovered all the weight he lost in the hospital, nor his good spirits. His mood had grown somber. We all thought this had to do more with Father than with the bullring, since Fernando had been signed for a year-long tour for the best *corridas* in Central and Latin America, where he would make a fortune. Father had refused to give Marion permission to travel down to Cordoba to meet his mother, and that had been a blow to his pride.

When they closed the door of Father's studio, I couldn't help lingering around. I wanted to listen in, not just out of curiosity, but out of anxiety for them. I was full of trepidation; I was awed that Marion had mustered the courage for this confrontation.

The door to the studio was a beautifully carved, heavy, double paneled piece, but it had never closed to perfection. *Another one of those shoddy jobs of sloppy national carpenters*, Father had described it so many times; but that served my spying purpose for the moment. I heard Marion and Fernando sit in the chairs opposite Father at the desk.

A silence followed.

Then Marion's voice, "We're here to tell you—"

But Fernando interrupted her. "No, please, Marion, let me." And after a beat, in a voice sober and rehearsed, he said, "Mister James, I would like to ask for your daughter's hand."

Through the chinks I could just barely see Father, his eyes on the desk and his hands with fingers intertwined at his chest.

"I am now signed for two years and I have enough savings to buy a good house, the deed of which will be entirely in Marion's name. While I live, I swear, she will want nothing."

A minute of uncomfortable silence passed. Then Father lifted his eyes, like two daggers of ice. "And what if you don't live?" he asked slowly. "Have you thought of that possibility? I mean, you've been gored twice in the last year, why are you so sure you won't die tomorrow? How can I give my daughter in marriage to a man who could be six foot under any day?"

Marion jumped from her seat and the chair screeched on the floor. "Father! How can you say that!" It was the high-pitched voice that always preceded her bursting into sobs.

"It's all right, Marion." Fernando interrupted her again in a level voice, taking her hand and gently lowering her back into her chair. "Mister James, it's true there is a risk, although many matadors get gored and live to old age. In a few years I hope to make enough money to retire; then I shall look for another business. But I love your daughter, and all I can offer her is what I have now."

Father suddenly burst into a growling rasp of laughter. A chill crept up my spine. I thought of pulling away from the chink and leaving the scene altogether. But then I heard the thundering voice.

"Why do you think I'm laughing? I'm laughing because all this sounds like a joke. Why would I give my beautiful, sophisticated, well-educated daughter to a man who is likely to give her a miserable life in dirty, dusty bullrings, with the daily anticipation of gorings and the chance of becoming a widow any day? Just tell me, why would I do that?"

There was a moment of frozen silence. Then Marion's chair screeched again as she stood up.

"Father, I am twenty-four years old and you can't tell me what to do. We thought we would be respectful, that's all. Fernando, let's go." She turned and marched toward the door, while Fernando followed slowly after her. I was going to run away from the door, but just then Marion burst it open and I stepped aside to let her pass. Fernando walked behind her and turned to close the door carefully. Then he stood facing me for a beat in the dimness of the hall.

"Why don't you say something to him? Why don't you tell him to go to hell?" I asked, deafened by the beating of my indignant heart.

He gave me a long, silent look. "I never had a father," he said after a moment and turned away, leaving the house after Marion.

That night, as I walked into the bathroom, I found Marion crying.

"What are you going to do, Marion?" I asked.

"I'm going to marry him," she said, wiping the tears from her bloodshot eyes in the mirror. "We already put in the papers." Then she sat down at the edge of the bathtub, rewrapping her robe around her bosom. "I wanted to elope, run away with him, but he said no, it's not in his code of honor. But I don't know if I'll be able to wait. I don't think I can be in the same house with this monster. I hate him. I can't believe the things he said today." She burst into sobs again.

Father had a way of smoothing things over when he had gone too far, like any good Machiavellian seasoned in political strategy. He announced we would have a big party in celebration of a significant contract his company had just signed with a German firm, and said we could invite all the friends we wanted. It would be a magnificently catered event: his new American secretary, Olga Morris, was taking care of that, with delicious food, wine, booze, and even a hired disc jockey. We were taken by surprise. Father had never been a lavish entertainer; he sometimes brought clients for lunch or drinks in the evening, and only allowed us small birthday parties and gatherings. Marion was cautious at first, but when Father said jestingly that she could also bring "her *torero*, without the bulls, please," she thought that this was his way to make up for their falling-out.

We'd never seen Father in such a good mood. The new partnership with the German firm was going to take his business to another level. He'd been working hard for the last twenty years to get to this point, and finally money and contracts were flowing into his company like never before. This moment represented the peak of his self-made enterprise, the realized dream of the young Englishman who'd arrived penniless in a remote, difficult land.

It was the end of May and we'd just finished our year exams and were ready to decompress. People started trickling in by eight, when it wasn't yet dark. The evening hung with that eternal twilight of summer solstice days. A haze like pink fingers caressed the garden, extending in soft strokes toward the distant mountains across from the veranda. The guests, a mixed crowd of friends from school and university, and Father's employees, stood around on the cool, plush lawn with tall cocktail glasses, exchanging social graces and soft laughter. The dress code was casual on our friends' side, with jeans and T-shirts, skimpy summer dresses, and shorts; and more formal with Father's employees. Olga Morris, a decadent belle from South Carolina with a lazy drawl, who'd just started working for Father, coordinated the catering by buzzing around between waiters with trays and the disc jockey, a weather-beaten, middle-aged rock-and-roller who blasted Michael Jackson's *Thriller* from large speakers at one end of the veranda.

When the evening dipped into a darker shade of orange and crimson, the swimming pool's underwater spotlights flashed up, making its oval shape shine with aqua-blue radiance. The crowd groaned, pleasantly surprised, and gathered around, mesmerized by the blue glittering surface. Then out of nowhere came a splash, followed immediately by another, and two figures slithered underwater until first one head and then another popped out on the surface. One was Julia's. The other was a short-haired girl with large dark eyes and a mocking smile, whom I had never seen before.

Julia struggled to catch her breath. "Alina!" she shouted, "I can't believe you pushed me in like this," but she giggled, splashing water into Alina's face.

The crowd laughed; and presently, one, two, three, and four more of our friends jumped into the pool with their clothes on, some even forgetting to take off their shoes. There was more laughter and splashing inside the pool. Someone threw in a ball, and a game of water polo began. Most of the other guests moved slowly back toward the veranda, searching to refill their drinks and settle into easy chairs to continue conversations. Waiters milled around offering *tapas* on trays and replenishing glasses of wine and cocktails, while guests mellowed into deeper states of tipsy placidity, and Tom Waits's voice crooned in the night air singing "Missing You."

The house stood behind it all like the magnificent backdrop of a delightful operatic moment. I gaped at the beauty of its silhouette against the cobalt sky, the whitewashed façade hung with creeping vines reflecting garden lights, all windows ablaze revealing red rooms with dark bookcases, gorgeous pictures, collections of ancient ceramic plates, vases thick with flowers on beautiful furniture.

"I don't think we've been introduced," a voice with a slight German accent said beside me. "I'm Marcus." I turned around to find a medium-height, muscular man in a cream summer suit; his face clean-shaven, with angular cheekbones and blue eyes behind gold-rimmed glasses. "I think you might be Anna, James's youngest daughter. Am I right?"

"And you are . . . ?" I looked at him suspiciously. There was something I didn't quite like about him, a keenness, a wolfish quality in the depth of his gaze. Or maybe just the way he looked at my breasts, which were somewhat apparent through my wet blouse that had been splashed over at the pool.

"Marcus Holsbeiter. I'm with Henningber und Berger, the company that just signed the contract with your father. I just moved to Madrid . . ."

"I see. Well, I hope you're already settled in," I began to say, but then I spotted Marion and Fernando walking into the garden, with Manuel trailing behind, carrying a guitar. I turned to Marcus. "That's my sister. I'll be right back." I hurried over to Marion.

She looked stunning in a red silk dress that clung to her waist and hips, and fell dramatically along her thighs to just below the knees. Draped over one shoulder she carried a shawl of black silk embroidered with red flowers ending in long tassels, a classical *mantón de Manila*, which Fernando had given her.

"It's scheduled for next Thursday at one o'clock," she whispered into my ear as I kissed her cheek. "I hope you can come."

"I wouldn't miss it for the world," I replied.

Then I saw Father walking toward us with Marcus. "Marcus, I want you to meet my daughter," he said, looking at Marion, but Marcus turned to me and said, "We were just introducing one another."

"I meant Marion, my oldest daughter," Father said, ignoring me. "She just graduated in architecture a few weeks ago. Marion, this is Marcus, he will be working with us as a partner from the German firm we just signed with."

"Nice to meet you, Marcus. Welcome to Madrid," Marion said quickly, avoiding Father's gaze.

"Marcus just arrived from Düsseldorf and I'd very much like to take him out to lunch next Thursday. I'd like you to join us; and afterwards you could show him around the old Madrid, to give him a sense of the place," Father said.

Marion blushed deeply and sighed. Then, after a quick reproachful look at Father, she said, "I don't think I can, Father. I'm getting married on Thursday." And turning around to Fernando, who was talking with someone else, she pulled at his sleeve. "Fernando, meet Marcus, he just arrived from Germany. Marcus, this is my fiancé, Fernando Rios."

The men shook hands. There was a moment of embarrassed confusion in Marcus's face. Then he said, "Congratulations!" Marion thanked him and, taking Fernando's arm, moved away to talk to another group. Father stood rigidly. His face was livid.

I said to Marcus, "Can I get you another drink?"

I walked quickly toward the catering table.

Julia, who had changed into dry clothes and combed back her wet hair, caught up with me. "Don't you think that Olga Morris is overdoing it with the booze? I mean, everybody looks drunk." I looked around, realizing she was right: the party was becoming a landscape of intoxication. People were sprawled on lounge chairs, many sat on the lawn or around the pool, wisecracking and howling with laughter. I scanned the crowd for Father and saw he had been joined by a group of employees who were chattering about some frolic I couldn't quite make out. Among them were his two mechanical engineers, Montes, a tough, muscular middle-aged man whom we hated for his dirty, sexist jokes; and Lopez, a sly, lanky fellow known for his bullying of other employees. Father's stare was vacant and fixed in the direction of the house. He paid no attention to the babble. Meanwhile, Olga Morris brought him another tall glass of liquor on the rocks, and stood by his side with her own cocktail, mooning at him from under her drooping eyelids.

"She's weird," Julia said. "She's been pouring him drinks nonstop, she's getting him really drunk."

"It'll be good for him to loosen up," I said, trying to conceal my disquiet. "Anyway, it looks like everyone is having fun." I wanted to protect Julia from the apprehension that was quickly building up in me. "I'm more worried about the music. If that guy has Lionel Richie and Diana Ross sing "Endless Love" one more time, I'll just scream!"

"Yeah, you'd think with his rugged rock-and-roll band looks he'd be playing more upbeat music," Julia said.

Across from us, the disc jockey flirted with one of Father's office girls and seemed to have lost interest in the music. But as I set to walk over toward him, I heard a deep, percussive, almost metallic chord tear through the air. Every head turned. Manuel sat upright with his guitar on one knee; the sweet, dark notes flowing from his fingers over the strings galvanized the air. The guests gathered around, entranced. The disc jockey turned the music down on his end. Manuel's fingers ran up and down the neck of the guitar; bright, dry notes played out swiftly and then held, as if suspended in the air, picking up again as the rhythm mellowed down, into a haunting, heart-wrenching melody.

It was as if the night sang through his guitar. On the horizon, a single streak of crimson lingered over the mountain peaks, loath to dissolve into the dark. Fireflies, like tiny swaying lanterns, shimmied in the air, as garden lights reflected on faces, inside pupils; while the fragrance of the night garden, heavy with honeysuckle and jasmine, invaded throats and lungs, pulsed into the bloodstream, intoxicating, like the lullaby flowing from Manuel's guitar.

It's a strange feeling when a beautiful setting is the scenery of a tragic moment. One tends to think of drama in the midst of storms, foul unsettling nights, or ugly scenarios. But when things happen within the perfect symmetry of beauty, there is an increased sense of pain. Maybe because it's unexpected. Maybe because, like a blade cutting flesh engorged with pleasure, it slashes to the quick, drawing heftier amounts of blood; while the mind, confused, is thrown deeper into frenzy.

I only saw Father's lunge from the corner of my eye. Then I heard the sound of glass smashing on the ceramic surface of the terrace, followed by the screeching of shards scattering around. The guitar stopped. A couple of women gasped. Marion screamed. I rushed over toward them. On the tiles, among the broken glass, a small pool of blood. Father's cocktail glass had cut Fernando's arm above the wrist. It was bleeding. Someone held it up in the air. A girl from Father's office brought out a scarf from her bag and tied it above his elbow in tourniquet fashion.

Father was being held back by Montes and Lopez. His eyes were bloodshot. "If you as much as touch her, I swear I will kill you!" he slurred, over and over.

But all of this was blurred by Marion's wails. She clung to Fernando's arm, hands smeared with blood. Montes and Lopez succeeded in walking Father away from the scene, while I pushed through the crowd toward Marion. But as I reached her side, she swooned before I could catch her, falling to the ground in a heap.

At that moment, everything turned to chaos. Arms, hands, and heads hovered over Marion, flitted over her senseless body, over

Fernando's hemorrhaging arm, wavered about the broken glass. Muddled discussions started on how to proceed.

"All right," I said, standing up. "Please, let me take care of this. Please."

Julia joined in. "Thank you, everyone, it's best you all leave now. She'll be fine. But I think we should call it a night." People backed off slowly, and I asked Manuel to help me take Marion up to her room. I followed behind his small wiry body as he carried her up the stairs and laid her on her bed. Fernando came into the room holding his arm; it looked like the tourniquet had worked and he had stopped bleeding.

"I'll get you a bandage in a moment," I said, covering Marion's body with a sheet.

"It's nothing," he said, "just one of those veins that bleeds a lot."

"Are you kidding? It's your main hand with the *capote*," Manuel said. "I'm taking you to the hospital for stitches. Meet me downstairs, I'll just fetch the guitar." He got up and left the room. "Your father is worse than a fucking Moor," he murmured as he passed me by, and I was taken aback by the hatred in his voice.

Fernando sat on the edge of the bed and took Marion's limp hand. "This can't go on. I'm hurting you more than anything."

Nanny hurried into the room. She'd just returned from her day off. "Go now," she said to Fernando, "and don't return until you're ready to make her your bride. Go!"

Fernando put Marion's hand to his lips one last time. I watched his haggard, ashen face as he walked out.

I ran downstairs to the terrace, a broom in hand. Most of the guests were already gone. Two waiters collected the remnants of drinks and *tapas*. I walked up to the disc jockey, who was wheeling his set away on top of a bulky dolly.

"Do you know where my father is?" I asked.

"He's in the library, with Olga and the other two guys. Sorry for how all this turned out," he said, and then added, "but thanks for the gig, anyway," and he disappeared into the passage that led to the street gate.

I turned to the terrace. All was silent. On second inspection, it had only been one broken glass and a few drops of blood. Strange, how my perception had magnified these elements just minutes before.

The table is strewn with remnants of lunch. Lamb ribs piled on plates, empty wine glasses, chicken sandwiches picked brashly apart. I'm still hungry and wonder if I might seek Julia and team up to go for more food. But maybe a strong cup of coffee will do the trick until the evening. I assemble some of the dirty chinaware and step into the kitchen. Constantine stands at the sink with a pile of plates on the side. He is putting on the flowery apron I had seen Delia cooking in.

"Is washing dishes also one of your duties as a sorcerer's apprentice?" I ask with a grin, as I dump my uneaten chicken into the garbage and pile my plate on top of the others.

"Not really." He chuckles. "It's just that poor Delia is kind of old to be doing this sort of thing on the job. She also needs to take her nap before we can go on."

"Pretty impressive attitude for a male attendant! By the way, how did you get into all of this to begin with?" I ask, while I poke around for the coffee pot among the clutter on the counter.

Constantine laughs again. "It's a long story, but in a nutshell, I was always one of those kids who doesn't fit in anywhere, the type who doesn't even drop out of school just because he really never went to school. I mean my mind was so absent, it didn't follow my body into the classroom. So one day someone gave me a set of old tarot cards and I was so stupid, I didn't even know what to do with them. But once, while my mother was hanging the washing, I was flipping the cards and all of a sudden . . ."

I look at him in amazement as he chortles away, splashing immoderate quantities of water and soap over the dishes. I hadn't realized how chatty he could be, hadn't even noticed how badly he stammered when speaking more than two words in a row.

I'm beginning to regret having asked about the launching of his career, when I hear my cell phone vibrate in my handbag a few feet away, and signal Constantine to hold on to his story until I return.

I step out into the patio. "Hello?"

"I need to ask you a big favor." Marcus's voice speaks in that hushed, urgent tone he always uses to coerce me into immediate business action. "I need you to drop everything and take care of an emergency. I know it's Saturday, I know you're supposed to go soon on vacation—"

"Hey, hey, slow down! Where are you, first of all?"

"I'm driving toward Düsseldorf. I left Helga and the kids at my in-laws. I just got this call, and I need to make it back. I'm hoping to reach the airport in a couple of hours and catch the next plane to Cádiz. But meanwhile, I need you to step in."

"What's in Cádiz?"

"There's a Liebherr tower crane stuck in customs. For some reason they don't have all the paperwork and they're threatening to ship it back tonight. If you show up in the next hours and vouch for it—"

"Wait! Marcus, I can't do anything today."

"Anna, this is major. It's a new client and I can't fail them. I really need your help."

"Sorry, Marcus. Not today. I'm also doing something important that can't wait."

There's a beat of silence.

Then he says, "I'm going into a tunnel."

CHAPTER 8

I snap my phone shut and throw it on the table. It slides among wine glasses and dirty napkins. I think of going back into the kitchen to make coffee, but the thought of engaging again with Constantine's unending tale puts me off.

I need to be alone, let my vexation wind down. I can't stand being harassed with urgent requests, expected to ride the winds in order to solve the problems of the world. Marcus is a virtuoso at this kind of appeal.

I walk away from the patio toward the pool. The midday sun refracts on the surface of the water, shooting blinding rays into my eyes. I walk up to the French windows facing the mountains. The old discolored awning has been extended over the terrace, and the crank handle is still dangling, dangerously close to the window-pane. Julia must have just lowered it and forgotten to put it away. But I can't be bothered right now. It's too hot to even step under the canopy of torn green fabric. I'm desperate to reach the seating area under the willow tree, far away from the house.

My mind returns to the tower crane in Cádiz, and Marcus's plea that I step into the situation. I know he'll convince me, if I let him. Do I ever say no to him? I know he'll call me again and again. It would be best to not pick up the phone at all. He'll just have to make different arrangements. He's got other people who can step in and give him a hand. Not easy to get hold of on a Saturday in August, granted, but hey, it just depends on how big of a compensation offer you make. And, if anything, he has the dough. So, let him deal . . . It all makes perfect sense, and yet why am I still loath to resist his request? On the surface we're the perfect business partners, but in the undertow of things, he always manages to place his priorities on top of the pile. Is it just him, though? Or is it my obstinate tendency to overindulge a partner who comes with a high maintenance cost? It's been years now since I've been pushing away that recurrent little voice whispering in my ear, *You don't really need him, do you? Wouldn't your end of things be easier, not to mention more profitable, without him?*

As I reach the willow tree, I see that the chaise lounge onto which I was hoping to flop is already occupied by Delia. She lies recumbent on her left side, one arm encircled around her head acting as a supportive pillow. Her eyes are closed; face placid with sleep. The long branches from the willow tree flounce from above, brushing lightly over her white-clad body. Frazzled, I sit on one of the chairs across from her.

The thick insistent buzzing of a bluebottle fly, one of those *moscas "cojoneras,"* or fucker flies as they call them here, distracts me for a bit as I jump up and swat it away with both hands. I settle again into my chair, surprised to feel all of a sudden relieved from my bad mood. Amazing, what a wrestling round with a fucker fly can achieve! For the first time I reflect that this *limpieza* might not be as crazy an idea as I thought in the beginning. Maybe we need to loosen up around here. Maybe I need more than anyone else to be delivered from my mental clutter, from all those rigid layers I've accumulated through the years. No one better than I knows of the deep cavities that lie underneath the façade of the energetic, efficient, down-to-earth Miss Anna Hurt. Has the time come to open them up and examine them in the light?

I turn my eyes to Delia. There's something so serene in the abandonment with which she embraces her rest. Her face, dappled by the long fingery branches hanging over, has the innocent, vacant beauty of the sleeping or the dead. The hand that's not nestled around her head is pressed to her chest. The rest of her body lies stretched over the chaise like a beluga whale. It reminds me of some of the pieces in an exhibit of ancient goddesses I saw in Basel a few years ago, a collection of round, curvy shapes of puckered stone. Most of them had no faces or no heads. But that didn't matter, because the fascination of the exhibit was about ancient, large, pear-shaped female bodies. The body female as a giver of life, with sacred orifices cut wide into the stone, large slits under the folds of gigantic abdomens; fearful gateways between the worlds. And here lies Delia, grossly voluptuous like all those Venuses of Willendorf or Hohle Fels. She only lacks the mammoth breasts and the fertility of a younger woman. But she probably has another kind of fecundity. That of the holy crone who no longer gives birth to single units of life, but whose body becomes a flesh sanctuary laid out for the reparation of human grief.

The holy crone! How small and insignificant my own body feels in comparison. I'm younger, my breasts are taut, my abdomen flat, the flesh in my legs and arms still full and fresh. But when it comes to my fertility? All my wasted female eggs have not yet produced as much as a child; what's worse, my modestly voluptuous curves cannot even boast a real lover these days. And it's not just me. The same can be said of Marion and Julia. I think of their beautiful eyes, smiling glances over joy-choked laughter filling rooms when we horsed around as girls. Where did our youth go? What happened to the Hurt sisters? Those gorgeous, sophisticated, clever girls everyone wanted at dinners and parties? Like our house that's seen other houses, less handsome, less spacious, with no mountain views, being sold, so have we seen all our friends and acquaintances, less dazzling, less passionate, get paired up, settled into marriages and good partnerships, while we were left behind with crushed hearts and broken stories. And it wasn't that we didn't have suitors, those were never lacking. But the best of life never seemed to curdle around us. It's not just about love either. What about our talents, our dreams of becoming great architects, painters, and actresses? Where did all that go? Why did a house like ours—full of music, of books and poetry, of beautiful art objects—not produce blossoming artists?

*   *   *

The days and weeks that followed the party were a jumble of nightmarish scenes. That night, long after everyone had left and the house had settled into silence, I heard Marion's bare feet walking toward my bed and felt her cold hand on my arm. As I opened my eyes, she hovered over me wearing the thin white nightgown Nanny had changed her into hours before.

"Anna, I heard noises in the garden, please walk down with me, I know he's here. He's come to get me." She pulled my sleep-drunk body out of the bed and made me follow her downstairs.

Like two ghosts we searched the garden. Marion pulled me along by the hand as we covered every inch of the grounds, her body in a state of high alert, scrutinizing the dark ahead. I remember thinking how still the night was, how the silent grass seemed to cling to my bare feet, tiny tentacles adhering to my soles like anemones, as if protecting me from moving forward.

"Look, someone's clothes ended up in the pool," Marion whispered. The moment I squinted to look down, a dull gleam of daylight shot through the dark, giving away the silhouette of a body in the water's depths. Marion's hands gripped my arms like tongs before she started screaming. I disengaged from her and jumped in. The chlorine burned my eyes as I opened them underwater. Before me drifted the amorphous shape of a man, his white shirt floating around his chest, his right arm slashed above the wrist.

The rest is somehow history. The exact cause of Fernando's death was never determined. First, there was a case opened against Father, since he had threatened and attacked him with a cocktail glass at the party. But the little evidence that could be drawn together was dispelled by Olga Morris's deposition in which, as we found later, she swore she spent the night with Father after the party, and had been in his company every single minute until the discovery of the body. When Father protested against her statement, she simply reminded him how drunk he was, to the point he'd been carried to his room by herself and Montes.

The whereabouts of Fernando between the time he left the house and the time he was found in the pool were also a mystery. Manuel, who had taken him to the emergency room, left him at the door while he parked the car; and when he returned shortly he found that Fernando had disappeared from the waiting room before being admitted into the triage office. The autopsy revealed high levels of alcohol in his blood, something that according to the pathologist could have seriously compromised his ability to control drowsiness when mixed with the strong antibiotics he was taking for the wound on the thigh that was still infected.

Then there was the conversation I'd heard outside the library window between Father's engineers. "Mister Hoooort"—that was how Montes and most Spanish people pronounced our "Hurt" family name—"those boys are just *gitanos*, Gypsies, all they need is a little talk from older men like us," Montes said, pointing at himself and Lopez and winking an eye at Father, who was slumped in a chair, besotted with unaccustomed drinking. "You just have to say, Montes, give him a little talk, if you know what I mean, and tell him to get the hell away from my daughter." But both men had been able to prove their whereabouts during Fernando's missing hours.

In the end, nothing came to anything. The forensic opinion of alcohol mixed with medication as the probable cause of a fatal fall pervaded. Fernando's body was sent back to his mother in Cordoba, to be buried. The investigation was closed and the whole affair declared to have been an unfortunate accident.

Meanwhile, Marion had a nervous breakdown. She lay in bed, collapsed for weeks, and all she could do was grab me, or Julia, whenever we were near, repeating over and over again, "Tell me it's not true, tell me he's all right." And she cried all day long. Nanny's abrupt dismissal didn't help either.

After dozens of Valiums and other similar pills, our family physician, Doctor Martinez, a gloomy man with a sallow face, recommended she be checked into the Clinica López Ibor, a trendy psychiatric clinic in the outskirts of Madrid. She stayed there for a couple of weeks, but when she returned home she went back to crying nonstop, until it was decided she would travel to London and stay with Aunt Kay, Father's sister, for a while.

Aunt Kay came to fetch her. We'd met her once, when we were very young and she had come to visit for a few days after Mother died. She was the only family member Father kept in touch with, and then not all that much. She was a tall, lean woman with translucent skin and pale blue, watercolor eyes. All the clothes she wore were in variations of peacock blue. She couldn't stand the heat, or the smell of Spanish food. She didn't want to leave the house or visit Madrid at all. There was only one thing she agreed to do, go to the Prado Museum to admire the horses in Velázquez's paintings. She was crazy about horses.

She was also very sweet. She looked into Marion's smashed-up eyes and said, "Poor darling, what a terrible heartbreak you are going through! But we will fix you, we will make your beautiful cheeks rosy again." Marion looked at her with indifferent, dreamy eyes. She was stunned all day long after the latest increase in her antidepressant medication.

Then Aunt Kay asked Father if she could take us all with her for a few months. "These girls are English, James, you can't keep them here forever."

"You can take Julia if you like, but I'll need Anna to stay with me."

Julia protested. "I'm not English, I was born here, this is where I belong. I don't want to go to London. I'm real busy at the moment."

I also protested. "I'm the one who wants to go, let Julia stay. I'll go with Marion." Something in me sensed it was my single window of opportunity to flee, to find another life. I had just been accepted into the Literature and Theater program at Saint Martin's School of Art. I wanted to study acting. I'd recently seen the movie *Blue Velvet* and I wanted to be like Isabella Rossellini. But Father wouldn't hear of it.

I stayed. So did Julia, who was, unlike me, ecstatic about it. She was getting together with Alina and attending the Escuela de Bellas Artes, the official art school of Madrid where they had met, and that was enough for her. She saw no need to go anywhere. Alina was now her main thing. They had become inseparable all of a sudden, and after a few protracted sleepovers that lasted a good number of days, Alina actually moved in, not just into the house as a permanent guest, but also into our room, the large double bedroom on the second floor that Julia and I had always shared. She and Julia spent the nights whispering and tittering under the covers in Julia's bed, ignoring me if I complained, colonizing the room further every day with their art projects, canvases, sticky, dirty materials, tools, and weird pieces of sculpture.

Finally, it was me who decided to move out.

I first tried Marion's room, but it was too charged, not just the whole gamut of *torero* paraphernalia slapped all over the place along with her belongings, but there was a heaviness in the air that didn't allow you to breathe. Sleeping in her bed gave me bad dreams, dreams about drowned horses, about *toreros* lifted up in the air by bulls' horns. There was only one other room I could go to besides Nanny's, where I didn't want to die of nostalgia, and that was Mother's old studio, the room where she had read and painted. It was now stripped of most of its original furnishings; a few bookcases, a round table, and a daybed were the only pieces left. Unlike my old bedroom, it had a window with a view to the mountains and I was happy with the idea of having my own space.

But I was unhappy at losing Julia.

Particularly at this time, when the household was still reeling with shock from recent events. It made me feel unbearably lonely. Julia and I had always been close. We knew each other's secrets, backed each other up, had spent endless afternoons and evenings playing together, oblivious of the world. Our room had been our fairy-tale castle since time immemorial, even more so after Marion moved out into her own, beautiful, grown-up room. Then Julia and I were left back in the old nursery that now became our exclusive *leonera*, or lion's den, as Nanny called it. Full of old toys, books, treasure chests stuffed with disguises and all sorts of strange and silly objects. Always cluttered, always a delightful mess. I remember poor Nanny picking up after us before bedtime, while we still ran around, impassioned by whatever the day's imaginary adventure might be. As we grew into teenagers the room grew with us. Now it was dresses and shoes, makeup, sports gadgets, erotic novels hidden away from view. But Julia and I stayed besties, confided everything to each other, shared friends, social outings.

How did all that disappear?

I had become a stranger to my sister, someone she had to tolerate in the house, because all that mattered to her now was to be as close and as alone as possible with Alina. Doors would suddenly

shut when I approached, backs turned. I was excluded from conversations and ignored at the table and the TV room. Alina had
abducted Julia. The house was full of their whispers and giggles,
they walked around hand in hand, swam together naked in the
pool, roughhoused in delicate feminine fashion, tumbling over each
other like kittens, punching and pinching each other's boobs and
crotches, and laughing, laughing. It was all fun and shamelessness.

I disliked Alina from the start. Her slick looks, her suave Cuban
drawl, her proud, round shape as she walked everywhere behind
Julia like a bodyguard, her mouth turned up into complacent grins.
But I had to admit I'd never seen Julia so happy. That shroud of
invisibility she had worn since a small girl, the look of misery in her
elusive eyes, her constant retreat into far-off corners to read or draw,
all that was gone. And instead there emerged a shining Julia, as if
she had finally opened up, as if every pore had unfolded and she'd
stepped into her full womanly beauty. Her strawberry-blond hair
glowed around her golden skin; her amber glance filled rooms with
the serenity that beautiful, self-assured women bring into spaces.

It wasn't only her physical beauty; that might have come of itself
just due to her age. She'd turned twenty-one; she'd reached her full
growth after having been a scrawny child most of her life. But it was
mainly her painting. In a few short months she went from painting
small watercolors of still-life motifs, landscapes and flowers, to taking on large canvasses. Filling them with thick strokes of vibrant
colors, red, green, bright orange, turquoise, to create abstract luminous landscapes or massive voluptuous female nudes with splayed
legs and open lips in the shape of volcanic craters. It was a radical
leap from any work she'd produced before. Teachers and students
talked about her in the art school. A gallery owner approached her
to take part in a collective exhibition.

Julia was flying.

At first, Father didn't seem to notice any of these changes. After
all, the house had become unstructured with the Fernando scandal
and Marion's departure, and, most of all, Nanny's absence. To begin
with, there was no one to cook, clean, or run the house. There was
havoc in the kitchen for weeks—none of us knew how to prepare
food, or do any housework. We lived on sandwiches, canned soups,

and the like. The place grew dirty and untidy; dust filled bookcases and shelves, cobwebs populated every nook and cranny. Everything became chaotic: the laundry room, pantry, cellar. Plumbing failed in bathrooms, moths invaded the bedding closets. For the first time ever there were leaks from the roof.

In the midst of this turmoil, Julia and Alina's relationship thrived, locked up in their atelier bedroom, rapt in their intimate world of love mingled with art. Julia's sense of herself as an artist flourished. She walked around the house in grunges splattered with paint, no shoes, no bra—and, I suspect, no panties either—her hair tied up in a careless knot, eyes consumed with inspiration. And Alina, always behind, the smug muse, adoring; but most of all, controlling.

This domestic turbulence also brought another person to the forefront of our household. Olga Morris. Olga Morris—whom we never ceased to call by her first and family names together, as a sort of defensive tactic against the persistent threat that she might enter our lives for real—stepped up to the task of trying to organize the house, initially at Father's request and eventually following her own agenda. She started by filling the refrigerator with Bimbo, the Spanish version of Wonder bread, cold cuts, peanut butter spread, Coca-Cola, ginger ale, TV dinners, and a whole range of American fast food she obtained through the PX, the grocery store at the military base in Torrejón, where she had friends. She hired a number of housekeepers, marched in plumbers and exterminators, hired and fired a few gardeners. But most of all, she tried to make herself agreeable, to gain our trust, and be admitted into our confidence, because the way she was moving in on us required that kind of strategy. She'd already become close with Father, having stood up for him in front of detectives and police. During the aftermath of Fernando's death, when Father was distraught over Marion's reaction to the whole affair, Olga Morris had silently moved into a higher position of power than she had been given when hired, and ended up acquiring substantial influence over Father and his business.

There was also the drinking. She brought with her shipments of booze, and made sure she had Father under the influence by dosing him generously during the languid evenings spent at the house, drinking cocktails in the garden or by the fireplace, listening to jazz. We were sure she was a long-standing alcoholic, and we hated the way she rolled her eyes when she was drunk, throwing back her head on the couch, her short platinum hair limp around her egg-shaped head, while she half whispered in her slurred, lazy drawl, "Oh, James, this is all so interesting! You have so much going for you."

She convinced Father to turn the library into an office so he could work more at leisure in the home, instead of spending his days confined to his downtown office. Consequently, she herself could also hang around the house all day long. And that's exactly what she did. She came early in the morning with the excuse of supervising the housekeeper, stayed for lunch, sat in front of the typewriter in the library, half dozing all afternoon, and served Father drinks as early in the evening as possible, so they could hang out in the living room pretending to discuss the business of the day. But she herself started drinking much earlier. And could the broad hold her liquor! We never saw her display any of the classical symptoms of deep intoxication. We only got to hear her slur her sentences while her small, flabby body sunk listlessly into chairs and sofas, and her crocodile eyes checked out everything under thick drooping lids. I'll say for Father that come ten at night, he would always get up and dial for a taxi to come take Olga Morris back to her place.

"Do you think he's sleeping with her?" I asked Julia once. She shrugged her shoulders, a thick paintbrush in her mouth, reluctant to pull away from her canvas and engage in insoluble hypotheses on Father's sex life.

"Of course he is," Alina said. "Why else do you think he can bear to have her around day and night?"

"She doesn't spend the night here," I replied.

"How can you be so sure?"

It was one of those rare moments in which I had been given access to my former room, and sat around with Julia and Alina in what had become their exclusive territory. I was annoyed at having Alina comment on the situation; I wanted to hear Julia's thoughts. But Julia never said anything these days, just allowed Alina to represent her as official spokesperson. I was becoming worried at how much power Olga Morris was gaining over Father and over our lives. Not to mention Alina's over Julia. Our household seemed to be going through a radical transmutation, both in form and content, and I was afraid there would soon be no place for me in the new order that loomed ahead. What would I do then? Or some sort of a civil war might erupt between Alina and Julia against Father and Olga Morris. Would I be forced to take sides?

"That's such a classic within the hetero world," Alina continued. "The women gain power through sleeping with the men. It's totally degrading, but then, what choices do they have if they buy into the male-dominated system?" She always talked like this; her feminism thrived on putting down men and heterosexual women. Later she'd be hostile toward Father, and display a friendly front toward Olga Morris. Of course, Father took no notice, because to him Alina was a nobody who was temporarily in the house to somehow help out, to accompany Julia, to fill the absences of Marion and Nanny. So he tolerated her, and paid her no heed. Even though he didn't witness all that went on between Julia and Alina, he had seen them occasionally kissing and sunbathing naked in the pool, and knew they were inseparable. But the idea they were lovers hadn't entered his mind. And if it had, it must have been stashed away instantly as a piece of ridiculous chimera.

"H-o-m-o-s-e-x-u-a-l-s? I've never met any in my life. I'm afraid they don't really exist; maybe a sick boy or two in boarding school or the army barracks, but they soon come to their senses when they grow up and get in the way of family," he said, laughing one day at lunch. "Who would want to bother with that, seeing it's already so complicated to be a normal man or woman? Preposterous!"

"There have been well-known poets," Alina started, disguising with difficulty the bitterness in her voice. "You'll be familiar with Oscar Wilde, or Sappho, even Federico García Lorca . . ."

"Nonsense! It's mostly yellow press! They might have had a crush or two, but, h-o-m-o-s-e-x-u-a-l-s? I really don't think so. People are ignorant, you see? They cannot understand passionate poetry, so they degrade it with base explanations."

Alina bit her lip. I saw Julia take her hand under the table as she said out loud, "C'mon, Alina, let's go have a siesta and read passionate poetry," and got up from the table to leave.

But if Julia having a lesbian affair more or less in the open didn't seem to touch him, something else did. Her painting. The moment he discovered the work Julia was producing, he pounced on her. I remember the first time he entered her studio room and saw one of her big canvasses. It was a picture in ochers and greens. In the middle lay the shape of a large yellow dog, belly up, basking under an emerald sun, its limbs dissolving in the surrounding sienna earth, while the saliva from its long protruding tongue collected into a green puddle on the side.

Father froze as he took in the dramatic sweep of the image. Then after a moment he said, "Julia, what happened to your beautiful watercolors? I mean, this is an interesting exploration, but it doesn't hold a candle to your other work. I think you might need to go back to your mother's pictures and take stock of how she worked. She was a true artist."

Mother had been a watercolor painter in her spare time. Her pictures were pale representations of garden motifs and languid landscapes in subdued pastel colors. They were very beautiful indeed, but sort of contained, their luminous transparency filled with a sense of anguish, maybe a projection of her exhausted lungs, in the style of romantic grief. She had never attempted any other medium of painting, she hadn't even owned an easel. But Father had always compared Julia's work to Mother's, pushing her to follow in her steps, and then never conceding any real praise when she succeeded painting in Mother's style. She was always one rung below. That was how he kept Julia under control.

All that was over now. Julia had erupted. Her awakening spurted out in dazzling colors and shapes that impregnated any blank surface within her reach. Paper, canvas, pieces of wood or carton, even the walls in her room. And Father started by giving her advice to pace her development, to go back to more classical techniques. He had never showed so much interest in her work, but now he would come up to her room every day and examine the pieces she had worked on. His tone soon became more nagging, badgering her about being careless, sloppy, hasty, until he started to criticize her openly. "This is not original, you're just looking at some of the awful work that passes for art these days, and having a go at it your-self," he'd say.

But for once Julia wouldn't listen to him. She looked like she was sure of her process. And she had Alina behind her, which was all that mattered.

"What would he know, really?" Alina would say when he'd left the room.

"The English haven't produced much decent painting, unless you're into those fluffy countryside pictures of Turner and Gains-borough." The awful thing was that Father knew. He was crazy about art. Not only did he collect every art book he came across, but he was a man who took art at the gut level as I have never seen anyone else do. He would take us to the Prado Museum and stand for hours in front of Giottos, Titians, and Albrecht Dürers. He would stand and quiver with emotion, travel along brushstrokes, fuse into colors, inside shadows. He would talk about the feelings the paintings sparked in him, how he got lost in Dürer's pale blue landscapes, cringe with Goya's nightmarish scenes, feel face-to-face with a Rembrandt portrait. It wasn't just classical art, either. Fa-ther was passionate about Dalí, Rothko, Kandinsky, and of course, Picasso. Had he had a choice, he would have studied art, he always said. Painting was the panacea of human experience.

So, why was he doing this? Even I knew that Julia was really on to something, that her work was strong. As I watched him go at her, I sensed his jealousy, his discomfort with her sudden glory. But soon I began to feel his deeper, darker jealousy toward Alina, the muse who had triggered these changes in Julia, who had pushed her through the doorway toward the discovery of her potential.

Lunchtime became Alina's probing moment. Rosita, our fleeting housekeeper of those particular months, had been forbidden by Fa-ther to cook Spanish traditional food, because in truth her cooking was the greasiest and saltiest ever tasted at our table. So she just served whatever Olga Morris had brought along, mostly takeouts from the Madrid branch of Kentucky Fried Chicken, or hamburg-ers from a place called The Hollywood Café. I was surprised that Father, the ultimate scourge of Spanish cooks, never said a word about the awful American fast food or takeout menus provided by Olga Morris. Once set before him, he worked through whatever had been placed on his plate with sheepish tenacity. The rest of us got high on Coca-Cola and only picked at our plates, while Olga Morris kept refilling her glass with wine.

"So, do tell me again why your family left Cuba," Father would start by asking Alina. "Did you say your father was working for Batista at some point?" He had homed in on the fact that Alina was excruciatingly ashamed of her family of Cubano *gusanos*, or anti-Castro Cubans in exile, and her radically opposed political views were one of the reasons she had moved in with us. She couldn't stand her parents or her brothers.

"My father did work for Batista's government, and then left Cuba after Fidel Castro came into power. He was promised they would respect his integrity if he accepted the new system," Alina replied cautiously, knowing how easy it was for her to flare up when discussing Cuban politics, and how well Father knew it.

"Well, I'm sure he was clever enough to realize that those types of promises coming from someone like Castro are as good as nothing. After all, the man is a dictator, and has no respect for the basic rule of law, so why would he keep a promise made to a former enemy?"

"He's an awful man," Olga Morris interjected. "Did you hear what he did? He just filled a bunch of boats with all the criminals he had in prison and the crazies from the psych wards and shipped them off to the States. What kind of a perverted mind would think of that?" she added, drinking the rest of her wine with a gulp.

Alina sighed, struggling to choose her words. "It's not like that. Castro took over a system totally corrupt and controlled by mafias. The revolution was the only way out of a government run through extortion, fraud, and crime. Batista kept people dirt poor and hungry, he tortured and murdered everyone who spoke out." She talked faster and faster as she went. I could see the heat coloring her cheeks, hear the increasing shortness of her breath.

Father let her finish, and then said, "Really? So what's the point of taking out one nail with another, as they say over here? Or was

Batista so bad? I mean Castro also murders, throws people in prison, extorts private property from decent citizens, chases out people like your father . . ."

Alina's face was now crimson with rage. "The revolution does not extort. It redistributes wealth, which is very different, excuse me."

"No, you're not excused." Father's voice was also in crescendo. "Don't you come to my house telling me about the redistribution of wealth. That's number one in nursery school. I'm all for the underdog, but if people want redistribution they need to go through the democratic process, they need to contact their political representatives, that's how we do it in civilized societies."

"And what of *societies with no civilization?*" Alina stressed her words by gesturing with her fingers. "Those packed with starving peasants, illiterate, living hand to mouth, dependent on despotic landowners and political crooks who profiteer by selling the nation off to gringo mafias." Alina was panting now and so worked up I thought she might start to cry.

"If that is so, in the case of negroes or indigenous people, they *need* to be taken care of by responsible landowners and church ministers until they can step into their own power, don't you think?"

"That's always been the colonial argument, hasn't it? The excuse to plunder and exploit other nations!" Alina was nearly shouting.

Julia got up from her chair and said, "This is a stupid conversation, I'm going back to my painting. Let's go, Alina." She grabbed Alina by the arm and they both left the table.

"Yes, go back to painting with your communist friend. See if Castro will allow you to paint freely, if he won't throw you in prison for using the wrong color." Father's voice trailed after them.

"That girl is very misinformed. Let me reassure you, James, that the States only supports democratic governments," Olga Morris said in her sloshed voice, but Father paid her no attention.

The war between him and Alina had been officially declared.

Many months later, after I'd already been working with Father for a while, and had immersed myself fully in his office politics, I came to understand their conflict from a new perspective. At least, from Father's side of the fence. Spain was still in the throes of a political transition toward democracy. There was unrest in some business sectors, strife going on between unions and employers. All of a sudden, workplaces that had been meek and acquiescent to impresario rule during the years of dictatorship quickened into a new social awareness, became restless, and started making demands. Cocky representatives arose among employees, and the air was filled with threats of strike. This generalized unrest was palpable in Father's business, maybe even more so for him because he was a foreign employer. So, yes, Father was troubled by all these changes and their underlying ideological fueling. But why take it out on Alina, a young, cheeky, self-proclaimed communist, a kid traumatized by her country's diaspora after dramatic historical events had shaken her life?

I could only wonder.

Meanwhile, the house became overwrought with their strife. Lunchtimes became unbearable. A second time under siege, her family having put her through the first, Alina's political discourse became intensified, almost obsessive, a torture to bear. And Father's rebuttal arguments poured out nonstop, exhausting everyone around the table. Even Olga Morris began to display signs of impatience that no amount of wine could appease. The rest of us had given up on interfering in their sparring. Theirs was a single-combat encounter. It was impossible to leave the table, too. It was one of the unspoken rules of the house that Father decided when the table talk was over. I could feel the silent fury building inside Julia. Her relationship with Alina was beginning to show symptoms of stress derived from these conversations.

Alina wouldn't yield either. Every day she came to the table with renewed energy and fresh arguments. It was this persistence that most annoyed Father. And a part of me started admiring Alina for this staunchness, for the fact that she didn't give in, a David in the form of a small, round Cuban brunette stepping up daily to an insurmountable Goliath.

The foil work only got hotter. "The thing about a revolution is not just about social and political reorganization," Alina said another day. "It's also about creating leaps in human consciousness, shortcuts in history. It's about new possibilities. Just consider Julia's painting. She's gone from nondescript watercolors to exuberant depictions, and she's done it by taking a quantum leap, not just in linear progression. Now, that's revolutionary."

This new argument was too close to the real sore between them and took Father's rage to a boiling point. "It's hypocritical to talk about revolutions and the wonders they might do for art, without mentioning gulags and concentration camps, don't you think?" Father snapped. He was realizing that Alina was a tough kill.

And then it happened.

One Sunday afternoon, I heard the front doorbell, and when I opened it I found Ventura standing there, his large overcoat puffed up by a blast of whirlwind swirling dry autumn leaves about the porch. He was the office accountant, a tight-lipped, lean, spindly man with a pair of thick glasses he was always wiping off with his handkerchief. He requested to see Father, and I took him to the study. Father closed the door behind them, commenting on the surprising timing of his visit. Sundays in Spain were sacred family-gathering time, never infringed upon. I knew instantly something major had brought him to the door. They spent a few hours locked up in the studio, and then the police came. After another long while of deliberation, Julia and I were asked into the studio to answer questions. Checks for hefty amounts of money had been cashed last week at the bank. Father's signature had been falsified. The checks could have only come from the filing cabinet in Father's studio at the house. Of course, Julia and I were clueless.

But Alina was arrested.

"Hey, wake up! Your phone has been ringing nonstop for the last twenty minutes." Julia walks toward me, my cell phone in her hand. Behind her, Constantine carries coffee paraphernalia on a large tray. He sets it down on the low table by the chaise, while Delia yawns and stretches out her body. "Constant, you can be a true angel when you try," she says, picking up one of the cups.

Julia hands me my phone, which has started to ring again. I push the hang-up button and put it on the tray.

92   *Susana Aikin*

"Bravo," Julia says, stirring sugar into her coffee. "But my experience of these calls is that they're a matter of insistence, and sooner or later . . ."

"Let's all just mind our own business for today," I snort.

The phone rings again. Everyone looks at me. Exasperated, I pick it up.

"Anna, listen. Please."

"Sorry, Marcus. Not this time. I'm taking care of something crucial."

"I'll pay you anything you want, I'll do anything . . ."

"Don't make promises you mightn't be able to deliver."

"Anna, this is not a joke. I really need you here!"

"Okay, but I already told you you're going to have to find someone else to help. I'm busy today. I have to run. Bye." I push down the power button until the phone goes dead. Julia sighs.

Everyone drinks their coffee in silence. Delia sips hers staring out toward the terrace. Then she puts down her cup. "Well, what can I say? A little romance in the air always cheers up company on a hot afternoon like this."

I look up at her, annoyed, but she goes on. "Do you know that Constantine makes the best love spells in the whole region? Totally guaranteed, no matter how impossible the situation. Isn't that right, Constant?" Delia breaks again into that thin smile that looks like it's trembling with muzzled laughter.

"You're too flattering, Delia," Constantine says, blushing.

I eye Julia with fury. Has she dared to share my private life with Delia? But Julia returns a no-I-haven't look. I get up. I hate to admit to myself that I'm fuming. "Where's Marion?"

"She's up in some bedroom," Julia says.

I make for the house.

"Don't forget your phone," Delia says.

I stomp off, while she turns to Constantine. "Let's prepare for the library and the study next. We'll need all the salt. And the big bags of sage."

CHAPTER 9

As I walk into the house, I hear a scream and a loud bang. A clatter of hard cascading sounds, as if a bunch of heavy objects were falling on the floor, follows. I hurry up the stairs toward the din that's coming from Mother's studio, my old adopted bedroom.

I push the door open. "Marion? Are you hurt?"

Marion is sitting on the floor surrounded by mounds of fallen books and a bunch of smashed wood shelves that seem to have collapsed on her. The room is thick with the smell of dust and old paper.

"I'm okay, I think. Just a bump on the head. I stood on a chair to reach up and everything came tumbling down." She dusts her dress and rubs her head as I help her up.

Amazing, how the entire structure of the bookshelf has come down suddenly; a small gesture like the pulling of a book was enough to make it crumble into pieces. Is the whole house coming to this?

"Shall I get you ice?"

"It's nothing. Look what I found. It's been lost among these shelves forever." She sits heavily on the daybed and opens the tattered cover of an old photo album. "Stop putting the books away and come sit with me," she says, and studies my face while I finish stacking the last pile. "Are you all right? You look very pale. Did anything happen? Has Julia been saying things to you?"

"Nope. Just hot, tired, and starved. Didn't get much lunch. But I'm not complaining." I slump on the bed beside her.

Marion scrutinizes me for a moment longer. "You know, you've a way of bottling things up, like your job is to carry everyone's stuff stashed somewhere inside you. It's not healthy, you know?"

"Please, let's not go there. I just want to get through the day."

"Okay," Marion says slowly. I know she is disappointed at my barring her from giving me one of those older-sister talks. But besides being chronologically a few years ahead of me, how is Marion older? She's never taken any responsibility for family affairs, has never put out any fires. She has to be taken care of when she goes into fits, feels pathologically overwhelmed when any piece of bad news is reported to her. All of a sudden I feel a hundred years old as I watch her get back to the picture album with the keen, light-hearted curiosity of a little girl.

"I haven't seen these photos in ages. Remember this one?" I glance over her shoulder and zoom in to the image contained in the black-and-white picture she points at. Mother and Father at their wedding, descending the stairs of the church of San José, a darkened stone façade carved with statues of apostles and saints. In the picture, Father is slim and elegant in his tuxedo, a long shock of light brown hair curling across his forehead, a beaming smile directed toward a small crowd of friends who throw confetti around. Mother stands by his side, her short, stylish black hair under a white pillbox hat adorned with a birdcage veil. She holds a bouquet of pale roses in her gloved hands, roses paler than the satin dress that runs tight along her slender body.

"How would our lives have been different if she'd stayed alive?" Marion says, something she's repeated unceasingly over the years. For a moment I study the image of Mother in the picture, and notice the deep yearning inside her long almond eyes. Of all the people in the shot, she's the only one gazing directly at the camera, and that makes this photo very strange to look at. As if Mother locks eyes with you, the viewer, with the intention of revealing something, of conveying a doubt, a sadness, a hidden piece of information.

How little we know about our mother, how few things she left behind. No diaries, no close friends, no friendly family members who could have informed us about what she was like, what she had hoped for, what made her heart quicken. Only her pale, watercolor landscapes. Our main direct source about her had been Nanny, since Father never talked about her; and as the years went by, Nanny's stories reminded us more and more of the stuff of novellas, and sometimes, just fairy tales. At some point we realized she had stored Mother away in the realm of legend.

Of course, there was also Marion, who was ten at the time of her death and remembered many details about her. Often I would go to Marion and ask her to tell me things about our mother, or ask her questions about her lifestyle. What types of food did she like? What did she wear when she went out at night with our father? Was she vain, being that she was so pretty? Did she ever cry? And Marion would then talk about her, but for some reason, my older sister never quite succeeded in conveying a rounded picture of our mother or her way of life—it was as if her own collection of memories was also fuzzy and incoherent. Then there was Julia, who also had some memories, although hers were mostly related to painting. How mother had taught her to mix colors, to wield paintbrushes. The box of colored pencils she once gave her. There was one cute anecdote Julia recounted over and over, about the morning Mother had her paint faces on discarded breakfast soft-boiled eggshells turned upside down in their cups—a man's, with a big moustache, and a little girl's, with rosy, circular cheeks—and how later they had taken strands of colored yarn and stuck them on top of the shells to resemble hair. And what about *my* memories? They seemed very different from my sisters'. I remember a pale, recumbent woman in a large bed. Her eyes swimming with sadness as she looked at me, as she touched my face with soft, cold fingers. She became increasingly sick after I was born, and hardly ever took care of me. We were told her lungs were very weak. She needed to rest all the time, and not be disturbed by us children. I remember asking Nanny at the market to buy me flowers so I could take them back to Mother.

Marion turns the page and another large black-and-white picture appears. Father standing by his old Triumph motorbike, clad in a bomber jacket and tall boots, leather helmet in hand, hair ruffled by the ride, a grin on his face. Behind him, a range of white high-peaked mountains tower over the winding dirt road below.

"He must have been around your age here," Marion says, pointing at the picture. "And he looks so much like you in this photo!"

"No, he doesn't," I snap.

"You always had the same eyes, and here it's just so obvious, and the smile . . ."

I glare at her, annoyed. Marion lowers her eyes in silence. But when I return to the picture and take in again his blue gaze, half-wondrous, half-startled, hardened over with the determination to shield its brittle, pained surface, I do feel a pang of identification, a sameness. A sameness if only in the fact that I too, like him, always felt that the thin membrane of my corneas left the deeper self unprotected, dangerously exposed. I also have strived through the years to glaze it over, to conceal emotion, doubt, pain.

How can I begin to deny that of the three of us I was the one who most resembled Father? Not just my eyes, the shape of the high cheekbones, the thin lips, the slender, compact body; most of my physical traits come from Father's family. Only the black, thick hair sets me aside. Not so with my two sisters. Down the years, as we learned to fear and hate Father, talk of this semblance between him and me became taboo among us, as if drawing similarities could result in some sort of defilement, in a contagion of his rage, of his tendency to inflict disquiet and torment in the lives of others. And now, why is Marion breaching this covenant?

"I'll just say for the man, he was good-looking in his youth," Marion says, and again it feels strange to hear this from my sister. We have for so long talked about our father with resentment, that his looks, his graceful figure as he stands by the mountain road, smiling at a companion, or just at the passerby who's taking his picture, has not entered my consciousness. I now consider his tall, slim body clad in Lindbergh-style pilot garb, his dimpled cheeks and piercing blue eyes. He was a handsome man, not only in his youth, but throughout his whole life. Although not exercise prone, his body remained trim, his hair never totally grayed, and his face, despite developing wrinkles and deep creases from the dry weather and the hard sun, remained firm. Only his rage distorted his countenance, firing up his eyes and setting his jaw, and as time went by, his face assumed a more permanent distraught look. But he never ceased to evoke admiration, with his English country-style clothes and his classic demeanor. Even when he was in the hospital at the end of his rope, crazy and desperate, nurses would come in twos, and stand at the door looking in, saying to each other, "Look at him, isn't he the most handsome man? He's like a movie star." Of course, we're talking about a geriatric ward.

But still.

Many people had wondered throughout the years why a man like him, handsome, driven, successful, had not remarried. After all, he was only in his late thirties when he became a widower, and there was no shortage of interested women swarming around him. Not just Spanish women, who might have coveted a foreign husband, but also women belonging to the American and British circles of Madrid, more modern, independent women, also looking for matches. But Father had kept himself secluded in his island, that is, in the house with his three daughters, for as long as he could hold it all together. And he made sure to keep other women out of the small kingdom he had so carefully cultivated.

The only woman to have crossed the line had been Olga Morris, who had made herself fit snugly, first in his work environment, and later in the house. Initially, all kinds of speculation went on about a possible affair between them, but since nothing was confirmed down the line, the gossip died down. Despite the fact that she stayed glued to him while she lasted.

The morning after Alina's arrest, we found out that Olga Morris had disappeared from Madrid leaving no trace. Further inquiries conducted in the bank where the checks had been cashed confirmed it had been her who presented the checks, had them ratified by the branch manager, and carried away the money. Because she'd been Father's head secretary and business administrator, the bank was used to dealing with her directly, and although surprised by the large amounts that were being cashed, it was assumed to be another one of Father's dynamic business transactions, and no further questions were asked.

Olga Morris was arrested three days later in Marbella, a million-aire vacation town in the south of Spain, totally drunk in a luxury hotel room and surrounded by the pile of sleeping pills she was probably intending to take. The money, save for a few thousand in her book bag, was missing. When interrogated, she refused to talk. The routine medical examination during her arrest revealed terminal breast cancer, which she admitted to having known about for the last eight months. After Father dropped charges, she was deported back to the States. The investigation to track down the money took a long time to arrive at conclusions. Long enough that I had most of it figured out before any official statement was issued. Sometimes the intuitive human heart is faster than police proceedings.

Weeks after she was deported, when looking around the desk she had occupied in the library, I found her old yellow leather purse in one of the drawers, the only personal item she left behind. Inside one of the plastic sleeves, there was a picture of a small boy with a narrow face, sad eyes, and limp straw hair. I then remembered her mentioning the young son she had sent to her mother in Rock-hill, South Carolina, after her divorce, because she couldn't afford to keep him with her. That instant I knew why she had taken the money and its probable whereabouts. The realization hit me like a lightning bolt, and then shame washed over me because of the fact that we had never, not even once, called her just Olga.

How much of this did Father know? Was he more involved than he admitted? That afternoon, weeks after the mayhem had finally quieted down and he and I were the only ones left in the house, I sat across from his desk in his studio and decided to ask him directly.

"Was there something between you and Olga that we didn't know about?" I was surprised at how adult I sounded. Not just how bold, but also how much I came across as an equal. There I was, only nineteen years old and questioning my father about his mis-demeanors. But then, at that strange moment, we were equals; like some unlikely pair that ends up cast away after a shipwreck, and become comrades-in-arms facing the calamity. So, yes, I had stepped up to a certain equality, and was determined to make use of it.

"Did you and she . . . ?" I repeated the question.

"That's neither here nor there," Father said sternly, but then he added in a softer tone, "but if you must know, no, not really, no, I couldn't say there was—" He faltered and then averted his eyes. In this gesture I saw not just the mortification he felt about the appearance of his relationship to Olga Morris, but also detected a sort of tenderness toward her, a trace of affection, something that surprised and shocked me.

"So, why are you dropping charges then?" I asked with a harsher voice than I had intended. All of a sudden I was furious at the thought of this scrawny, blond drunk having taken advantage of my father.

"It's complicated," he said, returning his eyes to mine. "Olga is a poor woman abandoned in a foreign country in total indigence by a ruthless husband," he added, and hesitated to go on while I waited.

"And . . . ?"

"And there's the cancer," he added.

"Did you know about it?"

"Yes."

We looked at each other in silence.

Spring was early that year. Outside the window, the untrimmed lilac bushes pressed their soft mauve blooms against the panes, and golden shafts of afternoon sunlight fell onto Father's back, silhouetting his head and shoulders against the wood paneling behind him. For the first time I noticed the lines on his forehead and around his eyes, his hair graying along the sideburns, and realized that Father was beginning to age.

Many times I have thought back on this moment, the first time I saw a glitch in his otherwise hard-hearted appearance, the beginning of a seemingly commensurate platform between us. In my innocence I had thought I was stepping into a protective role toward him. But there was no being at the same level with Father; he always needed to ride on top of things.

Only days earlier he had again played the callous, brutal role we were used to. And this time around, the consequences struck deeper and faster than ever before.

Alina had spent the night under arrest in the police station,

crammed into an overnight holding cell with prostitutes, drug dealers, and other poor street wretches. Not that she might have been
intimidated by this type of population, she was a tough cookie and
probably organized the group into some sort of protest or riot just a
few hours into the arrest. She was released the next day when the
police investigation was redirected to Olga Morris. After that she
didn't just not return to the house, but refused to see or to talk to
Julia again. She had had it with our family. Her cousin Camila, a
short girl with oversized hips and carrot-colored hair, scoffed when
she came over to pick up her belongings. *Fascistas de mierda.* Fucking fascists.

Julia was beside herself. She couldn't understand why Alina was
rejecting her as if she had had anything to do with her arrest. She'd
fought with the policemen who handcuffed her, and had refused to
let go of Alina when they dragged her into the police van. She
became such a problem that Father was told that if he didn't control
her, she would have to be taken in too.

That night she stormed into Father's study screaming, demanding to know how the hell he could even doubt Alina's innocence.
When Father retorted it had been the detective's conclusion and
not his, she was overcome with rage. "No, you had nothing to do
with it! I know you, you cunning bastard! I'm sure you drove them
directly toward that conclusion!" Father was chilled at her fury, and
so was I. No one had ever attacked Father like this.

"I hate you!" she said in a horribly hoarse voice. "I never want to
see you again, I'd rather sleep on the street, I'd rather whore myself
than eat at your table." This was not the Julia we knew. This was a
ferocious animal prepared to tear her enemy apart. Her brazenness
triggered Father's wrath and I could see his body swelling with violent might. He stood up.

"You dare talk like that in my house and you're out!" he said,
and I thought he was going to lunge at her. I jumped in between
them and covered Julia's body with mine. The three of us held our
stances in tension, watching one another and panting.

"Get out! Right now!" Father snarled.

"If you throw her out, I'm going too," I said, trying to sound
calm, although my legs were about to cave under me. Father glow-

ered at me, eyes burning with rage. Then he turned around and left the room.

Julia fell to her knees and vomited on the floor. Then she burst into sobs. Later, it took all my convincing skills to talk her out of going to the police station and camping outside for the night. For the first time in over a year, I slept again in our old room, close to Julia, who couldn't stop crying.

It was only the beginning of the nightmare. Alina's release from arrest marked the starting point of an intense rejection and smear campaign against Julia in the art school. Alina wouldn't talk to Julia, wouldn't even acknowledge her presence. People would start whispering when she walked into rooms. Julia became angst-ridden and restless. She stopped eating, couldn't sleep, started talking about dropping out of school.

"Can't you talk to her, tell her you had nothing to do with it?" I kept asking, incredulous of Alina's vengeful persistence.

"It's impossible to have a conversation with her. Every time I approach, she walks away," was Julia's answer.

"Can't you ask some mutual friend to mediate, to talk on your behalf?"

"I don't have anyone like that."

"What about that woman, Mananas? Remember you told me how she thought you were the greatest couple?"

"I wouldn't know where to find Mananas."

"Didn't she work in that bar, El Mojito, as a waitress?"

"What would I do, just walk in and say what? I only met her once."

"Julia, you need to do something. I'll come with you, if that's what it takes."

Julia perked up. "Would you?" It was the first time in days I had seen a flicker of light in her eyes.

That night we set out for El Mojito. We drove into town in Marion's burgundy Seat 600, which I had inherited after she moved to London. It had rained in the early evening and the cobbled streets of the older part of town glistened under the dim streetlights. It was after ten p.m. on a Monday, so most of the downtown appeared to be empty, save a few local bars where a handful of male patrons drank beer and watched replays of a soccer match. El Mojito, one of the scarce lesbian bars at that time in Madrid, was located in a narrow street in Chueca, a down-and-out neighborhood inhabited by older working-class denizens and a few Moroccan and Latin American immigrants. A decade or so later it would bloom into a cool 'hood gentrified by artists and young professionals, among which I would eventually count myself. But for now, Chueca was just a grimy, shabby-looking quarter, littered with garbage piles, its intricate network of dark, cramped streets running into each other in unpredictable ways. From the open windows and balconies above wafted pungent waves of cooking smells into the street, and the sounds of all sorts of family discussions and fights poured down below for everyone to hear. But not tonight. Monday was a hard fall after a long weekend of late carousing, and the neighborhood lay in a quiet slumber.

The entrance to El Mojito was a dark little door that first led into a sort of large corridor, to one side of which was a bar, backlit with a red glow; and then opened farther along into a roundish cave-like space with tables around a small, round dance floor. A swirling disco ball shot revolving shafts of color onto the walls; everything else was more or less in darkness, save for some candles on the tables. As we crossed the threshold, I was hit by a strong smell, a combination of alcohol and the dampened wood of old, dirty bars. Then there was the cigarette smoke that rose and curled up toward the domed ceiling. Everyone still smoked back then. It was considered cool and sexy. Julia and I were exceptions in that we had never been interested in the habit.

El Mojito was mostly empty, maybe a dozen women hanging around between the bar and the back room. Many of them were masculine looking, with short, cropped hair, and dressed in dark slacks and shirts with silver chains and bracelets as adornments, as was the lesbian fashion then. Everyone turned heads to check us out. The place was probably more of a membership type of hangout than an open bar, in the sense that new faces were the exception. I was glad we'd decided to wear jeans and plain tops. I would have felt even more singled out if we had dressed in girlie garb. We walked up to the bar.

"I'm looking for Mananas," said Julia.

The woman behind the bar, a large female with short black hair plastered with gel toward the back of her head, said, "That's me. How can I help you?" The bored expression on her face seemed to freeze Julia for a moment. Mananas waited for an answer, eyeing us wearily while drying a set of tall glasses with a cloth.

"I'm Alina's friend." Julia hesitated. "We met once, don't you remember?"

"Sorry, I don't; too many people come by every day." Mananas forced a little smile and held it for a beat. "As for Alina, she doesn't come around no more. Haven't seen her for months." She turned her back to us, and started replacing the dried cups on the shelf with extreme care. Julia and I stood, not knowing what to do next.

"Let's leave," Julia whispered.

"Are you kidding? Came all the way here, and leave just like that? I'm not sure I trust her." Then, turning to the bar, I said to Mananas, "Can we have two mojitos, then?" and drove Julia toward one of the tables. Mananas took a while to bring over the two fat glasses glazed with rum and lime, on the rocks, squashed mint leaves floating on top.

When I went to pay, she said in a half yawn, "Pay me later, when you're all finished."

No sooner had we settled down and started to sip our mojitos than there was a bustling at the door and a group of women entered the bar, boisterous with laughter and loud talk. The space became energized in an instant as the music changed from the Santana album that had been playing to a loud mambo orchestra. The raucous group moved into the back with drinks and settled among tables and chairs.

"There she is!" Julia's voice trembled. "I shouldn't have come. I don't have a good feeling about this."

Alina stood across the room with the group of newcomers. Although she didn't glance directly at us, I knew she was aware of our presence because as she stepped onto the dance floor, she began to take off her jacket making sure her body was turned in our direction, as if she were on a stage. She was dressed in khaki fatigues, the type used by the Spanish military, and a tight cream T-shirt that showed off her round breasts and slim waist. She chatted away and laughed loudly, and I knew Alina well enough to understand that she was warming up toward putting on a good show.

Meanwhile, maracas, cowbells, and conga drums interspersed with sax and trombone, electrifying sounds, filled the space with irresistible rhythm. I could feel the mambo beat throbbing stronger with every sip of my mojito. It pulsed inside my ears and along my veins. Julia was also drinking fast beside me. I ordered more drinks.

A group of women was already on the dance floor. They kicked and flicked their feet and swayed their hips to the music in wide, exaggerated movements. Then Alina walked into the middle holding hands with a partner, a tall, athletic woman with thick sensual lips and a short hairdo ending in a pigtail that curled on her shoulder. They turned to each other and began to dance, shaking their hips and stepping to the sides and backward. Because Alina was dressed in lighter colors and danced under the shaft of lights, she seemed to fill the floor. Her small, round body moved with a sensuality quite beyond what I had seen in her before. She danced in total abandonment, swinging her hips in flowing motion while her feet performed quick, sharp steps hardly touching the floor. Her olive skin glistened with beads of sweat pouring from her forehead toward her lips and downward from her underarms, moistening her T-shirt along the belly and under her breasts. Now and then she pulled her partner to her and rubbed her body lustily against hers, or brushed her cheek against her partner's open mouth.

Maybe it was the mojitos, but I felt my mind zooming in to her sensual curves, homing in on the perfect shape of her earlobes perforated with tiny diamond studs, inside the depths of her dark amber glance, seductive and jeering all in one. And for the first time I understood why Julia was so taken with her, why she had fallen into her irresistible magnetic field, how she could love her curvy, graceful body all night long. I turned to see Julia, red-faced and hollow-eyed, staring at Alina in a trance. And Alina was not just staring back, she was dancing for Julia alone. For a moment the room belonged to them, to their eyes locked in a harrowing, passionate glance, to Alina's body unfolding into waves of dripping desire, for Julia's parched mouth alone.

The song ended and the music mellowed down. Alina stood facing us. I thought she would come to our table and talk to Julia. But all of a sudden she turned to her dancing partner, took her face in her hands, and gave her a long, wet kiss. The other women on the floor cheered and clapped. Julia got up abruptly, her chair fell back and the mojito glasses that were on the table crashed on the floor. She was trembling. Everyone's eyes turned in our direction.

"Look who's left her rich daddy's closet to come and throw things around!" Alina taunted in a shrill voice.

"I had nothing to do with what happened. Please, you need to believe me," Julia pleaded in a broken voice.

"I don't have to believe anything. You're all chips off the old block. Hypocrites and Nazis."

"You don't mean this, you don't mean anything you're saying."

"Yes, I do. Beat it, *bollera de armario*, closet dyke, before I chase you out." Alina stuck out her tongue, then turned to her girlfriend and kissed her again. "I'll let you know that my new girlfriend is a policewoman. That's what it takes for a girl to be safe these days," she sneered, and turning around took a baton from the table behind her and flaunted it toward us under the light. Again, knowing Alina, it was hard to discern if it was a prop, or a real piece of her girlfriend's professional gear.

Meanwhile, Mananas, who was picking up the broken glass around us, whispered, "Why don't you all go away? It's not looking good."

"You knew who we were, didn't you?" I asked.

"Yep."

"Why did you pretend you didn't?"

"I was trying to drive you away, guessing what might be coming. And now, just get your sister out of here! I know how these bitch dykes can smash things up."

It was easy to lead Julia away, since she was in total shock. I held her by the arm and walked her out of El Mojito to the car. As we passed by the bar, Mananas leaned toward us and said, "Hey, don't take it so hard, she's mad now. You just need to give her time."

At that moment, I was grateful for the hope she was giving Julia, who stood shaking by my side. But over the years I have grown to resent her words and wished she had never uttered them, because that's precisely what Julia has been giving Alina all along. Time. And with that gift Julia has pawned the best years of her life.

Later that night I woke up with a dry cotton-mouth, and a headache like lancinating spears piercing my temples. The rum in the mojitos must have been rat poison at the very least. I groped my way down the corridor toward the bathroom for a desperate drink at the faucet, when I heard the racket. It was coming from Julia's room. I stumbled toward her door, and when I pushed it open, the scene before me made me rub my eyes in disbelief: Julia with a large kitchen knife, slashing her canvasses, smashing her school portfolio collection of ceramic nudes.

"Julia, what the hell?" I started.

"Don't you dare come in and interfere! All of this is going." Her eyes were bloodshot.

I stepped in. "This is no way to deal. Can't we talk for a minute?" But her eyes were gone, her pupils spiraled inward toward some dark place I had never seen before.

Father was already behind me. "What on earth is going on here?" he asked, and Rosita, who also stayed nights, peeked over our shoulders and started screaming at the sight of the knife. I tried to touch Julia's arm, but she yanked away from me and her face tightened into a threat.

"Step out, Anna," Father said. "Just close the door and let her be. I'm going to call Dr. Martinez." He walked away after saying to Rosita, "Shut up, woman, get the hell to your room this minute, and don't come out until I tell you!"

But I didn't step out. That would have meant admitting that Julia's lack of control was irrevocable. I hoped for a tiny window of discernment somewhere, in this surreal scene. I slid down to the floor by the wall and squatted, my head heavy and bursting, ready to throw up.

"Dr. Martinez will arrive with an ambulance and you'll get committed. Get ahold of yourself! This is *not* a game."

"I am not leaving anything around that reminds me of Alina. I don't want any of this, or this!" Julia screamed, but she had already put down the knife and was tearing a sketchbook apart. She grabbed the coil to stretch and bend it, when one end stuck her finger. She jumped back in pain, watching the blood pouring out onto her nightshirt.

"Fuck, fuck, fuck!" Hot tears streamed down her face.

I stood up. "It's nothing, Julia, let's wash it out." She clasped her finger as we walked to the bathroom, where I put her hand under the cold running water and wet a towel to dampen her face. "Let's change your shirt. We don't want them thinking you stabbed yourself." Julia calmed down, but in the aftermath of her frenzy she started shaking so badly I had to wrap her in a blanket. She refused to sleep in the bed she had shared with Alina. I took her to my room and put her in my bed.

When Dr. Martinez arrived an hour later, his grayish waxy complexion haggard with forced insomnia, Julia looked calmer, although exhausted. He prescribed Valium as always, the ultimate mental elixir of the time, and asked her to come into his office in the morning. He left, after casting a last sour glance at Father, as if he were beginning to suspect that it was he who needed treatment instead of his daughters.

A couple of days later, Julia packed a few belongings and moved out of the house into an apartment a group of her student friends shared in the city. She had no money and Father refused to let her take anything belonging to the house. But I was already working for him at the office and gave her all my salary behind his back, until she managed to pull her resources together.

It was just Father and I in the house now. Rosita only came a few hours during the day, mostly when we were both away at the office. In the evenings after work, Father and I would sometimes dine briefly together, and then each of us would get lost in our darkened, silent part of the house. The house was just that, dark and silent, with some corners like black holes pulling me into moods of longing, and the hushed garden peering in through thick panes at night, into my bedside lamp–lit room, drowning me in memories of sun-drenched moments, bustling parties, late swims, guitars.

* * *

"What was that?" Marion perks up, startled. "Can you hear it? It's Julia!" Muffled shrieks come from down below. I get up and listen out in the corridor.

"I don't care what you say!" Julia sounds flustered. "It's your job to handle every room in the house. That was the deal." I hurry downstairs and find her, Delia, and Constantine outside Father's studio. Constantine is holding a sort of metal bowl in his hands full of dried herbs. Sage, probably. Behind him against the wall are two big bags of salt piled up, together with the bucketful of water and the mop. Delia stands facing Julia, staff in one hand, handbell in the other. Her expression is impenetrable.

"What's the problem?" I ask.

Delia turns toward me, and she's about to speak when Julia cuts in. "Delia is just being difficult. She refuses to work inside Father's study until someone goes in first. Well, it's not going to be me."

"You've been designated to clear the paths in this *limpieza*," Delia says patiently. "I told you it would be your job to open every door and every window in the house before we even arrived. You requested the *limpieza*, and therefore you're the one who needs to lead the way. And you've done it everywhere but here."

"I already unlocked the door. All these rules are a pile of crap."

"I cannot clean this room if you don't clear the path. There's no way around it." Delia's tone is stubborn.

I approach Constantine. "What's going on?"

"Julia is breaking the energetic grid of the *limpieza*," he whispers back. "It's bad news. It could be even worse than if we hadn't started at all." I want him to further clarify this last cryptic statement, but my attention turns back to Julia, who is going off on one of her tantrums.

"I think we should call the whole thing off. I'm sick of having to take all the responsibility!" she shrieks.

"Julia, what's the big deal?" I ask her.

"The big deal is, I'm not stepping into that freaking den. I don't give a fuck if the *limpieza* can't go on," Julia says, her eyes red with fury. Then she screams at Delia over my shoulder, "I won't pay you a dime if you don't finish the whole house, this room included! Not even cab money."

Delia clicks her tongue. "Constantine, please bring a chair, it looks like we're going to be here for a while." Constantine brings a chair and she sits down ceremoniously, like a queen.

I take Julia to the side. "Hey, what's wrong?" I ask her in a softer tone. Julia looks at me, befuddled, and I see the agitation in the depth of her gaze. "Are you all right?" Julia doesn't say anything, her face is contorted as if she can't shake off an image or an idea. All of a sudden, the strange thought enters my mind that it's possible that the memories I have been entertaining in the last hour have not just welled up in my mind, but maybe in Julia's also, as if they were emerging from a different source than our individual brains, and impregnated the consciousness of us both, playing themselves out on a larger scale. In this sense, both Julia and I could have simultaneously relived the same scenes. Is the house regurgitating memories and engulfing us all in its own recollections?

Julia holds my gaze as if she were also contemplating a similar weird thought. "I'm not stepping into that room. I'm not putting myself through his shit." I see real fear in her eyes.

"Julia, we've come so far," I say, "we need to finish this."

"I'm not doing it."

CHAPTER 10

A scream pulls me out of Julia's stubborn gaze.

"Help, Anna! Oh God!"

"There she goes again," Julia mutters.

"Stop it! You're not making things easier right now." I turn away, annoyed, and make for the stairs. But at the second step my foot skids over a wet, slippery surface, and looking up I see sheets of water cascading down toward me. Marion stands at the top of the stairs, a metal piece in her hand. "It broke, Anna, I swear I only tried to flush it," she says with a mortified grin.

On the landing the water advances in gushes, rushes forth with the greed of a stream that has overflown its banks. It washes against the base of the corridor, where the wallpaper is curling up as if in dread of the avalanche.

"Marion, what the hell?" I yell, yanking the metal piece from her hand, and wade toward the bathroom.

"I thought it'd stop when the tank emptied out. But it kept flooding." Marion walks behind me, chattering away, anxious. In the bathroom, the sound of rushing water fills my ears as I ogle in horror the toilet overflowing from tank and bowl, a muddy geyser springing from under the house.

I gasp. "I've never seen anything like this."

I hear Delia's voice from downstairs. "It is written, *the gates shall be opened and oceans of tears will flood through.*" She pauses, and then adds, "I hope you didn't empty your bowels before you flushed, or else we would need to substitute tears for . . ." She chuckles. Constantine snickers.

Marion stares at me blankly. "I swear I didn't—"

Before she can finish, Julia walks in, screaming, "What the fuck? Water's already downstairs! What is it with you that you're always breaking things?"

"Stop shouting and help me find the shut-off valve," I snap.

A dim bulb hanging from the ceiling is the only source of light in the bathroom. For a few moments the three of us bump into each other while stooping and squatting in search of the valve. One of the vanity cabinet's doors under the sink breaks loose when Julia yanks it open. Marion hits her head on the metal edge of an elaborate mirror frame. My bare feet slip over the smooth marble floor. Marion has already tried to shut down the valve behind the toilet bowl, a piece of which ended up in her hand. A jet of brownish water spurts out of the rotten pipe with a deafening hiss.

"There has to be a main valve to the whole bathroom," I say, desperate, as I feel the water swishing around my ankles.

"Too many *womens* in the kitchen." Julia sneers. "Someone needs to leave." She gives Marion a sidelong glance as she crouches by the vanity cabinet.

"You mean me?" Marion snaps. "I'll gladly leave. I've more important things to do."

"More important than watching your house conk out under a deluge of shit?" Here they go again.

"Frankly, the house can go to hell, for all I care," Marion says.

Julia bristles as Marion brushes past her, nose up in the air. "That so? Then just get your fat ass out of here!"

"How dare you!"

"Could you two just break it up?" I say in a fury, stepping in between.

Marion clicks her tongue and leaves.

Julia gets back into the cabinet. "Revolting! It stinks in here. But wait! I think I got it!"

I dive down beside her. The inside of the vanity is thick with greenish mold along the exposed wall. A mist of fetid spores hits my face as I pull out a bunch of crumbling toilet rolls now sodden to the core, together with two plastic containers filled with yellowed shampoo bottles and other toiletry relics. Now we get a glimpse of dark corroded tubes of exposed plumbing at the far end, topped by a small hand wheel.

Julia turns it forcefully.

"It needs oil. It's too rusty," I say.

"Do you know where the main valve for the house is?" Julia asks. "Anna, we need to go down and shut it. Now! This thing won't yield." She pulls out her wet hands, red and swollen after turning the impossible wheel.

I stand up, panting. My feet feel puffy and cold in the streaming water. I plod out of the bathroom and down the corridor, holding on to the banister as I descend the stairs. Why do I always insist on walking barefooted when I'm in this house?

As I reach the second floor I see Delia and Constantine ahead of me. Delia is still sitting in the chair; her heavy legs and feet are drawn up and rest on one of the footstools that Constantine must have carried from the library. Constantine stands beside her, his trousers rolled up to his mid shins, although he's still wearing his shoes. On top of an adjacent chair, he's placed their magical accoutrements collection: the bowl of sage, bunches of white flowers, the coconut shell, a bag of salt, Delia's handbell. Why are they still here with dirty water flowing all around them, instead of having rushed off to a drier spot, is beyond my imagination. Now and then, Constantine mops water around Delia's chair in short, precise swishing motions. I see all this in a flash; it's a very weird scene, but I can't stop to think about it. The stream of water sloshes down around me, too. I need to pay attention to the stairs in order to reach the kitchen door and the garden as fast as possible.

Stepping into the sun-drenched patio feels like leaping onto another planet, away from the fetid, flooded house, grime running all over the unstoppable torrent. Burning rays of sun fall harsh on my head and shoulders, the soles of my feet dry quickly on the heated pavers. The water main is just where I thought it would be. At the foot of the thuja hedge by the gate, surrounded by browned ground creepers and long dry weeds. I pull up the stone slab and screw the valve shut.

When I return to the house, water is still lapping everywhere, cascading down the stairs and advancing into rooms off the landing, but Julia attests to the decline of the leak.

Now we just need to clean up.

"We'll have no water now," I say.

"No clean tap water, you mean," Julia says. "We've plenty of the other."

Half an hour passes. We've been mopping and vacuuming water nonstop. Delia has finally put her feet down on the floor, and Constantine, who still hasn't rolled down his trousers, must have returned the footstool to the library.

Delia leans on her staff. "Well, this was a spontaneous gift. I suppose we've been spared of cleaning that particular bathroom. Of course, we'll need to give one last sweep with salt water." She looks pensive for a moment. "It's always interesting how some spaces volunteer their own purification, while others resist like hell."

Constantine looks at her with a serious face, nodding in agreement.

I go up one last time to the bathroom for a final checkup. The smell of mold and rust still lies heavy in the air alongside the stench of rotten sewer. I open the small window over the bathtub, struggling with the handle. A tapestry of ivy appears behind the glazed glass, and the sun filters through, projecting quivering constellations along the pink marble slabs that cover walls and floor. This used to be mother's bathroom, the most beautiful in the house. A gleaming salmon-colored alcove with hand-painted porcelain fixtures and large mirrors in art deco frames. But now cracks, like dark, green-veined fingers, run along the walls and floor, as if the pink flesh of the original stone has been scratched by the years of neglect. The only remaining mirror is chipped at the corners, its surface veiled with large gray patches where the silver lining has been wrecked. I can recollect happy bubble-bath ventures with Julia inside the large tub, white foam flying over our heads among shrieks, while Nanny's

patience wore thin as she pleaded with us to step out into towels
and terry robes. The wide tub has no faucet now. Its bottom is a dry
bed of oxidized rust.

Marion walks in with a mop and a bucket.

"The house is falling to pieces," I say. "I hadn't realized it was
so far gone."

"I thought the real estate agency report stated that everything
was in good condition, including plumbing," Marion says.

"That was two years ago."

"Can things deteriorate that fast?"

"They say empty houses wither away once their inhabitants
leave. They just languish into decay."

"Heavens, Anna, you're suddenly in a very poetic mood."

"And you're in an unnaturally cheerful mood."

"Not at all. I just sense that things are beginning to move."

"Beginning to move?"

"You know, the cleaning is working after all."

"Really, by destroying the house through a toilet flood? What a
fine purge indeed!"

"Look—again, I'm sorry for anything I might have brought on,
okay? Now let me finish mopping here while you go down to Delia," Marion says, and nudges me gently so I will let her pass.

"Why don't *you* go down to Delia? You are *the eldest daughter of
the house*," I scoff.

"You know I can't face the study," Marion says, looking me
straight in the eye. For the first time I see some sort of alignment in
her fragmented gaze.

"What if I can't face it either?" I ask.

Marion sighs. "If there is a champion in the family, it's you, Anna.
But I'd understand if you refuse to take this on."

I watch Marion as she turns around and starts mopping the pink
marble floor. How did *the youngest daughter of the house* ever get to
this position of championship, I reflect, and find myself sliding
down that trodden path of regret I have traveled for as long as I can
remember. The path of coming to terms with having to accept responsibility for my family. A part of me still has a hard time understanding how Little Anna, the girl who lost her mother at five, was

designated to become a pillar of the clan, to take on burdens well beyond her years. And treated from the start as the voice of reason, the only one who could save a crazy family riddled with mad passions and erratic choices. At moments like these, I can't help but revisit my sisters' abandonment; how it's not just all weakness on their part, but also their willful indolence that has landed me in this forsaken position.

But there was more to it than my sisters.

For as long as I could remember, Father had complained about having no sons. "If only I'd had three sons! How much we could have done with the business! We could have conquered the world! As it is, what will happen to my company? Who will inherit it?" he wailed at mealtimes, during outings, in front of business connections and acquaintances. Having daughters was like a sweet curse, some sort of profitless responsibility, a burden to haul along in hardship. Marion, Julia, and I bore these comments with downcast eyes and mortified hearts, besides a good deal of embarrassment, when these words were spoken in front of others.

There was once a situation, however, where there had been a breach of this script. It happened during a vacation on the Basque coast when I was eight years old. Father and I had stayed late on the beach to watch the sunset while Marion and Julia returned to our rented cottage with Nanny. We had walked the length of the shore toward the lighthouse, hardly realizing how far we'd gone. Now we were hurrying back to make it in time for supper. It had been a coldish summer on that northern coast, and cool gusts of wind blew from the sea, giving me goose bumps over my sunburned skin. I turned to Father, who seemed to be lagging behind, and saw him standing clutching his chest with both hands. I ran toward him while he sat down on the sand, shivering, beads of sweat on his pale face, teeth chattering behind blue lips. I embraced his cold body in a panic, while he whispered, "It's nothing, Anna, just give me a moment," and then he lay down on the sand. I thought of covering him with sand, of finding a large stone that would still hold some warmth from the sun, but all was growing cold as the last rays melted into the horizon. I looked around the deserted beach in despair, and then spotted a small fishing boat gliding through the waves about a mile away. I stood up and ran toward the water, screaming at the top of my voice, but soon realized my shouts were being carried inland by the wind. I took off my red dress and waved it frantically at the boat. "Help! Help! My father is dying." Unheeding, the boat continued its dreamy cruising through the cobalt waves. I ran back toward the lighthouse in the encroaching darkness, taking turns between yelling and catching my breath, until the coastal guards spotted me from the road and came to my help. They took us to hospital, where Father was diagnosed with a severe bout of pneumonia, produced by overwork and stress.

Before being taken back home to Nanny by the guards, when I approached his hospital cot to say good night, Father said, "Anna, I think you saved my life today. You are very brave. We make a good team. You will always be my girl-boy." I swelled with pride as if he had bestowed on me a badge of courage. From that moment on, the girl-boy thing remained as a private, secret complicity between Father and me, something that excluded Marion and Julia, because "they were just girls" while I had earned a higher place in his regard, in that remote and superior world of men.

But some apparent privileges lead down indentured paths. Years later I would come to realize the consequences of our bond. Father with his girl-boy. I understand how this twisted term had held me captive and rendered me incapable of refusing him anything. And the first time I got a glimpse of what this meant was precisely in Father's studio, one afternoon back in the day, when it was still the stately, elegant room where he conducted business from the house.

It was my first meeting with Father as an adult. I remember gliding along the smooth, polished floor toward the plush, buttoned leather couch, and sitting opposite Father. He studied some paperwork on his lap, and took a long minute to lift up his eyes and say, "I called you in, Anna, because I need to discuss something important. Just bear with me for a moment," and returned to his documents.

I inhaled deeply in order to quench my increasing sense of anticipation, and looked around the room at the beautiful dark mahogany furnishings, the English desk with a green leather top, the hand-carved bookshelves neatly filled with books, the oil paintings on the walls. It had to be the happiest day of my life. The day before, I had received a letter from Saint Martin's with an unconditional offer to study literature and dramatic art starting in September, and ever since I had been mad with joy.

"Well, Anna," started Father, stacking his papers into order on the long coffee table. "First of all, let me congratulate you for having been admitted into Saint Martin's. I hear it's an outstanding school. I'll be happy to provide tuition and living expenses for you. However"—Father halted for a moment, took off his glasses, and wiped them off with one of those soft little white cloths—"I want to propose a better plan."

My heart fell into my stomach, while a vague fear started thickening around me like a fog. Father checked that his glasses were clean, put them back on carefully, and pierced me with his ice-blue irises. "I want you to take a gap year and work for me at the office. Learn the business; equip yourself with professional skills that will allow you to take over the company in the future. Then you can go study dramatic art and take it wherever you like. If you find it doesn't put bread on the table, as it happens frequently with the arts, then you always have something to fall back on. And who knows, maybe one day you might want to take over the whole company."

"But I don't want to work in an office, I want to study acting," I said, and felt my voice trembling, as the unsteady flutter of my heart radiated to every region of my body.

"What is one year? Nothing. At my age you will see it as a drop in the ocean of time. But it's a perfect slot to learn the workings of the business. I'll pay you well. I promise, Anna, you'll have no regrets. Why don't you start on Monday?"

"Can't we do it the other way around? I m-mean . . ." I stammered.

"No, Anna. *This* is the way we do it. It's my condition if you want me to foot the bill later on." The phone rang and Father walked over to the desk and picked up. He lifted a finger indicating that I wait while he spoke into the receiver. "Maloney? I've been trying to reach you. Do you have a moment to talk about this contract?"

The meeting was over. I fought back tears as I carefully folded the admission letter from Saint Martin's and put it back in my pocket. Nothing I could say would change Father's mind. He'd already made his decision. In fact, he'd probably made his decision a long time ago. I walked out of the study.

On Monday I started to work for him.

Delia's voice trails from downstairs. "Thinking about it is not going to help. Let's just get on with it, shall we?" I let her words reverberate in my ears for an instant, while the inexorable notion grips me once again: There's no turning back from what we've started here, we need to push forward till the end.

I take a breath and walk downstairs.

CHAPTER 11

Delia sits in her chair by Father's studio, slowly fanning herself. I feel the intense draw of her dark glance as I approach. Something in me shrinks and wants to slink away, like a cowed dog in the face of unknown shadows. There's the uneasy foreboding of some ordeal ahead, some albatross I should beware. But ignoring my disquiet, my legs just carry me along like soldiers, blind and undeterred.

I stand in front of Delia. "How do we proceed with the cleaning?" I ask.

"Someone needs to give access to the space, if Julia won't."

"Like me for instance?"

"It could be you. Were you the last person to close this door?"

"I think so. I had to get Father's documents when he was in hospital."

"Was that the last time anyone was in this room?"

"No, actually. The agency inspected the whole house, this room included."

"That doesn't count. You were the last person from the family to close this room, so you can be initiated to clear the way."

"Initiated? Can't I just walk in there?"

"You know the answer." Delia eyes me carefully from behind her fan. "There's no use stalling, time's running out. We need to be done before the moon comes up."

"The moon?"

"Yes, and today is full moon," Constantine adds, his voice full of a sort of eagerness. "Actually, a day before full."

I look at him, intrigued. But before I ask any questions, Delia says, "You should know this is for your own protection."

"Why exactly would I need protection?"

"You don't want to absorb any negative energy released in the cleansing, all right?" I nod like an automaton. All of a sudden I feel collapsed, something inside me has folded in, like an empty bag falling on itself. I'm incapable of putting up resistance.

Still, I need a moment to myself. "Can I go wash my hands before we start?" I ask.

"Yes, that's a good idea. Wash your hands. Thoroughly." I look at Delia, unsure if she's joking or for real. But those eyes now posing like black ravens are unknowable.

And of course there's no running water to wash hands with.

I walk toward the bathroom by the library, anyway. I close the door behind me and feel instantly safe. *What is it with bathrooms today?* I think. This one is a rhapsody in dark blues. I brush the palm of my hand along the narrow walls of indigo mosaic tiles and avoid looking at my reflected image in the slim mirror. I sit on the toilet seat instead and lean my elbows on my knees, bury my head in my hands. I need to shoo away my unease. I stare at the night-blue tiles on the floor paved in crisscross patterns. I've seen this image countless times, I know it by heart.

I'm an expert in idling inside bathrooms, my ultimate refuge from the blustering mundane. It all began after I started working for Father. I couldn't stand the office, with its mercantile banality, its ridiculous power games, the stifling smell of endless yards of wall-to-wall carpet, the long empty hours among functional furniture. I could only spend so much time immersed in this world before I felt I would explode. Like holding your breath underwater. Then I discovered bathroom breaks, the only venue to get away, to reconnect with reality. I used to smuggle a book into the bathroom, and lock myself in; a book of poetry mostly, poems being the most efficient way of getting a quick shot of sap, instant flashes of piercing beauty capable of replenishing the deadened mind. A few stolen stanzas from Rimbaud's "The Drunken Boat," or Neruda's "The Song of Despair." I stretched out my time inside the stall for as long as possible, until someone came looking for me or needing the toilet, and summoned me with a soft, cautious knock. After all, I was the boss's daughter, and everyone walked on eggshells around me, all smiles and graces, and delicate raps on the door.

The offices of MBE—Maquinaria Británica en España—Father's company, were located in the modern, upcoming quarter of Madrid called Nuevos Ministerios, a neighborhood of stylish apartment buildings with sleek façades and tall windows, where an increasing part of the international community was taking up residence or renting workspace. The company imported all sorts of heavy machinery for public works. The office was on the ground floor of a building surrounded by evergreen and rock gardens, an open space of over four thousand feet, with plush beige wall-to-wall carpet under modish desks and state-of-the-art electric typewriters, fax machines, telephone equipment, and even a computer or two. Father's personal office was at the far end, a large room surrounded by windows, some looking out to the gardens, and others looking out to his employees' desks. Opposite his mahogany corner table was an elegant sitting area behind which hung a large replica of a Kandinsky picture, a colorful juxtaposition of geometric forms, where circles, triangles, and linear elements interacted in a show of explosive vitality.

I had always thought bringing artistic images into a dreary mercantile reality was brilliant. In the beginning, every time I walked into the office, I couldn't but admire this combination of functional and artistic. But when I started working there I soon noticed that my perception became immune to all art and its stimuli, and that the territory of the endless beige carpet swallowed the whole space. Its whorl of sawdust yellow pulled at my eyes each time, abstracting my mind from all but my muffled footsteps walking across its tedious landscape. I learned to dread the beige wall-to-wall like nothing else in that office.

Besides Father, of course.

It was 1990 and Father's business was reaching its golden age. Contracts and orders poured in endlessly. At that time there were around thirty employees in the office—secretaries, engineers, accountants, salesmen, and administrative assistants. Everyone welcomed me politely the first day I came in to work. But Father took me immediately into his office, where I spent that day and many of the following, sitting around and bored to tears watching him interact for hours on the phone, aligning stacks of papers around his desk, and giving orders to everyone in short, clipped sentences. For the first four weeks he insisted I remain by his side and just observe him conduct business.

"Oh, if someone had given me this chance from the start, instead of having to learn everything from scratch," he kept saying. "There's no university in the world that can teach you the true golden nuggets of business. You are very privileged, Anna, believe me!"

Olga Morris was still working for him those first months, and her desk was just outside Father's office. She scurried in frequently, bringing papers and documents for him to sign, or just messages from clients she had talked to on the phone. She gave me friendly side-glances with her long-slit crocodile eyes and offered to make me coffee. But I always declined, intent on keeping her at arm's length. Every ninety minutes or so she brought Father a cup of coffee she made in the office kitchen, pouring boiled water over Nescafé instant coffee and adding Carnation powdered nonfat milk. She brought it over to his desk together with little pink sachets of saccharine, a product she had introduced, pitching it as a healthier alternative to sugar. The resulting beverage was gruesome, a thick, dark brown liquid tasting of dishwater with burned-coffee dregs. But everybody drank it by the gallon, and so did I after a while. It was the only drug available, the only escape from the relentless drill of pounding performance. Of course, there were cigarettes. Nearly everyone in the office smoked. Huge ashtrays sat on every desk, full of ashes and cigarette butts. Swirls of smoke rose from most lips toward the ceiling. Father was the worst of them all. He smoked constantly. He smoked Pall Mall, an expensive, imported brand. Sometimes he lit a second cigarette, not realizing he already had one smoking away in the ashtray. At the end of the day the whole place reeked of stale stubs.

There was a small, trendy hotel next door to the office, the Hotel

Aristos, with a bar and cafeteria on the ground floor where all the employees went for midmorning coffee, a sacred Spanish tradition impossible to eradicate, despite Father's ongoing efforts. Everyone visited the bar in twos or threes around eleven, drank coffee and ate a *bocadillo*, a local sandwich made with ham or cheese on a baguette. It was in this context that the real personalities and relationships revealed themselves. So, at midmorning coffee break, that first day, Silvia and Margarita, the two main Spanish secretaries, and Conchita, the receptionist, took me out for coffee to the Aristos and expressed their delight at having me on board.

"Hopefully you'll have a mellowing effect on your father," said Silvia, a dyed platinum blonde with a long face and pouting lips. Marina, the bilingual secretary who worked under Olga Morris, also came in and nodded curtly in my direction, but didn't join us. "Watch out for that one, she's a sourpuss," Margarita said. She was a shy, introverted woman with red hair and pimply skin. Soon after, Montes and Lopez, the head engineers, trickled in and shook welcoming hands with me, making chauvinist jokes.

"We work better around gorgeous women, don't we, Lopez?" Montes said, his small green eyes shining with lascivious glee. "Our professional performance is enhanced to no end." Lopez, a somber, more power-game oriented character, nodded in agreement but was looking ahead at a group of administrative assistants, one of whom was having an affair with him, as I would later find out. Even Ventura, the grim, withdrawn accountant, came in with his assistant and managed a wide jaundiced smile in my direction. But there were others whose hostile fronts I immediately sensed. There was a group of administrative clerks and assistants to the engineers, most of whom were young workers in their twenties, and who toiled the longest hours for the lowest pay. They seemed to be a more restless, discontented crowd than those whose families were dependent on their monthly paychecks. They probably felt disenfranchised and resented Father's domination. This younger crowd eyed me with distrust from the first day, and made no attempt to bridge their hostility.

Olga Morris was head secretary and Father's personal assistant, in charge of all correspondence with clients and suppliers. At least twice a day, she came in with a pad and pencil and took dictation from Father, then went back to her desk, typed it out on a big, clattery electric typewriter, and brought it back in to be approved and signed. I soon noticed that it wasn't so much dictation Father was giving Olga Morris, but more the spelling out of ideas or concepts for her to translate into actual language and jot down on her pad.

He would say something like, "Let's write a letter to Krupp acknowledging their performance report on our recent sales."

Olga Morris cocked her head and waited. Father would stack and restack papers on his desk. "You know, along the lines of . . ." A tightness would come over his face, as he fussed around looking for some paper or another.

After a few awkward seconds, Olga jumped in. "Should it say, *Dear Sir, Following last week's receipt of your excellent report, I am writing to thank you for the positive outlook on our sales stats, and to reassure you that our company will continue on the same line when it comes to . . .*" and she would recite the letter in one clear string of thought.

Father would look up in relief and say, "Yes, Olga, that's perfect. Whenever you can have it ready," and reassume his super-efficient stance.

In the beginning it didn't strike me as important, but as the days went by I started realizing that Father had extreme difficulty with written language, something he had learned to conceal very well, but was now apparent by the way he struggled with the wording of memos, sets of instructions, and letters. This was the reason why someone like Olga Morris was so essential to him, and before her a long line of super-efficient secretaries, perfectly bilingual, capable of coding the written elements of the business. This realization shocked me at first, but later intrigued me to no end. How did he manage to handle such a complex business operation without a basic command of the written language? I marveled at his capacity to get around his shortcomings, his power to rule over others and conduct an extremely efficient enterprise despite this basic lacking.

We had known for years that Father had never finished school, that he had a learning disability that today would be called dyslexia, but back then was punished as an act of noncompliance, or even contempt, by teachers and parents. Boarding schools whipped boys for academic failure, and his father, a strict, cruel man, made sure no sanctions and deprivations were spared to discipline his rebellious son. Father ran away from the family home at sixteen, and all trace of him was lost for a long while, until he reappeared fifteen years later, married to our mother and starting to create his small empire in Spain. In the meantime his own father disinherited him and handed over the textile manufacturing family business to his younger brother, Uncle Phillip, who drove it soon to bankruptcy. Father had never rebuilt the family ties. He traveled all over England for business matters but never stopped in Manchester to visit. Even Aunt Kay was surprised to see him in London more than once every five years. Father had never told us the whole story, but sometimes bemoaned the fact that he was never able to study, because he had to start working at a very young age. He also had a penchant for disowning his own success. When anyone flattered him for his business accomplishments, he would wink an eye and say, "Never forget, Anna, that in the land of the blind, the one-eyed man is king."

To Father, Spain was the land of the blind, a backward country with lazy, incompetent people who had to be not just coerced to do the work, but also disciplined and supervised most of the time. Father ran a tight ship to counteract these ingrained tendencies. No one was allowed to come in with excuses about failed missions, or jobs not impeccably accomplished. The consequences of inadequacy were met with sharp, demeaning reproaches and unpaid overtime hours to make up for the blunder. Everyone feared him, and underneath this fear ran a wide spectrum of feelings between hatred and reverence. They also admired him. He was the demigod who opened a door to a remote world through which poured an array of outlandish businessmen, and gigantic machinery with reams of instruction booklets in foreign languages. His despotism was mitigated by some with a whole set of legends that went around the office.

"Mr. Hooort, you sure can sell a donkey to a Gypsy," Montes said to him sometimes, when a couple of drinks at the Aristos had relaxed them. It was one of the jokes by which the staff flattered Father, Roma people being in Spanish slur lore the ultimate dealer rogues, the shrewdest merchants and swindlers. Father appreciated the comparison and enjoyed it each time, because he figured he was beating the Spaniards at their own game. He was king not just by power of rule alone, but also, and mainly, by virtue of his ability, a sort of topping meritocratic achievement.

But the sheer power of his rule still overran everything in the day by day. His commands and opinions were indisputable; nobody ever questioned anything he said. People walked into his office with a hesitant step, surrounded by a halo of apprehension. He would look up from his desk and pierce them with his ice-blue irises, waiting impatiently for a clean answer, or an efficient solution to a problem.

Silvia was one of his habitual victims. "How many God-forbidding times are you going to file a letter in the wrong cabinet? Where's your brain? Or should I ask, do you even have one? You can plan on coming in Saturday to reorganize all correspondence into the correct files."

"But Mister Hooort, I did it last month."

"Silvia." He raised his hand to indicate there was no possible argument in the matter. "Even if it takes a billion times to have it in perfect order. Order is essential to business." And with that, he waved her out of his office.

"Do you realize no one in this office looks at you directly in the eye?" he would say to me. "That puts them instantly in the position of suspects. They're either playing some antic to avoid doing their job, or else covering up some other misdemeanor."

There was only one person in the office who walked casually into his office, stood confidently, and looked directly at Father with an unflinching eye. It was Marcus. Of course, he wasn't technically an employee, he worked in the capacity of an associate representing Father's German partner. But that wasn't the whole explanation, since I had seen Father stare down clients, fellow businessmen and the like. There was something in Marcus that was fearless and unblinking, something I perceived as arrogant, big-headed, even smug. Something in the way he discussed matters with Father and even dared to contradict or correct him.

But Father seemed to enjoy him. "He can be a bit cheeky, but that only comes with the conceit of youth. Life will humble him. He is a clever lad. And hardworking. Two qualities I appreciate." Initially he encouraged me to watch him at work. "These Germans are sadly square-headed, but they get the job done. They're good workhorses, although terribly in need of creative spark. That's where an Englishman like me fits in," he'd say with a chuckle.

I shunned Marcus's company and his friendly approaches from the beginning. I watched his quiet, industrious presence around the office with an impervious eye, his supple, athletic body, broad-shouldered and narrow-hipped, as he leaned back easily in his chair, talking on the phone or typing his own documents, something un-heard of among other male workers. He kept mostly to himself. But with me, he wanted to linger if we met in the kitchen while procur-ing one of those atrocious cups of coffee. And I didn't just avoid all personal conversations, but also made sure I adopted a mean stance when he was around.

The first time I met Marcus in the workplace, I had been sent by Father to deliver some documents to the repair shop, a large garage area underneath the office building that the company had converted into a mechanical workshop. Here the engineers kept inventories of spare parts, and brought in small machinery and com-pany vehicles that needed repair. It was a bare, open space with a gray concrete floor stained with grease. Along the walls hung all sorts of tools, coiled cables, and connector cords on rows of peg-board, alongside calendars with busty women in bikinis sprawled over hoods of trucks and cars. In the back, metal racks held collec-tions of labeled machine parts. Strange, convoluted conglomerations of metal cylinders with jutting rods and colored wires sticking out, pieces I saw initially as unintelligible objects, but would eventually get to know well by name and function. Winch motors, rotary seals, torque converters, sprockets, and the like. This was the engineers' habitual hangout when they were not in the office, where they felt most at ease. It was a man's world. They lounged about in dirty blue overalls, cigarettes dangling from their mouths, going about their work with swearing and lewd joking, cleaning equipment and put-ting together engines and mechanical appliances.

I walked in, hugging the paperwork file to my chest. I felt small and out of place. Montes, Lopez, and their assistant Francisco stood looking under the open hood of a truck half hoisted in the air.

Montes turned around. "Miss Anna! What brings you down here?"

"I was asked to deliver the documentation for the Caterpillar crane that's being shipped tomorrow," I said.

"Oh, good! Let's see it." He looked quickly over the file. "But here's paperwork that still needs to be filled in. And it's in English." He snapped the file shut, bent over the truck and cried, "Germany! You're needed out here." The two other men stepped aside, and underneath the truck rolled out the body of a man stretched on a dolly. Strong, powerful legs emerged first, followed by the rest of the body clad in a tan overall, a tool belt packed with heavy wrenches and screwdrivers around the trim hips. Last came the head, and I recognized Marcus's hazelnut hair above the plastic goggles that covered his eyes. In a quick gesture he removed them and replaced them with the regular glasses he took out of his chest pocket. He leaped up from the dolly and stood facing me. His face and hands were smudged with dark grease. But something about his hair and tan overall, about his blue eyes and clean-shaven face, shone against the grimy setting of the workshop.

Lopez passed him a cloth and he wiped his hands.

He smiled. "Welcome to the underbelly of the business. Is this your first time down here?"

"Will you be able to fill in this document?" I asked, ignoring his question.

"If you give me a minute, I'll wash my hands."

"I don't have a minute. I need to go back. I'll leave the file with you." I put the plastic file in his hands. "You can bring it up later." I turned on my heels and left. As I stepped out, I heard one of the engineers whistle under his breath, as if saying, *Whoa, tough chick!* My heart fluttered as I hurried up the ramp toward the office.

If I was honest with myself, there was no reason for me to be locked into this aversion toward Marcus. My hostility could be linked to the memory of meeting him at the turning point of Marion's tragedy.

Or to the fact that Father had chosen him as a worthy distraction to steer her away from her matador. It might also be that I saw him as competition when it came to Father's consideration.

But Father only had thoughts for me. He tried hard to keep my attention focused on one aspect of the work or another, took me to meetings and lunches with clients, taught me the business database of the company and soon had me micromanaging certain small operations and projects. I was still overcome by tedium. The moment he wasn't breathing down my neck, my mind would wander away from the office, sweep past the immensity of the beige carpet and fly out the door into the vast beyond. The monologue I had prepared all summer in anticipation of the first audition at Saint Martin's still reverberated in my head. *A thousand years have passed since the earth last bore a living creature on her breast, and the unhappy moon now lights her lamp in vain.* It was one of Nina's speeches in Chekhov's famous play *The Seagull.* The words throbbed in my ears as if in a parallel reality while I listened to Father giving instructions, as I sat by his side in meetings, or read through technical brochures and written materials. *No longer are the cries of storks heard in the meadows, or the drone of beetles in the groves of limes. All is cold, cold. All is void, void, void . . .* I went over the text over and over again, clinging to the words as if they were a lost lover I was desperately struggling to retrieve. Or a disappeared continent, whose sounds and images I was determined to retain by incessant repetition. *Once in a hundred years my lips are opened, my voice echoes mournfully across the desert earth . . .*

Father would say, "Anna, are you with me? I need your full attention in this matter," and I would drag my mind back into his office, bring my eyes to focus on whatever paperwork he was pointing at, like a prisoner who crawls back into his dim cell after having contemplated the sky from the prison yard.

After a few months, Nina's monologue started fading away and I found myself having to confront the reality of the office as it was, a dry territory that had to be ploughed through day by day with the tenacity of the excavator with double jaws full of metal teeth we represented. This was the beginning of my extended visits to the bathroom with books of poetry up my sleeve. But despite this convenient escape mechanism, my underlying despair would sometimes peak.

Once, while pulling some documents out of a filing cabinet, I found a brochure on one of the products the company sold, Large Bored Piles. That was surely what I had been developing, sitting on my ass all these months and pacing back and forth on the dry wasteland of the tan carpet. I leaned my forehead on the open cabinet and uttered a laugh. It sounded more like a long croak, a twisted moan coming from a suppressed sob. I was wasting my youth, my thirst for poetry, for life.

"Are you all right?" Marcus stood close behind me.

"I'm fine," I said. "It's just that finding funny messages hidden inside the daily routine can be hilarious and pathetic at the same time." I turned toward him and held up the brochure to his face.

Marcus stared at the Large Bored Piles. "Umm, I don't really get it. What's so funny about this?" I was looking at his eyes behind the rimless glasses. They were a different kind of blue than Father's. A darker, calmer blue, the type you see in deep lakes surrounded by mountaintops. His skin was smooth, with close-shaved cheeks and chin. Strong jaws framed his well-delineated face. He held his lips tight in a way I had seen before, when he was trying to figure something out.

A gust of impatience overtook me and I put the brochure back in its file. "Never mind."

"No, no, I want to understand. Please."

"Don't you have piles in Germany?" I asked as I felt my mean spirit rising in my throat. "Piles in your butt? What would you call them, hemorrhoids?"

"Hämorrhoiden! Okay, I get it! I guess those exist everywhere."

"That's all it was," I said, closing the file cabinet drawer, annoyed at having engaged in the whole explanation with someone as slow as him.

"I wonder if we should add a price surplus to the product, in the light of this added advantage." Marcus rubbed his chin with his thumb. I looked at him, puzzled. "Bored-to-death hemorrhoids could be the most financially valuable, since they are, after all, the most rigid, the most reliable in the reinforcement of buttress structures . . ." He was mimicking the salesman for the bored piles who had visited the company a couple of months ago, a Herr Gottlieb Schwartz. An older, ceremonious German businessman with a strong accent who spoke with great solemnity about the brands he represented.

"Stop!" I was holding my sides and pealing with laughter. Everybody around was staring. Even Father was looking up from his desk and glaring through the glass window that connected his office with the rest of the space.

Marcus cut his parody short. "Let's return to our desks and bore our piles back into our seats," he whispered and walked away.

I wiped the tears on my face as I turned to leave. But Father summoned me with a gesture of his hand. "Now, Anna, please remember to be watchful of your behavior in the office. Too much camaraderie with employees makes it difficult to exercise authority."

"But Marcus isn't . . ."

"Yes he is. He's at a higher level, but he's still an employee."

"I thought you said . . ."

"Never mind what you thought. Return to your work."

Back at my desk, I avoided all eye contact with Marcus for the rest of the day.

That evening as we drove back home, Father looked intently ahead and gripped the steering wheel with unusual clout. "Anna, I don't want you to forget that you will inherit the business, that you will be a leading CEO. Hanging around with secretaries and engineers is below your station, and should be kept to a minimum. If you need something or feel lonely, you should come to me. *We're* the team, and everyone else works for us. Never forget it."

Friday night was the happy hour moment at the Hotel Aristos, when many of the office employees got together after work, had drinks and socialized. The evening started with light drinks, which got heavier as the hour advanced into the night. Gin tonics, martinis, and rum-and-Cokes then flowed freely, particularly if it was the end of the month, close to paycheck time. Younger and lower-paid employees like administrative assistants and junior secretaries left early, as did most of those with families awaiting them at home.

The heavy-duty patrons on these extended occasions were always the single senior secretaries and the engineers, who felt entitled to stay around and flirt openly, as well as criticize everyone else in the office. I disliked these gatherings, but it was difficult not to show up at all, given the pressure to join the crowd. So, I tried to keep them to a minimum, politely declining anything after a first small glass of wine and leaving as quickly as possible.

It was a few days later after the bored piles incident, at one of these happy-hour occasions, when Margarita, who became quickly exhilarated after a couple of drinks, walked up to me and said, "What about the German? Don't you dig him?"

"The German?" I echoed, taken by surprise.

"Yes, Marcus. Well, don't you?" she insisted in a slurred voice.

"Not really. Do you?"

"I do. We all do, but none of us have a chance in hell, 'cause all he looks at is you," she said, standing uncomfortably close to my face while her booze-heavy lids drooped over her drunken gaze. "D'you know he runs for an hour every morning before coming in to work? No wonder he looks so good!"

Silvia joined in. "The guy must be a beast in bed." She was the raunchiest female in the office and always made lecherous comments about the men. "I can't wait to find out and give you all the details." Both she and Margarita burst out laughing.

"Aren't you overrating him?" I asked, stifling my mirth and trying to sound cool.

"Hell, no!" both said in unison.

As I turned around I saw Marcus across the bar, standing in a group with the engineers, and paying no attention to whatever besotted conversation they were engaged in. Instead, he was looking directly at me and, as we locked eyes, he raised his cup in silent toast.

Because Father had asked me to pick up a set of files he had to work on during the weekend, I stopped by the office before going home. The place was dark and I flitted through the dimness toward my desk, where I'd left the documents. As I turned to leave, my eye caught a glance of Marcus's desk across the floor. An orange shaft of light from a streetlamp pooled over it through the adjoining window. Before I knew it, I was hovering over his workspace, observing how neat and organized everything looked, papers perfectly stacked together, pens and pencils grouped in a pencil holder, his calendar marked with bullet-point notes in precise, clean-looking handwriting. So different from mine, with doodling all over my paperwork and scraps of paper penned with soulful words or irresistible metaphors. I opened one of the drawers and rummaged through a few items: a calculator, a box of paper clips, color felt pens, a small audio recorder. I opened another drawer and found a blue-and-red striped tie, a tiny Spanish-German dictionary, and a tatty paperback. I pulled out the book. It was a Penguin version of *The Nibelungenlied*, with a picture of medieval knights in battle on the cover. I opened it randomly, and read:

> *A dream was dreamt by Kriemhild the virtuous and the gay*
> *How a wild young falcon she train'd for many a day*
> *Till two fierce eagles tore it; to her there could not be*
> *In all the world such sorrow at this perforce to see.*

A noise at the far end entrance door set my heart racing. I threw the book into the drawer and rushed to hide in the shadows behind a row of file cabinets. Marcus walked in humming, reached his desk with light, athletic steps, and scooped up his agenda. He was putting it into his satchel and turning to leave, when he noticed the open drawer. He took a step toward it, and stood examining the messed-up contents. Then he picked up the book and lifted his eyes, scrutinizing the darkness about him for a few agonizing seconds. My heart beat with such force I was sure I would faint even before he found me out.

But Marcus didn't move. After a moment, the pounding in my chest slowed down, allowing me to home in on the silence. We stood across from each other, I in the darkness, he in the orange hue of the streetlight, and I restraining my breathing while I listened out for his. I watched his shape silhouetted against the window, and for a few seconds, I wanted to stretch my hands and caress his shadow.

The sound of a car screeching and hooting outside in the street tore through the room, breaking the spell, and Marcus put back the book and pushed the drawer shut. Then he left the office with a slower, heavier step.

I slid down toward the carpeted floor and sat with knees pulled into my chest. How would I ever be able to face him at work on Monday? I was certain he knew it was me. Who else would pick a book in English out of his drawer? And why did he have an English version of *The Nibelungenlied*?

I thought of all sorts of excuses so as not to come into work next week. Nothing would do short of quitting the job, though. Sooner or later I'd have to face him. Although, come to think of it, other girls in the office, including Silvia and Margarita, who had the hots for him, might be snooping around his desk too. I had been told there had been instances in the past when these women poked inside the men's desks. Their findings fed the comical legends of office lore. A picture of his mother as a young girl was once found in Ventura's desk, and everyone had roared for months at his expense, seeing that, although well into his forties, he was unmarried and still lived with her. A fat wad of old lottery tickets, presumably unsuccessful, were found in Pablo's desk, an administrative assistant who was known as the office miser, had also contributed to the general mirth for weeks. And, after a martial arts groin cup was found at Jesús's, one of the engineers' assistants, oohs and aahs were still muttered by the women in the Aristos bar when he walked in. So maybe I would be able to scrape through undetected.

At last I left the office and walked down the empty street to my car. The tormenting anticipation of being confronted by Marcus besieged me. Just by the way my cheeks would burst into flames would confirm my indiscretion. My face was like an open book, and my eyes, tattletales of all hidden thoughts and desires. I moped around the house all weekend. At the last minute on Sunday, I thought of something.

I persuaded Miguel to drop me off at work on Monday. Miguel, or Michael Bradley as was his real name, was a boy I knew from the American School whom I had dated on and off for the last three years. I was never exactly hot for him, but he was sweet and sensitive, prepared to do just about anything for me. I asked him to walk me into the office and gave him a long, wet kiss in front of everybody, including Marcus. Then I ignored Marcus for the rest of the week, and we soon returned to the polite, distant relationship we had before, with no space for laughing about piles or raising cups across the bar. But underneath, a strain remained between us, a tension as we walked past each other in the hustle and bustle of work, as we sat across from one another in meetings with clients and providers, or stood in proximity exchanging notes or documents. The office became filled with our stolen glances; at any moment I could be assailed by spontaneous, uncontrolled blushing if I happened to be close to him and remembered the worn, yellowed pages of *The Nibelungenlied* hidden in his drawer. And the feeling that something had melded us together persisted, despite all efforts to gloss it over.

Later, when we were already inextricably entangled, and I looked back to recollect my first instance of desire, I returned to that sensation again, the merging of two shadows across space in the darkness of the office.

I'm startled by a sharp knocking at the door.

"Anna, just a reminder that Delia wants to start soon," Constantine says in his discreet, hesitant tone. I sigh. It always feels too short, the bathroom sojourn, a sort of hunger never satisfied. I get up and lean on the sink and open the faucet, forgetting that I cut off the water for the whole house minutes ago.

CHAPTER 12

Delia awaits me by the stairwell, patiently leaning on her staff. "Feeling refreshed and ready to go?" she asks, and I'm conscious of my grubby hands with no pockets to hide in. But now her eyes overflow with a sweet kindness and, as she pats my arm in passing, I once again get that whiff of treacle scent from her flesh. This time my mouth and stomach twinge with a sudden craving for sugar, a sure sign of my hypoglycemic brain plunging into angst. I walk on, ahead of Delia. But my mind is elsewhere. There's no pushing back the rush of recollection, once it's been unleashed.

The stakes were raised the moment Olga Morris defected with all the money. The office was thrown into chaos. I sat to Father's right at the long oblong table in the conference room as he explained in his difficult Spanish the consequences resulting from her hefty withdrawal of business funds. Every time he hunted for a word, or struggled with a sentence, he turned to me for translation, and toward the end of the meeting it seemed that I was doing the talking. Questions kept coming from every angle, directed at me. The bottom line was that the company coffers were empty. All payments including payroll needed to be withheld. The staff sighed and murmured. Father put an abrupt end to the meeting, saying he would travel to England first thing in the morning to secure a loan to cover the debt. Everyone dribbled out of the room, seething discontent.

Father said, "Anna, you're going to have to be in charge while I'm away." Then he turned to Marcus. "I hope you will be available to help if any situation comes up."

"Of course." Marcus glanced in my direction. "Although I'll be away most of the week supervising the training for the new dragline down in Málaga."

"Right. I suppose that cannot be postponed." Father stacked his paperwork into his briefcase and switched off the conference room lights.

That night I stayed late at the office while Father gave me instructions on the affairs I would have to deal with in his absence. By the time we were done I could hardly stand up, I was exhausted and intoxicated with the stench of his ceaseless smoking. I had never seen him this distraught. It wasn't just the money and Olga's disappearance; Julia had just left the house in a storm.

The next morning, he left for England, leaving me in charge.

At first, I refused to sit at Father's desk, but eventually, since most of the paperwork was there, as well as the phone lines through which he insisted on calling me every few hours, I resolved to sit in his place. I felt like a midget on a king's throne. Every moment of the day brought a humbling situation, with requests I was unable to fulfill, information on basic affairs I knew nothing about, conversations that were foreign to me. I realized how little I had learned in the past months, how well I had played the role of the dreamy, unwilling trainee at her father's enterprise. At first, everyone displayed patience, but after the second day, they began to tap their feet around me.

People were restless in the office, not just because of me, but because Father had already been absent for over a week and there was no news of money. Hushed conversations started to take place among groups in the kitchen, around desks or any other corner in the office. Even Silvia and Margarita, who had always posed as good friends, avoided looking me in the eye or saying more than a few words when I was around. Montes and Lopez had changed attitudes, the masquerading bonhomie they displayed when Father was around had faded, and instead their faces were pulled in grumpy, aggressive features ready to jump at any moment. Every morning I was hounded with the same questions about Father's return and news of reinstating the payroll.

The straw that broke the camel's back came on Friday afternoon when the coffee supply was finished at the fateful hour of three, the time when everyone needed a push to finish the week's work.

Conchita came into the office and said, "We don't even have coffee left."

When I looked in my purse to send her out to buy some, and saw that not even I had any money left, I decided to call it a day and send everyone home early for the weekend.

I was gathering my things to leave myself, when Montes stood at the door. "We need to talk. Everyone is gathered in the conference room."

I cringed. "I think we should wait till Monday. Father will be back by then."

"There's no guarantee of that. People need to talk. Now."

I had no choice but to be escorted to the conference room. All the other employees were there, gathered around the table. I looked around at their long, sour faces and sensed how they had been rallied against me. Some of them, like Silvia and Margarita, cast their eyes down as I looked at them. Many puffed at their cigarettes, and the smog in the room, filtered through the overhead neon lights, made me nauseous.

Lopez, leaning against the wall with his arms folded on his chest, spoke first. "It will be three weeks on Monday since we've waited to be paid, and haven't seen any progress. Everyone here needs to put food on the table. We can't wait any longer." The volume of his voice went up in crescendo, as if he were giving a political speech. Heads nodded around the table. "Our kids cannot go hungry. We've done our honest part of the work and now we need to get paid for it."

"I'm sorry," I interrupted him. "There's nothing I can do about this. My father—"

"It's your father who's responsible for this!" I heard Marina mutter at the other end of the table. "If he hadn't trusted that woman, we wouldn't be in this pickle." The group of secretaries huddled next to her mumbled in assent. She had been under Olga Morris's orders and hated every moment of it.

Lopez turned around and hushed the crowd. "Just a moment! Let's not get out of hand here. There's something that can be done." Then he turned to me. "Ventura tells us you have a signature in the main account and that there's been an entry this morning . . ."

Before he could finish, Ventura stood up. "I didn't suggest any of this, believe me, Miss Anna, this is not my doing." He seemed very agitated.

"The point being," continued Lopez, "that the sum is enough to cut checks that could cover half of what everyone's owed. We think you should consider this."

Ventura interrupted him again. "That money has been temporarily deposited by a client; it doesn't belong to the company. It would be very risky—" He faltered as angry heads turned toward him.

"Shut up, Ventura." Francisco scowled. "You're always throwing stones against your own roof!" Now everyone talked on top of each other, as if a fever had overtaken the group.

Montes came up behind me and said in his slick, suave tone, "Anna, I think it would be a good idea if you wrote some checks to calm things down. People are talking of not coming to work on Monday, even of going to the union and to the courts."

"But I can't do this without consulting my father." I was beginning to panic. It seemed that whole group was engulfing me.

"Aren't you in charge?" Carmen screamed at me from the tight knob of administrative assistants clumped together by the window.

Francisco walked up to me. He was young and cocky, one of the engineer assistants who always greeted me as an equal, but in an unfriendly sort of way. "You know we're hurting, don't you? You're not like your father. You need to help us." His jaw was clenched in a hard gesture. "Ventura, bring on the checks," he said without taking his eyes away from mine. "I know she's going to do this."

"What's going on here?" Everyone turned around to find Marcus at the door. There was a moment of silence as he walked into the room and stood by my side. "I thought I heard talk of signing some checks. Is this something Mr. Hurt has consented to?" he asked, looking around. He spoke in Spanish with a flawless accent. He was dressed in jeans, mountain boots, and a casual windbreaker, since he'd been on location all these days. He smelled of moist earth, maybe from the mud that had been spattered over his boots and calves. His presence was a slap of fresh air in this den of smoke, sweat, and gall.

"This is none of your business," said Francisco, confronting him. Montes, Lopez, and a couple of the women assistants booed along with similar comments.

Marcus turned to me. "Anna, I recommend you do nothing your father hasn't asked you to do."

Whatever residue was left of bottled-up emotions that had been festering all week burst into a rush of indignation and the crowd broke up into loud discussions.

Francisco grabbed my arm. "Anna, I recommend you listen to your own conscience instead."

"Let's stay civil," Marcus said, taking his hand off my arm. "And keep respectful distances."

Francisco lunged toward Marcus and pushed him. Marcus pushed him back. Then Francisco punched Marcus in the face. Marcus staggered back and his glasses fell to the floor. Everyone's head turned. Some of the women screamed. Jesús and Montes restrained Francisco, who shook them off and stepped back, swearing. Silvia picked up Marcus's crushed glasses from the floor.

Marcus regained his balance and thanked Silvia for the glasses. "All right, this is enough for now," he said, facing the crowd with a bloody nose. "The checks will wait until Mr. Hurt comes back. And if anyone wants to fight, I'll be waiting outside."

"I'm calling the police this minute," Ventura said, reaching toward the phone.

"No one's going to fight." Jesús nailed Francisco with his eyes. "Let's call it a day and wait till Monday."

The crowd trickled out of the room, browbeaten and exhausted. Conchita brought Marcus a box of tissues, and then left with everyone else. I collapsed into a chair.

Marcus pressed a bunch of tissues to his nose. "Sorry I couldn't be here earlier."

I was shaking. "They're so angry!"

Marcus sat down by my side. "You can't blame them. They live paycheck to paycheck."

"I felt so bad for them," I said, and burst into tears.

"They weren't exactly gentle to you, either. Don't worry, it'll get sorted out. Let me take you home." He helped me up from my chair and I went to get my things while he washed his nose off in the bathroom. We locked the office and walked out into the street.

"The funny thing is," Marcus said, frisking his pockets for car keys, "I said I'd take you home, but actually I can't drive for the life of me without glasses. I'm afraid you'll be the one driving a blind, nose-busted dud tonight."

We ended up at the house. I could have driven him to his place and kept his car until the next day, or just left him there and taken a cab back to the house. We could have done a number of things that would have made more sense than what we did. But he ended up spending the night. There was nobody home. Rosita was away on a family visit to her village. There wasn't a question of me being fearful of staying alone in the huge, empty house. I was shaken, but not afraid. It was that the moment we got into the car we both knew we didn't want to part. Nothing was said. Not even significant glances were exchanged. It was a feeling we both had in the gut.

We sat by the fireplace, and I threw in a bunch of sticks together with scrunched balls of paper, and lit a fire. We sat in silence for a while, savoring Father's most aged brandy. I studied his face, aware that his shortsightedness rendered him unsuspecting of my brazen examination. Shadows of flames danced across his features and his eyes looked larger and deeper without glasses. Different hues of blue gave his striated irises a marbled quality I hadn't seen before. Now that his nose had stopped bleeding, I saw that the punch had also cut his upper lip. A light brown, two-day stubble covered his chin and cheeks, and his body looked more muscular in these casual, construction-site clothes than in the suits he wore in the office. He sat in Father's chair with the ease of a large feline resting on a tree branch, relaxed but alert. I poked the fire and served more brandy. Then I curled into my own chair, dreamy with intoxication, while we talked through the night.

He parodied the mutinous office meeting and Francisco's assault until I was screaming with laughter. The scenario was a spaghetti-western saloon, and two crazy cowboys who fought for a last shot of whiskey among a disgruntled crowd of aged patrons and chorus girls. I was amazed at his good humor and lack of resentment over the incident. He assured me that growing up in West Berlin among mean neighborhood bullies had prepared him for much worse than anything Francisco could put him through. Then he asked about me, and I told him about Chekhov's Nina, and Saint Martin's, and how I was biding my time at the office until I could study acting. I went on and on, realizing after a while that nobody had ever asked me about my life before, and that I'd never talked about myself without bringing Father, Nanny, or my sisters into the account. He said he understood the heartbreak of unaccomplished vocation. He had tried to become a professional soccer player in his teens, but injured a knee and never made it past the regional leagues. Now, his consolation consisted in running every day and hiking on weekends. I watched his strong hands feed kindling to the fire as he related how he loved the rocky landscapes of granite boulders and pine forests in the Sierra de Guadarrama, the very same chain of mountains facing our house that I had grown up with. For the last year he had explored most of the trails in its sierras. He described the crunchy sound of pine needles under his feet on his trekking expeditions, when he climbed the steep paths toward the summits.

I can't say when I fell asleep huddled in my armchair. I only remember the image of Marcus watching the fire before I could no longer keep my eyes open. It was late morning when I woke up. The sun poured in through the huge French windows, tickling my face. Someone had wrapped me in one of the blanket throws we kept on the sofas. Marcus was gone. On the chimney mantelpiece was a note written in his clean, precise handwriting. *Keep the car until Monday. And thank you for the brandy.*

* * *

I follow Delia and Constantine down into the kitchen, where the ceremony needs to take place. After carefully closing all doors, they ask me to stand facing the altar, just a few feet away. To the side, Constantine starts lining up items on the counter: a cigar, one of the liquor bottles, a bunch of tree branches covered in thick green leaves, matches, and finally, an egg I see him take from a padded pouch in his backpack.

He catches me looking at him from the corner of my eye. "Don't worry about any of this. Just relax. It will be over quickly," he says.

I close my eyes and wait for them to begin.

CHAPTER 13

First softly, and then steadily louder, I hear Delia intone a song. After a moment, I realize she's reciting an Our Father, but in bizarre deep singing tones that remind me of a blues song or a spiritual ballad. I feel her circling around me and as I open my eyes, Constantine hands her a lit cigar, and taking it daintily with her right hand, she puts the lighted end inside her mouth and starts puffing out smoke all over my body. I am surprised at how nimble she seems as she slithers around me, now spraying me with a mist of cheap-smelling whiskey from her mouth, now going back to the cigar. In between puffs and sprays, she returns to her singsong prayer. I close my eyes once more, mostly as a defense against the alcohol spray, and now I feel something small and hard pressed against the top of my head. I can sense Delia's smooth cold hand behind it, and realize it's the egg I saw before on the counter, which is now being rolled down and rubbed against the back of my head, shoulders, spine, and finally all over my body. She rubs the palms of my hands with it and makes crosses over them. Then Constantine approaches from behind and strikes my shoulders with the bunch of branches, sweeps them heavily over my back and legs in downward motions. My flesh tingles under the feeling of soft whipping. A fragrance of something like eucalyptus is given off as the leaves beat on my skin, saturating my nose and lungs. The swishing sound fills my ears. For the first time in hours I feel light and relaxed, as if a weight has been lifted. Delia has stopped singing. I hear a snapping sound and watch her as she empties the content of the egg into a tall glass of water, a strange gray mass of mucousy matter that flops into the clear liquid and sinks to the bottom of the tumbler.

"Good, good. But not enough. Not enough," I hear Delia murmur, and she avoids my gaze when I eye her quizzically. Instead she seizes the branches from Constantine's hands and takes over the sweeping and striking over my body, chanting loudly again. Exasperated, I close my eyes again and yield to the gentle flogging that is now making my skin flare up and itch.

"Take me to the mountains," I said when I returned the car keys.

Marcus tilted back in his chair and eyed me through a new pair of thin gold-rimmed glasses. "Would your father approve?"

"Who cares about that?"

"You're aware there's a company policy against employees seeing one another after office hours?"

"No one has to know. Take me. Please."

Meanwhile, Father had returned on Sunday night and, after finding out what had happened in his absence, organized nothing short of an inquisition tribunal in order to question everyone and decide how to best discipline those responsible. Francisco and Lopez were fired, but everyone else in the office got a bonus in addition to their salary as a reward for the wait.

Father thanked Marcus, who had stubbornly defended Francisco until the end, and after seeing him out his office door, he turned to me. "Anna, you did very well, I'm proud of you."

"Without Marcus, I couldn't have done much. He saved the day," I said.

"I don't believe a word of that! Of course, it *was* his duty to help you. Anyway, how did you get home? I see your car was being repaired at the workshop over the weekend."

"Marcus took me," I said, and blushed.

Father searched my eyes. "I hope he conducted himself as a gentleman."

"He did," I said, and changed the conversation. Father had a fine nose for smelling out situations. I didn't want any more attention drawn to Marcus.

The week's wait was excruciating. Early Saturday morning, we met at one of the city exit roads to the sierra and drove in his car north to Navacerrada, one of the skiing resort areas closest to Madrid. The peak winter season was over, and it was easier to find solitary trails away from the trodden paths, after the snow had thawed. We drove up steep, winding roads surrounded by tall pine forests until we came to an open patch where it was possible to leave the car. Above us, the overcast sky was threaded with darker strands of heavy, leaden clouds. I wasn't properly dressed. I had no good hiking boots and my jacket wasn't even waterproof. We started on a trail ascending among pine trees and oaks. Marcus pushed ahead and I watched his strong legs pounding on the dirt path strewn with pine needles and granite shards. I followed his steps, dazed at the beauty of the forest and the crisp cool air that poured elixir-like into my lungs. Marcus waited when I fell back, and offered his hand when boulders hindered the trail. After a couple of hours we reached an open area of grasslands, an undulating sea of green sprinkled with lilac crocus flowers, the last haven at the foot of the sierra's summits. I threw myself on the grass, exhausted. Marcus brought out sandwiches and a water bottle from his rucksack. I lay surrounded by the pungent smell of juniper bushes, knowing I wasn't hungry for sandwiches. I reached for Marcus's head with both hands as he kneeled down to offer me water, and pressed my lips against his. Our bodies mingled on the pasture. Eagles cruised above our heads toward the mountain peaks.

But Marcus pulled away. "You're so young!"

"No, I'm not! I'm nineteen," I said, annoyed. "You're twenty-six, not that much older."

"My age cannot be compared to yours."

"Why is that? Because you were bullied in school?"

We were kissing again. Slowly at first, pecking at each other's lips and then with increasing hunger, while my body, caught between the cool plush grass and Marcus's warm pounding torso, thickened with desire.

Cold raindrops started falling on our hands and faces and, looking up, we saw the sky begin to darken as it prepared to down-
pour. We rushed back to the path, but the rain started drumming
down around us, hard and freezing. We found shelter under rocks
and waited for it to abate. I was soaked and shaking from the cold.
Marcus held me tight as we squatted on the soft mossy ground and
listened to the rain ravaging the forest.

It tapered off after a while, and we got up and continued on our
way. Fog had engulfed the woods, and the smell of ozone bounced
off the earth and the resinous trunks of trees. Marcus's warm hand
held mine as we traversed the damp veil of mist that hung over the
path. *If only this were unending,* I thought, *if we never got back to the
car, or to the city, or the office. If only this moment could be frozen in time.*

It was already dark when we reached the car. We drove down the
road and stopped at a large stone restaurant and hotel. A huge fire
blazed in the bar lounge. Very few customers were around, and the
barman explained that their television set was down, so everyone
had gone elsewhere to watch the soccer match. We ordered coffee
and brandy and sat by the hearth, warming up and drying off our
boots and jackets.

"Let's get a room," I said.

Marcus was silent for a beat. "Have you even been with a guy
before?"

"I've probably had more lovers than you."

He smirked. "You're used to having everything you want, aren't
you?"

I stood up. "Look, if you don't like me enough—" I made to
leave, but Marcus pulled me to him and pressed his face against
my belly.

The room was small. Dark red curtains draped a narrow window,
matching the frayed counterpane on the bed. On either side of the
metal headboard stood dim bedside lamps. The smell of mold hung
in the air. The barman, who doubled as hotel manager, made excuses for the chilled room temperature and switched on an infrared
electric heater in a corner on the floor.

As soon as the man stepped out, Marcus turned to me. "This is
not the place where I'd ever want to make love to you. Let's split."

"What does the place matter?" I said, burying my head in his chest. "You and I *are* the only thing that matters." Our bodies pounded, pressed against the chilled wall.

"You know this will change everything, don't you?" he whispered.

"I want everything to be changed." I knew the room would disappear the moment our lips fused again, the moment our bodies lay enfolded in each other's arms under the cold sheets.

I had been with other men, or other boys, to be more precise—Miguel and a couple others from the school—but nothing had prepared me for this encounter. I shivered as Marcus undressed me under the covers, warming me up with his hands and blowing hot breath onto my skin. I wanted to fondle him, but his nudity intimidated me. I didn't know how to start on his chiseled shoulders, his slim hips, his huge, beautiful cock.

I'd never seen such a male body. It felt smooth and elastic as he lay over me and engulfed me in a mélange of deep caresses. My own frame felt lightweight and elusive as he pushed through my tight tissues. I knew then that whatever sex I'd had before hadn't resolved my virginity, and that here I was being laid open for the first time, to be properly deflowered by my mountaineer lover. I surrendered to the mixture of agony and ecstasy, swayed by waves of bliss streaked with pain, while Marcus stifled my moans with kisses.

I remember reaching a threshold, a point where my flesh relented into a feeling of gushing abandonment. I opened my eyes. My mind flitted above the bed now encircled by the pink glow of the bedside lamp like a halo. I looked at Marcus, as we lay still, panting against each other. For a moment we swam in each other's gaze, drunk with the briny smell of love. Everything felt blurred, all matter around me seemed to be fading away, save for a smoldering point deep inside my belly where Marcus was locked in. I held my breath and clutched him tighter. I didn't want this to ever end. But ripples of unbearable pleasure were already bursting all over me. I blacked out for a few seconds.

When I came back, Marcus pulled out of me.

"What are you doing?" I asked, confused, my mind hovering over my engorged body.

He lay on his back, breathing heavily. "No one's ready for babies here."

"I told you I am on the pill."

"I'd need hard proof of that."

"You don't trust me?"

He drew me back to him, hugging me into his chest. "We're together now. I don't want any worries to come between us."

But a worry, like a tiny dark shoot, was already budding in my mind.

How would Father take this?

The following week at the office was surreal. I was so sore that I walked around dragging my feet. My mind kept flying back to the mountain hotel, playing and replaying every word, every glance, every second of our lovemaking. Worst of all, my womb turned every time at the sight of Marcus, or my nose detecting his body scent of mud mixed with musk, driving me insane. I had to rearrange my desk so as to be completely out of range from him. We had agreed to keep our escapade a secret, to pretend we were still cordial co-workers with nothing else going on. I tried challenging myself to act the role of the hidden lover, but I was terrified of Father finding out about us. Marcus was right. Everything had changed.

The office was busy after Father's return. Following the recent purge, everyone went about business with more diligence than ever. Things were back on track, and Father was intent on reorganizing the whole operation for increased efficiency. Sales and contracts skyrocketed once more. Confident of my reliability after my performance during his absence, he began to push me into more advanced responsibilities. But I knew he was always watching me, and his shift toward a cooler, more distant manner with Marcus was the sign that, if he didn't suspect much yet, he was preparing for that battle.

Why did he have to be so controlling? Couldn't he just leave us alone to pursue happiness whichever way we chose to? Why was he threatened the moment any of us showed signs of independence? We were women now, not little girls—did he feel we would desert him the moment we hooked up with a lover? Or did he want us to live eternally in his shadow?

Marcus and I continued to see each other on the weekends. I made out to join a trekking club that got together weekly in Guadarrama for trips. Every Saturday we would meet early and drive up to the mountains, hike up the trails and explore valleys and forests, and then find a small hotel to make love in all night long. Sometimes we would just have sex all weekend, leaving our room only for brief café or restaurant breaks when we were famished. We couldn't get enough of each other. Our bodies seemed to be made for one another. Just embracing was like entering a droplet of shared perception where we breathed together, climaxed together, dreamed together. Sometimes I woke up in the middle of the night and stared at the silhouette of his warm body sprawled on the bed beside me, wrapped in deep sleep, and felt he was just an extension of my own pulsing veins, of my own rhythmic breathing. And wondered how I had lived all my life without him.

There soon came a moment when we couldn't bear to be apart from each other. Then weekends led into furtive meetings during the week. Marcus's apartment wasn't a good option; he lived too close to the office and I was afraid we might be seen together. So I started sneaking him into the garden late at night, and we fucked like fugitives under the willow tree or at the far corners of the pool, always in areas steeped in shadows. I lived in a cloud of crazy bliss.

But not everyone was fooled by my secrecy.

"I know you're shagging," Silvia said one afternoon we happened to come across each other in the bathroom. "I know, 'cause your boobs have changed."

"Really?" I tried to sound detached.

"Boobs change shape when they get sucked on all the time." Silvia always made raunchy comments as her own peculiar way of bonding with women, comments that would have made me laugh in the past, but now felt vulgar, disgusting. I knew she was dying to get the gossip about my lover. I wondered if she suspected the truth.

"I'm just working out at the gym," I said in a cold voice. She gave me a look but didn't say anything else. She knew I had been lost to our former girlie camaraderie after the mutiny incident. When she left the bathroom, I felt like crying. Was my love with Marcus just another one of those seedy, venal affairs of adultery and fornication with which the infamous office legends were packed?

It was true, though, that my body had changed. I had lost weight and my waist had become very slim, whereas my breasts had filled out and my hips broadened. When I looked at myself in the mirror I saw a woman now. My face had opened with ripe, smooth cheeks and full lips, and my body was curvy and bold. Even my eyes had lost their round, childlike outline and elongated into almond shapes. I knew my new beauty was the doing of Marcus's lovemaking. Every time he held me in his arms I could feel his tenderness shaping me, perfecting me, making my every cell bloom.

But Marcus was growing more and more unhappy about our underground arrangement. He wanted us to be in the open, and we bickered about it all the time.

"I don't have a problem talking to your father up front. There's nothing wrong about being together," he would say, vexed.

"No, no, please. Let's wait for the right moment. Please." These conversations were torture; I just wasn't ready to face my fears. But Marcus wouldn't let up. He wanted, at least, for us to go to beautiful hotels, amazing spas, and similar spots. But most of the time we ended up in smaller, grungier places with spare, ugly little rooms and creaky beds, choices apparently forced by my paranoid obsession to hide from Father. I guess I had been traumatized by the way he had acted in the past when he found out my sisters had lovers. He had been ruthless, brutal, even lethal. I now sensed the same sort of danger lurking around me—I felt under constant surveillance, closely observed, and it paralyzed me. I was not only afraid for Marcus, but also for myself. But I couldn't put my finger on the exact source of my resistance to break away and leave behind everything that tied me to my father. There was a part of me that was stupefied.

At work, Marcus and I continued to go about each other stone-faced and courteous to the point of chilled etiquette. The Anna of the tattletale eyes died as I perfected my craft of masking my real self day to day, of hiding my pounding heart while, buried at my desk among paperwork, I thought of Marcus and his sweet lips brushing against my nipples or the way his hands wrapped around my waist as he penetrated my body.

In order to hide my consuming passion, I started making superhuman efforts to learn the business, forcing myself to come up with the most effective solutions to problems, with the most creative marketing action plans. I was suddenly the most enthusiastic trainee the office had seen. It was just a strategy to distract everyone's attention from what was truly eating me alive, but it bore good fruits in time, revealing my aggressive saleswoman's skills, by which I ended up being able to sell a donkey not just to Gypsies, but to my own father.

Julia also detected my change and made me confess the whole story.

"Why are you hiding? What do you have to lose? You don't need to live in the house, now you have my apartment. You don't need to work for him; it would be his loss anyway."

"I'm afraid he'll go crazy. I'm afraid he'll hurt Marcus," I'd respond in a daze. I didn't want any conflict. I just wanted to make love to Marcus for hours on end, and then sleep tight in his arms before I woke up to make love to him again.

"Don't be silly, Anna. Why give him so much power? What can he do besides throwing both of you out of the company, and you out of the house?"

"C'mon, you know him better than that! Is that all he did to you or Marion?"

Julia would then remain silent for a bit, but a while later she would take it up again. "Are you sure you want to work in that awful place anyway? Look at you! You're becoming a total square! Look at your jerky clothes, at those stupid pointed pumps. All these ridiculous, rich Daddy's girl accessories! What a way to waste money! Jeez, Anna, soon I won't even recognize you. Get out of all this while you can!" But listening to Julia's sound advice has never been my thing.

Then there was Father. Opening the door when I returned from my weekends, or sitting at the breakfast table the morning after I had ravaged Marcus at night in the garden. His pupils had a way of flickering every time he met mine after I had been with my lover, or when I lied about my whereabouts. Like a twinge of pained fear, followed by a hardening. And each time, as I averted my eyes and held my breath, I knew it was a matter of time. I knew it was coming.

No one was being fooled.

*   *   *

Delia sits in her chair by the altar; Constantine is putting away the ritual paraphernalia. No one speaks. The room is heavy with smoke from the paraffin candles, many of which are already consumed or close to extinction. There is a strong odor, a mix of cigar, whiskey, and the leaves they used on my body. I notice a new sudden clarity of mind. My eyes can move quickly around the room, can zoom in to the different objects on the altar, to their minute details. My hearing seems to have unfolded into different layers, I can hear the remote, raspy song of crickets in the garden as clearly as I hear the small noises Constantine makes beside me as he folds a paper bag into his backpack.

"Let's not lose momentum." Delia's words throb inside my ears and I reflect on the weight of their sound, as if they carry deep musical notes. Then I see her stand from the chair without the aid of her staff, her body looking young and supple for an instant, although the moment Constantine puts a cane in her hand, her mass seems to slump again into the old shape. I follow them as they walk up the stairs toward Father's study. I am wondering what I will have to do once we get there, but feel no inclination to ask.

We stop in front of the double paneled door and Constantine takes up the metal bowl full of herbs I had seen in his hands before, and lights it with a long stick match. The greenish mass starts smoking and the sickly smell of burned sage rises. Delia points her staff and Constantine follows the lines of the door frame with the smoking bowl as if he were drawing its shape.

Delia places a hand on my shoulder, and says solemnly, "Now, Anna, youngest daughter of the house, I ask you in the name of Eleguá, the opener of paths and roads, to give us access to this room by removing locks, opening doors and windows, so that we may bless it."

I take a step forward and place my hand on the doorknob. A flicker of trepidation freezes my fingers. Delia's hand squeezes my shoulder lightly. I turn the knob and push the door open.

CHAPTER 14

The first impression is an erratic pattern of light and dark. The old wooden venetian blinds are half drawn over the large window at the far end, and the blazing sun squeezes through the slits, creating a zebra effect over the walls and floor. As my eyes adjust, the objects in the room start taking shape: the desk by the window, the tall bookshelves, the chesterfield sofa, the wooden filing cabinets. Everything seems to be in place. Particles of dust dance in the shafts of light as I step in and walk to the window. A feeling of suffocation grips my lungs in the airless, oppressive silence that envelops me as I move through. The window opens easily, and clean hot air rushes in, pushing out the musty smell of the long closed room. I grope along the window frame to find the canvas strap that rolls up the blind, and pull it down hard. The blind hauls up with a sore, cranky noise and my vision is blanked out by a burst of white light. I turn around and get a different view of the room. Strewn all over are books and papers, stacks of newspapers and old magazines, cardboard boxes containing all sorts of unidentifiable things, documents and pictures pinned up on the bare walls, dark figurines standing on surfaces. Then the strap snaps in my hand and the blind falls heavily over the windowsill with a loud bang, and the room is enveloped in total darkness.

"Are you all right?" Constantine's small voice sounds very far away, although I know he and Delia are still at the threshold.

"I'm fine," I say, as I fumble around the desk to find the lamp switch. "But I'm afraid the blind is now permanently broken and there will be no natural light in here."

"Maybe I can fix it. I used to work for a company that made blinds and canopies and—" Constantine starts, but Delia cuts him short. "That will not be necessary for our purposes. Please switch on any light in there and leave the room immediately," she adds in my direction.

I'm jarred by her urgency and knock over the desk lamp. It falls to the floor, where it emits a small explosion of sparks as the bulb crashes. My hands turn to the glass cabinet behind the desk, and soon find its switch by the wall. A small, yellowed light shines inside the cabinet, illuminating a collection of African statuettes and Egyptian figures that startle me.

"This light is very dim, let me find another," I say, stepping back.

"Don't. Leave the room now," Delia says. I walk out of the study before they step in and close the door behind them.

I stand outside the study savoring my discontent. Something inside the room pulls at me with the strength of a magnet. I want to peek in; I want to put my ear to the door as I have done many times in my life before. But I resist and walk away. It's strange how the room has taken me by surprise, shocked me with its aura of clutter and neglect, as if I hadn't accessed its filing cabinets in the past years and accompanied the real estate agent as he inspected the house. But what is so surprising? Among other things, this room ended up being the depository of all that was left after the business was closed down, a cemetery of documents, archives, and all sorts of memorabilia of a lifetime of work.

Noises of someone unwrapping large sheets of paper or plastic coming from the corridor on the second floor divert my attention.

"Julia?"

No one answers. I walk up the stairs, which are still wet and slippery, and as I reach the landing, I see Julia ripping the wrappings off a large canvas she has taken out of the closet in the corridor opposite Mother's old studio. Other canvasses stand against the wall.

"What is this?" I ask.

"I don't understand anything. I thought all these had been destroyed long ago and . . ." Julia doesn't finish her sentence. We both look at the painting that emerges behind the ripped brown paper. It's a portrait of Alina. Actually, it's *the* portrait of Alina that made it to the collective exhibit and won Julia her reputation back in the day.

On the large canvas, splashed with green and orange, Alina lies nude on her stomach with round golden buttocks and splayed thighs in the forefront, her head and torso turned toward the viewer. A black-and-white toucan she holds in one hand pecks her on the red lips with the tip of its wide yellow beak while she stares at us with vacant, liquid eyes. This was one of the paintings Julia had slashed the night she was mad with pain after being snubbed by Alina. But now it appears to have been repaired to its original integrity, although on closer inspection it shows its carefully concealed scars worked over by skillful restoration.

"Who did this?" Julia asks, holding back her rage.

"Father did. He sent a bunch of your canvasses away to be restored. There's more in the attic. Don't you remember?"

"Of course I don't. You never told me anything about this!"

"I did too. You said you didn't want to have anything to do with him or the pictures ever again."

"I did not! Why are you lying? What's wrong with you? What else are you hiding?"

"Hiding! Why would I hide anything?" My head reels as Julia's hatred radiates through me. I'm not sure what's happening, I only sense Julia struggling with some unspeakable pain, and clawing around to get a grip on herself.

"I would have felt and acted very differently these last years, had I known about this." Julia's face is drawn and livid, as if the blood has drained out of her in an instant.

"Known what? That your father kept your precious artwork in the house all this time? That he didn't burn it all in a blazing pyre in some crazy act of revenge?" I'm the one screaming now and Julia's reddened eyes are beginning to overflow with tears.

"That he thought they were worth keeping," she says in a broken voice.

Julia turns toward the door at the end of the corridor that leads to the attic. She disappears up the narrow staircase carrying Alina's portrait. I want to follow her, but know she'd fight me back. I'd totally forgotten about these pictures. I do remember Father sending them off to a restoration atelier. Once they were back in the house, I lost track of them.

Fighting with Julia is always draining; seeing her upset is unbearable. When we were small and I saw her cry, I would run for my most precious toy and insist she accept it as a gift. A doll that had already lost an eye, an arm, and most of its hair was offered endlessly in this way. Anything was a small sacrifice if I could see my sister restored to balance, if those tiny, disconsolate eyes filled once again with wonder. Her last words still reverberate in my mind: *I would have acted differently, had I known that he thought they were worth keeping.* Now this was a real offering coming from Julia, she who had been so dismissive of Father all these years, his caustic critic, his most fearful detractor. So this is what lay underneath her animosity, the slashed acrylic body of Alina and Father's disdain of the brushstrokes with which she had caressed it into a portrait. Now, after Alina's careful restoration and her nudity accepted, admired, and wrapped, Julia's heartache was assuaged, and her past resentment reconsidered. Why hadn't Father told her about the restoration, sent her the repaired picture, or even just hung it on the wall as an act of reconciliation?

All of a sudden, I'm aware of all the things stored in the house. Not just the things still on display in rooms and on walls, like furniture, rugs, or pictures, but the collections of objects, books, photographs, postcards, souvenirs, and heirlooms, endless lists of mementos from our past, hidden away in closets, stashed inside drawers, hoarded up in the attic. And buried among the piles, what surprises can we find that will reveal different angles of bygone moments?

A cramping feeling of regret takes hold of me. I should have made an effort to put some order into the whole house during these two long years after Father's death. Even before his death, when the house began to slip into decline. All of a sudden the house's state of neglect hurts me, as if I had failed to attend to a child or an animal entrusted to my care and now found them sick or deteriorated beyond recovery. But in all fairness, when Father was alive the house was still the unconquerable lair of the demonic energy that possessed him. There was no way any of us could have barged in here with brooms and dusting cloths. The only thing to do was to flee, to seal the house in our hearts and minds, step away from its influence; from its dangerous, difficult memories.

I walk into Julia's old room; the room that was also mine, before I was ousted by Alina. The wooden blinds on these windows crashed down a while ago and now lie scattered around between the sill and the floor. The room is scorching hot. Blinding sunlight pours in through the glass panes. I shade my eyes and look around. It looks like it's been ransacked or evacuated in anticipation of a demolition or a diaspora following war. The beds' box springs stand on their sides by the wall beside the splintered head- and footboards. One stained mattress lies on the floor with metal springs sticking out through the cover. The old blue and lime carpet is curled up on all corners, splashed with stains of paint and glue. The walls are scratched and puckered with holes from the nails and tacks with which Julia hung her sketches and pictures. Dirty, broken objects, disfigured books and other junk is strewn around, now wet with the water that has flooded from the corridor under the door. I step on something squishy and bend down to pick up a small teddy bear lying among the mess. I recognize the grimy face with no nose button, and only stitched-in eyes. This used to be Marti, Julia's inseparable bedtime teddy from eons ago. Is it possible that the objects contained in this room go so far back? Isn't it pathetic that holding this grubby little piece of stuffed terry cloth is making me feel nostalgic?

I tried to return to our old room when Julia left the house after her fight with Father. It made all the sense in the world. It was the largest bedroom, the most beautiful, with its huge bay window bordered by a plush green seating area topped with seashell-stamped cushions, and a stencil trail of butterflies over the wall by my bed. But all its prettiness was gone by then. Julia and Alina had trashed it severely while using it as an art atelier, and it never felt like the old bedroom again. Taking up this bedroom again also made sense because it was the farthest removed from Father's, and I could sneak Marcus in at night. But that never worked out either. Marcus's dignity could accept romancing in the garden, but not inside the house when Father was asleep. I felt lonely when I slept in this room. I thought of Julia and Nanny; I was swamped by childhood memories that filled me with longing. It was like the space belonged to a time of innocence that had disappeared from our lives. I felt disenfranchised from my girlhood, troubled and insecure about my womanhood. After a few weeks, I returned to Mother's old studio. This bedroom then became a sad depository for all kinds of unwanted items in the house.

Across from the window is the large built-in wardrobe that became the storage for out-of-season coats and other discarded garments. As I approach it now, I see it's also stuffed with a jumble of leftover objects. Father's golf gear and Marion's old ice skates sit alongside moth-eaten blankets and taped-up boxes of small appliances. I try to close its mangled panel doors and struggle with the long handle of an ancient vacuum cleaner angled into one of the hinges. Some water has flooded into the bottom of the closet, creating a muddy residue along the base. I bend over to remove a wet clump of fabric wedged between the vacuum's handle and dust cover. As I pull it up to throw back into the corner, I recognize its touch. I hold it to the light as its damp weight unfolds its length toward the floor. My old emerald-green silk dress! It's been years since I last saw it. I can't believe it still exists. I don't think I've ever owned a more beautiful, provocative dress. I don't think I've ever paid more for a piece of clothing.

My body still remembers the feeling of its soft touch around the low shoulders and how its sleek wrap bandaged my waist and legs and fell down to my ankles. Walking in it was only possible in short steps, one foot in front of the other, thighs rubbing against each other, hips forced into sinuous sway. Heads turned in halls and rooms as I slithered along in this green skin.

All but Marcus's.

"Why are you leaving?" I ran down the stairs outside of the British Consulate, careful not to trip over the long silk dress. We were attending a cocktail party for Business Week, organized by the chamber of commerce.

Marcus stopped ahead of me and turned around. "Don't you think I've paid my dues for the evening? Or should I wait it out until midnight, looking on while Mr. Anderson and his partners swoon all over you?"

"What's your problem? This is just a business gathering!"

"Really? There's always *some* sort of business around you." He took a step closer. "You've finally become an accomplished actress, you know that?"

I slapped him on the face, hard. Marcus rubbed his cheek for a moment.

The embassy porter walked toward us. "Is there a problem, miss? Should I call security?" I shook my head and he moved away.

"Look." Marcus undid his bow tie and stuffed it forcefully into his pocket. "I'm just a simple guy, I'm not cut out for complicated plots. There's only one thing that's plain right now: There's not enough space in your life for me. And I'm thinking it's time for me to clear out."

I stood shivering in the cold air, hugging the green silk around my ribs. I hated him. I fought with that part of me that always wanted to bury itself in his chest. "Do whatever the hell you want. I don't care!"

I stomped back up the stairs into the building, fuming.

Only eighteen months ago we had been so close that pulling apart from each other to reenter our separate worlds was unbearable. There had come a point where no matter how much we tried, however impeccable the strategizing of our hiding, our togetherness was impossible to mask. It was as if the aura of our belonging pulsed into rooms and wrote itself all over walls with the certitude of sunlight pouring in through windows. Everyone's silence reflected this knowledge. It should have been a sign to blow up the bunker I had created around us. But I didn't. I held fast to my game plan.

Father then decided it was time to act. He started by marching in from the fringes, his heavy machinery directed toward the difficult, delicate target of destroying the core of my affection. He had refined his cunning and understood that direct warfare would only draw me closer to Marcus. Firing Marcus was no option either. He was the employee of our company's German partner, very well considered and key in personnel training of field equipment.

First, he tried to get me out of the company. Come April, he insisted on my taking up the degree at Saint Martin's in September, assuring me he would take care of all expenses, and that he would rent a nice flat near the college that I could share with Marion. I sat listening to him as he tried to convince me of the importance of a college education and the need to spend time in a big metropolis like London, feeling stunned at the thought that the offer I would have died for less than a year ago now sounded like an empty, dreary scheme in which I would just wither away pining for Marcus. Nothing made sense without him. Acting and Saint Martin's could go to hell as far as I was concerned. I wanted to stay in the now, and the now was the electrifying flush that galvanized my every cell when I stood in the presence of my lover.

After weeks of employing every possible form of persuasion with no result, Father took a different approach: He decided to spoil me rotten. He upped my salary, he bought me a new car, he introduced me to the crème of the Madrid British and American circles, took me on business trips all over Europe, buying me gorgeous, expensive clothes in Milan and Paris, booking vacations in places like Monte Carlo or Venice, dazzling spots where he would indulge me to no end. And I, instead of resisting, let myself be traveled, wined and dined, pampered to death, thinking I was immune to his seduction. But I wasn't. I learned to enjoy this high life and began to relish being paraded around by him in social circles, making an impression on the men he introduced me to, all those he thought might distract me from my lover.

But there was no pulling me away from my sweet love. I was just settling into a schizoid, compartmentalized life, where the office, Father, and my social life were on the outside, while on the inside I carried Marcus tucked away in a hidden shrine. After returning from trips or supercilious social gatherings, I rushed to meet him in dark streets, or at one of our sierra hideouts, in surroundings always more silent, always more real, and wondered at the simplicity of his handsome, strong body, of his down-to-earth conversation, or the way in which lying in his arms felt like home.

In an effort to bridge the growing gap between my two selves, I began to dream about planning our escape. It started as a game. We would sit up on the bed and pull out a bunch of maps that Marcus carried in his car and I had stuffed into his backpack. We sat around and planned trips, at first to all the mountains we could think of, the Pyrenees between France and Spain, the Alps in Switzerland or the Atlas Mountains in North Africa. Then the planning expanded to more exotic places, like the rainforest in Brazil, or the Land of Fire in Patagonia.

"Let's go live in a faraway country," I said.

"I could get a job as an engineer in a bunch of different places."

"What about Tanzania or Kenya?"

"There's lots of work in African countries."

"Or South America. Peru, the Amazon."

"We can also live here and travel all over." He pulled me into his warm body and we rolled over the maps, which rustled and crinkled under our weight. "But will you be able to leave your house, your father?"

"We can elope."

"Eloping *is* leaving your family."

"Father would never talk to me again if I eloped."

"I doubt that. After a while . . ."

"You don't know him. There's no going back with him."

"You're too scared. He's just a father, what can he do besides staying mad for some time?"

"I'm scared he'll split us up."

"He won't. I'll always come back for you."

And he joked, comparing himself to Siegfried, the hero in *The Nibelungenlied*, invincible after having bathed in dragon's blood, save for one small spot of vulnerability on his back. And that spot was reserved for me. "Nothing can break us up if we decide to stay together. Not your father, not anyone or anything else." He might have been older than me, but he was naïve too.

Father was sending Marcus away on training jobs as often as he could. He started with postings around the Spanish peninsula. The company had expanded into new lines of equipment, one of which was shipyard machinery that demanded supervised installation in faraway ports, such as Galicia and the Basque Country. In the past those jobs had been given to Montes and our other Spanish engineers, but now Marcus took on most of the traveling, sometimes spending a week or more away and returning exhausted, only to be immediately given another assignment. Father was looking to create overwork and discontent, so that Marcus might complain or even quit the job, or at least his commission at our company. But Marcus did all the work without objections, rendered accounts and field reports with immaculate correctness even in the face of Father's taunting attitude. Father had become short-tempered and cutting with him, always trying to find a way into provocation. And those West Berlin neighborhood bullies he grew up with must have been something, because I've never seen anyone as impervious to Father's affronts as Marcus. Particularly if I happened to be around, Father would probe him to the limits.

"This job will be tough, but it'll land well on your résumé," he was once saying as I walked into his office.

Marcus sat across from his desk. "Tough? As in field logistics?"

"Tough on all counts: logistics, human element, comfort level. Think of a prospective rig in the middle of the desert, with temporary accommodations filled with non-English-speaking Chinese workers. Heat, dust, Muslim law, Spanish chaos. The whole gamut."

"I see," Marcus said. "Do we need to go there for a full three weeks?"

Father smirked. "Afraid so. Someone needs to keep an eye on these chinks, we don't want them to disgrace our pumps and then be blamed by the Algerians. But you'll be fine, your countrymen had a lot of experience down in those sand fields during the war, Rommel and his cronies. You'll tame a bunch of Chinamen all right."

Marcus stared at him. "I'm not sure what that would mean, but I'll do my best." He got up and left.

He was being sent down to a place in the middle of the desert called Ain Tsila, in Illizi, a southeastern province in Algeria, close to Libya and Tunisia, where a Spanish company we had teamed up with had a contract to do exploratory drilling. This was the first time Father ventured into oil-rigging equipment, something very much in demand in the north of Africa in the nineties. These were difficult but profitable markets that Father had disdained in the past as dangerous. But now the demand for oil and natural gas was going through the roof and opportunities were rampant. Father was in touch with an affiliate of British Petroleum and Algeria's national oil company, Sonatrach, and hoped to participate in future provisions of equipment for two desert drilling rigs in that area.

"I don't want you to go."

We had lain together holding each other tight for hours and had not even had sex. The sun had gone down a long time ago but no one had bothered to switch on any light. His packed bags, his special boots and other desert gear, lay around at the foot of the bed. It was one of those rare occasions when I had gone to his apartment, since he was leaving for the airport at four a.m. For the first time, I was full of apprehension at his departure.

"It'll be fine."

"No, it won't. I've seen this company at work, they're unreliable. Why didn't you refuse? He can't make you do this."

"Don't know. He keeps challenging, and I keep taking up the gauntlet. Whoever stops first, loses. One of those stupid male games."

"Marcus, call it off."

"Too late."

"At least, promise me this will be the last time."

"Promise me you'll stand up and say, *Dad, I have a boyfriend.*"

Checkmate. I felt like crying and clung harder to his body. On the bedside table a digital clock flashed red numbers at my tired eyes. Two fifteen a.m. In one hour we would have to get up and start getting ready to go. He to the airport, I back to the house, to sneak in through the back door and pretend the next day I'd had a great night's sleep.

"Promise you'll come back."

"That I can promise."

We lay in silence, listening to each other's breathing.

The three weeks extended into four and then into six. It was very difficult to get in touch with Marcus outside of the office. I could only read field reports sent by fax, ask casually about the progress of the drilling. On the sixth week, there was an explosion in the rig that injured a number of workers and the whole operation was temporarily called off. Marcus returned to Madrid. He hadn't been hurt in the incident but had contracted typhoid fever. He was hospitalized and lay delirious for days, exhausted with malaise. I could only visit him twice at the hospital, and that had to be done together with Conchita, the receptionist, as friendly company representatives. A private nurse had been hired by the German company to ensure around-the-clock supervision of his progress. The second time I visited, Conchita talked nonstop with the nurse about soup recipes, while Marcus and I looked at each other across the room. He had dark rings around his eyes, and his face was sad and drawn. The pale green room smelled of antiseptics and a pungent disinfectant reminiscent of chlorine mixed with rotten pineapple. I sat in the small chair by the window, my rib cage reverberating with every pang of my heavy heart. I so wanted to rush over to him, to cover his face with kisses, to wrap myself around his depleted body. Only when we were leaving did I approach the bed and, as I pulled out a bottle of water and a book to leave on his table, Marcus clutched my hand and held it tight against the edge of the cot. We stared at each other for an agonizing moment. Conchita waved goodbye from the door and I pulled my hand away. "We'll come back tomorrow. Sleep well and get better," I said in a sweet, neutral voice and left.

The next day I sat in the office, a bundle of nerves and guilt, under Father's constant surveillance. *This is the moment to step forward*, the voice kept whispering in my head. *This is the moment to demolish the whole edifice of lies and deceit.* I sat biting my nails and listening to the rain strumming on the windowpanes. Unusual stormy weather was sweeping over Madrid that fall, and unexpected leaks had brought out the smell of mildew and dampened sheetrock around my desk area. I thought of Marcus alone in his hospital bed.

"Anna," Father said, walking out of his office, "seems like you'll have to fly to London in the morning and take our dossier to Paul Anderson for the BP meeting."

I stood up. "I couldn't, really."

He cocked his head. "But this is important. Afterwards, you may visit Marion and take her out to lunch. On me, of course."

I dug my nails into my fists and swallowed into my dry throat. "I thought I would go see Marcus in the hospital. He doesn't have anyone in Madrid."

"Marcus is fine. He's being officially discharged tomorrow or the day after. You can see him when you return. I already have your ticket." He held out the ticket for me to step away from my desk and take it, while he drilled me with his icy eyes.

"Can't we send an international messenger? It's cheaper, and—"

"Anna, you need to deliver this personally to Paul. Who else am I going to trust?" His eyes flickered with that aching twinge I so much dreaded. "We're a team, Anna. Let's not forget that."

A feeling like sand sliding down an hourglass overtook me. As if I were being drained of all strength, of all determination. Something that was already brittle and thin broke inside me that moment, like a small twig.

I took the ticket.

Nothing was ever the same after Marcus's return. It took him quite a bit of time to recover. He had lost a lot of weight, not just with the typhoid, but even before, during the long weeks working at the rig. I met him at his apartment, which now I felt I could visit casually. Something had changed in him. He looked sinewy and older. He seemed troubled and distant. He talked about the hardship of working in the unbearable heat, of the miserable, inhumane conditions the Chinese workers were kept in, of the terrible solitude of the desert. The accident at the rig had been very dramatic. He had helped in moving the wounded and organizing the rescue mission. Our lovemaking felt strange. I struggled to find a way to confess my angst while Marcus clung to me, distraught. His body felt rattled and slow. As I searched his eyes, I saw the wounds that the desert and the raging fever had left on him, and my betrayal felt monstrous. But we never talked about my trip to London; I never asked him if he had expected more of me while he was at the hospital. For the first time, a screen of smoke rose between us.

We never quite resumed our escapades outside the city. We now met at his apartment or even at the house, when Father was away. The playfulness of our physical encounters was gone, and now our lovemaking just deepened into dejected tenderness. I began to feel smothered by him. His patience had worn thin, and he started demanding more of my presence. He relaxed his reserve with me at the office, which was a way of defying Father. He couldn't stand my flirting and teasing other men in front of him, during meetings or events where we could never engage in personal conversations. We soon started getting into squabbles and rotten little scenes, after which both of us were sore for days. Then we would pine for each other again, and end up in one of our hiding places making desperate love, as if on the verge of losing one another forever. And all the time I knew that my betrayal was the wedge that kept our split open.

Why couldn't I just confess and ask to be forgiven?

Why couldn't I turn to Father and say, *You know very well Marcus is my lover?* I can only think of Father's look when he flitted his eyes between the papers on his desk and my gaze, a clabbering swirl that swept up all my courage, all my sense of selfhood, all the uniqueness that had just been bestowed by Marcus's warm embraces.

There was also his unswerving seduction. "You understand, Anna, that you will end up inheriting the whole business and the house. It would only be fair pay for all your work. Then you can choose to be generous with your sisters if you like. You are the only one who is making herself worthy of it all." With words like these he would frequently lay his empire at my feet in a seemingly nonchalant gesture, like a desperate king prepared to toss it all in one sweep, anything to cling to the slippery object of his affection. But I was quite taken with his offerings, they satisfied my vanity, they flattered my conceit.

And so my allegiance swayed between my father and my lover. It had become a pendulum out of control through which I bounced from one to the other, magnetized and threatened by both.

"I still hold the position of ecstatic slave, but I suspect I'll end up just as your dog." Marcus leaned back against the bed's headboard with palms clasped behind his head. His sense of humor had turned bitter. This was one of his recurrent, annoying jokes.

"Why are you always saying this?" I asked.

"I feel I'm just the instrument of your revenge."

"My revenge?"

"Your revenge, as in getting back at your father."

"Why would I get back at my father?"

"Electra complex? You tell me."

I jumped up in fury. "Are you saying you're jealous of my father?"

"I don't even know who's jealous of whom anymore."

"Very funny!" I started dressing in silence.

He got up from the bed and rocked me in his arms. "Marry me, Anna."

I was overtaken by panic. "You know I'm not the marrying type." This had become my own joking way out of these conversations that were becoming more and more frequent.

"Come live with me, then. We don't need anyone. We can set up our own company, we can get a house in the mountains . . ."

I wasn't ready to make that type of change, to break up my current life, to leave the house, to fight with Father. I was drowning between two different, opposite loves. I could choose to break my father's heart, or my lover's. I was afraid of Father, but I was also afraid of Marcus. His love threatened to engulf my identity, to dissolve me into the magma of our unending ardor.

Marcus dropped his arms, sat down on the bed, and slumped on his back over the mattress. He lay motionless, staring at the ceiling. "You know what this is beginning to feel like? The last days at the soccer league, when I was still allowed to play, even though the noose had already been fitted around my neck. No matter how hard I tried, no matter how much I wanted it, it wasn't going to happen."

I went over to the bed and lay by his side. "C'mon, Marcus, it's not like that."

"No, it's not like that," he said after a beat. "It's worse, 'cause my love for you is so much greater than anything I ever felt for soccer. But maybe that's always going to be the fate of guys like me. We shoot too high, we want the sky, we dream beyond our means. That's why we're doomed to lose out."

I took his face with both my hands and drew his lips toward

mine. "Don't say that." But Marcus resisted, holding me by the wrists, and then pushed me away.

He lay for a moment more in silence, listless with dejection. Then he jumped up and stood by the window, looking out while he pulled up and zipped his jeans. "I guess we're back to our old dilemma. Where to have a decent incognito breakfast in this town."

I should have known he was reaching the end of his rope.

Our fight outside the consulate was the last. Marcus kept his word. He disappeared. In less than a week his desk was empty, his phone disconnected, his apartment cleared. All the proper, plausible explanations fell in place: He was being called back by the German company and sent to an Asian construction site. No note, no call, no forwarding address. Vanished.

I waited at first. After a period of rage, in which I hunted down every track of information that could lead to him, without success, I fell into despair. I felt eviscerated, emptied out of all life. During the day I wanted to scream, emit long wails like those of Greek tragedy heroines directed at distant, unfeeling gods. At night, I just throbbed with loneliness, wondering how I would ever get my body to forget Marcus's hands, if it would be possible for my brain to erase the deep blue tunnels of his eyes. In the morning I dragged my limbs out of bed, heavy with dejection.

The spring months moved into summer and my restlessness was unbearable. I couldn't stand the office, least of all the garden at the house, with all the hidden corners where we had so many times made love under bushes and flouncing willow tree branches. I was irritable with everyone, especially with Father, who played the role of innocent bystander of my inexplicable affliction, but couldn't conceal the smug scowl of victory that spread over his face. The view of the mountains from the veranda became too oppressive to withstand. Micro images of yellow lichen on speckled granite boulders, of tiny chipmunk feet scurrying up a tree, or drops of sticky sap dripping down rockrose bushes, stuck like needles in the cornea of my memory, reminding me of our past amorous ramblings.

In September I went to visit Nanny. I had only driven north to see her a few times since she left the house some three years ago. I found her bedridden, horribly emaciated and aged. As soon as I entered the room, I rushed to embrace her, and then sat at the foot of the bed and wept. I told her the whole story.

"*Mi pobre niña*, my poor girl," she said. "This is what happens when you put two young people in the same space. When I was a girl, families with sons never hired pretty servants if they wanted to avoid trouble. I remember my sister cutting my eyebrows before I interviewed at your mother's house, and even then . . ." She paused midsentence while her chest heaved. "There's nothing for it, girls and boys always find each other."

"But, Nanny, this is different."

"There's nothing new under the sun, *niña*." She patted my knee with her cold, bony hand. "But don't worry, time cures everything." She closed her eyes, exhausted. She was dying.

Time didn't cure my grief; the only thing time did was teach me to encapsulate it. I dug my heels into the company, working day and night with feverish intent. I was the first one in the office in the morning and the last one to leave at night. I followed my father into offices, business lunches, exhibition fairs, quarries and construction sites like a general marching into battle. I sat for hours with accountants and lawyers. I learned by heart the specs and technical details of all construction and recycling machinery, mining equipment, tower cranes, dumpers, pumps, concrete molders, scaffolding, mast climbing platforms, and any other piece of useful articulated metal that came my way. I impressed people when I stood up in meetings and recited information on equipment in two languages to back up Father's business and marketing plans. I became some sort of a phenomenon in the industry, a living database of information that fascinated clients and manufacturers alike. I walked into construction sites wearing a hard hat with the same ease with which I swept into lavish drawing rooms or corporate parties dressed to the nines. I flirted my way around in this male-rooted landscape, exercising the same manipulative seduction on the humblest worker as on the most stuck-up millionaire CEO. And Father sported me proudly among throngs of tough, shrewd businessmen with poker faces and thin, cynical smiles. We became known as an invincible team. The handsome, ruthless Mr. Hurt, and his beautiful, brilliant daughter. No government contract escaped us, no private enterprise commission resisted our snare. It was like we were king and queen of the industry for those years. Everyone was in awe.

In my downtime I locked myself inside the house. I sat by the fireplace in the library and wolfed down lines of books. Novels, history, poetry, architecture, science, anything I found on the shelves I read compulsively to the point of indigestion. On occasion I would date men, even go out with one for a few months, but nobody captured my attention for long, no one felt worth getting involved with. Sometimes, exhausted and full of ennui after a long day, I would lounge in the old leather armchair facing the fire and watch the flames devour the wood, transforming and reshaping the pile into battlefields, towering infernos, mysterious cities and barren, incandescent landscapes. Then Marcus's eyes and lips would float above the glowing cinders, pulling the old wound out of the recesses of my heart, and I would go to bed aching with failure and wretchedness.

A whiff of smoke hits my nostrils and travels down my throat. Something is burning close by. My first reaction is to go down to the study, where Delia and Constantine are still locked in.

CHAPTER 15

I put my ear to the door and hear the handbell.

Delia is humming another strange song: "*Eleguá, Santo bonito / Eleguá, Caballo negro / Caballo negro, bandera colorá / Ay Mayumbao, Ay Mayumbao.*" (Eleguá, beautiful saint / Eleguá, black horse / Black horse, red banner / Oh, Mayumbao, Oh, Mayumbao.) Meanwhile, Constantine is sweeping, swooshing the coconut around the wooden floor. The smell of burned sage is lingering around the door; they're probably parading the smoldering bowl around. But the whiff I got earlier is different, like a smell of burning fabric or old paper.

Upstairs, the door to Marion's room is ajar. I push it open and a cloud of smoke hits my face. After a few seconds, I make out Marion at the far end. She is standing close to the open window, and on top of the desk by her side stands an oversized ceramic bowl where flames dance surrounded by thick smoke. Marion is throwing papers and small objects into it. Letters, postcards, bullring memorabilia. She has brought down the collection of posters and pictures plastered on the walls for so many years. They lie piled upon each other on the bed, and on top of it all the black Andalusian wide-brimmed hat she used to wear when going out with Fernando.

"What are you doing?"

Marion's eyes are intent on the flames. "I'm getting rid of all this clutter. Useless memories."

"If you want to burn stuff, why don't you do it in the fireplace?" The smoke makes me cough.

"The library and living room are off-limits now, don't you know? Until they finish the *limpieza*." She turns to me with feverish eyes, and I know she might go haywire any moment. "And why would you give a damn where I burn this?"

"Look what you're doing to the room!"

Swirls of smoke reach upward, blackening the ceiling above the bowl.

"The house is gone anyhow." Marion returns to her pyre. "And this is my room, so get the hell out!"

"If anything catches fire, we have no water to put it out with!" I'm beginning to feel frantic, but Marion doesn't pay any attention, she just keeps feeding the bonfire.

I look around for a blanket or any other piece of thick fabric, as the only other plausible means to put out a fire with. But the room just stares back at me, threadbare and desolate. The once bright delicate flowers scattered over the blue-green wallpaper are now faded. The long curtains, torn to shreds. The rosewood sleigh bed has no bedding, an old dusty sheet just covers the mattress. I take a step toward the wardrobe, but Marion rushes ahead of me and grabs the door handle. "Don't you dare!"

I freeze while she opens the wardrobe and yanks out a black-and-red piece of fabric. She takes it to the pyre, and I recognize the *mantón de Manila*, the embroidered shawl with long tassels Fernando had gifted her the day before the party. She throws it into the bowl, but it is too large to fit in completely and most of it dangles down to the floor. It catches fire quickly, producing thick coils of smoke together with the smell of toasted naphthalene. The flames travel down to the tassels.

"Are you nuts? You're going to start a fire!"

"Get out of my room!" she says, picking up the loose ends of the shawl with her bare hands and folding them over the bowl.

I rush downstairs, reach the study and knock hard on the door. "Delia, please, I need you." There is a moment of silence.

"You know, you can't really disturb us when we're doing the work." Constantine is whispering through the door. He looks at me with his strabismic eye through the slit between the panels.

"It's an emergency," I say, stepping back from the image of his skewed eye.

He sighs as if my request was a heavy load to consider. But Delia says from the far end of the room, "It's fine, Constant, we're done here."

"True, but you know I like to pick up my things in order—"

"Open the door," Delia commands.

The door opens and Delia walks out of the darkness, leaning on her staff.

"Make me some coffee, dear. As strong as you possibly can," she says as she trudges past me.

"The thing is . . ."

"I know what the thing is. Just get the coffee."

I turn toward the kitchen while she starts on the stairs, one step at a time, heaving herself up while holding the banister with her free hand, until Constantine comes to her aid.

"The order of the elements has been reversed," I hear her muttering under her breath. "I was expecting earth to follow, not fire."

"Won't that quicken results?" Constantine asks in a hushed tone. I can't believe I can hear their whispered conversation as if I were in between them, although I'm more than twenty feet away.

"It could. But now we need to watch out." They reach the top of the stairs and turn to Marion's room.

My mind is reeling for reasons I don't quite grasp, as if my brain were fogged and spinning away from rational thought. I reach the kitchen that reeks of burned paraffin from the zillions of candles that are nearly all out by now. I realize that the coffeepot is still full with cold coffee, so I pour it into a large mug and put it in the microwave. I am burning to go upstairs and find out what's going on. I stir more than plenty of sugar into the coffee and make for Marion's room.

Julia joins me outside the door. "What's going on?"

"I think Marion is going into one of her fits."

"Oh shit."

I push the door open and we walk in. Delia and Constantine stand around the pyre side by side with Marion. Constantine shakes one of the maracas I have seen earlier on the altar in the kitchen. It makes a rattling cascading sound that repeats itself endlessly into a loop. Delia prays, "*Santa Bárbara bendita, Santa Bárbara bendita.* Blessed Saint Barbara, Blessed Saint Barbara." She has a necklace of red and white beads in the hand that holds the staff, now tilted toward the pyre. Now and then, she turns to Marion and says, "Don't stop, keep feeding the fire! Changó is fire, Changó is thunder, Changó is lightning! If you feed him now, he won't be hungry later."

Marion approaches the fire with a large photograph in which she is standing with Fernando dressed in glittering matador costume, and feeds it to the flames. Her eyes light up with a sort of madness.

"What the hell?" Julia turns to me. "This is insane. Is she leading her on to burn down the whole place?"

I look at Julia as she turns her face back toward the scene inside the room and feel surprised at her detachment. I don't want to say to her, *You started all this, why do you complain now?* We are well past the moment for reproaches. Instead, I reflect on how strange it is that Julia seems to be all of a sudden totally uninvolved in the process, while Marion and I seem more invested every minute. Right now, I know exactly what Delia is doing. She's pushing Marion in the direction she thinks she wants to go, knowing that there is nobody like her to do exactly the opposite of what she's told.

Julia shakes her head. "This is ridiculous! I think I'm going to split. I don't see the point anymore."

"Hell no, you don't split! You're staying until it's all done, even if it's to help sweep up the rubble."

Julia leans closer and whispers, "I don't mean leaving for good. I just want to take my pictures home. It'll only take a couple of hours."

"No you don't! No one leaves until it's over!"

"Sorry, but you don't tell me what to do!"

We glare at each other for a moment. "If you leave now, I will never trust you again," I say, and from the corner of my eye I see Delia looking at us with a disapproving eye. Then she shakes her handbell in our direction.

Meanwhile, Constantine is carefully stomping out a few burning pieces of paper that have fallen on the floor.

Delia turns to him and coos, "Gentle, be gentle with Changó." Constantine slows down.

Marion watches as the photo burns, first opening a brown hole in the middle and then devouring the entire image up to the edges. Soft, flaky sepia cinders float up to the ceiling. Marion turns around and, picking up the black wide-brimmed hat from the bed, places it on the pyre. I think it's going to flare up, but in fact it seems to stifle the flames underneath. Smoke puffs around the brim and wafts out the window.

"What else will you burn for Santa Bárbara?" Delia asks Marion, and puts the bead necklace around her neck. "May Changó bless you for bringing on the sacred embers."

"That's all. I'm good for now." Marion sits on the bed looking haggard, and stares out the window.

"*Ay, Changó, Changó, dios del fuego y la danza.* Oh, Changó, Changó, god of fire and dance," Delia sings and shakes her hand-bell. Constantine answers with his maraca.

"All right, let's have that coffee," Delia says after a beat, sitting down on the only chair left in the room. "Marion, tell me about this handsome man."

"There's nothing to tell. He's been dead for so long."

Just as I'm going to take the coffee mug over to Delia, I hear a door slam on the opposite side of the corridor. It's the door to Father's bedroom, which always bangs when the wind blasts through the hallway from the opposite window. Why is there wind now? Last time I looked out, the thick haze of midday swelter had lifted from the garden, and the afternoon promised to slide into a blushing basin of quiet.

"Here, I'll take that cup if you go close it," Julia says, and takes the mug I've been holding in my hand long enough to make the coffee stone cold.

I walk to Father's room, and I'm about to secure the door when

I figure I should also close the window, and step inside. The window's old frame looks lopsided and distended; it takes pulling and pushing in hard to lock it down. Another strong gust will break it loose again. I turn around and look at the stripped bed surrounded by white walls. It faces the mountains through the window I just closed, a stark eye staring out into the world with no curtains, no drapes. I am always surprised at the sober atmosphere of his room. This used to be my parents' bedroom before Mother died, and no doubt very different then to what it is now, possibly a warm, soft haven for the end of each day. But I have no recollection of that time. I have only known this bedroom as it is now, spartan. Funny how of all the lavish, ornate furnishings of other rooms in the house, this one, the master bedroom, is bare, austere to the point of harshness. No one has talked about this room today. How come the study is considered a much more difficult place than his bedroom? One would think that the space in which a person sleeps and dreams, or lies awake tossing and turning all night for years on end, would be far more charged than a place where one just works and conducts business. But no controversy has arisen on the subject of cleansing this bedroom. I guess Delia and Constantine have already whisked through it, swept it and sanitized it with their magical trappings. Without a word.

The bed is a simple wooden frame. Above it hangs the only picture in the room, a coarse oil painting of a country boy leading a horse in a field. The horse is a bay draught horse with thick white-stockinged legs, and the boy walks barefoot with trousers rolled up to his knees. They walk together into a dim sunset, careless and tired, after a long day of plowing.

Right now there are no furnishings other than the bed, no bedside table, no small bookcases, not even a chair. Someone must have removed them all. But no one has touched the contents of the wardrobe that runs sideways to the bed. Inside still hang his suits, his ties; on the floor still stand his shoes. I fear to open it and look at these things. The white walls around me create a strange silence, a sense of chill. Father didn't die on this bed, but somehow, when I look at the bare mattress, I imagine the silhouette of his body lying very still with hands crossed over his chest and head slightly tilted toward the ceiling, like the stone statue of a knight carved over an ancient tomb. Despite his fierce personality, or maybe because of it, some people saw Father as something like a knight.

I remember when we arrived at the large halls of the mortuary and located the parlor where the wake was being held, how surprised we were to be assailed by a multitude of faces, many of them unfamiliar, who talked about Father's generosity. How he had given them money during hard times, or visited them while sick, or protected them in the face of bullying landlords and corrupt officials. Some were old employees, others older members of the Madrid British circle, and others just neighbors and distant acquaintances, like a niece of Nanny's who told us he had sent money for monthly and medical expenses for years until she passed. The small community that gathered around his open casket knew him as the man who could scream and humiliate, chastise and bully, but also soothe and protect. But we, his daughters, only knew him as a man to be feared and avoided, as a man we chose to punish in the end through purposeful neglect. I remember stepping away from the wake, and pacing the long marbled corridors outside while remorse bit into my guts, overriding my grief. Surely of the three of us, I had been the hardest on him.

I had been the hardest because I had been the closest. And for the longest time. Not only that. I had been the daughter he most loved. My desertion and my sustained resentment became the cruelest punishment he ever received. Neither of us ever talked about it as we sat in awkward silence on my rare, brief visits to the house years after I had left, and we drank tea looking at the near empty fireplace or at the dimming evening light outside the windows. The man I had been in awe of, the man who had shown me the world, was now reduced to my personal prisoner under house arrest, and I could visit him at will or let him rot for months. On those occasions where I condescended to go, I was cold, dismissive, bored. But the rancid pain for all we had shared during the years we had worked and lived together surrounded us like a fog.

Back then, there had been a world full of splendor that only he and I inhabited, that not even Marcus had been able to permeate.

I remember smiling to him over the table, above wineglasses and conversations of clients or business acquaintances, locking eyes with him in that familiar space only the two of us shared. A space lush with images, witty words, and treasured sounds. I remember tongue-tied moments when we reveled in music as we drove home from a meeting, from the airport, or through beautiful country roads in the French Riviera. Brahms's Violin Concerto in D Major, Haydn's piano sonatas, Satie's Gnossiennes. I remember looking for him at cocktail parties, combing crowds until I spotted him, and then admiring him from afar, so handsome in his spotless black tail suit, as he stood with others, sipped champagne, or spoke to older, beautiful women. Not everything was his possession of me. Or his seduction. I was in the game too.

So when did I turn on him? What made me decide to strangle our precious bond? All I can say is that anything beyond the number two is a difficult love proposition. Choices need to be made to trim it down to something manageable, however imperfect. And love, even as it glorifies us and makes us shimmer with radiance, can also bring out the darkest parts of the self.

"Guess who's back in town," Father said one Sunday morning at the breakfast table. He sat drinking tea behind his newspaper. "Marcus Holsbeiter. He's been posted back in Madrid by a new German firm that sells steel windmills and all that new environmental nonsense."

My heart punched at my rib cage with a zest I hadn't felt in seven years. "Environmental nonsense? That's the future!"

"All right. You can tell him that. He's proposing we market them together." Then he added after a beat, "I've invited them to lunch."

"Them?"

"Him, and his wife. Tuesday at Horcher, one thirty p.m."

My head reeled as I left the table. His wife! My newly found joy fell flat on its face. I spent the day in turmoil. I considered canceling the engagement. However, on Tuesday morning I got up determined to sail through the lunch. Despite everything, the prospect of seeing Marcus again filled me with a brutal thrill. I dressed up in a sexy plum-colored suit and expensive snakeskin pumps. I dabbed my lips with an aubergine-colored lipstick that went well with my short black hair.

Horcher is one of those ridiculously priced, *ancien régime* style restaurants that, for some reason I had never understood, was considered the best dining establishment in Madrid. It was proud to have maintained until recently the tradition of dressing their personnel in elaborate red lackey uniforms and having them ceremoniously place special cushions under customers' feet before serving the table, a practice I considered nauseating and always refused. But it was classical in the high business community to close important deals there, so I was one of their regular customers.

I arrived fashionably late, and as I was being led to the table by the benevolent maître d' with the long gray sideburns, I saw Marcus and Father stand up from their chairs to greet me. The moment I met Marcus's eyes I felt my guts would fall out of my body. My heart thumped out of control up through my throat. I made a beeline for him with the intention of embracing him, but he just offered his hand and a cool cheek to kiss politely, as was the custom in Spain. Even as I pecked him, I felt that odor of his, that musk mixed with mud, envelop me like a cloud, invigorating me like an elixir that brings life back to a benumbed patient.

"Hello, Anna." His words hung in the air while I fought to harness my exhilaration. He looked healthy and strong, handsome as ever.

"Hello, Anna," a singsong voice echoed. Marcus stepped to the side and a blond woman with translucent skin, almost like an albino, offered a small beautiful hand that rested on mine like a fairy's. We were introduced: Helga, Anna.

"I am so glad to finally meet you," she said. "You're quite famous in German business circles." She was dressed in drapes of ivory and soft pastels that gave her aura a dazzling white sheen, hard to pierce with the eyes.

"Really?" I tried not to sound acid.

"The most talented woman in the industry, they say."

We settled at the table and I studied the menu I already knew by heart. I was about to say something mean against businessmen and their nicknaming of female colleagues, but when I lifted my eyes and saw the expression on Helga's face, so loving, so lacking in malice, my whole façade crumbled. I knew I would never be able to hate her.

A casual business conversation was started on the subject of turbines and how they might be introduced in the market. We talked for a while about a possible collaboration while I studied Helga from the corner of my eye. Everything about her was pallid, her thin, shoulder-length blond hair, her very white skin and dreamy blue eyes, the pearly hue of her arms. Her beauty didn't just come from her pretty features, but from a sense of frailty. She was delicate, refined. There was a vulnerability in the openness of her gaze, in the sweet curl of her lips, that made her immediately endearing.

"Anna, you're barely touching your food," Father said, packing in his course of venison carpaccio with grain mustard and spicy figs. "Would you like to order something different?"

I abandoned my fork over the mound of endives and cranberry salad. "I'm on a diet."

"With your great figure? I still haven't been able to throw off the extra weight after the second baby."

The sound in the room ceased. I looked around dazed. I could see lips moving without emitting any noise. Mute figures of waiters came and went. A queasy feeling crept into my stomach and I thought I was going to retch. I lifted the serviette to my lips and excused myself.

That night I rang Julia's doorbell at three a.m. She opened the door, annoyed, her red jumbled bed-hair spiked around her head.

"Please. I need to spend the night here."

"You mean what's left of the night."

We went straight to her bedroom, a messy mixture between a painter's studio and a monk's cell, and lay on her narrow bed together. My body was rigid; I couldn't even cry as I told her about the lunch.

"The strangest thing is how different we are. We have nothing in common. I don't understand how he chose a woman so unlike me."

I guess the pain came from all the times I had searched for Marcus in other men, waiting to find the same tenderness in another lover's glance, even the shapes of his arms, the lines of his hip bones running down another male belly. What a wasteland strewn with boyfriends and lovers I'd left behind in this useless quest.

Julia hugged me. "I thought you were over him. It's been so long."

"I don't understand it either. It's as if he'd never gone away."

"Can't believe the bastard had the nerve to come settle back in Madrid as if nothing'd happened." Julia yawned. "And call Father to make a deal. It's fucking sick in the head. Like he returned to continue their little game, another carnival shooting-round to win the girl neither of them can have. Makes me want to barf."

"Julia, I don't think I can travel with him to get this contract."

"Don't you dare go anywhere with him!" And she dozed off.

The following week, Marcus and I set off to Düsseldorf to negotiate a contract with the German firm. We arrived at the plush offices of Nordemex at Friedrichtrasse in the center of Düsseldorf, and sat around a large glass rectangular table in tall black chairs. There were eight attendees, between company executives and board members, and only one other woman besides myself, sitting at the far end and taking notes on her computer. I was by far the youngest person in the room. I was introduced as co-owner of Maquinaria Británica en España. Cold eyes stared at me as I started a PowerPoint presentation of marketing specs of windmills and steel turbines for the Spanish market, as well as distribution strategies that our company could implement. I spoke in English and Marcus translated into German. The Q & A lasted a couple of hours, by the end of which I was exhausted, but happy to realize I hadn't left one query unanswered. A boring but necessary lunch in an elegant restaurant down the street sealed the deal. They agreed to sign a marketing contract, granting all of my terms.

Marcus took me to the hotel we were staying at overnight and then left, saying he had to visit family and we would meet again at six a.m. in the lobby before going to the airport. I went up to my room, took a bath, and lay on the large bed for a nap. When I woke up it was already dark. I went down to the bar and ordered a glass of red wine. I sat in the sleek leather chairs surrounded by subdued reddish lights. Gray-clad waiters milled around small groups of patrons engaged in hushed conversion.

It was eleven p.m., well past bedtime for a sleepy German city like Düsseldorf, when I went up to room 207 and knocked on the door. It took a few seconds to open. Marcus stood in loose tartan pajama pants and a white T-shirt, his iPad in his hand. Behind him floated the sweet, sad notes of Keith Jarrett's *Köln Concert*.

"Everything okay?"

I stood in the somber corridor, looking in at his figure against the warm glow of bedside lamps. An old scene flashed in my mind like déjà vu. I, behind dark file cabinets, and he, in the yellow pool of streetlight with that tatty, beautiful paperback in his hands. Ten years had passed since that moment where our shadows mingled for the first time. Back then I had fancied him as the young, wild falcon I was going to tame. But now I no longer knew who the falcon was, and who the falconer. Where I stood at the threshold of his room in the dim corridor of a commonplace expensive hotel, I had nothing to offer, I no longer owned a shadow. I was just a beggar with empty hands defiled by vexation and long years of sorrow.

Marcus shifted his weight. I looked at his bare, clean feet on the carpet. He searched my eyes, waiting for an answer. Blood pulsed thick in my veins, gushed down my belly, trickling down into my knees, my legs, into my feet swollen after hours of wearing stylish corporate pumps. I knew that if I stood here for a few more seconds he might say, *Come in.* He too was pounding. I could feel it in my gut. Even the sweet little ghosts of his children playing in corners behind him could not shake the momentum that was rolling toward the impending ridge.

"I . . ."

An elevator door dinged at the end of the corridor. Marcus and I stared as an old venerable couple stepped out and shuffled their way down the hall. We looked at each other again, but something had switched. A small sober voice whispered in my ear, asking if I knew what I hoped to gain by crossing this doorway, and what brutal piece of machinery I planned to cut my losses with when the moment of reckoning came. Its cool, tinkling sound, like the elevator ding, poured over me like a jug of water. Was I looking for a one-night stand, or was I conniving to become the mistress of a married man? The mistress of *my* man.

And then I knew that if I stepped into the room, if I as much as looked into his eyes, embraced his body, felt the pulse of blood along his loins and arms, clambered up toward that soft, thick cloud from which we always listened to our billowing breath below . . . If I were to plunge into this right now, with me struggling to pace my desire, a famished demon, fast and reckless to reveal my flaked-out mind . . . To do all this, and he not be mine, I think I would go mad.

I turned to leave. "All's good. See you tomorrow."

"Sure."

Marcus took a while to close his door. Once in my room, I fell into my bed, crushed.

Next morning at the airport I sat across from Marcus in an uncomfortable plastic chair and stared at him. He looked so rested, a man contented with his lot in life. I'd hardly slept. I hadn't touched any food since the corporate lunch. My eyes smarted from insomnia, the dryness of my lips extended into my throat and lungs.

He lifted his gaze from his laptop and grinned. "Congrats again for yesterday's meeting. Your pitch exceeded all expectations. Those guys are the toughest sell."

I jumped up. "Marcus, do you think I give a shit about any of this?" I threw my posh leather briefcase at him. People around us turned their heads and stared. I stomped off down the terminal hall toward the bathroom signs. There was a long line at the women's room and I stood slurping my runny nose and tears into the back of my throat.

"Are you all right, dear?" said an overweight, blond woman standing behind me.

"Just my allergies," I said in my atrocious German.

"Aren't they awful? I used to have them too."

I left her in mid-sentence as I dashed into the next empty stall. I stifled my sobbing while flushing the toilet a number of times. I leaned my head against the door's cool metal surface as thick tears seared my cheeks. What had I been hoarding all these seven years besides this festering longing? What did I care about contracts or money, expensive clothes, ridiculous cars, or stupid business trips if I didn't have Marcus? What was the meaning of gaining the whole world if I couldn't sleep curled around his back, listening to his deep, soft breathing all night long? I would gladly take on a job cleaning public bathrooms, if I could just go back to a dingy little room with him at the end of each day.

I arrived very late at the gate where Marcus had been patiently waiting with my briefcase, in case he needed to miss the plane too. We didn't speak as he walked behind me down the jet bridge into the aircraft. Neither did he look into my eyes when we sat and fumbled with our safety belts, not that he would have recognized the deep red holes I hid behind the dark sunglasses. I made to sleep leaning against the small oval window the whole flight.

When I reached the house, I took two sleeping pills before crashing on my bed, although it was only one in the afternoon.

"Miss, Mr. Marcus on the phone," Lolita, our new maid, said from the door.

I squinted against the sunlight bursting in through the window. It must have been after ten a.m. the next day. I made to move, but my body wouldn't respond. I had no muscle power. My limbs were dead.

"Tell him I'll call back later." I buried my tear-pooled eyes in my pillow. "Please, draw down the blind before you leave." I stayed in the same position for the rest of the day, motionless save for my eyes, which flooded rivers into the bed linen.

In the late afternoon, Father returned home, and seeing me in this state called Doctor Martinez. He must have been the last doctor doing house calls in the whole of Madrid. After taking my pulse and pressing the stethoscope on my chest and back, the old, sallow-faced doctor sat in the armchair facing my bed and sighed.

"Are your cycles regular?" he asked in a tired voice. I nodded yes.

"Has there been an accident, a piece of bad news?"

I opened my mouth to say no but my treacherous eyes burst once more into a torrent.

He sat for a moment, opened his briefcase, took out a prescription pad and wrote a few fast words. Then he called Lolita, who was only a few feet away listening behind the door. "Take this to the pharmacy immediately."

He shot me a sad, benevolent look before leaving.

Lolita returned promptly with a small box of pink pills and a glass of water, and gave me two to swallow. Before she turned to go, she gave me a coy look and said, "Miss, I didn't want to say in front of the doctor, but I think you could have some heart problem. My brother had angina and he also lay in bed collapsed."

"Thank you, Lolita. I need to sleep now," I said, turning toward the wall, and she stepped out quietly.

The smart little bitch! How accurate her perception, or how astute her spying. Wasn't this the final stage of my broken heart? Wasn't that fist-like, muscle-clustered organ inside my rib cage disintegrating? Had it not become a slab of flabby meat coated in the nauseating, iridescent foil of decay? And why would I have a need for a heart anymore if it wasn't to beat for Marcus? I reached over to the bedside table for the medication box and extracted the information pamphlet. The section on clinical pharmacology read: *Exerts anxiolytic, sedative, muscle-relaxant, anticonvulsant and amnestic effects. Covers a variety of symptoms arising from conditions of spring depression and vital sadness.* I read again, *vital sadness.* Yes, I wasn't hallucinating, it actually said, *tristeza vital.* I threw the box of pink pills across the floor.

It took over three weeks for the medication to kick in and for me to sober up. Doctor Martinez returned a good number of times and I heard him speak with Father down in the hall about long-term exhaustion and a nervous breakdown. Father refused his suggestion to check me into a clinic.

Julia visited and brought me chocolates, books, and a set of watercolors and paper. Marion, who had just returned from London, sat by the bed holding my hand, and said, in her beautiful, marble-tongued English, "Anna, just hold on, you'll be just fine." She sounded like Aunt Kay.

But I didn't want visitors, gifts, kind words, or phone calls. I just lay on the bed stunned, staring up at the ceiling for hours, observing how the pink pills rearranged the landscape of my storm, how day by day they pulled together the different fragments of my pained confusion, and arranged them carefully, thoughtfully, meticulously, like the fitted pieces on a Rubik's Cube. And how hard they worked at blunting the raw, exposed stems of my nerve endings! Marcus, Helga, their beautiful babies, the cozy kitchen smelling of warm bread, the adorable pastel nursery, their snug family bed, all floated away into remote vignettes of silly, ingenuous fantasy. Finally, I was won over by the proficiency of these small pink industrious agents of benumbed, empty bliss.

And behind their shield I started planning my revenge.

The evening I had decided to go back to work, I was still hanging out in bed when Father knocked on the door and came into the room.

"How are you feeling, Anna?" He had been quiet all these weeks, checking in all the time to see if I needed anything. He walked to the window and stood there looking out into the sunset with hands clasped behind his back. A long swath of rusty orange tinged with crimson laced around the darkened, distant mountaintops. He turned and walked toward me, stopping at the bedside table. I watched his hands as they picked up the small pile of books by the lamp: *The Diary of Alice James, A History of the Black Death in Europe, The Poems of John Donne.* He put them down again and sat in the armchair facing the bed. We looked at each other for a moment. My eyes felt hot and drowsy, and his were drawn, shadowed with a strange anguish. He averted his glance.

"I've been thinking, Anna, that you might want to take time off, travel for a while." His fingers fidgeted over the flowery fabric of the armrest. "I feel I might have pushed you too hard all these years. I should have insisted on your going off to college, it's not too late if you still—"

"You didn't tell me he had two children."

Father froze. I slid down farther into the bed and waited.

"I told you he was married, and it follows that if a man marries . . ." He faltered. The last ruby glow of dusk flashed through the windowpane before the air dissolved into cold indigo. Everything turned into inky silhouettes against a darkening sky.

"Still. You didn't tell me."

A few seconds passed. Father pulled himself up in the chair. "We don't have to work with him, if you're not comfortable. I can secure similar equipment . . ."

I switched off the bedside lamp. "I need to sleep now." He left the room.

I had already decided to put myself far away from his reach.

Another gust of wind pushes against the window, rattling it. Invisible streams of air sift through the cracked frame and swirl into the room. The door opens and Julia walks in with her cell phone in her outstretched hand. "It's for you."

"I can't take this call."

Julia pushes the phone into my hand. "Deal with your shit like everyone else. And ask him not to call my phone again."

I walk out of the room and down the stairs. "Hello."

"Can we talk for a minute?" Marcus's tone startles me. It sounds close, intimate.

"Please, don't insist. I can do nothing today. Can't you contact someone else?"

There is a silence. Marcus is waiting. Waiting for me to turn it all around in an instant and whip out a brilliant solution. His silence exasperates me, like a mute metronome browbeating me into action. All of a sudden, the fact that I've never turned down any of his urgent requests shames me. I'm always there for him, bending over backwards in ways I wouldn't even dream of for my own business deals. Like a good old doormat, happy to be gratified by the mere weight of his feet on the unshorn surface of my undying allegiance.

"Listen," I say. "I always back you up. I can't continue to function this way. I'm rethinking our teamwork. I'm not sure it's working for me anymore. I want out."

The stillness at the other end of the phone intensifies for a beat. Then Marcus says, "All right. Let's pretend I accept what you're saying. Let's pretend we don't work together anymore. Still, I think we need to have a conversation about what's been hanging over us for a while."

"I don't think we need to have any conversation at all." I'm try-ing hard not to raise my voice. "I think it's time we accepted that this"—I falter for a second, my mouth is dry and the fog in my brain is whirling—"that this—whatever it is we're doing—isn't working. Particularly for me."

"Particularly for you?"

"Yes, for me, Marcus. I think you understand who's the weakest party here when it comes to—"

"You, the weakest party?" I am detecting traces of indignation in his tone, and I'm fuming, fuming like I haven't for years, but my voice, instead of delivering my words like a deft knife, begins to break up as I say, "Like you don't know how I've cornered myself into this charade." What am I doing? How long is it since I've al-lowed myself to assail Marcus with emotional language?

Another moment of silence. "Are you okay?"

"I'm totally fine. It's just that"—I'm beginning to stammer, I'm beginning to shake—"I'm realizing how many years of my life I've poured down the drain." But I can't say anymore. My temples throb, my chest aches.

"I could probably say something very similar," he starts, but I cut him off in a breathless rush. "Please! I'm not listening to any of this. I just want you out of my life for once and for all, all right?"

"Okay, Anna. I'm boarding a plane to Madrid as we speak. The moment I arrive, I'll drive right over there, 'cause it might be over, but we're still going to talk."

"You won't dare! Besides, you don't know where I am."

"Yes, I do. I know exactly where you are. And nothing's going to stop me from coming." He clicks his phone shut. I stifle a sob and throw the phone at the wall, where it breaks apart and scatters over the floor.

Julia's face appears around the wall at the top of the stairs. "You won't believe how Delia's handling this," she says, and then sees her phone. "What's your fucking problem? You think everyone can afford a new phone every month like you?"

I raise my hand in her direction to indicate I can't deal with any-thing right now and walk away. I hear her run down the stairs behind me and pick up the pieces. "Stupid crazy bitch! You're just like your father. An arrogant asshole incapable of holding back your rage."

I feel the sting of her words, they lance me right in the lungs, freezing my breath for a few instants. I want to lash back, engage with her as I haven't done since we were girls, but I can't go there. Her assault seems trifling compared to what has just happened. The pain from my exchange with Marcus is still throbbing inside my chest, unabated, and I just can't explain why it's thrown me into such agony.

CHAPTER 16

I walk into the darkness of Father's studio. I push away the piles of books and papers that clutter the sofa and lie on its parched leather surface. Why on earth would I walk in here at a moment like this? But I just did, right into the belly of the beast. I close my eyes and fold my arms over my face, while the strange dead air of the room envelops me and I drift away from the madness upstairs, from Marcus's voice.

How long is it since I've been working with Marcus in the farcical capacity of business partners? Maybe five years? Six? Is it already six years since he returned? I'm always confused about time when it comes to him. But yes, that's more or less when I left Father's company. The time I finally challenged my father, conjured enough cold blood to abandon him, to quit the business and leave the house. The time I moved to downtown Madrid to start my own life over.

At first, Father was furious. "Who would think of moving back into the smog and clatter of downtown? It's a ridiculous idea! Reverting to the old grunge, to the squalid quarters. People lived like rats in those buildings when I first arrived in Madrid." But the part he couldn't stomach was my leaving the company. "Why would you leave something that's yours? Why would you throw away something that has taken me decades to build? You can have it all, the premises, the client portfolio. I'll transfer everything to you."

I ignored his pained, flustered look and ordered another dry martini. A delicious April sun tickled my face as we sat on a terrace café in my new neighborhood, where he had been humbled into visiting. I didn't need any of what he was throwing at me. I already owned the essentials. And much, much more. He had fast-tracked me into a soaring business career and now I was like one of those martial art disciples who has surpassed their teacher and stands strong and invincible in the presence of an aging, once proud and unassailable fighter.

I had made quite a lot of money in the last years, so I bought a large duplex apartment in the same neighborhood where Julia and her artist friends lived. The space belonged to a young architect who had connected two old apartments through a wide, sweeping spiral staircase. On the second floor, the master bedroom stepped onto a terrace, from which sprawled a landscape of terracotta roofs, a maze of tiles in russet, sienna, copper, titian, and any other imaginable shade of red and brown. The flat skyline of the old Madrid extended infinitely toward the south under clear blue skies. A puzzle of architecture condensed by history. No mountains in view, no plush gardens packed with larks and nightingales. Just narrow cobbled streets and small uneven piazzas populated by famished sparrows, under a canopy of ceramic crisscross patterns sprinkled with church steeples. It was like moving into a different country.

The neighborhood had been one of the old popular enclaves of downtown Madrid where artists like Julia and her friends had moved to some years ago, but was now being taken over by young professionals, gays, and hip groups looking to reinvent the ancient quarters of the city. There was still a contingent of modest dark-clad senior citizens coexisting with the buoyant newcomers. Small boutiques were sprouting all over out of the tiny, seedy shops that were once grocery stores or five-and-dime dens. Old bars and *tascas*, some of them over a hundred years old, filled up on the weekends with beautiful, rowdy, young people. The same went for streets in the spring and summertime months, when carousers stayed up late drinking and chatting in outdoor cafés. The gay movement had taken hold in these streets and their annual parade was beginning to attract followers from all over Europe and the rest of the world.

It was a fun place for me to live in. In the evenings after work I'd hang out with Julia and her friends at the outdoor cafés in the Plaza de Chueca, a small, irregular-shaped square that was the focal point of the whole neighborhood. We would chat and drink *cañas*, or small glasses of beer, basking in the lazy mood of the long summer evenings, watching the pink twilight glide above the plaza's earthen roofs, over the white façades with ornate balconies, while swallows darted overhead calling frantically at each other. Later, when deepening shades of blue encroached around the small square, and illumined windows popped up in shops and overhead apartments against the indigo air, the plaza would still be swarming with its picturesque population. Pale, gothic-clad youths, loud troops of swank transvestites, and old neighborhood women dipping croissants in their coffees while engrossed in malicious gossip.

It had been a long while since I had felt lighthearted and upbeat again. What better moment to start anew, to put away the past?

But I wasn't done with the object of my affection.

I got hold of Marcus on the phone. "I'm leaving MBE and starting my own company. I hope we can modify the contract to include this change. I'll take up any extra legal expenses." We had finally negotiated a contract with the German company Nordemex for the distribution of their wind turbines in the Spanish market, and I had decided to take it away from Father's company and represent the merchandise myself with Marcus as a business associate.

I paced around my new empty living room as we talked, sliding across the white marble floor speckled with gray. Tall windows with wrought-iron balconies looked at other windows with balconies across the narrow street. Net curtains were in order here. And the beautiful French-style fireplace with ornate scrolls and leaf carvings at the end of the room would not be used as such, it would just remain as a prop.

"Anna, the guys at Nordemex don't care how you organize it. They want to work with you, not with MBE," Marcus replied. For a moment, I wanted to laugh. It all sounded like a game, he and I talking serious business.

Marcus added, "But are you sure you want to do this? I mean, on the trip to Düsseldorf—"

I didn't let him finish his sentence. "I think we're both adults and we can do this. In fact, I'm sure we'll be great partners," I said. "I'll fax you the new contract tomorrow so you can review it before I send it over to Nordemex." I hung up the phone. Yes, this was the tone. And this was the game. We would be adult children playing business instead of house.

Father was dismissive. He couldn't accept that his pride was under the doormat. "It's not going to work with the Germans, you know. They're very self-serving as I've found out through the years. One always has to be on the watch-out with them." He didn't dare mention Marcus. He knew I would have just gotten up and left.

Despite his predictions, the association with the Germans worked. And the affiliation with Marcus proved to be a great success. We became good business partners, developed substantial projects together, got amazing contracts, made money. Strange how effortless, how easily we moved through this dense, insidious world of heavy machinery. Sometimes it felt like a dance. We didn't really need each other at all. I could work alone, or for anyone I chose to and represent anything I wanted, my reputation was so established all over. He could keep pumping German machinery into the Spanish market, where the demand was unwavering. But we stuck together. Sometimes we split commissions at a loss, other times we failed to secure deals because of our joint venture, but the projects and contracts kept coming our way. We each worked out of our own space and although we only lived thirty minutes away, we didn't see each other for weeks or months at a time. Most of our communication was done through telephone, fax, and later email, messengers, deliveries, and whatnot. But most days I got to hear his voice on the phone, that husky, intimate sound in perfect English tinged with the slightest trace of German inflection. That was my daily dose of paradise.

"You're soooo fucked up!" Julia stared at me through narrow drunken eyes across the low glass table. We were sprawled on facing sofas in my huge, elegant living room. "You could have anyone you want, you could create whatever life you wished for yourself, and you're still holding on to this son of a bitch like there's no tomorrow."

I wanted to say, "Look who's talking," but decided to let it go. I wanted to avoid the old dispute that always arose when we started on our third bottle of wine, while hanging out together late at night. Julia was living with another girlfriend, but still thought of Alina. When confronted, she often said, "At least I'm not having a perverse affair through the retailing of awful machinery," and never ceased to admonish that "It would be much healthier if you had a proper fling. That way you might have a chance of getting him out of your system." But that was precisely what I didn't want. The point was to make sure Marcus stayed in my system. He was already an indelible part of me. I thought of us like those braided trees whose trunks have fused together after years of growth and now are just one single inseparable column.

I refused to listen to Julia over and over again.

But who was I fooling?

Although the business collaboration with Marcus was going strong and we were consistently on friendly terms, not all was well on my front. Soon my old restlessness crept up on me again, taking me to long hours in the gym, keeping me out at night partying and drinking, driving me into bouts of desperate dating. It was when I started going out with men again that I saw how much I had changed. I had become entrenched in loneliness, my heart had surrounded itself with a hard, airtight sheath. I found myself treating boyfriends and lovers with indifference, knowing ahead of time I couldn't love them, using them to buy time toward a stupid, imaginary moment of deliverance that I knew would never come. I felt like a grand harlot when I turned them away after they confessed their affection, or when I wanted them to leave my bed in the middle of the night after they had satisfied my desire. Later, I would lie sleepless for hours, loathing my emptiness. Not all was well.

Then there was Helga.

In the beginning, Helga had made innumerable efforts to befriend me, inviting me to dinners at their place, to birthday parties, to outings with her children. I always gracefully declined. She had whined about it earlier on: "Anna, I would be so happy if we could be friends. I hardly know anyone in Madrid. And I like you so much!" But she had finally accepted our casual, distant relationship, and now on those rare occasions when we happened to meet, she would be her usual discreet, sweet self. My attitude was one of polite deference; I tried to interact with her as little as possible. For a long time I was in denial of the fact that I was as much a part of her life as she was of mine. That there was no escaping our entanglement.

Once in a while we had to entertain visiting German clients who traveled to Madrid for business. They were crazy about flamenco and always wanted to be taken to a *tablao*, an establishment where *cantaores* and *bailaores*, singers and dancers, got together and put on a show. One of their favorite places was the Café de Chinitas, a touristy but well managed restaurant that had flamenco shows. I disliked these outings, but they were a must in the realm of business hospitality. Marcus usually brought Helga along and I would show up escorted by one of my ephemeral boyfriends. This one time, I had enticed Marion to come instead, since she was a flamenco pro and good company to help stave off the pesky client we were entertaining for the evening, a guy by the name of Wolfgang Viehmann, who had a crush on me and kept asking me out each time he came to Madrid.

We sat at our table in the dark, narrow dining room under large windows decorated with elaborate iron lattices that faced the street. Ahead of us stood a small wooden stage, decorated with a tapestry of antique embroidered Manila shawls associated with flamenco dancers' dresses. Underneath the bright-colored birds, roses, and carnations knit into the silk stood a row of simple wooden chairs where the performers sat. They would start by handclapping and singing, until one of the women with hair in a bun and a tight dress layered with ruffles stepped forward onstage and broke into a round of dramatic heel tapping. Then a wiry man with a ponytail and a black tuxedo undershirt would join in and they danced together to singing and guitar playing.

After a heavy supper of grilled suckling pig—where I only ate cheese and salad—we sat sipping wine and listening to the featured singer of the evening, El Niño Candela, as he stood on stage and sang in a broken voice to soft handclapping and emotional strumming of guitars. "*Aaaay, aaaay! El castigo que te mando, es que cuando estés durmiendo con otro, estés soñando conmigo.*"

Wolfgang drew close to me. "Please, translate what he's singing."

I had been distracted and now struggled to listen to the words again. "Your punishment will be," I translated, "that when you're with another you'll be thinking of me—or something like that." It was an old Spanish poem that had been reworked into different genres of songs, although this was the first time I had heard it in flamenco.

Wolfgang turned to Marcus. "*Fantastisch! Ist dass genau*, is this accurate?"

Marcus thought for a beat. "Wouldn't it be more like, when you're sleeping with another, you'll be dreaming of me?"

I considered his choice of words. "Actually, yes, that's more exact."

Marcus raised his cup, and the smile I knew so well danced in his pupils. My heart thumped.

"*Ach so leidenschaftlich!* This is what I find so passionate about you Spaniards," Wolfgang said in his lame English, and gave me an insinuating nudge. I was ready to move into rejection mode with this moron, when I froze. Helga was looking at me across the table. She had also been listening to the translation, and had interrupted her conversation with Marion about Roma Gypsies. Her eyes, always those aquamarine basins of sweetness, were fraught with a harrowing sorrow. I had never thought she could pale any further, her skin was so translucent and white. But her countenance was drained and withered as if an agent of death had passed through her and robbed her of all freshness. We held each other's gaze for a long moment. I looked in dismay at her shrunken light, at her pained acquiescence to the truth she had just understood.

"Where can we go dancing after this?" Wolfgang nudged me again, showering his wine-drunk breath all over my face.

I whipped out my cell phone. "Oh my God! I nearly forgot! I have a teleconference with Chicago in thirty minutes. I'm going to have to run home if I want to make it. I'm sorry to leave like this." I scrambled around for my things before anyone could react, excused myself once more, and ran out of the restaurant into the street.

I was getting into a cab when Marcus walked out with my coat. "Here, you're forgetting this. Do you have to leave? What's the rush?"

"Sorry, this is really important. I need to talk to Fitzgerald about the new wind farm project. And oh, please get that guy off my freaking back. Tell him anything you want."

"It's not my place."

"Yes, it is. 'Cause if you don't, I'm not showing up at the Munich fair." I jumped in the cab and banged the door shut. We whizzed down the street toward my place.

Once in my apartment, I dropped my coat and bag, and sank to the floor. Helga knew everything. She had fathomed the underlying current that was going on between Marcus and me. Why was it that it didn't matter how much we tried, however much we sacrificed, we never succeeded in hiding our affection? Everything we were together ended up written on every gesture, every glance, every song, even across the high vault of the skies. And what about collateral damage and innocent victims? Up to this moment I had felt as the outsider looking in on their idyllic marriage and charming fairy-tale family life. Now the tables had turned. There were others out in the cold looking in, possibly more desperate and hopeless than I. She might be sleeping with him every night, but he was still dreaming of me. I felt her pain rolling her thin across her kitchen floor and living room, nailing her at the extreme corners with sharp, pointed tacks. If it came to choosing between my man sleeping with another woman or dreaming about her, I would doubtless choose the first. In a thousand years. For the mingling of shadows is the hardest thing in the world to disembroil.

But would I really choose to just be dreamed of?

When I open my eyes again the room doesn't seem dark anymore. I get up and walk to the window, tripping over a few books and soft objects lying on the floor. Constantine has done something to the strap, tied a knot and secured it to the sill, so that now it's possible to pull the blind up a bit and get some light streaming in through the chinks. If this much can be obtained, then why not go for all? I hold it with both hands and haul it with all my strength. The heavy blind pulls up and before it threatens to fall again, I drag over one of the auxiliary small tables by the desk, and prop it against the window frame.

I lean out of the window and take in the golden hue of the afternoon. It must be well past six o'clock and the thick haze of the midday swelter has lifted from the garden level but still hangs on the distant mountains like a misty veil. I can see the pool from here, its dark waters swaying with green algae and murky scum from its depths. Then I catch sight of her, standing quietly at the corner, removing her sandals and peeling her burgundy dress off her body, hanging it on one of the nearby bushes, together with her mauve bra and lilac panties. I want to rub my eyes. Marion, naked, lowering herself to sit on the stone edge of the pool, her long black hair covering her big, soft breasts, her pubic bush small and fuzzy among the round thighs and pink hips. She, who has always been so modest, so demure, now stands up again, stark nude, and holding the pool rail with one hand, lowers herself down the steps, slowly, into the water.

Chapter 17

A sudden gust of cool wind slaps me on the face. I look up and see heavy clouds gathering above where minutes ago the sky was a smooth runway, a clear blue airstrip toward an endless firmament. The amber evening light turns down a few notches, transforming into opaque ochre. The garden shudders. Marion swims toward the center of the pool, her hair floating behind, like a wavy, long trail dress. Her slow movements create concentric ripples in the water that extend to all corners. The darkened light encroaches on the pool, deepening the green color of bushes and trees, shading the white stone around it, blackening the waters. But Marion doesn't show any signs of wanting out.

A second gust hits me, and then rushes in through the window, sweeping a bunch of papers off the top of the desk. It may be time to close the window. I step down and take hold of the auxiliary table's legs and pull them away from the window so I can shut it. It seems to be stuck under the weight of the blind. I pull again with both hands, placing a knee on the window frame to lever myself, but there's nothing doing, the table is caught and will not budge. I try to wriggle it from an angle with both hands, and at the third tug, one of the wooden legs breaks off and I stagger backwards, falling on the floor with a loud thud. The glass cabinet beside the desk crashes beside me, the glass door smashes on the floor, its contents clattering all around. A sharp sting cuts through my thigh, and when I sit up and look, I see a gash like a long claw mark that the jagged edge of the wood has left on my flesh. Or is it one of the shards from the glass cabinet? It bleeds.

"Are you all right?" Julia's at the door.

"I fell and scratched my thigh."

She hesitates to come in. There's her fear of the study, as well as the lingering red cloud of our recent fight.

I pull myself up holding on to the desk and walk to the sofa, dragging my leg. Julia scoots in and helps me sit and lift the leg over the coffee table, onto a pile of books. She kneels beside me and looks at my thigh.

"This looks nasty! What did you cut it with?" She's holding the flesh around the gash. It is bleeding more now. I feel her strong, slim hands on my thigh. She doesn't look me in the eye. I know she's chewing on what she said to me minutes ago.

"It's nothing. I just need to wash it off," I say.

"Yeah, like we have clean running water to wash anything off with. If you got hurt with one of the nails, you need to go to hospital for a tetanus shot."

"You're kidding! How would you get tetanus inside an office?"

"You can probably get almost anything inside this office."

I laugh and look around. Even in the dimming evening light the place looks filthy, dust is settled over everything like a mantle, and grime shines in patches on the surface of furniture. And then, all these strange, dark statuettes of carved wood. How did it all get like this?

"I think I've seen some rubbing alcohol around," Julia says.

"You're not serious! You know how much that hurts?"

"Are you going to be a little girl now, whining about a bit of alcohol on a cut? I might be able to find peroxide. But that's the best you can hope for. Otherwise, it's the emergency room."

"Aren't you blowing this out of proportion? It's only a gash," I say.

"It's bleeding all right. I'm going to ask Marion to go to the pharmacy for stuff. You're lucky I just put this in my pocket." She pulls out a small packet of Kleenex and makes a compress with the tissues, pressing it to the gash. "In the meantime, stay put." And she leaves the room.

"I'll come with you," I start to say, but she's already disappeared.

I have an uneasy feeling creeping up on me. It's quiet in the room, in a bizarre sort of way. I wriggle to accommodate my hurt leg by moving it into a different position. The back of my thighs stick uncomfortably to the couch's leather surface. My whole back is sweating. It's hot and heavy in the room. I remove the tissues from my thigh and look at the gash. It's almost stopped bleeding; it doesn't look very deep. A close inspection of the edges convinces me that it wasn't made by the wood but by broken glass. The cut is a clean slice, a thin, wry smile upon my thigh. And the blood is dark, a carmine red, and thick, close-knit, as if reluctant to be shed. Like my tears.

I look toward the fallen cabinet. Pieces of jagged glass lie around among scattered objects, dark pieces of sculpture and small statuettes. My first thought is how upset Father would be in the face of this disaster scene. This glass case had always been his treasure cabinet. It was a tall, slim antique mahogany display cabinet with an inlaid-wood, glass-fronted door standing on Queen Anne cabriole legs. The cabinet itself was a piece of art. It always held his most precious possessions in the way of antique objects and small pieces of sculpture. Every time he traveled he visited art auctions, flea markets, and antique dealers, and always returned with something. Something beautiful or interesting that would fascinate him for months on end, that would be displayed in this cabinet close to his desk, within his range of touch and vision. For a long time, the central piece of the cabinet was the marbled head of a Greek goddess he bought in Sotheby's in one of his trips to New York. The end of the nose and chin were slightly fractured, but the round face and strands of hair pinned around the head were intact. Her beautiful soft features gleamed through the watery reflections beneath the marble surface, and her eyes, smooth and vacant on the outside, smiled inwardly above her parted lips. He also had an ancient Greek kylix, a drinking cup he acquired in Athens from an antiquarian, a black ceramic piece depicting an orangey assembly of gods in a banquet scene on its curved exterior. A fragment of the torso of the satyr Silenius standing on one leg, and a collection of Roman silver coins, were among the other cherished objects kept in the glass case. Those were the years of his craze for Greek and Roman sculpture. He had some books too, a few small, parchment-bound, handwritten medieval treatises on theology and medicine, and an exquisite reproduction of the book of hours of the Duc de Berry, decorated with colorful miniatures and gilded calligraphy. These were the pieces he thought of as his gems, ceremoniously showing them to guests and spending hours talking about their graces.

But at one point all these objects had been removed from the cabinet, and allocated around the house in different places, left to gather dust on bookshelves in corridors, in the library or the living room, on top of the dining room mantelpiece. Dark statuettes and other somber pieces had replaced them behind the glass, all of them coming from his trips to Egypt. A collection of tin-glazed earthenware shabtis, those funerary servant figurines found in tombs, together with green soapstone hieroglyph-inscribed scarabs and a wooden mummy mask, weathered and pockmarked, propped up on a stand, replaced the former items in the glass cabinet. Then other things less defined, like strange pieces of cloth, small scrolls, amulets. At the center of it all, a group of four slender bronze statuettes, all very similar but of different sizes, their elongated heads ending in the tall headdresses of priests and long spade beards. Their slim figures seemed in the act of striding forward, bearing enigmatic gift boxes in their long, thin hands. This was just the glass cabinet, but the room was full of books on the history of Egypt, on the Valley of the Kings and its treasures, and myriad travel books on Cairo, Alexandria, the Egyptian desert, and the Nile. In the last years of his life, Father had become obsessed with Egypt. And because none of us visited him that much by then, it took us a while to recognize how taken he was with anything Egyptian.

Julia walks in quickly with a plastic bottle in her hands and a bag of cotton wool. "You're going to get it from Delia, she's on her way," she says.

"Get it from Delia! Why?"

"You're not supposed to be here. This room was already done."

Julia unscrews the bottle and throws the bag of cotton wool on the table.

"What is this? She's become our governess or something?"

"I tried to tell you before. She's taken over." Julia grabs my leg and pours alcohol freely over it. It washes over the gash, stinging like a burning trail of gunpowder.

I howl. "Oooow! Stop! What are you doing?"

But Julia is undeterred. "Hold still for a moment! You're making me spill it all over." The alcohol is splashing over the coffee table around my leg. I swat Julia's hand and she steps back, bottle in hand.

"Well, at least I got some of it into the gash," she says with satisfaction. "Jeez, you're such a crybaby. For all your brilliant business skills—"

"Shut up! You just wanted to get back at me for the phone," I say, blowing on my thigh to diffuse the alcohol, which I don't dare wipe off with my dirty hands. It still burns like hell.

Julia laughs. "We're even now, plus I've saved you from gangrene."

I try to swat her again from the couch but she jumps back. We're little girls again, and she's teasing me to make me cry. Where is her sad, sullen face of a few hours ago? It's been replaced by that impish, malicious smile Marion and I used to call the red she-devil grin, and beware everyone when it starts dancing on her face. The wicked side of the scrawny girl who used to hide in corners with her pad and colored pencils. She can be up to any amount of mischief. She used to throw all of Marion's undies out the window into the street when they fought. She used to bury my dolls under bushes or thread pages of my favorite picture book into the blender together with my chocolate milk. She could do anything to me this moment. She could sprinkle the rest of the alcohol on my face, or threaten to burn my hair. Only Nanny can save me now.

"Julia, if you dare . . ."

Heavy footsteps interspersed with a cane thudding on the wooden floor approach the study. Lighter, scurrying sounds trailing down the stairs in the background follow.

Delia enters the room. "Who said you could come in here?" She

THE WEIGHT OF THE HEART 205

is thunderous, her face portentous with lifted eyebrows over fierce eyes. "And spilling blood! Didn't I say no one can go into rooms that have been cleansed until the whole house is finished? What *is* wrong with you girls?"

"Where can we go? All the rooms are closed by now." I am amazed at my defensive tone and the fact that I'm actually intimidated by her towering presence.

"I don't care where you go. Get out of the house! Sit outside! Holy Child of Atocha! Am I ever going to be able to finish this job?" Delia is exasperated; she opens her arms as she talks, even lifts the cane off the floor. "And you," she roars at Julia, "go help your sister out of the pond."

"Out of what?" Julia changes her red she-devil grin into her other classical expression of sad-girl-who's-never-hurt-a-fly-in-her-life.

"The pool! Where else?" Delia is fuming.

Constantine scuttles into the room, breathless. "Calm down, Delia! I'll take care of this. Why don't you sit for a minute while I walk her outside?"

"Are you also out of your mind? Don't you see she's cut? Now we need to close the wound before she can move." She stares at Constantine for a moment, takes a deep breath, and then says, in a calmer voice, "What do you have in your medicine bag?"

Constantine studies his sandals. Above them stem his sharp, bony ankles followed by thin, pale, hairy calves. I can't believe he still hasn't rolled down his trousers. "As a matter of fact, Delia," he stammers, "since this wasn't an up-front healing job . . ."

"Constantine!" Delia stomps her cane on the floor. "How many times have we gone through this! You need to bring everything along at all times!"

"Sorry, Delia." He looks on the verge of tears.

Delia flashes angry eyes around the room. First at me, then at Constantine and finally at Julia, who's still at the door listening in, but dashes off under the umbrage of her gaze.

Delia paces around. "What's the saying? *El que se acuesta con niños amanece meado*, if you go to bed with children you'll wake up pissed all over." Delia turns to the window and stands for a moment looking out. Wind is blowing in. It lifts her black hair in undulating waves, it flaps her white dress against her body and then swells it up around her large shape like a sail. Could there be so much wind coming in through the window? Am I just tired and drifting into dreamy visions?

"That's the problem with growing old. Everyone around starts feeling like a child." Delia sounds sad and forlorn. When she turns again toward the room, her anger has vanished.

"Surely, you have something," she says. "Agrimony, prunella, burdock?" Constantine's gaze remains lowered, but from my angle I see his strabismic eye roaming around the room with the monocular focusing of a chameleon's. As if it were doing all the thinking for him.

"No aloe in the garden?" Delia waits, but Constantine is mute. Then, something clicks inside him and he says in a small voice, "I've only seen thistles."

"Blessed thistle? I guess that's what the Orishas want then. And that's also the punishment they are bringing your way for not being on top of your duties."

Constantine lifts one red, mortified eye toward her, while its strabismic partner rolls around the window and finally falls upon my gashed thigh. "Sorry, Delia."

"Don't sorry me. Sorry your fingers as you're picking the blessed thistles. And make sure you come up with a damned good poultice paste." Delia's dark liquid eyes sweep the room like a fierce bird of prey and descend once more on Constantine. "And now, move! We're out of time."

Constantine leaves the room after emitting a small mortified sigh. A blast of wind streams through the window and slams the door behind him.

"Oooh, the South Wind, laughing at me again!" Delia says, turning toward the window. "Laughing at my cranky, mean old age! Always a humbling teacher." The room is quiet now. Outside, the song of the cicadas has died down. A distant rumbling pulsates through the house. I long to get up and walk outside, but I feel trapped. Paralyzed, like a small prey in a den full of invisible predators.

"The storm is approaching. Good, good." Delia turns to the desk, where the cabinet lies in shambles. She stoops over the broken glass. "What do we have here?" She bends over and picks up the fallen pieces one by one, setting them with utmost care on the desk. She stands the bronze gift-bearing figures in line and then steps back to look at them. "Charismatic little messengers, these. I wonder what they carry in their boxes," she muses.

She stands across from me, leaning with both hands on her cane. "Your father was an interesting man, wasn't he? Tell me about him."

"He loved art."

"He did, did he? More than he loved his daughters?"

"Well . . ." I falter.

"Well?" She waits for my answer, her eyes moist with a sort of challenge. I know what she's trying to do, I know where she wants to take me, but I feel drained and dampened. For the first time today I am anxious to have all this done and over with, to go home and fall on my bed, cool cotton sheets under the air conditioner, and drift into sleep.

I also know she's not going to let me off that easily.

Delia walks around. She pauses by the large bulletin board mounted on the wall, where different cuttings depicting Egyptian reproductions of hieroglyphic art are pinned up, forming a chaotic collage of enigmatic images surrounded by pictograms.

Father's initial fascination with the desert had led him to the valley of the Nile and the string of ancient pyramids and pharaonic tombs along its riverbanks. Then followed his infatuation with the ancient civilization and its enigmatic art, his subsequent trips to the Valley of the Kings, his visits to burial chambers, his obsession with mummies. Among the enormous collection of books on Egypt and reproductions of Egyptian art he had bought in his last years, he had acquired a reproduction of the *Papyrus of Ani*, one of the manuscripts of the *Egyptian Book of the Dead*. The long scroll depicted the stages of death in striking polychrome images surrounded by hieroglyphic writing, which contained instructions and spells to help the deceased in their journey through the afterlife. A few of its pages that were at some point torn from the large book are still stretched out and secured with pushpins on the wall.

"I thought your father was a Christian," Delia says.

"He was Protestant," I say.

"But he was looking for something he wasn't getting in church, wasn't he? Something special." Delia unpins a few pieces from the board. "These are curious, but the text is in English. Will you read them for me?" She slumps into the old green leather wingback chair by the sofa and lodges her cane's handle on its arm. She smoothes the pages of the papyrus over the coffee table. I bend over and examine them. One depicts a ceremony in which a mummy is being held upright at the entrance of his tomb by Anubis, the jackal-headed god, while a group of priests touch his face with a long, spooned blade. The English caption at the bottom of the page reads, "The Ceremony of the Opening of the Mouth." I translate for Delia. She's interested to know what is the meaning of the little winged figure that travels down a vertical shaft connecting the entrance of the tomb to what looks like the burial chamber below.

"'The opening of the mouth,'" I read, "'is performed to give a voice to the deceased and to liberate his ba-spirit so it can reunite with its mummy and start its journey in the afterlife.'"

"I see," Delia says, tracing her finger along the vertical shoot where the birdlike figure travels. "They help the spirit out of the body. And with actual instruments. Intriguing. Is there a closer picture of the tools they're using? I'm sure I could use something similar in my own work." She takes the picture and pulls it close to her eyes. She studies it for a moment, then looks at me. "Your father was on to something here. How did he die? Was he sick? I thought he wasn't that old."

"He was seventy-two."

I tell her that on his last trip to Egypt, after he traveled down to Luxor on the Nile, he had stayed in Cairo for a few weeks and become ill, to the point where he had to be transported back to Madrid in a Red Cross aircraft and hospitalized immediately. It was the beginning of August and the three of us were in different vacation spots, so it took us a couple of days to return to the city. He never left the hospital, and he never received a convincing diagnosis. It looked like a tropical disease at first, a case of inexplicable, extreme dehydration later, and finally, a cerebrospinal inflammation of unknown origin. He was never able to tell us what had happened to him. He died four weeks later.

Delia listens intently. "I am truly sorry," she says. Then she asks, "How did you and your sisters take it?"

I stare at Delia but don't answer her question. Instead, I stay inside my head. I remember the three of us feeling devastated. Unbearable grief mixed in with the sense of guilt we all felt because somewhere deep down we felt liberated from a father who had embittered our lives. That much was obvious in the uneasy glances we exchanged during the hours that followed his passing. Later on, Marion acted more conventionally bereft, while Julia openly admitted relief. But I felt stunned. My cold indifference of the last years turned instantly to remorse. Was there really nothing I could have done to bury the hatchet? No gesture of atonement I could have accepted in order to forgive the past?

CHAPTER 18

My mind plunges into murky waters of painful recollection, like a diver hurled into the cold depths of oceanic limbos. Father's arms punctured with needles, connected to tubes, IV drips, catheters. His body emaciated, rigid on the sterile bed. His eyes staring out of his face, in mute terror. And his ears seemingly deaf, indifferent, while his hands felt limp as I squeezed them on that last long, unending night. To have him die without a word of reckoning, without an explanation. I sat on the plastic chair adjacent to his bed, feeling sick under the thin tube of fluorescent light, my lungs bruised with unexpressed grief. Julia paced outside along the pale green corridor. She looked in now and then, with a haggard, drooping face. Marion sat on the small sofa by the window. She had filled the room with flowers during the last days and brought innumerable boxes of chocolates, the contents of which she now nibbled at distractedly.

The young night nurse with the pink piggy face and chubby fingers walked in and whispered, "The doctor has agreed to put him on morphine," and Julia rolled her eyes from the door, her lips gesticulating big words without sound. "About fucking time."

What had happened to Father on that last trip? It had been his fifth trip to Egypt, and he had embarked on it without telling anyone. I had called the house minutes after he had taken a cab to the airport, and Lolita, who still tended to the housework three times a week, answered and reported that he had only told her he would be back in three weeks. Three weeks! That was a long time to hang around Cairo and the pyramid routes. Organized trips were normally a week or ten days long. And to go in the month of July, when the country's scorching temperatures could easily hit beyond one hundred degrees Fahrenheit. He was no longer traveling under the auspices of the Spanish Association of Egyptology. He had fallen out with them, after launching into unending squabbles over petty matters, as he so often did with everyone around him, until they suspended his membership. When later I combed all documents and paperwork in this room in search of clues, I found nothing besides a hotel bill on his credit card statement among other expenses, and a couple of printed emails where he corresponded with a certain Hammed El Yussuf. In the emails, El Yussuf offered to rent him an apartment in Giza, in a neighborhood called Nazlet el-Samman. There was a picture of the apartment that showed a sparsely furnished living room opening onto a large adobe terrace looking out onto the pyramids of Giza and the Sphinx. But he never made it to Hammed El Yussuf's place. Instead, he stayed in a small, cheap hotel in the Cairo quarter of Mohandeseen, the Zayed Hotel, the same place from where the international Red Cross had repatriated him. The Zayed Hotel personnel had been very gracious when I called up, giving me a heartfelt, although foggy, account of Father's days locked in their room number 24.

"Miss Hurt, your father was a nice gentleman. But he stayed in his room for many days before we realized he was not well. He refused food, and didn't want the cleaning lady. Miss Hurt, please, if you want to come stay at our hotel, we will welcome you. We are so sorry for your loss." I looked at the website picture of the circumspect concierge with droopy eyes and cropped black hair behind a fake malachite counter, who might well be Mr. Karim Rashid, the Zayed's spokesperson expressing his condolences. I clicked on the photos of some of the rooms as I gracefully declined his invitation. Small cheap-looking beds covered with red-striped counterpanes against sandy walls stuccoed with imitations of pyramid reliefs. Why did he stay at the Zayed?

A strange choice for a first-class traveler like Father. Maybe, at that point, he didn't care about anything anymore.

What was it with Father and the desert? He, who took the battle against my love for Marcus to the desert, did he end up losing himself in the same torrid dunes where he had tried to torch my heart and break my lover?

It all started after the company got involved in providing equipment for oil rigs along the northern coast of Africa. After Marcus's experience, I refused to get involved in that department and focused solely on public-works machinery and mining equipment within Spanish territory, leaving Father in charge of desert rigs. He started traveling to the different sites along the Sahara in Algeria, Libya, Mauritania, and Egypt. When the pressure of Islamist militants started building up against international companies rigging the desert, Father moved the company business away from controversial areas like Algeria and Libya, but still kept ties with the Egyptian drilling scene by dealing directly with their National Petroleum Corporation. The extent of his business transactions with them was modest but constant, and although it didn't bring in proportional benefits to the efforts needed to keep the bond going, Father was intent on maintaining it that way.

From the beginning he was mesmerized by the desert. Despite the heat, the uncomfortable dwellings, the mounting danger around the rig settlements, there was a gleam in his eyes every time he returned from a trip. He was in rapture when he talked about the desert night skies, the profound silence, the shifting landscapes of sand dunes. His skin was always red and burned after a trip, making his ice-blue eyes stand out even more in his face. Sometimes I thought I saw a glimpse of madness in his fixed stare as he recounted anecdotes about the resilience of camels on the long journeys, or the beauty of palm trees surrounding oases in the middle of nowhere. He had once met a nomadic group of Berbers in Tunisia who gave him and his travel companions shelter for the night, after their jeep broke down on pathless sandy territory.

"Desert Berbers are noble and trustworthy, you can see it in their eyes. It's rare to see deeper eyes than those of the Berbers," he said. "For people who have nothing, their hospitality is exuberant. Even if they only offer you a few dates, it feels like you're tasting the most delicious food in the world. They make you feel like you belong to their tribe." I looked at him in surprise. Only a few months ago he had rambled about those *A-rabs*—who, in his book, included all inhabitants of northern Africa—intent on boycotting Western civilization through their resistance to selling oil at decent prices. Now, all of a sudden, he had touched their souls through their eyes, through their kindness, and had been moved. But I paid him no attention. To me, the desert was reminiscent of Marcus's ordeal, a wasteful sacrifice that had left a bitter taste in my mouth, that had broken something that would never be made whole again. I hated the desert even more after Marcus left and I had to deal with my own desolation.

"Only someone with no imagination whatsoever could not fall in love with the desert," Father would say, referring to Marcus without naming him, maybe in an attempt to assuage my grief after he was gone. "Forget the rigs and all their hardship. Just to walk out at night and look up above and see a perfect map of the constellations shining down on you like you're the only being left on Earth. To wake up every day and see a different landscape of dunes and know that they move and change shape all the time, whether you can grasp it with your eyes or not. Who wouldn't be transported by that?" And he insisted I accompany him on trips, but I always refused. It would take me years before I understood how this very desert had affected our lives, how it had been the crossroads where I had lost my lover, and my father had begun to lose his mind.

His increasing trips to the Sahara had a deep, insidious effect on him, and it all began to set us apart. He lost interest in the things we shared: trips to European cities, visits to museums, classical concerts and theater plays. And I became more and more obsessed with finding ways to live with my broken heart. By the time Marcus returned to Madrid, Father had removed himself from most social activities and become somewhat of a recluse between the house and the office, outside of his desert traveling. His old, angry persona now alternated with increasing spells of absent, fixed gazing through windows or into empty space. His focus on business matters began to dwindle. By that time, I was practically running the company single-handedly. So when I left, the whole operation shriveled down to half its size in less than two years. Father had lost the drive to prosper and develop the business. He had been fired up while we were growing up and while he was training me, thinking I would inherit the company. But now he didn't see any point. I had been his last card.

What did the desert hold for him? I've never stopped wondering. I remember flinching when looking him directly in the eye as he talked about the vast regions of golden dunes under the dazzling sun or the pointed white light of stars. I remember holding my breath, paralyzed with vertigo, as if I were leaning over an abyss and watching strange, disconnected scenes unfold before my mind's eye. Vertical rods of blinding light shooting down, searing the corneas, frying the mind; brown, parched, protruding tongues of camels, lizards, of defeated men gone crazy with thirst; and sand, burning sand sifting over and through everything, sliding out of Father's fists and pouring out into the wind. Maybe the burning sand running through his fingers was the image of his deepest, hard-bone truth. For all his passion, for all his yearning to possess and to belong, his life had unfurled as a barren territory where nothing ever took root, where nothing could be grasped and held for long, where isolated experiences with generous, welcoming Berbers might just be shimmering mirages of a desperate mind. And in the end those sands burning through his fingers were only the yield of his rage, of all the years spent consuming, desiccating, reducing to ashes all he touched, all he coveted and loved, like a King Midas of sorts, obsessed not with gold but with the possessive greed of a heart that sucked in everything around like a black hole.

Maybe the empty landscape of the desert was also a mirror of his loneliness, of his extreme isolation at the end of his life. He had no friends, no real family ties. His life had been emptied out after his three daughters left the house in rancor. But it was not just at the end of his life. As long as I could remember, Father had been lonely. Lonely sitting in the cold living room while we, as girls, milled about with Nanny in the kitchen, warm with smells of baking, with laughter and silly gossip. Lonely in the office, in the beautiful office with large windows pouring over gardens, while around him employees struggled with their tasks and seethed at his overbearing power and superior know-how. A lonely man in his passion for art, in his jealous possessiveness of his daughters, in his journey through an exile that landed him in Spain, a foreign territory whose gifts he never was able to fully embrace. I used to think of him as a lonely boy too, a boy scourged and whipped into corners, a boy turned fugitive from sheer misery. And then later, I witnessed him also as a lonely old man, as a destitute dying man, destitute because for all his riches, for all his accomplishments, for all his beautiful house, he died alone, far away from the hearts of the daughters who stood around the hospital bed, far away from his Manchester home, in the suffocating heat of a Madrid August afternoon.

Poor Father. A part of me had always felt pity for him, always wanted to protect him. Even as a little girl, when I saw him come in late from work, his face gaunt, his shape frazzled, and he stood by the door looking in at our three little beds to say good night, my heart would beat painfully against my ribs. Why the straitlaced distance, our small bodies rigid under the covers instead of jumping out of bed, insubordinate with affection, to rush over and embrace him, jump around him in welcome, as children and puppies do? We never touched Father's body. An occasional peck on the cheek, a shy pat on the arm or the back, was all. Neither did he touch us. Taking my arm to help me out of a car on our way to a party or a meeting was exceptional. His love was in his fight to provide for us: food, a beautiful house, a bountiful education. His gifts, money and things money could buy. But his passion could only be channeled through jealousy, through possession. And loving him back was difficult, a balancing act between standoffish devotion and a terror of disappointing him. Even as girls we knew that we had a wounded animal for a father.

"Everyone thinks they are Romeos and Juliets, but no one knows how hard it is to come by real love. The love that never dies. Like that between your mother and me," he said once, during the time when I was grieving for Marcus. I remember looking at him, surprised at first, since he never spoke of Mother, and then feeling the sting of his words. There were standards of perfection akin to the consecration of high art that he applied to everything and that were impossible to reach. Nothing was ever good enough. In this book, my love story with Marcus belonged to a lower strand of passions, there was something worthless and pointless in it, it would never be approved. But it couldn't be vanquished. Neither could it be suppressed. So we started living in a bubble of hypocrisy, fogged up by the duplicity of thoughts and words. I became a fabricator, a weaver of whole tapestries of deceit, and he, a sly receiver of corrupt legends. Anything to avoid the naked truth. I used to return to the house after weekends of furious lovemaking with Marcus, with face and body visibly swollen from all his mauling and his kissing and my whole aura stinking of his bodily juices mingled with mine, and I would walk up to Father right here, in front of this very desk, and feed him lies about my whereabouts, about the sweet girlfriends I had slept over with, about their mother serving breakfast. And Father would listen quietly and nod approvingly, careful to avert his glance, because we both knew that if he ventured to meet my gaze, his pain and my shame would merge, combust and burst, exploding our bell jar. We were trapped in the delusion that the truth would tear us apart, but it was deceit that consumed us, swallowed us up like a marsh of slime and quicksand from which we could never pull out again. Not even when I left the house and the office in a tornado of bitterness did I confront him about his role in the devastating outcome of my love story. Instead, I just informed him, stone-faced and ice-hearted, giving supercilious reasons for my decision. Neither did I ever find out if he understood the resentment I had built over the years under the idyllic father-daughter relationship we both wielded on the surface. How my love for him had been infringed by hatred for his dominance, for his arrogance, for the way he felt entitled to meddle in other people's lives, in his daughters' love lives, crushing our hearts and conniving to destroy our lovers.

At the end of it all, where was his victory?

And where was mine, for that matter? Of all the years shunning him, neglecting him, throwing cold eyes over the shriveled image of his defeat, what did I gain? I had yet to understand the consequences of my vendetta.

*   *   *

A coppery light enfolded Father's office the last time I visited, when I swung by, unannounced, to drop off a set of keys. It had been a while since I had last been there, well over a year. I was surprised at first, and then shocked to find the large space empty. There was nobody at the reception area. I walked down a line of vacant desks, wondering if I'd forgotten it was a bank holiday or some equivalent Spanish saint's feast, until I came up to Ventura's desk and realized business was being conducted as usual, whatever that meant.

The old accountant got up from his seat with a great deal of difficulty, a smile spreading across his yellow parched face. "Miss Anna! So good to see you back!" I shook his hand, horrified at how much he had aged. His whole frame trembled, his limbs quivered spastically as he steadied himself against the desk. "Don't mind my shakes, it's just a bit of Saint Vitus's dance, as my mother calls it. What to do? We're all getting on. And you? How are you?" His sincere glee cast a dark cloud over me.

"Where is everyone, Ventura?"

"It's been only Silvia and me for a while now," he said, blinking. "We had to downsize, you know, after you left . . ." I looked around at the desolate space, at the once busy, elegant office that drew all sorts of international business people and big-ticket contracts. Empty and dimly lit, the place looked decrepit with its shabby, outmoded furniture and its begrimed walls. Even the beige wall-to-wall carpet I had so dreaded back in the day was worn out. But its degradation only gave me a pang of angst. All was tinged with a sinister air of aged neglect that made me shudder. For the first time I was slapped with the extent of my magnicide. After I left, Father lost the drive to push forward, and let the ship go adrift. My abandonment had the effect of starving the company of vitality and sustenance, and it had trickled down to nothingness through resignations, layoffs, and the severance of contracts. It wasn't just my walking away, I also took with me the best clients, on purpose. Now, laid before my eyes, was the collateral result of the revenge I had planned against Father. I had intended to draw blood, but ended up casting a whole net of misery and decay.

"If you need to see your father, Miss Anna, he's over at his office." Ventura stared into my face with affection but also with curiosity. Was he asking himself for the hundredth time what had actually happened for me to walk out one day, to never return again?

As I made my way to Father's office, Silvia emerged from the kitchen with a cup of the legendary appalling coffee in her hand. I recognized in an instant the smell of the acrid grind drowned in powdered milk. At least one element seemed to have survived intact the ravages of time.

"Anna! Blessed are the eyes! Where have you been?" She stepped back, gesticulating in admiration. "Look at you!" She made me turn around to show her my dark red evening dress, and I felt ashamed of my fashionable trappings, the dazzling Coach bag and my new Kenzo shoes. She had aged too. Her dyed blond hair looked straggly and disheveled, and huge tawny bags of skin hung under her eyes above an orangey sweater covered all over in tiny balls of fuzz. But there was true affection in the open smile that revealed her nicotine-stained teeth.

As I kissed her on the cheek and exchanged a few pleasantries, I caught sight of him over her shoulder. Father, sitting behind his desk, swathed in the brownish crepuscular light that poured in through the window. He was dressed as usual, in a perfect suit and tie. A wavy lock of hair hung over his forehead as he looked down at a stack of paperwork. The image pierced me like a spear across the solar plexus. A neat little figure trying hard to focus, lost in the immensity of his empty office. Empty of business, of bustle, of life. A picture of the past. Rotting. In sepia.

Having slayed him would have been kinder.

I had finally stepped up to the plate and proved myself to be my father's daughter. I could also be cruel, vindictive, coldhearted in the heat of rage, and then live on to struggle awkwardly with the consequences.

And so it was that a few weeks later I found myself on the same page with Father. Literally. In front of the page of the *Egyptian Book of the Dead* written for the scribe Ani, where an image of a sideways-kneeling Anubis pointed his dark jackal face toward his hands holding the tiny pendulum of a huge weighing scale, from which hung two dishes.

"What is he weighing?" I asked.

It was six months before Father's death and I had walked one night into the darkened study and sat on the armchair by his side. I tried to hide my disquiet at his ashen face, as he hoisted himself up from his lying position on the chesterfield sofa. I had come into the house late that evening in a fit of spontaneity, without notice, and become alarmed at the gloomy façade, with no lights on the porch or in the windows. I walked through the kitchen, staircase, and corridors, turning on light switches, my anguish increasing as I realized that something else, besides this lurking pool of darkness, was encroached about the house. There was a heaviness churning in the air, a feeling of strange elusiveness that made rooms and corridors seem larger than I remembered them, as if spaces stretched out ahead of me, even in the darkness, hindering my advance.

Where was Father?

A dim light in the studio at the end of the hall answered my question. From the door I could see his slim, recumbent body on the sofa.

Why so quiet?

I put extra weight on my feet as I stepped into the room. "Hello, Father! It's awfully dark in here!" I turned on a few lamps around the room. Father shaded his eyes and raised himself into a seated position.

"Having a bit of a nap?" I tried to sound cheerful as I sat on the armchair by his side, but I knew he hadn't been sleeping. "Aren't you cold?"

It was freezing in the room, one of those discarnate Madrid February evenings where the frost was already gathering to lay its icy mantle over the land. "Shall I make you a cup of tea? Don't you want to light a fire in the drawing room?"

Father didn't reply. He just sat there, stunned, looking at me, or through me. A couple of minutes passed in uncomfortable silence. I stared at the large open book that lay on the coffee table in front of him, and examined the terrifying black pointed dog-face of Anubis, his long muscular thighs as he knelt one knee on the ground, holding the minute pendulum of the large scale while surrounded by a host of sideward figures and strange animals.

"What are they weighing?" I asked again.

I wanted to engage Father's attention, have him snap out of his trancelike silence. Talking about art was always a safe arena with him. But I was also curious about the two bizarre objects weighed against each other on the scales.

Father groped for his glasses on the table, put them on, and looked down at the page. He seemed to come back to life as his eyes roamed over the polychromatic pictures. "They are weighing his heart against a feather," he said at last in a tired voice.

"His heart? Whose heart?" I said, but remembered instantly that we were looking at a reproduction of the *Papyrus of Ani*, the *Egyptian Book of the Dead* written specially for Ani, so it had to be Ani's heart, whoever he might have been. "Weighing it against a feather? How would a heart ever weigh as little as a feather?"

"That's how light it has to be to enter the afterlife," Father said in a matter-of-fact way, and pointed to another figure, standing behind Annubis, who had the head of an ibis and a pen and tablet in his hand, with which he seemed to be taking notes on the procedure. "This is Thoth, and he records the results," Father said, and moved his finger toward another figure standing under the scale, a horrific animal in the mixture of a crocodile, a lion, and a hippopotamus. "And here's the Devourer, who snatches the heart if he doesn't pass the test."

"But how's the heart going to weigh less than a feather?" I repeated my question with the incredulity of a child.

"That's it. It's quite impossible," Father said. "But there's some sort of a trick, a spell the deceased might quote that might help with his plight. Read it, down here." I started reading to myself. "Out loud," he insisted.

" 'Oh heart which I had from my mother, O my heart which I had upon the earth, do not rise up against me as a witness in the presence of the Lord of Things; do not speak against me concerning what I have done, do not bring anything against me in the presence of the Great God.' " I reread it to myself in silence.

"Why would the heart speak out?" I felt like a stupid infant in the face of an inscrutable oracle. I watched Father's hollowed gaze through his glasses and wondered why his pupils were so contracted, pinhead small, when they should be dilated in the midst of all this darkness. He was staring at the sturdy heart, as it sat upright on the scale holding its breath against the lightness of the feather. So, if the heart could be trusted to keep silence in this awful momentous instance of judgment, there could be a chance of redemption. But again, why would the heart be so eager to speak up, to confess its murdering moments, its dark thoughts and desires?

"The heart cannot live with remorse," Father said, as if reciting some text. "It would rather speak up and fall into damnation, than carry its burden into eternity." He was silent for a beat and then added, as if to himself, "But what good does that do anyone?"

His eyes were lowered, his thin face haggard with a gauntness I had never seen before. Was he weighing his own heart? Was he memorizing the spell?

Never had I felt so close and so removed from Father than in that moment, both of our heads bent over the *Papyrus of Ani* at the center of the dim yellow ring of light around the leather sofa in his study. Our bodies so close to each other, and yet so distant. Hurting to reach out, to breach the gap, and yet incapable. And the darkness around us, so fierce, so menacing, like the Devourer waiting to snatch our hearts. Not just his.

Mine too.

CHAPTER 19

"Are you still with me?" Delia whispers. I'm not sure if I hear it in my head, or if it's coming from her lips. I have drifted into a slumber, and when I open my eyes I feel her gaze intent on mine, and realize she's been watching me all this time, however long it's been since I've passed out. Watching me with those raven eyes like black lakes of unnerving scrutiny. Has she been watching my thoughts, or even the images that are swelling up in my memory? I flinch at this possibility. And yet, there's a certain soothing at the odds of being peeped on in the midst of cramping pain. Like an unexpected sharing, an opportunity to dissipate a portion of torment away from the self.

I look around the room. The light inside the study has become opaque, a sort of light brownish yellow that tints everything with the sepia sheen of old photographs, the same light as in the scenes of my recent recollections. It's strange how the mind can travel through time using impressions affected upon the senses, like gliding vectors across the tectonic plates of memory.

A whip of distant lightning flashes through the window, and then follows the rumbling of thunder, heavy growls tailed by the wind flogging the trees outside, rattling the loose wood in the blinds. But the rain is still being withheld. The heavens heave and lurch in the agony of overdue labor. The room sweats.

I lean back on the sofa, drained. I feel hot and sticky, a small animal left to desiccate upon a withered plain. I turn on my side, and lie outstretched on the sofa with head resting on the buttoned leather arm. My temples are throbbing now, and my thigh aches with a sore thud that pounds from the cut. I want to close my eyes. I need water.

The door opens and Constantine walks in with hurried little steps, a gleaming reddish-brown bowl in his hands. Julia follows behind with a white bandage. The wind rushes in with them and sweeps through the room, an angry hiss that blows close to the floor, and bangs the door shut again.

"It's ready, Delia." Constantine is his diligent apprentice-self again. He sets the bowl on the table, near my leg. I recognize the old copper mortar that has been in the kitchen since I can remember. The piece that Father always claimed to be a Russian apothecary mortar more than a hundred years old. He used to fly into a rage every time he caught Nanny, pestle in hand, in the act of crushing some herb or spice that she intended adding to the food. How could she be as insensitive as to use a precious antique in the commonplace act of pursuing a recipe! Because the piece came from Mother's family and had been used in the kitchen forever, Nanny could never understand his regret. Now, its yellow glint hurts my eyes. And the sour, metallic smell of the copper travels up my nose toward my brain. It makes me sick to my stomach with its sweet, earthy scent. Like blood.

Julia sits by me. "Are you all right? You look pale."

"I am very thirsty, and I have a headache. Is there any water I can drink?"

Delia motions Constantine to take up the mortar again. "Just let us put this over your wound so you can leave the room." Then she says to Constantine, "Very good you found a copper bowl. Our Lady of La Caridad del Cobre always provides. Did you bring a spoon to spread the poultice with?" Constantine nods.

Julia bristles by my side. "Wait a minute! You're not putting that stuff on her leg! It's a bunch of prickly thistles he's mashed up together, and I saw him spit into the bowl!"

Constantine exchanges glances with Delia. Then he takes up

the mortar and pulls it to his chest, as if protecting it. "Excuse me, but no such thing happened. I used a bit of sunflower oil to make the poultice," he huffs, offended.

Julia jumps up from her seat. "I think we've been through enough bullshit today. I'm taking my sister to the hospital right now, and that's that!"

"I'm not going to the hospital, I just need water," I say, and my words reverberate in my head, adding to the pain that now throbs in amplified, unbearable sweeps.

"Yes, you are! You're coming with me right this moment!"

Delia takes up her cane and rests her chin on its handle. "I'm afraid this is not your call, Julia. You chickened out a while ago, but Anna's following the course. She's the one to decide."

Julia glares at Delia for a beat, then kneels down beside me. "Let's get out of here, Anna. I don't like this. I don't trust them anymore." She's pleading. I look at her as through a fog. My head is exploding. I see her concern, I see her fear, but it's as if we're on different planes. Where I am, there's no exit the way she wants to take me. The pain throbs inside my temples, and my thoughts are caught in a narrow tunnel, pressed against clingy, ropy walls.

"I just have a migraine. I need to take a painkiller and get a bit of sleep." Just articulating these few words is excruciating, like tearing at deep membranes in the vortex of my head.

"Anna! You hit your head when you fell, you can't go to sleep! You've never had a migraine in your life. I'm calling an ambulance this moment!" I hear Julia on the verge of screaming.

"What on earth is going on here?" A figure draped in a long whitish cloth, like a bed sheet tucked around her like a toga, stands at the door. We all look at her in awe, even Delia. Marion's wet hair falls in black curly waves down the sides of her body. Her face is serious, beautiful, like the marble statue of a Roman matron. Water drips to the floor from the fringes of her cloth, around her bare feet. Her voice commands again, "What is the problem?" She walks toward me with an imperious stride, holding her toga drapes to her body. Julia stands up and gives way as Marion sits on the sofa close to me and takes my hands.

"Oh, darling, you feel so hot!" She brushes the sticky hair away from my forehead. She hasn't called me darling for at least fifteen years, and her hands feel cold and soothing. "This girl is dehydrated and exhausted. We need to get water immediately."

"We need to get her the hell out of this goddamned house is what we need!" Julia says.

"Don't be ridiculous. Take my car and fetch water. She has to drink before anything else," Marion says, still pressing her hands along my face and throat. The throbbing in my temples abates.

"You don't understand! They're trying to put some weird-ass poultice on her wound," Julia shrieks.

"A poultice?" Marion examines my gash and then looks at Delia.

Delia smiles over her cane. "It's only thistles. In our tradition they're healing herbs and spiritual protectors. Blessed thistle is a liver tonic, good for infections. It's given to breast-feeding mothers. What harm can it do?"

"Anna, are you all right with this? Do you consent to having this herb put on your wound?" Marion's eyes are soft, loving. Her skin is cool next to mine, she smells of ferns and moist plants. I want her to embrace me, to pull me to her bosom, to lull me into sleep.

I can hardly move but I manage to nod. "It's fine."

Julia screams. "She's feverish! What does she know?"

"Julia, stop this. Go get water. Now." Marion doesn't even raise her voice.

Julia shrinks and stands for a moment, hanging her head. "You know, this is also your fault. You didn't bring any food for us. She hasn't eaten anything the whole day."

Marion turns to her again and stares her down, but gently, with the patience a good mother uses with an unruly child. "Please, Julia, get us water."

"And Advil," I manage to say.

Julia clicks her tongue and leaves the room.

"Thank you, Marion." Delia takes the mortar from Constantine's hands and holds it in her own for a minute, closing her eyes and moving her lips as if in silent prayer. Then she takes the spoon and dips it into the poultice. Meantime, Marion and Constantine lift me from the sofa into a seated position and place my leg on the coffee table once again. Delia sits in the armchair and reaches over with a spoonful of green greasy paste. A shudder of trepidation gets hold of me as the spoon approaches my thigh. But Marion is holding my hand and I feel no pain as the cool spoon spreads the goo over the gash. Just a little heat around the edges of the cut.

"Good." Delia says. "Now you need to leave. Get some fresh air while I seal this room again. Can you get up?"

"I can walk her out and sit her under the willow," Constantine says.

"All right, but make it close to the house. The storm will be here any moment."

Marion squeezes my hands. "Can you go out with Constantine while I change?" I nod. I've taken to just nodding, I realize I don't need to talk, I don't need to initiate movement, everything is being done for me. It feels like being a small child again, carefree, even in the face of complications.

Constantine offers a hand and together with Marion they pull me up from the sofa. My head starts pounding again as they walk me to the door. The moment we cross the threshold, I feel disoriented.

Marion says, "I'll be back immediately," and she hurries down the corridor.

Constantine threads his arm through mine and holds my elbow with a strong hand as we cross the French doors that lead to the garden. His clothes, his hair, everything on him and around him reeks of burned sage, making me nauseous, as if my stomach would turn inside out in an instant. We walk quickly, faster than I can handle at this point, and I sense how much effort he is putting into pulling me along. My body feels like a dead weight.

"Sorry to rush you, but we're running so late," he says. "And me, letting Delia down with all my petty mistakes. Sometimes I don't know how she puts up with me." He's talking to himself while he pulls me along. "You see, no one understands Delia's work. I bleed when people treat her like a phony elder. Like she's going to pull out a tarot deck or give you a love potion made out of candy. Delia is so much more. She works with people, she helps them overcome their heartaches. Whatever's blocking their lives. She's a powerful healer. She's a liberator of souls. If people just knew." He rattles on, but I'm having a more and more difficult time focusing on his words.

The air is oppressive as we step out of the house, as if the barometric pressure has dropped and is weighing down on my diaphragm like lead, stuffing my lungs with an unbearable feeling of cotton wool. I look up for a brief moment and see the mass of clouds above, like a whorl of gray and yellow, a swirling, angry smog. Its raging blaze presses on my eyeballs, hammering streaks of pain into the middle of my brain. I am dragging my leg now, and I can feel the bandage Marion tied around my thigh beginning to get loose, slipping off. We walk over the terraced area, and when we reach the scorched patch of lawn I want to ask Constantine to stop and let me catch my breath, but I can't inhale, I can't open my throat to talk. My knees bend and then he turns to look at me, while I slide down over the charred grass. He towers over me as I fall into a heap.

"Delia! Delia! I think she's being claimed," I hear him say, before his voice turns into a strange hum streaming out of his lips. My ears are about to explode as if I were being pushed down through vertical miles of water. My lungs are paralyzed. Constantine holds my face with both hands while he accommodates my head on the ground. I look into his eyes. Into the pupil of his strange, strabismic eye, which roams around for a while until it locks with mine. His left eye into my right. It feels like a painless insect sting. A quick, sharp perforation of a membrane, my membrane, a taut sheath extending around my body and hemming it in like a drop of water. Constantine is also surrounded by his own membrane. It connects with mine through the tiny hole that has just been pricked. Sweet air streams through the puncture, and I suck at it with desperate greed until it fills my head and my throat. I realize I'm breathing through Constantine—every time his membrane expands, mine receives a delayed pulse of luscious air. Constantine is also changing. His ugly, pointy face is transforming into the semblance of a horse. A handsome, sorrel horse with moist chestnut eyes and a long blaze reaching down to his wide nostrils. The horse snorts and turns, canters away, while I sink into the parched ground that is opening around me like a crater, in jagged movements like spastic waves. I fall through the crack and under the surface, the soil sifts over my body as if it were coarse, heavy flour. My hands grasp at the shriveled lattice of roots that emerge around me as I slip down the tunnel, to no avail. I tumble into a cool, blind space. Now, as I lie on the soft bed of soil, I know I am underneath the house, I can feel it pounding above me with the echo of every sound. Delia's unsteady steps as the South Wind pushes her out the door in Father's studio, Marion's soft silk dress sliding down her body, Julia placing gleaming plastic bottles of cold water on the hall floor with a thud. The house is over and around me. Its base surface stretches over the periphery of my body, grows out of it at some level, inseparable, like the shell of a huge snail. I am still connected with the large breathing membrane, although it is not a membrane anymore, but a breast. A huge breast of earth with a thick pointed nipple that I suck at with all my strength for a few drops of air. Delia's dark, laughing eyes spill over me, bathing me in tender mirth, and I realize it is she who is feeding me from her breast, a mammoth black Earth Mother towering high against the sky.

But then, as I look again, it's not Delia, it's Mother holding her soft creamy breast over me, cooing, while she nudges her pink nipple into my mouth and rocks me into her bosom. I begin to breathe.

CHAPTER 20

Fat raindrops fall on my face. I feel them tumbling over my cheeks and into my eye sockets. One or two roll into my parted lips and I savor that most sweet substance on Earth. Water. Its cooling tang hallows the taste buds in my tongue, infuses the whole cavity of my mouth with grace. Life is back. My pain, I realize, is gone. And I feel fresh, renewed, as if I had slept through a long, comforting night.

I blink my eyes open against a sky of lead streaked with feeble veins of lightning. Thunder follows like dissonant drums, a cacophony of grumbling still reluctant to release the avalanche from its overdue belly. Just one fat drop at a time. For now.

Around me kneel Marion and Constantine. Delia stands at my feet, leaning on her staff and looking down. Her eyes have a new expression, one I have not seen before. Although set in my direction, they look beyond me, spellbound, tiny sparks flaring up now and then on their dark surface as if she were reading the meaning of a strange revelation playing itself in front of her.

"Anna, are you all right?" Marion holds my wrists. "Oh, I shouldn't have left you for a second!" Her velvet brown irises quiver with unease, on the verge of tears.

"I'm fine. I'd like to drink water, though." My voice is back. My lungs are open. I push myself up on my elbows, but Marion presses me gently back down. "Don't move just yet."

Julia bounds toward us with two large bottles of water in her hands. "What happened?" she shrieks when she sees me on the ground. "Did he do anything to you?" she says, pointing at Constantine. She drops the water bottles and rushes to me with an angry, flushed face. Constantine stands up with a pained look and joins Delia.

"No, no," I say, "he only tried to help me."

"Julia, stop your hysteria! How could you even suggest anything like that?" Marion says. "Anna came down with convulsions. I didn't know she was in such a bad state. Poor thing."

"Convulsions? Who goes into convulsions without being epileptic? I knew we had to take her to the hospital!" Julia turns to Delia. "I've known you for a very long time, but bullshit aside, that thing you put on her wound . . ."

"Can I please have water?" I say, sitting up.

"Fine, drink," Julia says, uncapping one of the water bottles. "But you're coming with me to the emergency room right after." She holds the bottle to my lips and I circle my hands around its frosty body and swing it upwards with all the eagerness my thirst can muster. The water gushes down my throat and into my stomach as if into a black hole. I can feel the unbearable craving down to my very cells as I suck it in.

"Hey, take it easy!" Julia pulls the bottle away, and then turns to Delia. "I'm taking her, no matter what you say, no matter what any of you say."

"Julia! Julia, look at me." Delia nails her with gentle but firm eyes. "You can take her to the hospital if you like. It's all fine. But you have seen people being mounted by Orishas before. In all of our masses Alina brought you to. This is just what happened. After a deep cleansing, the Orishas can take you up for a few minutes. They honor the brave of spirit with gifts of vision. That's all. It might have been you, had you done the work. But you quit midway, you missed out on the best part. And that's why you're feeling so jittery, so distraught." She's smiling again, Delia, curling those thin scimitar lips behind which she seems to be trembling with irresistible mirth.

For a moment, I think Julia will continue to fight; she's not one to go down without being clubbed to the ground. But Julia just looks at Delia meekly, even sheepishly, as if the reproach had hit the right chord. Then, I see her lowering her eyes in dejection. "Sorry, Constantine, I didn't really mean what I said," she starts, but Constantine cuts in swiftly, "Don't worry, I've had worse things said to me."

I drift away from their exchange. I'm aware of a sudden silence in the air. Nothing moves, the small sounds of the garden have ebbed into stillness. The atmosphere around us has become a dark shade of metallic gray, like hematite. It galvanizes the air with scintillating tension. Now everyone's eyes are focused on me, looking at me from a sort of distance. As if they were seeing something ghostly. Even Julia's.

"What?" I begin to say.

"It's here," Delia answers.

Then it breaks open, the sky above. A bolt of lightning like a jagged javelin rips the heavy gray belly, followed by a deafening crack of thunder. Rain begins to fall, hard, fast, pelting around us like bullets, soaking us in seconds.

"We'd better get you inside." Marion scrambles to her feet and helps me up. Julia gathers the water bottles. As we run to the house, the water is already forming rivers along the ground beneath our feet, and the dry, caked earth is beginning to dissolve into mud. I turn back to see Constantine pulling Delia's arm while she walks against the rain, her face turned upward, shielding her eyes with one hand. Once they reach the house, we close the French door behind us, as the wind picks up, driving the rain hard against the façade, strumming it in gusts against the windowpanes. Marion locks the door. We stand looking out at the rain splattering around the house, mesmerized by its knifelike patter playing upon the surface of the land as if it were a drum. The wind whistles around the house, down the chimneys, rattling windows and doors. Water falls in thick vertical sheets over the swimming pool and the patio, drowning the garden, whipping the long branches of the willow tree.

"Hell!" Julia says. "To think of all the drought we've had this year! I haven't seen a storm like this in a long time."

"It feels like a monsoon," Marion says.

I'm sodden to the core. We all are. Amazing, how in just minutes we've been drenched by what felt like bucketfuls being thrown from the top of the world. My thin cotton shirt sticks to my body and rivulets of water drip down my legs. We're all standing in puddles.

"Let's go to the library and light a fire," Marion says. "We can sit for a bit and dry ourselves while the storm abates. I found a bunch of old towels in the linen wardrobe."

"Thank you, but Constantine and I still have to clear the altar," Delia says. "We could use one last cup of coffee, though, now that we've come into water." She says *come into water* as if she were saying *come into money or riches*. Of course, she means *drinking* water. But right now, coffee sounds good and the kitchen even better. It's probably the coziest room in the house, putting aside the paraffin smog created by hours of candles burning. But my teeth are chattering. All of a sudden I'm overcome by chills.

"I'll make the coffee." Julia looks at Marion. "You take care of Anna."

We start trooping toward the kitchen when a loud cracking sound followed by a blasting explosion of crashing glass deafens us. We turn around, bewildered. The large French window has been smashed and shards of glass shoot around the room like shrapnel. Delia takes a step in front of me, opens her arms as if to shield me, while everyone else huddles behind. Jagged fragments of glass fall over furniture and slide along the ceramic floor with screeching sounds, while the wind howls into the room and jangles the French door before it splits and streams out of the multiple broken lattice panels. Then the awning crashes down outside, its soaked green tarpaulin sprawled over the terrace along with the mangled aluminum rods. The long, heavy crank handle is spiked through the French door that is now hanging off its upper hinge.

"Holy shit!" I say, looking over Delia's shoulder. We all stand frozen, just feet away from the crashed glass.

Then Marion says, "Who was dumb enough to leave the crank handle hanging?"

And Julia and I answer in unison, "One of these days that bloody piece of a botched rod is going to smash up the whole window!" before the three of us burst into laughter.

Delia and Constantine turn to us in surprise. "What's so funny?"

"Just that we must've heard our father say this every day of every summer of our lives," Julia says, still in splits.

"There you go." Delia smiles, looking toward the window. "His prediction finally became true. Although I would've thought the lightning was more to blame than the handle."

The rain has quieted down. It falls in soft pitter-patter rhythms along the eaves surrounding the house. The sky is clearing up, the dull ashen layers of clouds are being torn into long strips, revealing the dark red gleam of a blood-orange sun that sinks behind the line of mountains.

I look back at the large latticed window, its panels ragged with broken glass, the door torn and hanging like a huge open mouth gaping out toward the violet dusk that now descends over the garden. Who would have thought that the awning's cracked handle, a humble piece of metal, rusty and forgotten in an abandoned garden, would have become the unsuspecting implement in the opening of the house's mouth? I search for Delia's eyes. I want to plunge into those dark layers of scintillating wisdom and know that she is thinking the same thing. Delia returns my gaze and for a brief moment I see a smiling sparkle of kindred understanding, but then she locks her eyes back into their old hermetic surface, those obscure mirrors that bounce back my reflection.

"The *limpieza* has been accomplished," she says solemnly. "It has been a good one. A very good one." Behind her, a crescent moon just a day away from full newness rises over the night sky.

CHAPTER 21

"You can't leave without telling me more about what just happened to me!" I'm aware of the despair underlying my voice. I've asked twice already, but Delia is busy reorganizing the contents of her big brown bag and doesn't even look at me.

We're in the kitchen. Constantine and Delia are gathering their things before they leave. No one has made coffee. It seems that some of the house's electric circuits have come down in the storm, and the electric range is out of order, along with multiple lights in the house. Julia has gone, flashlight in hand, to figure out the circuit breaker.

I address Delia once more across the table. "What is this *being claimed by the Orishas*? Who are the Orishas?"

But Delia, who's now bending over her small suitcase, is adamant in her silence. I stare at her with beseeching eyes. A part of my brain is still trying to hold on to the images of the vision I had out in the garden, but I can already feel them slipping away like sand through open fingers. As dream sequences that fade, once the dreamer crosses over to reality upon waking. Losing the concrete imagery of the experience doesn't take away the astounding awe I feel has been opened inside me, like a magical eye I never knew I had, which holds me spellbound to the cryptic messages contained in my vision. It's the codes to interpret these messages that I'm hanging on to by the fingernails; they're also slipping away, swallowed up into the quicksands of the coarse upper layers of my brain. Soon, only the memory of a sacred fog will remain.

"Delia?" I insist. "Talk to me."

She turns to face me with an exhausted expression of indifference. She looks old now, Delia, her eyelids are heavy over her glazed eyes. Why am I harassing her? The thought crosses my mind that this is not the Delia I've known all these past hours, this is a hag-and-bones version of herself, a bunch of old clothes discarded from her true, vibrant soul.

"This is not a good time for this. It's late for Delia, she's had a long day," Constantine says from the other end of the kitchen. "Besides, we're only an hour away from curfew at the nursing home." Then he adds in a loud voice, as if speaking to a deaf elderly person, "We need to get moving, Delia."

Marion and I sit at the table, now a wasteland of hardened spattered wax from the consumed candles, squashed cigar butts, and empty liquor bottles, all covered by a layer of mauve ash from the burned incense sticks. Constantine is still clearing selective elements from this altar's aftermath scene, such as postcards of saints, plastic statuettes, cowrie shells, and colored beads, together with the coconut-shell halves that held them. Marion sits by my side and pulls at my hair with the old musty towel she insists on drying me with.

"Come on, Delia, it's not fair," I insist. "You made me go through the whole thing without any warning. Give me *some* explanation, tell me anything."

"Was it *that* terrible?" Marion asks. "May I ask what happened when you collapsed in the garden?" She is unfolding a bunch of old, faded pieces of clothing from a pile, trying to figure out what would be the least ugly apparel I could trade my filthy, wet T-shirt and shorts for. "I'm dying to know what happened to you," Marion insists. "Can't you talk about it?"

"I'm not clear anymore," I say. "It's faded away. I remember not being able to breathe and then falling into a strange place, somewhere around the house, and Mother pulling me out."

"Like a rebirth!" Marion says.

"Mother? What did she look like?" Julia asks, coming down the stairs.

"She looked very pale, with pitch-black hair. Her eyes were huge gray pools of water. She looked into the distance."

"Did she say anything?" Julia sits down. Her face brightens up, expectant.

"No, she just sang this little song." I stop for an instant to retrieve the lyrics and the tune: "*Luna, lunera, cascabelera, toma un ochavo para canela.* Moon, moon, sleigh bell moon, take a farthing for cinnamon."

"She always used to sing us that song! Remember?" Julia says, and she and Marion exchange smiling glances.

"I don't remember her singing at all," I say.

"Poor Anna, you never spent much time with her, did you?" Marion says.

We all sit in silence for a moment while I mull over Marion's words. In truth, I mostly remember Nanny as my primary caretaker growing up—I spent lots of time in this kitchen and following her around the house as she did chores. Mother was always bedridden, exhausted, or feverish. When I was taken into her room for a visit, she would caress my face and hands, whisper sweet nothings. *My little Anna. My teensy flower. My bright star.* She had little energy for anything else, never mind singing. Most of the time she was out of breath and would begin to cough if she talked for too long. Now those whisperings echo again inside my head. *My little Anna. My teensy flower. My bright star.*

Across from me, Constantine packs things tightly into the compartments of his rucksack and inside multiple plastic bags. Cleanup time is when he's at the height of his perfectionism, apparently. He puts aside the bucket and mop they've been using on the floors, as well as the straw hearth broom he's been sweeping and swishing the coconut with, in every room in the house.

"You can't reuse any of these. You have to use brand-new ones each time," he says. "So I'll take them with me and dispose of them safely." The thought crosses my mind that they were never brand-new items to begin with, but I let it go.

A few moments ago, I saw him sweeping up the coconut with the straw broom, into a brown paper bag with utmost care. Now he seals the bag, pressing its outer edges into a neat cuff, and puts it in my hands. "Burn this when you make a fire. And make sure you don't open the bag." Then he motions toward Delia and whispers in a conspiratorial tone, "We need to let her be. After jobs like these she needs to check out for a few hours. I've got to get her out of here as soon as possible."

Marion overhears him. "I'll call a cab then." She dials on her phone.

Constantine blushes. "We'll also need to get paid."

"Of course! I'll get my purse. Please remind us how much we owe you," Marion says.

Constantine looks even more flustered. His crazy eye roams around the floor while he seems to be doing some complex mental arithmetic.

Julia reaches for her backpack and extracts a wad of bills from a side pocket. "I got it!"

"Go ahead, we'll pay you back later," Marion says.

"No, no, let me pay for this. I think I owe it to everyone after having been the best of my bitchy self for most of the day." Julia approaches Constantine. "Delia said two fifty for the job, plus a hundred for you, plus fifty for the cab. And here's an extra fifty for you. Okay?"

Constantine's face goes dark crimson as his hesitant hands receive the bills.

"Okay?" Julia repeats.

"It's just that . . ." We all hang on his words. "It's just that I spent an extra 2.50 euros on the coconut, plus 1.60 coming and going on the subway to the Mercado de la Cebada, the only market in the old Madrid where you can get it at this time of year. Then there was the broom. It has to be made of old-fashioned broomcorn, you know, and they're hard to come by these days."

"All right, all right, here's an extra fifty for your troubles," Julia says.

"Well, the broom was twelve euros and . . ."

"Take another twenty and let's call it a day," Julia says, about to explode from exasperation.

Constantine looks unhappily at the money that Julia thrusts in his hand. He's about to open his mouth again when Marion says, "Here's another fifty from me." And then, intuiting Constantine's unyielding technique, she points to the door. "Oh, I think the cab's at the gate!"

Constantine sighs before he gets his backpack, the mop and bucket, plus the broom and a bunch of plastic bags from the counter and heads out the door. Marion and I help Delia up from her chair and walk her slowly out of the kitchen and up the ramp that leads to the garden gate. She drags her feet and holds her large brown handbag tight against her chest. When we reach the cab, the driver opens the door, and she stands for a moment before getting inside.

"So nice to have seen you girls again," she says with a vague smile. "You all look so pretty."

I embrace her large, puffy body. It sags in my arms. I search for that smell of quince jelly and treacle that has soothed me through-out the day, but instead I only find the musty, sour smell of old flesh. "Thank you for coming out, Delia. Can I call you tomorrow? Can I come see you? I have so many questions."

"Yes, dear, call me. I think there is a public phone at the home." She gets into the car with immense difficulty. We stand by the gate until they drive off.

When I enter the library, Julia is already making a fire. She has piled up a whole load of dry pine cones over a mound of balled-up old newspapers and is applying a long matchstick to it all. Multi-colored flames sputter around the paper and then start crackling as they reach the cones. Marion sits on the edge of the sofa opposite the fireplace.

"The old trickster!" Julia says, as she builds a tepee-like struc-ture of thin logs around the burning cones. "They're a good team, those two, they know how to bounce off each other to squeeze cli-ents. They always put on the same little skit at the end."

"C'mon, Julia! You're not telling me that's your real opinion of them, after you pushed to bring them in, had them make a mess of the house and nearly drove us all insane," Marion says. "You're just mad at Delia for some other reason."

"It *is* my true opinion of them. But they always trick me into thinking they're for real when they want the job. Then I slowly wake up as the thing progresses and, by the end, I just pay them as much as I can to get rid of them."

Marion laughs as if she were listening to utter nonsense. "You're crazy!"

"It's true, Marion. I'm sorry I brought all this on. I'll clean and fix up the house and contact the real estate agent again as compensation."

"At least it has brought the three of us back together," Marion says.

I sit on the leather chair by the fire. I rest the coconut, wrapped in the brown paper bag, on my lap.

"You're the one who's the trickster," I say to Julia. "First you bring on the trick and then you trick us into disbelieving it, right?" Julia laughs, and I continue on my rampage. "You're full of shit, Julia! I'll never trust you again. And now, no matter what you say, I shall proceed to follow to the letter the original instructions for the burning of this artifact."

"Whatever." Julia sits back on a low stool by the sofa, her face stretched into a big grin. "We just paid a shitload of money, and if you want to play it till the end, hey!"

"As for the shitload of money," Marion says, "at least it's rendered some excellent and immediate results, whereas all my years of therapy . . ."

Julia laughs. "I'm glad you're also satisfied."

I want to glare at her, but a part of me is amused. I'm relieved at the lighthearted mood we're all sharing at this moment. And, of course, I know my sister Julia's side as joker, as con artist. She was always able to swindle Marion and me into believing all kinds of crazy things just to get the best of us. The old, annoying equivocator. She's just playing us now. Or is she?

I place the coconut on top of the wood pile with care, and sit back to watch the brown paper darken around the edges and flare up, revealing the ropey, striated surface of the coconut husks. The flames snap and crinkle as they circle around it in long tongues. The room is soon infused with a smell of burned coconut.

"This turns out to be a real gift, since we don't have a lot of wood." Marion smiles, staring into the fire. "But we do have wine. Two fine bottles of Marqués de Riscal I bought today."

"And some leftover Cuban rum from the lavish table of the Orishas!" Julia sniggers. "If you give me your car keys, I'll fetch it all." She prances out of the room.

"You never really know with Julia, do you?" Marion muses into the fire.

"You also think Delia is a fake?"

"It's difficult to make a judgment on someone like Delia. Let's just say it's been a *very* interesting day. I'm actually very impressed. I certainly got to clean out my closet." Then she adds in a whisper, "I suspect this might be something Alina has demanded of Julia before their upcoming reunion. I don't know. Those two."

Marion watches the flames for another moment, and then turns toward me with a crumpled piece of faded purple cloth she's picked up by her side on the sofa. "Look what I found for you!"

"Where on earth did you find this relic?" I say, unfolding what turns out to be a one-piece outfit of shirt with shorts, the sort of romper we used to wear around the house as teenagers on summer days. "Oh my God, it must be over twenty years since I've seen this!"

"Go on, wear it!" Marion says. "You have to change out of that filthy T-shirt and the wet shorts. And it's such a great color for you."

"I don't think it'll fit."

"Of course it will. You haven't put on as much as one pound all these years. I don't know how you do it."

In a few quick movements I pull my T-shirt and bra over my head and step out of my shorts. I stand stripped down to my panties by the fireside, where its blazing glow soon warms up my skin. I look at the one-piece, trying to remember how to slip it on.

Marion stares at me in amazement. "Look at you! What a gorgeous body! Your boobs haven't moved an inch! And that waist!"

Julia walks in with a tray full of wineglasses and bottles. "Ooh!

Striptease time! Wait a minute! I want to try that too!" She puts down the tray, peels off her clothes, and yanks the romper off my hands. I take a lunge toward her and we spar, each pulling frantically at the piece of clothing.

"Julia, stop! You're going to rip it!" I say, annoyed.

We used to be like this a long while ago, three girls in a room, mostly in Marion's room, trying on clothes and accessories, playing around, confiding secrets, wisecracking about boys and dates, while whole wardrobes of fine clothes in beautiful colors flew from one end of the room to another, and makeup, scarves, hats, and all sorts of shoes lay strewn over the bed and across the floor. Friday and Saturday nights were many times like that, as we got ready to go to parties or hang out with friends. "What shall we wear tonight?" was the triggering question, and soon we would all be cavorting around closets and drawers. Most of the time, Julia and I would be naked, or stripped down to our underwear, unashamed, while Marion, always more chaste, coy about her older—then more beautiful—body, wore one of her kimonos or a bathrobe in ladylike fashion. Those were days before Marion fell in love with Fernando, before Julia met Alina and before I even knew Marcus existed. The days of innocence and sisterhood.

Marion's cell phone rings inside her small book bag on the sofa. We all freeze.

Marion fishes the phone out of her bag. "Who can be calling at this hour?"

But I know exactly who's calling at this hour, and my heart thumps uncontrollably in my chest.

"Oh, hello, Marcus! It's been such a long time." Marion gives me a significant look, while I scramble to pick up the romper from the floor, and clutch it to my chest as if to shield my nudity from the eyes of a stranger who had just walked in the door. "Yes, here she is." Marion gives me the phone.

"Oh God! We'd forgotten about *him*," Julia mutters as she slips back into her clothes.

"Anna, I'm at the gate, but the buzzer doesn't seem to work," Marcus says, as soon as I put the receiver to my ear. I want to take a large draft of air into my lungs but my rib cage is fluttering to the tune of my fast-beating heart and won't allow any further distention. Both my sisters stare at me with sharp, attentive eyes. I take a step away from them, away from the glow around the fireplace, into the darkness at the far corner of the room.

"Anna?"

I let his voice sing inside my head, like I've done all these years every time we talked business on the phone, the last venue of intimacy we have burrowed ourselves into. In all those conversations about machinery, contracts, and clients, only a few moments had to elapse before the divorce between outer meaning and inside feeling started to happen. Then the talk would split into separate threads. The words, in their practical description of business terms, would sort of precipitate into a lower layer and continue unfolding with a perfect sense of their own, while another form of subtle energy rose above it all, a deep, warm feeling of togetherness, a cloudy space where no words were necessary, where communication just hung on the music of the voice. The voice as a pure, abstract musical tone capable of moving the heart along the whole range of the emotional spectrum. In those moments, I would float around the room, away from my body seated at the desk or sprawled on the bed, and tune my whole being to Marcus's voice.

"Are you there? Did I lose you?"

And now I'm wondering, was this all in my head? Was it just my dream body floating up to his, across material boundaries, beyond satellite dishes and radio waves? Was I delirious when I felt our subtle bodies entwine and curl around each other as we talked?

"Give me a couple of minutes. I'll be out there," I say, and click the phone shut. I walk toward my sisters, toward the glowing brightness that radiates out of the fire. I'm about to enter its circle of light, away from the darkness, the same way I'm about to walk out of the shadows of my dream life and step into the glaring reality that Marcus and I have been avoiding all these years.

"Don't you dare go out to him. Ask him to come in the morning. Who does he think he is?" Julia starts.

"Leave her, Julia. She needs to do this," Marion says.

* * *

The anointment ceremony takes place by the fireside.

My two sisters help me into the romper. It fits, but it's absurdly short, above the gash across my thigh. The buttons in the front only come up to the point just between my breasts. I start to complain, and I'm about to decide that I will return to my old clothes when I see the wet, greasy pile on the floor and realize there's no turning back on this matter.

"At least it doesn't give you a wedgie," Julia says. I know she's trying to make me laugh. I must look pretty grim at the moment.

"We need to tidy you up a bit," Marion says. "Julia, get one of the hand towels and that last bottle of water." Julia brings a towel and tilts the water bottle over it to wet it. Then she dabs my face with it, and afterwards rubs my hands and legs. Marion takes a comb out of her bag and straightens my matted hair.

I look at my reflection in the huge gilded mirror that hangs above the fireplace. My features, lit from below by the firelight, are ghostly. Shadowed eye sockets and hollow cheeks, thin lips. My body looks dehydrated and gaunt. A sad princess groomed by her two ladies-in-waiting, who are at their wits' end to make their lady presentable. I am going out there to meet my knight in armor after a decade of self-imposed house arrest, the variety where the heart is locked up in dungeons of pride and insurmountable obstinacy, while the rest of the body pretends to live in the world. The situation is momentous; physical appearance doesn't really matter at all. I want to think that only my determination matters. The resolve to free myself from the fixation that has been smothering my soul all these years.

Marion rummages through her purse. "Do you want to put on some lipstick? It's a subtle mauve." I shake my head. She brings all sorts of other items out of her bag. "What about a little spray of Yves Saint Laurent's Rive Gauche?"

"Of course not, Marion!" Julia says. "What a slutty thing to do— let her just go out there being herself."

"There's nothing slutty about my makeup, it's very understated," Marion says.

"Still. Just because she's meeting a guy—go slap some lipstick on? How tacky can that be!"

"You wouldn't understand, Julia, you're in a different kind of game."

"Really? Don't you know I'm considered a lipstick lesbian *in my kind of game?*"

And they go on, my sisters, back and forth, jesting and taunting each other, while they play around with their life-size little-sister doll, pulling at my hair and straightening my dress. It's been a long day. Giving my plight undivided attention is hard. But then, they're still in step with procedure. A certain ritual needs to be followed, elements of adornment studied, unctions applied in order to shield the contestant against faintheartedness, against despair. The sad princess needs to take up arms. I'm not meeting Marcus or any knight in armor, I'm preparing to battle against this fourteen-year monster that has hardened my arteries, necrotized my brain. I'm preparing to amputate my own tissue. A pang of anguish cramps my rib cage.

Marion turns to me. "Are you all right? You look so pale!" She folds me in her arms.

"Anna, you don't have to do this," Julia says.

Marion looks into my eyes. "Do you love him this much? Even after these many years?"

Her question echoes in my brain. Love, what kind of blanket word is that? What kind of word would encompass all of desire, tenderness, lust, affection, capricious want, yearning, devotion and every shade in between? Isn't there a way to express what still pulsates after *love* has risen and fallen countless times, burned itself over and over again, to the point of leaving no ashes? I know love as in the way I lost myself to Marcus in that mountain hotel, fusing body and soul with him on that cheap, creaky metal bed. I have tried so hard and for so long to retain every image, every whisper of that night, to ingrain it all in my gut, etch it all over my skin like the tattooed pictograph of a legend. But who can hold time? Time always runs along, and we failed to run with it. Instead, we floated adrift like boats without oars on the ripples created by that moment, until we ran aground on the shores of languor. Had our love story been bold and out in the open, would we have ended somewhere else? Probably. But here we have been all these years, paralyzed, stuck in the swamp between the water and the land. And now I'm anxious to crawl out, to pull out like a fish striving to morph into a different creature. Ready to trade gills for lungs.

"He's calling again, Anna," Marion says, but doesn't pick up her phone.

"I'm all set," I say.

"Here." Julia slips out of her sandals and offers them to me. But I decline.

I'm going out there barefoot, alone.

CHAPTER 22

The street outside the house is dark and deserted, the air still hung with moisture from the rainfall. A couple of old-fashioned lampposts throw small pools of yellowed light over the sidewalk. Marcus leans on one of the poles a few feet across from the gate. His muscled figure, slanted, with crossed arms, exudes intractable patience. He's dressed in jeans and wears his shirt untucked, which gives him a laid-back, disheveled look I've not seen in a while. That, and the fact that his hair is longer. It curls over his forehead, sprinkled with gray.

I step out onto the sidewalk and stand against the old metal gate. My feet stick to the pavement, and as I look down I realize I've stepped into a big clump of purple glob that was once fruit hanging from the mulberry tree above; now it's all slumped over the sidewalk, with its sweetish, rotten stench filling the air.

Marcus looks at me, puzzled. "What on earth happened to you?"

"Nothing. We're getting the house ready for sale."

He points at the gash on my thigh. "You're hurt."

"Please don't," I say, raising my hands in defensive gesture. "Don't touch."

Marcus steps back and leans on the lamppost. "Are you all right? You're crying."

"No, I'm not!" But I *am* crying. At least, tears are streaming down my face. I want to think it's about the emotion of laying eyes on Marcus again. But it's not. It's about fear. The fear that precedes a battle where any victory that lies ahead is messy and unclean, at best.

I dry the tears off my face with the back of my hand.

"Are you in pain?" Marcus asks.

"It was just a small accident. I'm fine."

"Are you sure?" he asks again.

I nod.

Then he adds, "Can we talk for a minute? Can we step inside?"

"No, sorry, the place's a mess. Julia and Marion are still around, and . . ."

"Okay." Marcus sighs, puts his hands in his pockets and stares at his sneakers. "Not the ideal place, but I think it's best we talk anyway." He looks up. "I'm sorry I pressured you before, about going down to Cádiz. I understand dealing with the house is a priority."

"Did you cut short your vacation just to come and tell me this?" I ask.

Marcus laughs uneasily. "No, I thought I might save the day. But I already lost the crane. They're sending it back tomorrow morning."

"You could still scoot down there and salvage it. You've always had a way with those custom guys."

"Maybe." Marcus thinks for a moment. "I also realize how much I lean on you in some of these dealings. I want you to know I don't take you for granted." The back of my neck stiffens with a sense of upcoming danger. He's moving in. I can feel it in the warmth he's packing into his words. "I know I've offered before and you've refused, but I'd like to revise the terms of our agreement."

"Thank you, that's generous. But I'm done. Working together is just not—working for me anymore," I say. "It's not even work. It's my life in general. I need a change. I'm thinking of going away, traveling with Julia to Florida and then going to Melbourne, where Miguel has set up a school. Staying for a while. Maybe even looking at the possibility of starting something over there." I'm rambling, making up plans as I talk, pumping myself up with a false sense of power, a mirage of resolve.

Marcus paces up and down as I've seen him do many times when he's figuring out the logistics of a complex deal. "So, you're leaving."

"About time, don't you think? I've been working nonstop since I was nineteen."

"Nineteen," he echoes.

We're both silent for a beat. Then, in a sudden sweep, Marcus rushes toward me and embraces me. It's an awkward move. It takes me by surprise. Our bodies clash and heave against each other as we stumble against the wall. I start trembling as I feel his body heat against mine. Marcus holds me tighter, buries his face in my neck. But my shaking only increases, I feel like a limp puppet in his arms. The vibration starts at the feet and travels in jerks up my body. Like a current, electrifying my conduits of perception, memory storage, attention. My body feels like a screen on which all impressions of pleasure, pain, all the waiting, the treachery, the despair, everything we've lived through together is simultaneously projected. The reflections mix and intertwine, they morph like fast-forwarding images of cloud formations, rattling my frame to the point I think I might fall again and convulse, as I've just done in the garden. But Marcus holds me fast, upright against the stone, until all impressions and images snuff out one by one and bring me back again.

I stand for a beat in his embrace. My body feels warm, the smell of his sweat fills my lungs, my belly throbs against his. Where is this taking me? I disengage from him.

Marcus steps back. "Can we go somewhere? Have a drink, eat something?"

"Marcus, I came out here to tell you that we should cut all ties. That we should call it quits, call it a day."

Marcus paces again with his hands in his pockets. "You want to call fourteen years a day?" He smirks, and I pull my eyes away from his face. I don't want to be caught in his smile. It's always his first line of attack.

"Yes, I do. I want out. I've had enough."

"What about me? What if I said I don't want to lose you?"

I'm dumbfounded for an instant. Then, it tears out of me like a bolt.

"You don't want to lose me? You broke my fucking heart!" We're both left staggering in the wake of my scream. But there, I've articulated it at last. It's flown out of my mouth like a furious bird that's been struggling for freedom for as long as it remembers. It's opened its wings and cut through the air like a burning arrow.

"*I* broke *your* heart?" His even tone highlights the hysteria in my voice.

"Yes, you did! You left me, just like that. I didn't hear from you for seven years, and then you came back with a whole family. Who would do that? I mean, why the hell come to Madrid? Of all places on this goddamned earth?"

"Oh, I broke your heart, and all the time I thought it was you who didn't consider me good enough to be your boyfriend, let alone your husband." His eyes are bruised with hidden rage, with anguish. "Who really left who, Anna?" He looks away, chews on his words for another beat. "Did I do anything but love you?"

Something folds inside me and I begin to blink as I try to hold on to his gaze. "I was so young, I was stupid, I didn't know what I was doing, I didn't know how to express"—I falter at the edge of tears, but regain composure—"how much you meant. How you were the only thing that mattered."

We look at each other for a long moment.

"And now?" Marcus asks.

I sigh. "I've finally understood there's no going back."

"Who's talking about going back?"

I don't want to, but I snap again. "Marcus, you're not going to leave your marriage! And I'm never going to be your mistress, okay?" All of a sudden, I'm mad, I'm defiant. I'm wielding my words like a whip. Marcus looks away toward the end of the dark street. I can feel the throb of his hurting.

We've been here before, Marcus and I, feeling each other's pain across space, with little or no chance of soothing each other at the level that would befit our true feelings. When I stood at the entrance of the cemetery chapel taking condolences from the small community attending the funeral, I spotted Marcus across the narrow cobbled street of the necropolis. They had just wheeled in the dark, bulky coffin containing Father's remains, together with the collection of gigantic, ghastly flower wreaths that Marion had ordered for the service. Marcus stood in the distance, holding hands with his beautiful little boys, eyes gutted with grief for me. We stared at each other for a harrowing moment, before Helga came flying into my arms.

"Anna, we're so, so, so sorry! We have no words," she said, and embraced me. She embraced me fully, with the all-encompassing soothing bosom of a mother, of a best friend, of the most loving wife of my very own beloved. I stood in her arms, feeling the weight of her thin chest against mine, her albino blond hair tickling my throat and cheeks. It must have been the loneliest moment of my life. I tore my eyes away from Marcus, thanked Helga, and walked inside the chapel where the service was about to begin.

Now, I study my dirty toes enmeshed in the squishy bed of mulberry goo, not sure of what to do next. The truth has trumpeted through me, but what does that do for the dejection we're both feeling? I never thought I'd have summed up our situation into such a vulgar jumble of words. Being a mistress. Leaving a marriage.

"I'm sorry. It's not what I really wanted to say. It's just that I don't see any way out," I say.

Marcus thinks for a moment, his head bent over his chest. Then he looks up. "Helga and I have talked."

"Talked?"

"It's been hard for us all these years, you know?"

"Don't you dare hurt Helga!"

"Hurt her? I already wronged her by marrying her when I was crazy for you."

"What about the children? I can't be in the middle of this. I won't do it."

"Anna, *I'm* doing this," he says, then he adds after a moment, "but I still need to know . . ."

"Know what?" Where do I get the energy to sound so angry? My heart is beating fast. I'm quickly losing ground. A part of me is dissolving into the pavement. Another part is screaming to follow him into the gates of hell.

Marcus sighs. "All this is my fault. I should've taken this step a long time ago, instead of ruining a bunch of lives with my guilt and wimpiness."

Ooh, how I want to kiss those lips, breathe into his nose and mouth and taste every drop of tenderness that purrs out of his throat. Instead, I step away and try to laugh out loud, but my laughter dies into a croak. "I refuse to listen to any of this!"

I slump against the gate, slide down to the pavement, and bury my head in my hands. "Why is everything always so difficult?" I say. My brain is burning; all my resolve is turning into madness. I'm utterly exhausted.

Marcus squats beside me. "Hey, hey," he whispers, and touches my face. "Let me take you into the house. You need to rest."

I place my hand over his and press it to my cheek. His warm, strong, cushioned hands, the hands I've watched so many times screwing fierce pieces of machinery together, digging into dark, grimy engine mouths to insert a valve, to connect a piston pin, always with precision, with solicitude, a deft surgeon operating on metal patients. The hands I've also seen cupped around his children's bodies, holding little hands, wiping mouths, spaghetti faces. How did I ever imagine I could win any battle against these hands?

"I can't go anywhere," I say. "I only want to lie down and sleep." I feel lost. Caught between prostration and failure. I slide my whole body down onto the pavement. The flagstones feel warm and wet as I slump over them. The street looks vast and hugely somber from this angle. The foliage of the trees blots out the streetlamp's phosphorescent lights. All is stone quiet. It's the end of August. The city is empty.

Marcus takes me by the arms and tries to pull me up. "C'mon, Anna, let me carry you inside. You're not well." But my body is a dead weight and my arms slide away from his hands, they fall to my sides. He tries to hold me up by the shoulders, but I shrug him off. "Leave me alone."

"Anna, you're the one being difficult now," Marcus says.

"I'm always difficult." I close my eyes. I can feel the mulberry glue sticking to my hair on the side of my head. "Anyway, I have nowhere to go."

Marcus sighs. "All right, if you won't come up, then I'll have to descend to your level." And he gets down on his knees and lowers his body onto the pavement alongside mine. We're lying on our sides facing each other. "At least now we're square with each other," he says, and puts his arms around me. Our faces are in shadows, dappled by glints of lamppost light filtered through the mulberry leaves. The rotten fruit reeks around us like a drunken fog. I want him to hold me closer, to kiss me, fondle my wilted body; but we only stare into each other's eyes.

"Anna, let's not fight this anymore. I can't live without you. It's all I know."

" 'Tis all you know?"

"Yeah, all I know."

"All as in all?"

"Just all."

A long time ago, when we were lovers, we used to lie so close together, hold each other so tight, that sometimes I thought we would weld into one piece, one beautiful projectile of amalgamated metal intertwined with lips, breasts, bones, and a pair of twinkling diamonds set at the exact points where our pupils had smoldered into each other.

"Listen, Anna, the truth is Helga won't have me anymore. She's served me with divorce papers. She says she won't live with a man who's in love with another woman, and she's right. I've been a shit husband. Now I'm a free man in spite of myself."

I'm incredulous. "What? When did this happen?"

"This past week, in Germany."

"Why didn't you tell me?"

"I'm telling you now."

A car vrooms around the corner and screeches to a halt a few feet away. Harsh lights shine on our faces, blinding us. We sit up in confusion. Metallic doors open, a harsh voice says, "What's going on here?" Heavy boots walk toward us, followed by clinking, jingling sounds. I shade my eyes and recognize the red neighborhood security patrol car. Two men dressed in dark uniforms tower over us, one tall and lanky, baton in hand, and the other short and squat, arms akimbo. Marcus and I scramble to our feet.

"Don't move!" the short guy barks. "Vicente, call the police."

I recognize this short man, he's been on the job for a while; he's always had a soft spot for Julia and me.

"No, no, Paco," I say. "Please, don't. Everything's all right."

"Miss Anna?" He looks at me, startled. I can't imagine what I look like this instant; the man is having such a hard time recognizing the chichi Miss Anna he has always known.

"Sorry, we were just . . ." I mumble.

But Paco is incensed. "Who is this man? What was he doing? Has he hurt you?" He looks fiercely at Marcus and his hand wraps around the gun tucked in his belt.

"I can explain everything," Marcus says, standing up.

All of a sudden I want to laugh, laugh so hard that I'm having a difficult time keeping a straight face as I get to my feet and step between them. "Paco, it's all right. He's my friend," I say. Then to further pacify Paco's furrowed face, I add, "He's my boyfriend. *Mi novio.* I'm sorry we were misbehaving." I'm back in control. I'm commanding Paco and his colleague to back off.

Paco is not convinced. "Are you sure, Miss Anna? This doesn't seem right. I mean the way you look," he says, eyeing me up and down, concerned. "Has he threatened you against talking?"

"No, no, it's not like that at all. It's just been a long day, I've been cleaning the house, and . . ."

Vicente steps in. "We've received a complaint from a neighbor about violent behavior in the street. We need to report this to the police in any case."

Marcus reaches for his wallet. "Let me give you a card with my information."

Paco takes the business card and looks at it suspiciously. Maybe the German name sobers him up. He returns the card. "If you clear out of here in the next thirty seconds, and we see Miss Anna inside the house, we'll take her word for the incident," Paco says with a stern face. "Otherwise, the police will be here in a few minutes and you can explain it all to them."

Marcus and I look at each other with a pang of mirth mixed with sorrow. *You see, Anna, it's not just us, the world always seems to come in between, to entrap us away from each other,* he says with his eyes. Yes, Marcus, it's clear now that this Earth is not wide enough to hold the likes of you and me; it's not perfect enough to reflect our true fate written above. It can only refract our constellation, splinter it into variations of mangled, broken tales. But then, neither does it have enough power to tear us completely apart, does it?

I want to rush over to Marcus and hug him, cling tight to his body even if it'll get us arrested, I so can't bear to lose him again. But Paco and his colleague won't have it. "Please, sir," they say, as they flank Marcus and walk him to his car. "And be assured we'll be watching until morning."

Marcus sighs. "Get some rest, Anna. I'll come get you first thing tomorrow."

"No, no, meet me at my place in three hours."

"But that will already be morning."

"All right, morning then."

The two security guards watch with crossed arms as he drives away.

Paco turns to me. "You sure you're good, Miss Anna? I hope you understand that this is in everyone's best interest. Let me see you into the house." He pushes the gate open and lets me in.

"Thank you, Paco."

He nods, his face smug with accomplished professional and gentlemanly duty.

CHAPTER 23

The house is dark and silent. I walk toward the library, and as I pass through the living room, I stop and stare at the broken window. I cannot walk up to it, as I would like; it would be my bare feet against the myriad shards of glass scattered all around. A graveyard of crystals with the moonlight shimmering on each and every broken piece, giving the room the feel of a ghostly constellation, a mangled reflection of faraway star formations shining up above. There's always a softening of features when faces are played on by the light of night, so different from the harsh, unrelenting disclosure of sunlight. This is how I see the room, with its open, broken mouth and jagged crystal lips parted toward the cooling night. The house has exhaled, breathed out all toxic memories, and now rests under the moonlight, with that rejuvenated, simple beauty displayed by the dead. No more fretting to do, no more tormented fury to withhold. The show is over.

Now, it's just silence.

A sweet scene awaits me back at the library. My two sisters are huddled around the fireplace, whispering and laughing softly, drinking from large crystal cups filled with burgundy wine. They've pushed aside sofas and chairs and piled up rugs and blankets on the floor before the fire, where they lay sprawled as if on a large bed, the way we used to with Nanny, when Father was away. They've lit candles to take the edge off the darkness that now fills the room. They turn expectant eyes toward me as I walk in and slide onto the carpeted heap between them.

"What happened?" Marion asks.

"Did he accept your resignation?" Julia asks.

"Nope."

"What did he say?" Marion asks.

I shrug. Where would I begin?

"I am going to need your car in a couple of hours, though," I say.

Julia and Marion ooh and aah, laughing, poking fingers in my ribs.

"How did I know it?" Julia snorts.

Marion pulls at the goo in my hair. "Wow! There was a tumble in the hay and all!"

"Can't trust that one to let go of you," Julia says.

Marion laughs. "C'mon, Julia, give the guy a break! Who'd want to lose Anna?"

"Who am I to criticize?" Julia sighs. "Still holding on to my own story like a freakin' barnacle."

"It seems to be a family trait." Marion motions me to move closer, puts her arm around me and presses her cheek to my shoulder. Julia reaches over and pours me a glass of wine.

We lie in silence, staring at the fire. The wine floods into my body like a stream of nectar, loosening up strained tissues, pumping sweet, bubbly sap into my fatigue. I struggle to keep my eyes open.

The ravenous flames that towered over the coconut a while ago have given way to smaller tongues that lick away at the incandescent mass of wood. The glowing pile crackles softly as it breaks down, creating different shapes in its collapsing structure. The embers now form a sort of beehive configuration, with rows of glowing cells lying on top of one another, crumbling, caving in, and toppling over each other. And within the effulgence of every tiny chamber of the hive, a small scene plays itself out. Fernando being gored by the bull and Marion bending over the lips of his wound; Julia's pensive brush-strokes delineating Alina's curves; Father's hands locking Egyptian statuettes in the cabinet; Marcus and I climbing, reaching for ever-receding sierra peaks, making love, while red, burning earth falls away at each pounding of our bodies. The house is here too, with its smoldering rooms filled with scenes of love, of rage, sadness, or jesting; snippets of human stories in each vanishing little alcove, re-enacted time and time again since the beginning of the world. All of them muffled in the sounds of the burning, crackling, and hissing, the dull hum that sweeps up all the music, the laughter, the pain, the poetry, and the fury into the swirling column of smoke rising above.

I think of the fire as the energy that consumes and reconfig-ures matter, the energy that shapes it along its relentless destiny toward death and transformation. Human passions, like fire, also consume and reshape us, they take hold of us and spend us in mer-ciless progression. We sway in the grasp of their power, dreaming empty dreams about freedom and self-willed changes, unconscious of our true shackles, of our dark prisons. And just sometimes we may come across strange opportunities to bend the course of our fate. May we be lucky to identify them and brave enough to follow them through to the end.

"What are you thinking about, Anna?" I hear Marion ask be-side me.

"Nothing. Just nonsense that comes with wine on an empty stomach."

Marion raises her cup. "Let's have a toast." She thinks for a mo-ment. "To the Hurts!"

"Marion, you're not pronouncing it properly." Julia laughs. "We're in Spain, it's the Hooorts."

"It sounds terrible," Marion says.

"I love it," Julia says.

"Me too," I say. "It always reminded me of the onomatopoeia of an exotic trumpet note."

"Precisely," Julia says. "It's exotic, if anything English ever was."

Marion raises her cup again. "Here goes, then. To the Hooorts, a lineage of obstinately passionate, impossibly wistful individuals!"

Julia giggles. "That was a bit much too much, Marion!" Her cheeks are flushed, she's slurring her words. "Me, despite all I said before, I'll toast to Delia and Constantine, for their weird but awe-some ways," she says. "And to Anna, as always the boldest, for carry-ing the day to the end." A drowsy smile dances in her pupils as she raises the cup in my direction and takes a sip. She's plastered too.

"And you, Anna, what will you toast to?" Marion asks.

I think for a moment. I'd like to toast to Marcus, to our undying patience for each other, to our unbroken bond. To the poetry I've stifled through the years and the way it's fed this crazy love. To Father, whose warfare unwittingly fueled our passion. But most of all, I want to toast to the night that gallops fast toward the morning sun and will soon bring the return of my lover.

I'll toast to tomorrow.

My sisters look at me, and wait. Their gaze is tinged with disquiet. They can feel my pulsing transport. Are they afraid I will slip out of our newly found sisterhood?

Tomorrow. The sound unfurls along the base of my tongue toward the tip, in a long, lazy, wavelike motion that fills me with unease. *Tomorrow* is the word I've been clutching all these years, clawing at with the same frenzy of one who'd try to hold the wind. What's tomorrow? That dim, unreliable light bobbing ahead that mesmerizes the traveler and pulls her away from the beauty of the trail below. Whatever sweetness tomorrow could hold for me, whatever promised bounty, nothing could beat this moment that is already escaping into the dusty twilight of the past. It is here and now, with my heart bursting in my chest and my gaze spilling over with the light of my lover's eyes, that my body tingles with the certainty that, if I were to die right here, in this very instant, I would be taken at the crest of my happiness, at the peak of my flight.

Shouldn't this be what I raise my cup to?

I say, "I'll toast to this amazing moment. To our freedom, after everything that has happened this day. And to the three of us, that we may always stay close."

Marion and Julia smile, they relax. We clink our cups and drink.

Outside, the wind rustles in the trees, swishing long branches into gentle beating against windowpanes. Flurries of thin air stream through the old cracked frames, making the room quiver. The crystal beads of the chandelier above jingle.

I close my eyes.

The house, of course, is also clinking its glass.

$\mathscr{A}$CKNOWLEDGMENTS

This book would have never come to completion without the invaluable help of my amazing agent and good friend, Jeff Ourvan, and Kensington's brilliant editor, John Scognamiglio, both of whom I need to thank for their editorial help, keen insight, and ongoing support for bringing my stories to life. Also thanks to Kensington production editor Carly Sommerstein, who made sure to put the perfect finishing touches on the novel's text. Instrumental also in the writing of this novel have been the members of my New York writers' group, who have read and critiqued my writing relentlessly until it became the book it is, particularly Dawn Rebecky, Aaron Parsley, Tom Walsh, John Casey, Judy Karp, Maureen Meehan, Monika Patel, David Ranghelli, and Jeremy Goldstein.

A very special thanks to my mentor at Manchester Metropolitan University, Livi Michael, for her continuous support, and to my colleagues Helen Steadman, Nicola Ní Leannaín, Bee Lewis, Fin Gray, Marita Karin Over, Zoë Feeney, Sue Smith, Jane Masumy, JV Baptie, and Kate Woodward. Also to my other colleagues and friends of the British and American Madrid Writers Circle, who took me in and made me feel a part of their amazing literary group: Felicity Hughes, Joseph Candora, Ryan Day, Anne MacMillan, and Lance Took.

I am also grateful to my brother, Nicholas Aikin, and my sisters,

Helena Aikin, Carola Aikin, Olga Aikin, and Anabel Aikin, all artists themselves, and always enthusiastic of any individual or collective family projects. To my cousin Nancy Condardo and to my friend and writing colleague Carlos Mayor, both of whom have supported my writing from the start. A special thanks to Melissa Burch whose friendship is essential to my artistic endeavors, and to Sally Ekaireb, who has stood by me in every instance of struggle and success.

Last but not least, to my cool sons Ivan and Daniel, and my lovely daughter-in-law, Paola, always supportive of every artistic project I undertake.

THE WEIGHT OF THE HEART

Susana Aikin

ABOUT THIS GUIDE

The suggested questions are included to enhance your group's
reading of Susana Aikin's *The Weight of the Heart*!

DISCUSSION QUESTIONS

1. In the novel the Hurt sisters' family house is haunted with memories from the past that make it difficult for them to make any decision about the property. Do you believe that houses and other structures can hold memories of past events? Or do you think that memories are solely attached to people? Have you ever had any experience where you felt an imprint of something that might have happened in the past attached to a particular space?

2. Different cultures have, and have had in the past, different ways of dealing with people's problems. In the novel, Delia is a Cuban Santería priestess who believes that cleansing the energy of the family house will help liberate the Hurt sisters from their unresolved emotional issues. How do you feel about alternative ways of dealing with personal dilemmas and difficulties? Have you ever tried any alternative way, besides classical Western psychotherapy, to tackle any personal situation?

3. In the novel, James Hurt is an accomplished entrepreneur and self-made man, who is nonetheless insanely possessive of his three daughters and a master manipulator over their choices and their lives. Have you ever come across anyone like him? Do you think there is a tendency for powerful parents to overwhelm their children and dictate their lives?

4. What about children engaging in toxic loyalties toward manipulative parents, as Anna seems to do in the first part of the novel? What do you think makes her behave as she does? Is it just blind love and admiration for her father, or fear? And fear of what?

5. How does the absence of the mother affect the structure of the Hurt family? Do you think that if the mother hadn't

died earlier on, James Hurt would have established the same controlling relationships with his daughters? Can you think of any other stories or novels with similar father-daughter relationships?

6. Anna hides her relationship with Marcus from her despotic father in order to protect her lover, but ends up paying a hefty price for it. What do you think made her act like this? Do you think she could have done things differently? Can you think of any other love stories where passionate relationships are concealed? Do they always end tragically?

7. In the beginning of the novel, Anna and her sisters are at odds with each other, but as the "cleansing" progresses, they slowly bond again. Do you think their lack of solidarity was a result of their father's abuse, or on the contrary, do you think their father was able to better exert his tyrannical power over them because of their lack of unity?

8. The title of the book, *The Weight of the Heart*, implies issues of accountability and guilt over circumstances that maybe could have been dealt with very differently. Do you think that Anna's coming to terms with her own responsibility in past events and relationships is the tipping point of her healing process? And do you think that James Hurt's revelation of his feeling of guilt toward the end of the novel redeems him in our eyes as readers?

Printed in the United States
by Baker & Taylor Publisher Services